GILDED DREAMS

The Dragons of Sin City

Thora Woods
Shannon French

This book is dedicated to Benedict Cumberbatch. Without his dedication and talent, I never would have developed this insatiable attraction to giant murder lizards.

Thora Woods

I'd like to dedicate this book to the three Toms. If your surname isn't Hiddleston, Hardy or Sturridge, you're the wrong Tom.

Shannon French

CONTENTS

CONTENT WARNING

The following book contains material that may not be suitable for all audiences. This is a romance novel intended for readers 18+, and contains scenes of explicit sexual content. This includes same sex encounters (MM), as well as descriptions of kink and fetish activity including but not limited to: degradation, forced orgasm/overstimulation, Daddy (honorific) kink, and Dom/sub dynamics.

This book also contains themes and descriptions that some readers may find triggering in nature. This content includes, but is not limited to: violence; coarse language; discussions of self-harm/suicide, including suicidal ideation; descriptions of physical, verbal, mental, and emotional abuse; sexual assault (non-penetrative); discussions of body image, and degradation thereof; enslavement and trafficking; loss of parents; mentions of incest/pedophilia (non-graphic); gambling; and non-consensual magical coercion.

Prologue

Dominic

Las Vegas - 1930

The train whistle screams, the last chugs of the wheels slowing to a stop. I look up from my poker hand as the brakes sigh in relief, steam billowing across the platform. Movement in the saloon's bar room ceases as everyone turns to watch the latest batch of souls unload from the cars. I breathe deep, smirking at the sharp mix of human sweat and magic that floats through the open doorframe. Fresh meat.

My companions gather up the chips and cards, our game coming to an abrupt end. I have to admit that I'm a little disappointed by the interruption. I was well on my way to winning Darrel's soul. But there will be other opportunities for a small prize like that. There's a new scent in the air, like lightning and pine and something sweet. It's oddly familiar, making the hairs on the back of my neck prickle. Someone interesting has finally rolled into town.

I push my chair back from the table with a screech, eager to identify this particular newcomer. My footsteps are heavy on the dusty wooden floor as I saunter out to the covered porch. The train depot across the wide unpaved road is a frenzy of activity. Porters are pulling off luggage and cargo from the cars even as passengers try to get their bearings. The sun is high and bright, the dry air hazy from the heat. Most of the souls aren't dressed for the desert, layered up in jackets and flannel. A man from the Boulder Dam project shouts above the din, instructing anyone who signed up for work to make their way to the company office up the road.

My gaze sweeps over the crowd. Mostly human, but with the occasional shifter or other supernatural trying not to draw attention to themselves. Overwhelmingly male. Unattached. Perfect targets for my brand of business. I'd have to let them get settled in before I tempt them to my club, of course. Best to wait until they're bored and looking for a bit of excitement to liven up their evenings. And then I can show them one *hell* of a time.

I'm disappointed for a moment, sure this is just another load of common prey when *they* step down onto the platform. The pair stands apart from the crowd, in more ways than one. For starters, the men are huge. They are well over six feet tall, if not closer to seven feet. The taller of the two is broad as well, with shoulders that strain against the tweed jacket he's squeezed into. His reddish-brown hair is slicked back and gathered in a neat ponytail at the nape of his thick neck, with his chin and jaw covered in a matching, full beard.

The man beside him is only an inch or so shorter than his massive companion and with leaner proportions. His sharp face is clean-shaven and ridiculously handsome. Dark hair with a touch of gray at the temples sweeps back from his forehead in the current fashion, though I'm sure with a face like his, any style would look complimentary. His suit is charcoal gray, tailored perfectly to fit his unusual frame.

Unlike the brute, there's a certain ease about the way this one carries himself, a confidence that is earned rather than assumed.

The crowd parts and I realize there's a third member of their party. This man is of more average height, maybe just about six-foot, but he looks tiny next to his friends. His posture isn't doing him any favors either, but that's not what's striking about him. His hair is so blond that it looks white in the glare of the sun, despite being hidden beneath a wide-brimmed fedora. With his hands deep in the pockets of his slightly too-big jacket, his arms stay tucked tight to his sides.

My predator instinct picks up on his body language, nearly salivating at the feast before me. The little one would do very nicely for my collection. And maybe I can bag his friends in the process.

I push off the frame and lope down the stairs into the packed earth street, thumbs hooked through the front two belt loops of my trousers. As the trio descends from the train platform, I linger nearby, pretending to read one of the signs pasted to the bulletin board as I strain to hear their hushed conversation. At first, it only sounds like gibberish until I pick up on a few key words. They're speaking Russian. Interesting. A muttered incantation, and then their conversation becomes clear.

"Not much here," the brute mutters, his voice rough and deep.

"The council said as much. But that works in our favor," the dark-haired one replies.

Council? Are these government men? But why would the government hire Russians? I keep my attention locked onto the board as they wander past me, too absorbed in their conversation to pay me any mind. I inhale, trying to discern more of their scents when my blood runs cold. The inside of my nostrils burns like I've just huffed from an open barrel of bathtub moonshine. Strong magic, old magic. The kind I've only ever experienced once before, though that one hadn't been nearly as potent as what these three carry.

Dragons.

Images flash through my mind. Memories from decades in the past. My spine tingles, forcing me to stand up straight as if a long-forgotten sergeant has just ordered me to attention. Suddenly, I'm sent right back there, to the pits and shadows. Forging incantations, too young to understand they won't be enough. Death and destruction tangle with my deep routed lust for the chaos surrounding me. I breathe deeply, their scent... it brings it all rushing back. But I'm not some wide-eyed, fresh from the hellfire demon anymore. I'm hardened by war just as they are.

"Gentlemen!" I call out in English, laying on the charm and a fake Western accent as thick as I can manage.

The trio turns to look at me, and even at a handful of paces away, the strength of their magic is nearly enough to make my eyes water. I keep my smile in place, tipping the brim of my ten-gallon to them in cordial greeting.

"If y'all are looking for a place to stay, I'd be happy to take you to the finest inn we've got," I offer, keeping my spine straight.

The dark-haired one lifts his chin, and we lock eyes. His irises are a true purple, a color I'd only seen in gemstones and clothing dye. I flick my gaze to the brute, catching the flash of something in his midnight blue eyes, similar to a bolt of lightning. A white-toothed grin peeks out from below his auburn mustache, but his jaw is too tight for the look to be friendly. The little one, on the other hand, doesn't bother disguising his contempt. His pouty lips curl into a sneer, but he keeps his head down so I can't make eye contact. So I look back to the monster concealed beneath the charcoal gray suit.

"And who might you be, friend?" he asks, his English smooth if only slightly accented.

"Friends call me Dominic," I reply, rolling my shoulders back and grinning.

"Dominic."

The lead dragon repeats the name I gave him like he's testing it for something. If he's looking for a lie, he won't find one. It might not be my true name, but rather the one I've picked to go by in polite society. A demon knows better than to give that out to anyone, let alone strangers, and least of all, dragons.

"You may call me Viktor, Dominic. These are my... associates, Felix and Gavril," the leader, Viktor, says, motioning first to the little one and then to the brute with an elegant wave of his long-fingered hand. "If you'd be so kind as to direct us to lodgings, we'd be happy to repay the favor with a drink."

Ah, now *there's* a carefully worded request. Someone knows how to play the game. I grin to myself and nod, motioning them to follow me as I lead them back across the wide street to the saloon. The bar room has cleared out slightly, but most of the dozen tables spread throughout the space are full. Their posture stiffens under the ratcheting tension as my new friends realize that not a single patron or employee in this establishment is human.

"Our little watering hole is home to many interesting folks like yourselves," I explain casually, dropping myself into my usual chair in the back corner.

The dragons perch carefully on the spindly wooden chairs, and I almost laugh. Gavril especially looks comically out of place at a standard-sized card table, even as he tries to play it cool. Viktor, however, settles into his seat like it's a throne, a king ready to hold court. Unfortunately for him, this town already has a de facto mayor, and I'm not looking to give up my position so soon.

I motion to SueAnn, the Seelie Fae owner of this inn, for a round of drinks and she flashes me a smile. She might own the building, but she didn't do it alone. Her contract isn't up for a few more years, but I'll have to be on the lookout for someone to take over. This is a prime spot, and I'd hate to lose it.

"So is this your tavern?" Viktor asks casually, crossing one long leg over the other.

"Naw," I drawl, grinning to myself. "I run my own little club a few blocks up. A place where the hard-working boys at the dam can unwind after an honest day's work."

"I see," Viktor mutters, eyes narrowing suspiciously. Something tells me I'm not his first demon. Not that I should be surprised. He's not just an old soul; he's one of the big boys. Not the oldest I've met, but old enough to know a threat when he sees one.

SueAnn arrives with a tray of drinks and Viktor immediately pulls out a crisp bill from his wallet, well above what drinks in this town would cost. It's not a foreign currency like I'd expected. These men came prepared.

"What brings you to Las Vegas, friends? You don't exactly look like the day laborer type," I ask, trying to keep my tone casual.

Gavril chuckles, and the hairs on the back of my neck stand up. There's a distinct air of danger about him, like he's one wrong look away from tearing the building down around us with his bare hands. A loose cannon, unpredictable. My least favorite type of being.

"We're here on a business venture. Now that the governor signed that gambling bill, we'd like to see if we can make it in the casino business," Viktor answers, not even acknowledging his companion's demeanor.

I lift my chin and take a long drink from the pint glass in front of me. It doesn't escape my notice that none of them have even glanced at their own beverages.

"We've got more casinos than cows around here these days," I joke, but none of them so much as crack a smile.

"Does the herd include your own establishment, Mr. Dominic?" Viktor questions, sounding for all the world like he gives a shit. But I can see the wheels turning in those unnatural purple eyes. Dragons never change.

"No, not me. But there are plenty of others that won't take kindly to newcomers edging in on their pasture," I retort, spine stiffening.

"Any good farmer knows that too many heads of cattle can lead to overgrazing. For the benefit of the whole, it is often necessary to cull a few...unruly herd members."

Viktor and I lock eyes, and I don't dare to look away. I don't know who these fucking dragons think they are, but if they think they can come in here and intimidate me, then they must have a few screws loose.

"And I'm to assume y'all are good farmers?" I drone, gripping my glass tight.

Viktor's grin sends a shiver down my spine. I half expected to see rows of razor-sharp fangs in his mouth, smoke leaking out from between them with the hunger blazing in his eyes. But instead, his teeth are normal, if too white.

"Oh, the best," Viktor says lightly, making the other two laugh low in their throats.

I blink, eyes flicking between the three. Gavril was impossible to ignore, but I'd all but forgotten about Felix. But now that he's made his presence known, I suddenly feel outnumbered.

Abruptly and in unison, the three dragons stand and straighten their clothes. Felix and Gavril start for the door, but Viktor lingers for a moment. I stay seated, even rocking back in my chair to avoid having to crane my neck to look into his face. The cool impassiveness of his expression almost unnerves me, though I don't let that show.

"Thank you for showing us around, Dominic. I'm sure this won't be the last time our paths cross," Viktor says in almost a whisper.

As I open my mouth to respond, the slick bastard turns on his heel and marches out the door, his two companions trailing close behind.

I know enough about dragons to know their very presence here threatens everything I've worked so hard to achieve. Whatever those three are up to, I can only hope they keep it as far away from me as possible. With any luck, they'll grow bored with this backwater train stop and move on to more fertile pastures like dozens before them have. In the meantime, a few good wards never hurt.

CHAPTER 1

VIKTOR

T he lights of Las Vegas glitter like a thousand neon stars, spreading out below my feet. The first time I looked out over this balcony, I'd been awed by the sight. These days, there's nothing but passing awareness. Each entity below, from the dazzled human tourists to the hotels lining this mile or so of desert oasis and everything in between, moves exactly as they are supposed to. Exactly as my pack and I have directed them to move. All but one.

Somnium.

I can see that godforsaken building from my perch, a dark spot in the invisible web of power we've woven since we came to this lawless, backwater railroad rest stop nearly one hundred years ago. Every moment since we've arrived has been dedicated to our plan, and step by inexorable step, we've exerted our will over this land and made it ours, a shiny, gilded mecca for the outcasts and degenerates of the supernatural world, as well as the human. But that club and its bottom-feeding demon owner have eluded us. Every night, I step out onto this balcony and see the same damn building. My eyes are drawn to it as if the flashing lights and bustling streets are meaningless in our failure. Failure is not a word I take kindly to. Until now, it hasn't been in my vocabulary, and I don't plan to keep it there for long.

My hands grip the cool steel railing, the cuffs of my shirt riding up just enough to bare my wrists to the nip of the wind. Familiar heat bubbles below my skin, and I can sense the ridges of my scales against the undersides of my forearms. My flesh feels tight and itchy as I try to will my dragon form to retreat. I refuse to let that persistent cockroach from Hell get the better of me, even unknowingly. My kind has always treated any demon presence like an infestation. Stamp it out before it gets its claws dug too deep. We've let that menace exist for too long. But no more. Every other square inch of this city belongs to me and mine, and I won't allow us to trip this close to the finish line.

"You can't set buildings on fire with your eyes, Vik. But I love watching you try."

I whip around to face Gavril, the hulking smartass currently leaning against the doorframe to the living room of our penthouse. The warm lighting from inside casts his monstrous figure in a tantalizing silhouette, highlighting the wide expanse of his shoulders and the grip of his hands on his biceps as his arms cross over his glorious chest. The mere sight of him is enough to make me forget my anger and consider entirely more entertaining ways to spend my evening.

"Judging by that look he's giving you, it'll be me who gets to watch a show tonight," Felix mutters from behind Gavril's back, silver eyes glinting with unassuming mischief.

He skirts around our larger pack mate, loping across the concrete floor with bare feet. His pale skin almost glows in the dark, but as he reaches my side, the blues, purples, pinks, and yellows of the flashing lights below scatter a masterpiece across his cheeks. As he looks out toward Somnium, a little frown pulls at his perfect Cupid's bow of a mouth, and I momentarily lose myself in his profile. He's angelic, the most inhuman looking of the three of us. I have to tamp down the urge to bundle him in my arms and do whatever it takes to soothe his troubles. He's not a fragile, wilting violet, despite his appearance.

"We need a new plan." I take a deep breath, eyes still following Felix as he settles himself into a seat at the patio set to my right. He tucks his legs up underneath him, elegant hands bundled in his lap.

"Plan? Is it time for another 'P'?" Gavril straightens, a new spark of chaotic joy lighting up his midnight blue eyes.

"Oh, for fuck's sake," Felix groans on a sigh.

"Hey, all I'm saying is that the first four didn't work. And if politeness, politics, pussy, and priests did fuck all to make him leave, we can always try good ol' fashioned petroleum. Who's up for some arson?"

Gavril thrusts his hand in the air, but Felix and I give him matching deadpan stares.

"First, brick doesn't burn. Second, and arguably more important, it doesn't work that way and you know it." My hand moves to scratch at my furrowed brow, aching with tension.

I catch Gavril shrugging out of the corner of my eye. "Worth a shot," he mutters to himself.

He closes the distance between us, coming to stand on my other side. On instinct, I reach out and lay my palm on his arm, feeling the pulsing urge to do *something* coming off him. I understand his restlessness, even if we can't indulge it. The magic we're working with is old, and the rules are clear. If we want this to work, we can't take shortcuts. Loopholes, however...

Gavril shifts his weight closer, seeking out more of my touch subconsciously. I push a little, easing his discontent for the moment. I'll work out the rest of his excess energy later, after we've settled on the next steps.

"I spoke with Sly about those charms. He's willing to

work with us," Felix says, lifting himself up off the chair and drifting closer.

"And his price?" I ask, already knowing the answer.

"Casino credit, of course, and maybe some loan forgiveness," Felix replies, rolling his eyes.

I grunt noncommittally, but Gavril chuckles. "You mean he doesn't want me to break his other leg?" he asks sardonically.

Unable to help myself, I smirk. Not too long ago, the mage thought he could play with the big boys. I can't say I didn't enjoy putting him back in his place. But we can't always rely on fear alone to keep him loyal. Especially not when we're dealing with a demon.

"I'll consider it. He can have my charity, and just maybe, if he can deliver on his end, then he can earn my forgiveness," I say mildly.

Gavril sighs again, but he can get his kicks somewhere else. We're running out of options. This mage could be our last hope of acquiring Somnium, and the last thing we need is Gavril snapping him in half for the sake of entertainment.

"So we're really doing this?" Felix asks simply. "You know he'll figure it out eventually."

"You might be giving him too much credit there," Gavril replies, twisting away from me just far enough to ruffle Felix's hair.

Felix bats the hand away, but his smile undermines the glare he tries to throw Gavril's way. Instead, my pack mate tucks himself against my side, and I wrap my arm around him before kissing the top of his white-blond head.

"We shouldn't underestimate our enemy, Gavril. He might be a demon, but Dominic hasn't survived for this long by chance. We've accounted for every possibility, though. So, yes, he may figure out what's happening, but it hardly matters."

I stare out over our territory as I speak, finding the squat brick building and narrowing my eyes at it. It's beyond time we did something about that pest.

"By the time he does, it'll be too late," I growl.

CHAPTER 2

Lyra

T he hazy air of Somnium pulses with the steady beat of the electronica track Mercedes chose for her dance tonight. Or is that Lexus? I can never keep the Car Girls straight.

"Hey, sweetheart, can I get a Sex on the Beach?"

The slurred voice pulls me from my thoughts, and I turn to stare into the middle-aged face on the other side of the sticky bar. His cheap suit is askew, mouse-brown hair mussed. Emerald is hanging on his back like a barnacle, batting her clumped-together fake lashes like her life depends on it. I give the pair a quick, tense smile before turning to the wall of liquor bottles behind me.

Right. What's in a Sex on the Beach again? Vodka and... what else...

As I reach for a bottle, a disgusted scoff stops me. I turn and give a bland look to the patron, waiting for the inevitable order change.

"You don't have Drako's here?" he asks, half disbelieving,

half exasperated.

I grit my teeth in an expression I hope looks like a smile and not a grimace, swallowing my retort. We don't carry anything from the Drakona brand, least of all their locally distilled vodka. Even being caught with one of their casino chips in your pocket will get you tossed out and banned for life. There's been a weird back-and-forth proxy war between Dominic and the Drakona boys, going back as far as I can remember, though I'd never cared enough to ask why. That shit is well above my pay grade. Though if I had a nickel for every time someone bitched about our "No Dragon Product" policy, I would have skipped town years ago.

Emerald takes over, soothing her mark's ruffled feathers as I pour a generous amount of the bottom shelf gasoline Dom tries to pass off as vodka into a glass, adding just the barest splash of orange juice, and…

"Pineapple juice, Lyra. Beach means tropical," Trish, my bartending partner for the evening, mutters as she comes over to get ice for her own customer.

I lunge for a bottle marked pineapple juice, but a gentle hand comes down on my forearm.

"No, honey. No." Ginny, my roommate and best friend here in Hell, is smiling at me from across the bar, gold eyes full of her signature *bless your heart* kindness. "Peach schnapps and cranberry, baby. Vodka, orange juice, peach schnapps, and cranberry. Get it together, ladies."

Throwing her a grateful look, I finish the drink and pass it over to the man. He takes it and thankfully retreats for another dance. I push a few flyaway copper strands out of my face as Ginny comes around to mix her own drinks, cursing the humidity again. Everyone says Vegas is a "dry heat," but the pool of sweat between my tits that refuses to evaporate into the oversaturated air begs to differ. I know Dominic makes enough money from this shithole to afford better climate control. It's not like he's paying for labor or anything.

"You'd think I'd remember this shit eventually," I sigh,

my sarcastically wistful tone making the other girls laugh.

"We should start tattooing the recipes on your forehead. There's enough room," Trish snipes, a little too bitter for the joke she's trying to make.

"We'd be better off tattooing them on all the cock you suck, baby girl. You'd see them more often, and maybe you'd actually learn something." Ginny jumps in before my temper even has the chance to bubble, and I can't help my satisfied grin at the look of shock and horror on Trish's face before the girl flounces away to help the next customer.

Ginny and I make hard eye contact for a moment, affection for the wolf shifter swelling in my chest. I've been working for Dominic the longest out of everyone, but she's a close second. Girls like Trish will be gone soon enough, but me and Ginny...well, we're in this for the long haul.

"How are you feeling, baby girl?" Ginny asks, voice a little lower than her usual volume. She's the kind of woman who's used to making sure she's heard, loud and clear. It's just one of the reasons me and her get along so well. Neither of us have the time for assholes.

"Oh, you know. The usual," I groan, wiping my hands, sticky with peach schnapps, on my thighs.

"You didn't get much sleep last night," Ginny adds with an arched eyebrow. "Tossing and turning all night long, and for all the wrong reasons." There's a hint of mischief in her all-knowing eyes.

"There's not been many people round here worth tossing and turning with." We chuckle knowingly.

"The pool has been a little on the dry side lately, ain't it?" She shakes her head, sending curls of hair fluttering around her shoulders. "But I wasn't born yesterday. I know that ain't what's bothering you."

I groan, hanging my head back and staring up at the ceiling. Ginny can read me like a book. Must be a benefit of being a shifter or something. Whatever it is, it's frustrating as hell. I can't hide a thing from her.

"I can't explain it, Gin. I just feel…" My voice trails off, blending into the bass as it rattles my bones.

"Off center?" She fills in the blanks, as always, tilting her head to the side to study my face.

"Something like that."

Ginny finishes stacking her drinks and heads off across the room, holding the tray close to avoid spilling on anyone. When she slips behind the black velvet curtain, my heart squeezes slightly. I can't place the reason, but watching her walk through that portal never gets any easier. I don't dream often; it doesn't really make sense in a place like this. But when I do, I dream about getting the both of us out of here. Running off to some place where the sun shines in summer and the snow falls in winter. We'd have a little cabin in the middle of nowhere, surrounded by endless open space. Every night we'd drink in front of an open fire until our skin turned pink and our eyes glazed over. It would be calm and quiet and ours. It's a pipe dream. Neither one of us is making it out of Somnium alive, but it's nice to play pretend every now and again.

I scan the dark room on the other side of the bar, my eyes skating over the dancer–definitely Lexus; she's the one with the lips tattooed on her ass–on the stage and onto the dazed men in the seats along the edges, fishing for more cash to throw at her. Behind the stage on the opposite side of the room from the bar are the DJ booth and Zane, the wolf shifter working tonight. I take my time dragging my eyes up and down his bare chest, wondering idly to myself what the sweat rolling down his pecs would taste like. But movement out of the corner of my eye pulls my attention, even if I wish it didn't.

The heavy velvet curtain parts, and a young woman, human by the size of her, stumbles out, supported by one of the Dream Lounge servers. She's got tears running down her face, but her expression doesn't indicate if those are happy or sad tears. A first-timer, then.

"When can I come back? I need to come back," she babbles as she trudges by me toward the door.

"We're open every night, my dear. And if you join our members club, you're welcome to come back as often as you like."

I shudder and turn away from the bar, my stomach roiling. His voice grates like a thousand rusty razor blades against my eardrums, and the scent of his cologne makes me swallow back bile. Dominic continues his sales pitch for a few more minutes, and I pretend to be busy dusting the bottles.

I want to block out the sugar-spun lies he's feeding this poor woman, the same shit he's been peddling for decades, but it's almost impossible. Live out your wildest dreams and deepest fantasies in a safe space, with no limits or judgment. All for a small fee, and a dash of your soul to power them. A grain of sand, hardly anything at all. There's no obligation or contract, so what's the harm? You can quit anytime you like.

When I can't stand it anymore, I throw some dirty towels into an empty box and shoulder through the swinging door to the backstage area. Down a flight of stairs, I make my way to one of the storage rooms and ancient washer/dryer in the far corner. The music is muffled down here, but the lighting is just as shitty. A glance at the wall clock makes me groan. We're still five hours from closing, but it might as well be an eternity.

Taking my time, I head back to my post, dragging my feet. I try to pull my black t-shirt down a little, but it refuses to move below my belly button. My black jeans only come up so high, so I'm left with a pale muffin top poking out awkwardly. I consider going to my room and finding a hoodie, but the three flights of stairs down and then up again wouldn't make the snide comments I'd get worth it. I could wear snow pants and a parka in July and not be bothered, as long as the humidity stays low. But when it feels like I'm stuck in Satan's Swampy Ass Crack, the extra layer would be more of an annoyance than a help. It needs to storm in this city before I drown on dry land.

I stop under one of the ceiling AC vents in the service hallway behind the bar, closing my eyes and turning my face up toward it for a moment. It's barely running, but I'm still grateful for the slight relief. However, my slice of bliss is interrupted by a deep chuckle. I raise an eyebrow as Braxton, one of the bouncers, steps into the hallway. He rubs a thumb over his plump lower lip, not even bothering to hide the lust in his aqua eyes as he scans me up and down. When he gets within arm's reach, I don't move. If he needs to get by, he can figure it out. The hallway is plenty wide enough for the two of us.

"You free later, Guppy?" he asks, his gravelly attempt at a pickup line making me snort.

"Seriously?" I deadpan, cocking an eyebrow.

Braxton is beside me now, and I have to stop myself from wrinkling my nose. Tritons like him always tend to smell like a pier, and not in a good way. This close, I can see the fishlike scales along his hairline, blending seamlessly into his muddy locks. He's new, only a month or two into his year-long contract, and he's still fucking his way through the staff. Strippers trade gossip like baseball cards, so it only took two days before his package was added to the dressing room power ranking board. Definitely in the bottom half, but with a fun ribbed pattern that a few of the girls swear made them see stars.

"I get off at six. We could go grab breakfast, and then I could scramble your eggs," he goes on.

It takes all my concentration not to laugh in his face. That certainly isn't the sleaziest pickup line I've heard, but it's damn close. On any other day, I might have flirted back, maybe even taken a ride on the Bologna Sea Pony to see what the fuss was about. But I'm sweaty enough without needing to engage in extracurricular activities.

"Maybe another day, Brax," I sigh, starting to move away, back toward the bar.

His hand on my upper arm stops me in my tracks and I stare down at it. The fingers are short, not long enough to wrap around the jiggly flesh, and I can see the webbing between the digits. His skin is cold, clammy, and his grip is much too tight to be friendly.

"Don't be like that, Guppy. We could have fun," he says, trying to stay casual.

Gritting my teeth, I swallow the growl building in my throat. I look him up and down once, not liking the way he's trying to loom over me. I'm small, only coming up to his chin, and he isn't the first guy to try to use his height advantage to intimidate me. But you know what they say: the shorter the woman, the closer to Hell.

I bring my opposite forearm down hard on his wrist, and he recoils with a hiss, giving me the space to pull my leg back and kick out at his kneecap. He yelps as it bends just a little too far the wrong way, staggering into the wall and clutching it.

"Having fun yet?" I sneer, stepping back to admire my handiwork.

"Fat bitch," he spits, trying and failing to stand on his bum leg.

I fake a yawn. "Okay, Fishface. Have a shitty day," I chirp in my fake customer service voice before bounding away.

It takes less than four minutes before a snarling Dominic is at the bar, glaring daggers at me. I purposefully ignore him for as long as I can, knowing how much that grinds his gears. Dominic and I have a hate-hate relationship on the best of days. It's only a few lines of legalese in my contract that keep us from tearing each other limb from limb, but there's nothing that prevents me from being as absolutely infuriating as possible.

"Lyra Spanos, I know you can fucking see me. Get your lard ass over here, now," Dominic barks, his oil-slick tenor carrying over the country-rock music blasting through the speakers.

"Did you hear something?" I ask rhetorically, but Trish knows better than to get involved in this. Though I do catch her pressing her lips together to keep from laughing.

"Now!" Dom demands again.

With a groan, I resign myself to the lecture. I look around the room, trying to find literally anything to focus on other than my boss. Ah, yes. The DJ. Zane is still shirtless, and he's looking my way now. At least we can eye-fuck each other while Dominic tries to chew me out.

"You broke a bouncer's leg," he starts.

"Not even bothering with foreplay, eh, D?" I snark, leaning forward to rest my elbow on the bar, propping up my chin with my fist.

"Lyra—"

"He put his hands on me. Besides, it's not like you won't be able to find another sucker to replace him," I sigh, staring at Zane's rippling abs. Is he flexing them for me? I bet he is.

"You say that every time. I'm just supposed to believe that guys like him are trying to get with someone like you?"

The open contempt and disgust in his voice isn't anything new. Still, it irks the hell out of me that even after a hundred or so years working for this Prick on a Stick, his comments about my body still hurt. I know I'm not the ideal female figure, not with the size of my ass and tits, and the way my thighs rub together. The tips of my pointed ears aren't as long as the other fae I know, and I've never met one, man or woman, under five-foot-eight. By all accounts, I should be tall, willowy, graceful, like Sapphire, the dryad currently entertaining the men drooling all over the stage. Instead, I'm barely tall enough to lean on the bar top, and too chunky to be anything other than a shitty bartender for the rest of eternity.

Dominic's words fade into a drone at last, and I drift. I let my mind take me away from the strip club I'm trapped in for the rest of my life to a place where no one puts their hands on me unless I ask. Somewhere that doesn't smell like a department store perfume counter fucked a high school boy's locker room. A place where I never have to pretend to know how to make a martini again. A place where the sky stretches from horizon to horizon, not a cloud to hide the ocean of stars, and I can breathe freely once again.

CHAPTER 3

Felix

I keep my back to the wall of the casino, eyes scanning every face that passes, cataloging them almost instantly. A few familiar ones, but for the most part, simply tourists. Ignorant humans who either have no idea what sort of creatures are around them, or know and just don't care.

My phone vibrates in my pocket with my alarm. I silence it with a push of a side button before heading toward the bank of elevators. It's been a slow day, but that's fine with me. I can always find ways to liven things up once I'm back with my pack mates. My skin itches a little, like it's just a hair too tight on my bones. I roll my shoulders as I approach a gaggle of gawking wolf shifters as they stare straight up at the ceiling. One of the young ones steps back suddenly, and I suck in a lungful of wet dog smell as I just barely dodge him. Though his pudgy hand brushes my side, and his gold eyes look around wildly, trying to find me. But the cloak of power I've gathered around myself renders me completely invisible, and the young wolf scrambles back to his pack, face drained of blood. I smirk. Hopefully, he'll watch where he's stepping from now on.

I pass the bar and scan the faces out of habit, slowing as I recognize a pair of fae males, one with gold hair, the other with blood red, their heads close together, speaking rapidly. Maybe today won't be so uneventful after all.

"—chicken out on me now, Lynk. This was your plan," the light-haired one of the two is saying once I'm close enough to eavesdrop.

"Yeah, well, that was before we've been sitting here for three hours and haven't seen any of those scaley bastards," the red-head, Lynk, hisses, eyes scanning the room behind them nervously. He looks right at me for a moment, completely oblivious.

I slip my phone out of my pocket, concentrating to make sure the device is cloaked like the rest of me as I pull up my message thread with Gavril. Depending on how this goes, I might have some new chew toys for him to play with.

"We have to do this, not just for us, but for the others. We won't survive for much longer if we don't get some relief. And we're paying dues for a reason. The least they could do is hear us out," the blond goes on, his tone wavering slightly as he tries to convince himself as much as his friend.

Now I'm officially curious. I slip behind a nearby pillar out of view and drop my invisibility shield, sighing with relief as the pressure on my skin dissipates. I imagine this must be what Viktor feels when he loosens his vest laces at the end of the night. Throwing off my hood, I shake out my wavy hair before smoothing it flat. When I peek out from behind the pillar, the fae have turned their backs to the room and are ordering another round of drinks.

I step out and lean sideways against the pillar, hands in my pockets, waiting. It doesn't take long before the fae turn around to scan the room, and they spot me immediately. Their faces pale, but they don't run, which is odd. They preen themselves instead, straightening sleeves and collars, tucking away loose hairs. I let them sweat for a moment before pushing

24

off and crossing over to them.

"Is there something I can help you gentlemen with this evening?" I drawl casually, fighting to keep my shoulders back instead of hunched in my usual posture.

"Yes, Mr. Devereaux, actually. Um, there's—" Lynk clears his throat, swallowing hard.

I look him up and down. He's dressed well, wearing an unwrinkled button-down and pressed slacks. His hands, however, show years of hard work. Callouses and cracks, with a permanent black stain under his fingernails. A smith of some kind?

"We wanted to discuss...well, we wanted to ask if there was any way you or your partners could..."

The blond trails off as I similarly scan him, keeping my face purposefully clear of emotion. Up close, this fae is much brawnier than his companion, and I spy dozens of scars up and down his forearms. There's a persistent odor of blood and meat around him, strong enough to cover the citrus zing of fae magic I'd expected. A butcher.

"What we mean is that we have a problem, and we wanted to...get your help," Lynk picks up, the strength fading from his words.

"Help with what, exactly?" I question softly, so low they have to lean in to hear me over the ambient clamor of the casino.

"A new clan has moved in. Dryads. And they're interfering with our businesses," the blond goes on, sounding more confident now.

I remember Viktor mentioning something about that real estate lease being finalized a few months back. We'd made it clear to the newcomers how things work in this town, so I'm even more curious about what could possibly be so amiss to drive these two here to beg for my pack's help.

"We've noticed they're doing a lot of business after dark; people in their Sunday best coming and going out of back doors," the blond goes on.

I perk up at that. Finally, something interesting. "Has anyone you know been inside these back doors?" I question.

They both shake their heads. "We didn't want to overstep. But I've been in this town long enough to know when something isn't right. And this isn't right." The blond sets his jaw, sitting a little straighter.

God, I didn't think there was any integrity left in this desert. I almost feel bad for him. It won't be long before that honest streak gets him killed. But it won't be me and mine that teach him that lesson, at least not today. I slide a card out from the back of my phone's case and hold it out for them.

"You were right to bring this to our attention, gentlemen. I'll make sure Mr. Kulikov and Mr. Russo are informed. Call this number in a day or two, and give the person who answers your information. We'll be in touch before the end of the week with next steps."

They nod and I give them a smirk before leaning past them to wave down the bartender. "Their tab is on the house," I instruct, and the bartender nods curtly.

The fae try to speak, but I just chuckle. "Next time you need our help, don't wait for us here. Just go to the concierge desk and leave a message. A lot safer than sitting at the bar insulting our mothers," I comment, turning on my heel before they can puzzle out my meaning.

I jump into the private elevator, scanning my ID card as I go. It's closing in on seven p.m., and tiredness settles deep in my bones. It's been a long, boring day and using my power for extended periods of time always leaves me feeling somewhat worn out. I roll my head from side to side as the car moves steadily up through the floors.

The second the door slides open, I'm met with the welcoming scent of garlic and rosemary, followed closely by the sound of Gavril yelling at the television.

"Let me guess, your stocks went down," I quip with a smile as I make my way inside. Viktor must have finished up work early, standing with his back to me as he chops the ends off a bunch of green beans and tosses them into a skillet.

Gavril doesn't move from his position on the sunken couch. The TV's on silent, and he's sitting with elbows leaning on his knees. His bear-like hands are bundled beneath his chin.

"If you know so much about stocks, why don't you share your knowledge?" Gavril snaps as though he's furious, but the smirk playing on his lips tells me otherwise.

"Mind your tone," I reply, coming to a standstill behind Viktor. My hands reach out to run down his sides, and I nestle my face into his back, drawing in his scent as if I need it to survive.

"Long day?" I ask him, as he takes hold of the skillet's handle and tosses the green beans so they don't burn. A cloud of steam rises as I pull him closer and press a gentle kiss to his shoulder.

"Long enough," he groans, a palpable air of stress around him. Reluctantly, I let go of him and hop up onto the counter by the stove. I pick aimlessly at a resting rack of lamb smothered in a herby crumb.

"You used pistachios this time," I comment, nodding in approval.

"How many times have I told you not to taste before I've plated?" Viktor turns his face to me, just enough that I catch the playful smile on his usually straight lips.

"So far? Every night this week." I suck my finger and thumb into my mouth, savoring the flavors. "Wine?"

Viktor nods toward a crystal decanter on the kitchen island. "A '93 Bartolo Mascarello Barolo. Not my favorite, but it pairs well."

"Such a snob," I muse, hopping down from the counter and pouring myself a large glass. Viktor grins wildly as he salts the vegetables and plates them. Gavril stands from the couch and meanders over to us, picking my wineglass out of my hand and downing the lot in a few mouthfuls. He lets out an animated *"ahhh"* as he licks his lips.

"You're an animal," Viktor chuckles, carving the lamb with expert precision.

Usually, I'd be thrilled to get home and sit down to dinner with my pack, but tonight there's something toying with the far corners of my focus. My tiredness is quickly dissolving into impatience, yet I can't quite put my finger on why.

"You're disappearing into that head of yours," Gavril says, gently pushing my hair back from my face. People always think he's nothing but muscle. Just the guy we keep around to do the messy work. But Gavril is so much more than that. Inside, he's soft and caring to a fault.

"I came across a couple of fae," I admit as we sit down at the table. Viktor takes his place at the head, as usual, whilst Gavril settles in beside me. Warmth radiates from him in comforting waves, and I naturally lean against his arm.

Viktor stills, knife and fork poised above his plate of food. "Trouble?"

"They were fine, but apparently, they're having some issues with a clan of dryads who have recently moved to the area." I chew my food slowly, relishing the balance of herbs and spices Viktor has used.

Viktor draws in a long breath, stress settling on his wide shoulders. "I will add it to our list."

"Between Somnium and the population growth, we're lucky we even have time to eat," Gavril scoffs, his plate almost clean. "I'll handle the dryads."

Even the mention of Somnium has me tensing up, but I try to mask my emotions. If I'm going to manage to sneak out later, I can't risk Viktor getting suspicious.

"The fae seemed pretty shaken up," I reply. "They said they'd call with all the info."

"I'll let admin know I'm waiting." Gavril dishes up seconds for himself and tops up our wineglasses.

"I trust you'll deal with the dryads peacefully," Viktor muses, eyes locking with Gavril's.

Gavril lifts and drops his shoulders in a shrug. "If they show me respect, I'll do the same."

"We don't have time for distractions." Viktor's words hang heavy in the air, dangling between us like some sort of pendulum. Time is ticking by too quickly. If we don't make our move soon, our hourglass will be empty of sand, and we'll be right back where we started. The restlessness in my gut solidifies into resolve. We need more intel, and if my contacts aren't getting what we need, then I'll just have to do it myself.

CHAPTER 4

L it with a neon red glow, Somnium is not unlike many of the streets outside. It's unforgiving, casting its patrons in a ghoulish light. Combined with the thrum of bass, you'd be forgiven for believing you'd stepped foot into the seedy underbelly of Hell itself.

My steps slow as most of my concentration goes to keeping my invisibility shield up. With each breath of stale air I take, my shoulders feel weighted down, and there's a dull ache spreading in my ribs. It's like squeezing through a too-tight space, playing a full-body game of Tetris as I'm forced to manipulate each part of my body into an unnatural position. All of this sends a clear message: I'm not supposed to be here. Whatever wards Dominic has put up around this place are strong, and once again, doubt creeps in. I knew it would be risky; that on the surface, this was a bad idea. But we've worked off rumors and innuendo up to this point. It was high time we had some solid information about what the hell goes on here.

A stage, that's arguably more well-lit than the rest of the dive, is currently occupied by a leggy blonde human. She spins around a sturdy pole with elegance, tipping and bowing to the leering men occupying the surrounding seats. It's overly warm in here, even with a subtle draft blowing out from the AC. The floor is sticky underfoot, like walking on a carpet of discarded gum. It takes me a second through all the distractions to remember that the dancer on stage and the assortment of lecherous audience members are not why I'm here.

Rough scales tingle just beneath my skin as I move past the central stage and toward the private rooms in the back, just beyond a heavy black velvet curtain. There are a few seconds when I glance from the entrance over to the closed-off area, and then back again. The space is vast, cluttered, yes, but much bigger than it should be. There's no way the average-sized brick building my pack and I studied over and over could contain all of this. And the amount of magic it would take to power the wards, as well as these space-stretching spells, would be astronomical. How can a demon like Dominic be doing all of this?

Questions swirl in my mind as I step through the curtain behind a server. I can't linger, but I need answers. Loud music gives way to sultry chatter, and suddenly, the noise of the club is coming from the ceiling rather than behind me, as I'd expected. I draw in a long breath, and the bitter undertones of dark magic stifle the air like rotting fruit. To my left, there's a hallway with scantily clad attendants slipping in and out of curtained alcoves. I need to get closer, but the longer I stay in this place, the harder it becomes to focus. The realization that I've snuck in here without Viktor or Gavril's knowledge makes the sudden panic that I'll do something rash, overwhelming. I hadn't considered that my curiosity would grow and fester to the point I would find my way into the lion's jaws. If my cloak were to disappear, I'd be up demon creek without a fucking salt circle buoy to keep me afloat. But in for a penny, in for a pound.

"I promise you, there's no catch," a familiar voice chimes somewhere in the distance, behind the drapes and off to the left. A few feet, maybe. Close enough that his unplaceable accent is impossible to drown out.

"Just a touch of your soul and I'll see to it that you'll be flying high in no time, darling."

Dominic.

I imagine he spins the same bullshit every night. Empty promises framed with bright-eyed smiles.

"You'll never even know it's gone, trust me."

My strides increase in speed until I'm peering around a corner into an open space. Another bar lines one side, but there are no liquor bottles piled high on the shelves behind. He's there, the demon bastard himself. Wearing a suit that's at least thirty years out of style, he's not what most people would consider conventionally attractive. His average height and build make him supremely unassuming, but there's malice to the way his dark eyes and slicked-back hair glint in the blood-red light of the club. A spark appears between him and his prey before it disappears into a vial. *A grain of sand.* That's how he describes the amount of soul he needs to acquire to make their experience unique. Those pinches add up fast. I've seen these people queuing down the street before Somnium has even opened, itching to get inside for their next escape. They always have the same empty stare, visibly sleep-deprived and desperate. Cracked shells of who they once were.

I'm about to step closer, to finally witness the process we'd only ever heard about, when a wave of nausea hits me like a freight train. I backtrack out of the lounge and through the curtain to the main club, shaking my head to clear it of lingering tendrils of magic. But then something new catches my attention, a scent so unlike anything I've experienced before. My movements stall as I spin tentatively on the balls of my feet, gaze darting past the clientele in search of the piece that doesn't belong.

A crash from the main room pulls my attention, and my

heart jumps into my throat. I should leave. Now. My shield is draining my reserves, and I can't be caught lingering here, especially if a fight is about to break out.

"Watch where you're fucking stepping, bitch!" An enraged man, human by the looks of him, is up on his feet beside a low armchair. The dancer he'd been patronizing scuttles off, cash in hand despite not finishing her dance. The human's hands are balled into furious little fists at the end of his doughy arms and, even with his short stature, he's towering over someone.

A flash of red hair catches the light before a sticky drink tray launches against the man's temple. He recoils, mostly in surprise, I presume, since I can't spot any blood. There's a loud cackle of laughter as he falls back into his chair, and I finally get to see the other participant in this spat.

"What? Too busy trying to find your micro-dick to pay attention? Sure you didn't drop it somewhere?" Her voice is such a stark difference to the face-melting bass amidst the chaos. I take a cautious step to the left to get a closer look without accidentally bumping into someone.

A tiny speck of a woman has her hands firmly settled on the soft mound of her wide hips. Her petite face, surrounded by a mop of unruly red hair, stares at the man like she's about to nip at his damn ankles. They're about eye level now that he's seated, but that doesn't stop her from looking down her nose at him.

"1985 called while you were busy disappointing Ember, by the way. They want their acid wash jeans back. Did you get dressed in the fucking dark or something?" She picks up her tray with a peculiar kind of grace, growling at the man in the soaked jean and khaki shirt combo. With a flick of her hair over one shoulder, she flounces back toward the bar, slipping under the bar hatch rather than opening it.

The Dream Lounge is long forgotten as my feet follow my curiosity toward the bustling bar in the main room. I dare to step close enough to overhear the fascinating little spitfire as she talks with her co-worker.

"You know Dominic is going to have your ass. That's the second one tonight," another bartender hisses in the direction of the firecracker, whose face is a delicious shade of annoyed pink.

"Fuck Dominic," she grunts, lips pursed. "If he's not going to stop these scumbags from touching shit they shouldn't, then I will. And he can kiss my lily-white ass in the meantime."

"Lyra..." The second woman shakes her head, sucking her teeth while she fills two glasses to the salted rim with cloudy liquor.

Lyra. A name like a song. I whisper it to myself, luxuriating in the feeling of the syllables dripping off my tongue. It's a name that's meant to be sighed, to be moaned, to be screamed at the peak of ecstasy.

I mentally shake myself at that last thought. I haven't felt like this in years. Why now? Why her?

As if answering my own question, my body warms. Humming with the proximity to her and leaving me weaker than any dark magic ward ever could.

"It's better for me to stay behind the bar, anyway. I hate this table service shit," Lyra goes on, drawing my focus again.

My eyes remain glued to the redhead as she dusts off the bar with a dirtied cloth, scrubbing the same sticky spot with vigor. I study the delicate veins and muscles in that arm as she moves, making the simplest of tasks look hauntingly majestic. Heavenly, even. An angel caught in the sharp-taloned grip of purgatory itself.

The second bartender raises a fair eyebrow in her direction. A silent, skeptical question that makes Lyra chuckle and shake her head.

"It's not better for me. It's better for them. It's safer for everyone if I'm contained by this thing," Lyra replies, slapping the bar top and making the other girl laugh.

I can't help but smile too, and I dare to take another step

closer, until I'm standing in front of her, only the bar between us now.

Lyra bites down on her lower lip, as if considering something, until a dazzling smile lights up her features. Capillaries expand and fill with rose blood, a maiden's blush spreading across the bridge of her nose and the rounds of her cheeks.

The longer I stare at her, the more my chest tightens. This time, it isn't the dark magic wreaking havoc on my body. I clasp my hand down against my stomach as the muscles jump and twitch with a sensation akin to nervousness. Something tugs, deep inside me, that I can't quite put my finger on. It coils and knots like thick rope. Instead of the rough grip of scales beneath my skin, there's a fiery heat spreading down through my extremities. Like being pulled into a bath of scalding water.

A fraction of an inch away from the mystery redhead, the words spill out from between my lips.

"Who *are* you?"

Lyra stiffens, whipping around to look at the place where my head ought to be. For half a heartbeat, I let myself get lost in the golden green of her hazel eyes, the long copper lashes framing them, the perfect slope of her nose, and the dart of her quick tongue as it slides out to wet her parted lips. But as her hand reaches out, I have to pull back before she touches me. And despite every stiffening fiber in my body telling me not to, I bolt.

CHAPTER 5

GAVRIL

Viktor and I pull into a parking spot outside of Sly's shop, the sun bouncing off the dark-tinted windows of our town car. The strip mall is a few blocks from the main drag, and nothing about the building would suggest it houses a powerful mage and his wares. Squeezed between a Papa Johns and a nail salon, The Sorcerer's Source has no front window display, just black curtains and neon signs depicting a palmistry chart, a crystal ball, and a steaming cauldron whose smoke blinks on and off in a steady two-second beat.

Overall, tacky and mundane. Just like the man himself.

Leaving Antony, our driver, behind, Viktor and I cross the short distance to the front door, which I pull open for my pack mate to let him enter first. He gives me a small, secret smile, one he'd never let anyone outside of our pack see, and my heart skips a beat. There's a flash to his purple eyes, an ember I hope stays lit through this chore. I follow behind, taking a minute to admire the view of Viktor's ass in his perfectly tailored charcoal gray suit.

The door closes with a soft chime, but we don't break our step to look at anything on the crowded shelves to either side of the main aisle. Most of the junk is for human tourists, crystals and tarot cards, and a few books one might normally find in a mundane spiritualist store. The real prizes are the items in the locked glass cases lining the walls. The amulets and artifacts that contain real magic and curses, if the rumors are to be believed. Sly isn't exactly known for his strict moral compass when it comes to making a sale.

The man in question is behind the glass-topped display counter, staring at Viktor and me as we maneuver our large frames through the space until we come to a stop before him. The mage is human, but the aura of magic around him is substantial. He's lanky, with tan skin and a long neck, giving him the appearance of a desert lizard, especially as his bright green eyes go round as casino chips, his Adam's apple bobbing as he swallows hard. I cross my arms over my chest, flexing a little, just to watch him sweat.

"Glad to see you up on your feet again, Slyvester," Viktor starts, his soft Russian accent giving the pleasantry just the barest hint of a threat.

Sly's eyes flick to me, and I grin, looking him up and down. I've lived on the sounds of his begging for a week, and it takes a lot more effort than I'd admit to stop myself from ignoring Vik's decree for no violence today just to hear it again. Guys like this weasel talk a big game, but they all shit their pants when faced with a real predator.

"Yes...um, doing very well, thank you, Mr. Kulikov. Wha-What can I do for you...g-gentlemen this fine afternoon?" he stutters, not-so-subtly wiping away some sweat from his upper lip.

"My associate informs me that you've agreed to lend your talents to a little project we've got. I'm here to finalize the specifics," Viktor continues, settling his shoulders in a more comfortable position.

Sly frowns for a moment, and I shift until I can lean

against the counter, supporting my weight on one palm. I tsk under my breath, pushing a little of my power through the metal frame of the glass case until it arcs out in a bright flash, zapping the back of Sly's hand. He yelps and jumps backward, nearly toppling a stack of wooden crates. Vik shoots me a chastising look, but I only grin.

"Did that *spark* your memory, Sly?" I tease with a waggle of my eyebrows.

My stomach jumps at the annoyance simmering in Viktor's amethyst gaze, the tight clench of his jaw. I lost my voice of reason many years ago, so there's nothing in my head to stop me from wanting to turn that simmer up to a full boil.

Sly swallows roughly and rubs his hand, a small red mark appearing where my lightning hit him. I consider doing it again as his silence continues but, unfortunately, he gasps and nods vigorously.

"Yes, yes. Now I remember my conversation with Mr. Devereaux. Sorry about that–yes, I remember. The charms, yes, of course," Sly rambles, edging toward a curtain-covered doorway ever-so-slightly.

I clear my throat dramatically, and the mage freezes. Viktor lifts his chin, assessing for a long heartbeat, and I watch Sly's knees start to knock. Unable to help myself, I push another pulse of electricity from my fingers, down into the floor, through the wires, and out of the outlet just behind the mage. The bolt hits him square in his lower back, and I barely hold in a chuckle as his limbs twitch erratically for a moment before he collapses against the display case. Viktor flashes me another look, a warning. Oh, good. He's caught on to my game, even if he's not thrilled to be playing.

"One of our associates will pick you up and bring you to the work site," Viktor states, speaking before I get the chance to send any more sparks. "The items we need you to empower will be waiting, as well as any supplies you may need. Our associate will oversee the process and bring you back to your humble abode. Once we receive confirmation that your charm works as discussed, I'll make sure my accountants are informed that your account has been balanced, and collection attempts will cease."

His bored tone sets my inner chaos gremlin into a frenzy. My fingers itch, longing to close into fists and bury themselves in Sly's face. That would certainly entertain both me and Viktor, at least for a while. But no. We need him whole and fully empowered for the project. If he has to expend magic to heal himself, then he might not have enough juice for the charms. Stupid humans and their limited magic reserves ruining my fun.

Sly swallows hard, visibly shaking. "What sort of items are we talking about? I don't do weapons, and with a spell like this–"

Viktor chuckles, a dark sound that stops the mage mid-sentence. "Nothing like that, Sly. Though I'm not sure why you'd be worried if we did need you to handle a few firearms. You pay us your dues on time," he says, waving a hand.

"Yeah, but my dues don't stop the feds from raiding my shop," Sly mutters, rubbing his back.

Viktor looks almost offended by this puny human's doubt, and I growl a little louder. Sly backpedals, rattling off almost incoherent apologies, but Viktor's stern expression silences him again.

"Your role here isn't to ask questions. Unless you'd like me to reconsider my offer," Viktor says, no veil covering his threat now.

Sly shakes his head, holding up his hands in a gesture of surrender. "No, I'll do it. Just want to–I just–never mind. I'll do it. You don't have to worry about a thing," he says, looking away.

"You're right; I don't," Viktor replies, cold as a Siberian winter. He glances at his watch before sighing. "Pleasure as always, Slyvester, but we must be on our way. Our mutual friend will call on you this evening. Don't make him wait."

Viktor doesn't acknowledge any of the parting

platitudes Sly spouts off, simply turning on his heel and heading toward the exit. I linger for a moment, the impulse for violence too great to ignore. Giving Sly a wink, I zap him one last time, his body dropping to the floor like a sack of potatoes as he convulses. My laughter follows me out, and I'm still smiling as I step back out into the desert heat and slide into the backseat of the car with a satisfied sigh.

Viktor's silent for several minutes as we leave, but I don't care. I know I'll pay for my antics later, but, my God, it was worth it.

"You know what I want to say," Viktor starts at last.

"That I shouldn't play with my food?" I suggest flippantly, offering him an innocent pout before I turn to look out of the window. Crowds roll by, tourists and punters, all seemingly unaware of our presence among them.

Viktor gives me one of his practiced sighs, the kind that could make lesser men drop to their knees and beg for his forgiveness, but I just smirk to myself. His hand on the back of my neck makes me jump, before I go limp and gasp, a flood of cool ice filling my veins from each spot his fingers dig into my flesh. My instinct to fight, to tease and struggle, disappears, my eyes drooping as Viktor's will crushes my own with ease.

"I gave you a strict command, Gavril, and you disobeyed me. You clearly need to be taught another lesson in obedience, don't you?" he growls, dragging me down so he can speak into my ear.

I moan softly, cock jumping to life in my jeans. Fire replaces ice in my blood, and I lick my suddenly dry lips.

"Please," I breathe, trying to twist to face him. But I'm still frozen under the weight of his will.

"Please..." Viktor prompts, squeezing my neck.

"Please, *Daddy,*" I gasp, cock throbbing as waves of pleasure running through my body, all stemming from the hand on my neck.

"When Felix gets home, he's going to help me take you in hand, *my heart,*" Viktor promises, nipping at my earlobe before shoving me back to my side of the vehicle.

The loss of his touch and command leaves me aching, but not nearly as much as the pounding between my thighs. I adjust myself as best as I can, a stern look stopping me from letting my hand linger for too long. Thankfully, we're pulling into the underground garage, and I'm almost vibrating in my seat with anticipation. I throw myself out of the door and jog to the elevator, hammering the call button over and over, even as Viktor takes his sweet time coming to my side.

"Not so fast," Viktor says calmly, loosening the knot in his tie as we step inside the car. The doors of the elevator close, leaving us both standing beneath the fluorescent lights.

"You take one step inside and then you get down on your knees like a good boy. Understood?" His tone is a mixture of promise and poison and although he always keeps a steady head when we play, I still get that exhilarating zing of fear.

A short elevator ride later, we're back in the penthouse, but before I can catch him, Viktor is moving toward the kitchen, shrugging out of his suit jacket and rolling up his sleeves. I follow him like a lost puppy until he shoots me a cool stare. Viktor nods to a spot beside the elevator doors, just once before he goes about fixing himself a drink. I know better than to throw myself at him, or to beg for forgiveness. Yet the longer Viktor leaves me with a raging hard on, the more I want to break a few more of his rules.

I'm reluctantly settling into my place on the floor when the elevator rings, and I turn to see Felix stumbling out of the car, eyes wide. All thoughts of climbing Viktor like a tree flee my mind, my pack mate's visible distress taking precedent. I stumble to my feet, but Viktor is already at Felix's side. Our hands are brushing at his hair, his face, and his back, trying to soothe him. But his silver eyes are far away.

"What's wrong? Are you hurt?" Viktor asks, words clipped with worry. His eyes travel up and down our smaller friend, trying to find any evidence of injury.

Felix shakes his head, shoving out from our grips and

moving to the wall of windows that looks out over the strip. He stops and leans against the glass, hands pressed flat on either side of his head, like he's trying to melt into it. Viktor and I share a look of concern, moving hesitantly to his side.

"Who *are* you?" Felix whispers, not even aware of us anymore.

"Who is who, *my soul*?" Viktor prompts gently.

I can see Felix's face, and he's staring out into the middle distance, the glare from the last rays of the setting sun not bothering him in the slightest. I try to follow his eyeline and swallow as I realize he's staring at Somnium.

"Did that slimy bastard do something to you?" I ask, gripping Felix's shoulder tight in barely contained panic.

Thankfully, he blinks, coming back into himself before shaking his head. I relax a little. Not that I don't think Felix could destroy that demon six ways to Sunday, but doing so could very well threaten to unravel all of the work we've done.

"She's a woman...no, not a woman. She's...something else..." Felix starts, trailing off with a wistful sigh, cool eyes dancing in a memory neither of us can see.

Viktor and I look at each other again, this time in alarm. The last time Felix caught a bug like this for a woman, we had to flee France in a hurry. For some random woman at a strip club to suddenly break a two-hundred-fifty-odd-year streak might be more disconcerting than the idea of Dominic seeing him on the premises.

"Who is she, Felix? You're not making any sense," Viktor questions with a low snarl of frustration.

"Who, indeed, Viktor. Who is she, indeed," Felix sighs cryptically before going silent again.

I swallow and step back, running a hand down my face. Viktor keeps trying to needle Felix for more information, but I give up, heading to the kitchen to mix us all a round of drinks. My thoughts are troubled, a frown pulling down the corners of my mouth. It's not quite jealousy settling into my gut, but apprehension. There isn't a single doubt in my mind about where Felix's loyalties lie, and that's with me and Viktor. But we can't afford distractions, not when we're this close to finally achieving our goal. So I'll just have to make sure Felix forgets her, at least until after we've dealt with Somnium. Once this is over, then we'll have plenty of time for distractions. And how I do love a good distraction.

CHAPTER 6

Lyra

The sun is just dipping low behind the barrage of neon lights and rooftop terraces, casting this side of the strip in a warm orange glow that's more comforting than its artificial counterpart. It never really gets dark here. The flickering stars in the midnight sky are often replaced with strobe lights at casino entrances and the reflection of flashing billboards in the distance.

I like this time of day, somewhere between day and night, when the streets are eerily quiet. Like the sweet calm before the storm. Usually, I sit up here on the roof of Somnium, watching the rest of the nocturnal creatures wake from their slumber. But tonight, I don't have time for such luxuries.

It's a Saturday, easily Somnium's busiest night, and we've got a full house of dancers, DJs, and no doubt an animated Dominic already pulling *dreamers* in off the streets. A bitter taste of bile rises in the back of my throat as I try to convince myself that it's time to head downstairs, into the pit.

Standing up from my spot on the rooftop, I dust off my

black jeans and head for the door. I take the stairs two at a time on short legs, convincing myself that the quicker I get to work, the quicker tonight will be over. I can busy myself with restocking the fridges behind the bar and getting the chairs down from atop the tables. Maybe I'll even catch a glimpse of Zane setting up. It's humid enough that there's a good chance he'll be strutting around topless, and I can steal a glimpse or seven of that magnificent chest of his.

When I walk through the storeroom and into the expanse of the bar area, I'm surprised to find a sweaty Dominic with his head in the sink by the dishwasher. One hand, with knuckles covered in a slimy smattering of dark hair, is partially buried in the ice bin. My mouth parts in silent outcry as he gathers a handful of ice and runs it over the exposed skin at the back of his neck.

"There's a health code violation if I've ever seen one," I choke out bitterly, frozen on the spot by the hatch.

Dominic turns his head just enough to look at me, swiftly melting ice sliding out of his hands and into the sink below.

"Oh, fuck off, Lyra," he curses, foamy spittle gathering at the corners of his mouth like he's parched. As if on cue, he points to one of the liquor bottles. "Pour me a white zinfandel."

I'm used to my stomach doing disgusted barrel rolls at the sight of him, but as I study him now, the nauseous roiling only gets worse. His face is tinged gray with an angry crimson flush around his ears and, if I'm not mistaken, there's a tremble in his limbs like he can't quite find the focus to stay still. He's been like this for a few days, maybe going on a week, but with the house lights up, the change is even more obvious. I spin the top off a warm bottle of white zinfandel, purposefully ignoring the chilled bottles we keep in the fridges, and pour a hefty measure into a glass. With a fake grin, I slap the glass down on the counter beside his waiting hand.

"One white zinfandel, I hope you choke, have a pleasant day." The snarky clip of my words comes naturally around

Dominic, and I revel in the irritation brewing in his beady little eyes. The others might not have realized it by now, but Dominic can't force me to be courteous. Unlike other bosses, he doesn't have the ability to cast me aside with a snap of his stubby fingers. He's forced into this eternal damnation just like I am. Hell if I'm going to make it easier on him.

"You're a real piece of fucking work," he grumbles, swallowing down the pink wine with a grimace. He sets the glass back down when he's done and wipes the spilled droplets from his mouth with the back of his hand.

I lean my hip against the bar, crossing my arms over my stomach as I survey him with a newfound curiosity. There's definitely something different about him. He looks sickly, weak. Like he's succumbing to a fever. Hopefully, the cause is long-winded and painful.

Dominic turns around to face me, pointing one finger in my face and forcing me to breathe in a lungful of the putrid perfume he's giving off. Before he can say whatever he was about to, I reel back, coughing. "Fucking hell, Dom. What is that?" I manage to get out between hacking retches. My hand moves instinctively to cover my nose and mouth, but I still gag against my open palm. "You smell like hot shit and sauerkraut."

He just growls and lowers his hands to his sides, clenching his fists. "I don't have the time or the patience for your insults, Lyra. Not today. Not to-fucking-day."

Dominic barges past, and I narrowly avoid coming into contact with him. "Funny, with a face like yours, I figured insults were given a designated time slot. Do you need me to book an appointment next time?" I shout at his retreating back, earning me a middle finger over one shoulder before he disappears behind the curtain to the Dream Lounge.

"Is he gone?" Kiera, one of the other barmaids, pokes her head through the entrance, her fair hair tied back in a bun at the base of her neck.

"Yeah, with a bit of luck, he won't come back," I reply

with a chuckle. "Were you hiding outside?"

I cover an empty liquor case with a garbage bag before shoveling out the contaminated ice. I couldn't care less if anyone who was stupid enough to come here catches whatever funk Dominic has, but I'm sure as shit not going to have this toxic stank cloud hovering around for the next several hours.

"Damn right I was. Did you smell him?" Kiera winces, shaking her head and shivering with disgust. "I don't know what the fuck is going on with that guy, but I hope he figures it out, and fast. Gross."

We share a laugh as I work, even if I'm trying not to hurl. After chucking the ice into the dumpster behind the building and refilling the ice bin from the industrial ice maker in the back, I realize Dom's stench is still lingering. Sighing, I grab a bottle of bleach and start filling the sink.

Hours pass and Dominic doesn't resurface. The club is bustling with men and scantily clad women, most of them grinding and twirling to the heavy bass coming from Zane's DJ booth. I'd been right about him going shirtless and currently, my eyes are watching his taut stomach wind in time with the beat. Every now and again, his dark eyes find mine and his thick lips twist into a devilish smirk.

I spend the best part of all night admiring him from afar, waiting to see if he'll do more than just make eyes at me, but with no success. Time to take matters into my own capable hands. By the time his fifteen-minute break comes up, I've already filled a glass with water, and am shoving through the crowd toward the booth, climbing the short stairs as he takes off his earphones.

"You should rehydrate," I shout over the music, holding the water out to him and lingering there just long enough that his hand rubs against mine in passing.

He guzzles it in one long pull, the muscles of his throat

working until the liquid is gone. "Oh yeah?" he asks, rubbing the back of his hand against his lips. There's an empty look in his eyes, like he hasn't quite grasped the word, so I make a mental note to stick to a vocabulary with a two-syllable maximum.

Zane follows me back to the bar, leaning his burly forearms against the sticky surface, palming a second glass I set in front of him, but not drinking it. Instead, his fingers dance along the sides, gathering up the condensation before he licks them clean. My head tilts to the side as I admire the digits, taking just a moment too long considering what they'd feel like toying between my thighs.

"I've seen you here before," Zane says, boyish charm lighting up his masculine features.

I frown momentarily, stopping myself before I can roll my eyes at the lame opener. If I'm planning on mounting this guy like a giant Sequoia, I need to at least try to play nice.

"I've seen you, too," I reply casually, flashing white teeth and a poke of pink tongue. It works. Zane's eyes go straight to my mouth, and I take note of the jump of his pulse in his thick throat. Oh yeah, I've got him.

"You want to take a break with me, right?" I ask with a soft smile, tilting my head to the side to be as charming as I can possibly be.

There's a pause as I watch his face closely, waiting for him to pick up what I'm putting down. And I can see the moment the lightbulb switches on behind his eyes. It's almost too easy.

"Yeah, that sounds good. We should take a break together," he drawls, running a thumb along his lower lip."

I open the flip top on the side of the bar and motion to the door behind me that leads to the employee-only area. And just for the hell of it, I give him a firm swat on his perfect ass, earning me a low growl and a playful snap of the teeth. "Really, Lyra?" Keira chuckles, shaking her head.

"What?" I hiss back, pushing Zane through the door and

toward the storeroom.

"I swear you've got more game in your pinky finger than half the guys or girls in this place," she replies, and I flutter my eyelashes in response.

"What I lack in size, I make up for in sheer force of will," I say with a wink before following my prey through the door.

The second I get Zane down to the second floor and under the spiral stairs, I jump on him and wrap my arms around his wide shoulders. He's hard and burly, which isn't uncommon for wolf shifters, but it still makes initiating the first move almost impossible for my five-foot-three frame. With a dip of his head, our lips clash in a battle of teeth and tongue. It's sloppy and a little miscalculated, but I'll let it slide for a guy that looks like he just walked out of a health and wellness magazine.

"Take off your pants," I order between kisses, his large nose poking me in the eye as he tries to fumble with his belt.

"You don't waste any time, huh?" Zane chortles, sounding a lot like he just hit the jackpot.

I'll admit, I know I'm a catch. These guys swan in here with their big talk and big game and never expect to be conquered by a miniature redhead. I enjoy playing into their surprise, their disbelief. Like they can't quite believe their luck.

"What can I say, I'm enthusiastic," I grunt, shimmying out of my own jeans before jumping up to wrap my chunky legs around his midsection.

The beginning of my arousal is already pooling in my lower stomach. A flutter of excitement makes my insides tingle as a rush of warmth travels down to the base of my spine. Zane's hands are fumbling at my bra, but I save him the bother and push the cups up over my tits. The burn of his rough chest against my peaked nipples is exactly the kind of shit I've been craving these last few days. I needed this. To feel *this*. Like I'm not just a shell working behind a fucking bar.

Just as Zane's mouth latches around one nipple and he

sucks softly, I freeze. That warm tingle I'd felt seconds earlier has vanished, leaving an unsettling chill in its wake.

"What is it? Someone coming?" Zane asks breathlessly. The big guy has backed me up against the wall, his growing erection against my stomach.

"I don't think so," I whisper. The suspicion that we're being watched is almost too hard to ignore.

Almost.

My mouth lands on his as I reach down between our bodies just long enough to twist my panties to the side. If anyone is watching, we're about to give them one hell of a show.

CHAPTER 7

Felix

I swore that I wouldn't go back to Somnium unless I was directly ordered to. Now that our plan is in motion, it's too risky. We have to keep our distance, or else Dominic might catch on and we'd be back to square one all over again.

But I couldn't get her out of my head.

Lyra. The redhead with a mouth like a sailor and more spirit than I've seen in a single soul in decades.

I don't know how I got there, but I'm standing outside of the club, lingering in the shadows of an alley that overlooks the back entrance and dumpster. I've been doing anything and everything to keep myself from this exact spot for over a week. I'd even taken a few shifts on the casino floor, catching cheaters and card sharks for Gavril to have his wicked way with. But nothing has been able to get those gold-green eyes out of my head.

It must have been some sort of trick, a spell on the building to make everyone inside seem infinitely more attractive. There was enough magic there that I could have missed a glamor spell in the shuffle. And Dominic would stoop to such cheap antics if it meant earning a few more pennies. That is why I've been picturing her laugh, her hips, her breasts every time I close my eyes. It had to be.

I've just about talked myself out of this and into going home before I get into trouble when the back door opens, and there she is. In the orange glow of the setting sun, her hair looks like dragon fire. My stomach drops before jumping sharply into my throat. She's too busy hauling a box of ice into the dumpster, so I can observe her without needing to use my power to cloak myself.

She's wearing black jeans again today, ones that cling to her curves like a second skin. God, I'd give anything to take a bite out of her round ass, and other places. As she stretches out onto her tiptoes to reach the top, I get the opportunity to see the curve of her silhouette. Breasts that sit heavy on her chest, down to a waist that I'd love to wrap my hands around, wide hips, and thighs I want to suffocate between. The perfect woman in every way possible way.

My eyes have only begun to drink their fill of her when she heads back inside. Panic lurches in my gut, and without thinking twice, I slip into my power, shielding myself from view, and follow her, just managing to sneak through the closing door. It takes some effort to avoid colliding with the dancers as we walk through the backstage area, but the crowd thins as we round a corner into the service corridor behind the bar. I only breathe a sigh of relief once she's back behind the safety of the counter.

The evening passes in a blur, and I even spy a few people turning in the fake drink coupons we made. I know I shouldn't stay. It's busy, and anyone could bump into me and give me away at any time. It's easier to maintain my power tonight, which is a good sign. That means our plan is working and Dominic's power is weakening. But I can't leave her, not when I find the perfect vantage point at the end of the bar, a little nook between the last stool and the wall on the opposite side of the lift top entrance. I'm out of the way of the servers and patrons, but I still get to watch Lyra to my heart's content.

Everything about her entrances me, even when it shouldn't. She doesn't treat the customers with anything beyond cold indifference, sometimes even edging into outright contempt, but she always has a smile and supportive shoulder pat for the dancers and the other employees. She doesn't give a shit if she can't remember the recipe for a rum and Coke, and won't let anyone bully her into apologizing for her mistakes. She's stubborn and funny and fierce and incredibly sexy.

About halfway through the night, my eyes itch, and I have to resist the urge to let my head droop and rest against the wall as the need to sleep sinks over me. It's late, past midnight for sure, and between the hour and the strain of using my power for so long, it's getting harder to justify lingering. Vik and Gav will probably wonder where I've been. But the idea of leaving Lyra alone bothers me. She's had to fend off too many wandering hands already, not that she can't handle herself. But the crowds are getting rowdier, and the idea of something happening to her makes my stomach clench.

I'm pulled from my half-asleep haze as she leaves the safety of the bar area, heading toward the DJ booth, a glass of water in her hands. I want to follow, but her path takes her through the thickest part of the crowd. I can't risk it, even as my heart hammers. But it's easy to pick her hair out from the sea of color, and I watch her climb the stairs to the booth, conversing with the DJ for a moment before the two head back to the bar.

As the DJ leans forward and starts speaking with Lyra, my eyes narrow. Even if I couldn't smell the wet dog in the air from my hiding spot, his dark eyes and bulk give the man away as a wolf shifter. Lyra can do better than the mutt, surely. But to my astonishment, he maneuvers behind the bar and through the employee door, Lyra right behind him.

My feet move before my mind can catch up, as I'm too busy sorting through the rage and disbelief flooding my system. I lose them for a moment, and I glance up and down the hallway, deciding to take the stairs to my left rather than deal with whatever chaos might be waiting in the backstage area. My footsteps are muffled by the music thumping through the walls, and as I descend to the lower level, I catch a whiff of wet dog that makes my nose crinkle. I follow it down the hallway, passing the open doors to several storage rooms, until a breathy moan makes me freeze. Finally, I spot them, tucked into the shadows under the steps of a wrought-iron spiral staircase.

I suck in a sharp, silent breath. My cock has been half hard all night, but now it comes to full attention. I don't know what manifested first, my ability to make myself invisible, or a voyeur kink, but the two are inseparable now. I tuck myself behind a shelf with a gap at the perfect height for me to watch without being seen if my shield should suddenly drop.

Lyra jumps up into the wolf's arms, most of her pale skin hidden behind his bulk, wrapping her strong legs as far as she can around his waist and pulling him to her. He groans, an arm coming up to support her before he moves forward, pressing her into the wall. I can see her face now, the impatience pulling down her dark brows making my jaw clench. How dare he keep such an exquisite creature waiting?

"You're so wet, baby–"

"I know, Zane, so don't make me wait," she growls, hands clenching on his bare shoulders.

The wolf, Zane, laughs, which only sets her off more. She grabs a handful of his shaggy hair and yanks backward, making him yelp. When she bites his throat, I have to stifle a groan. How lucky is he to get to feel her like that, to have her mark him as hers, even for this quick romp in the shadows. I slip a hand under the soft waistband of my thin cotton pants, palming my cock and stroking slowly. Hot fluid covers the head, and I spread it down my thick length, squeezing the base until my knot swells.

Lyra's head flies up in a gasp as Zane's hips roll, and her

eyes go wide for a moment before the lids slide down, her lips parted in pleasure. The corners lift as Zane sets a hard, fast pace. Her nails drag along his back as she writhes, whimpering with each hard thrust.

"Oh, fuck yes. Right there, don't–don't slow down. Don't stop," she grits out, brow furrowing.

"You feel too good, babe. Gonna blow if I–"

"Slow and deep then, and hard. I'll do the rest," Lyra sighs with a frown.

Another flare of rage makes my cock pulse. This pup could never satisfy a woman like Lyra, not in a thousand lifetimes. She deserves a man who can make her see stars without her needing to lift a finger. The wolf tries, even stepping back to allow Lyra to arch her back and rub her clit in furious little circles, but his technique is sloppy.

I pump my fist along my length as I imagine what a beauty like this little spark would look like speared on *my* cock, hanging on for dear life as I drive into her over and over, hitting her exactly where she needs, sending her screaming over the edge. I wouldn't need to pace myself, to fight my orgasm, because her pleasure would always come before mine. She wouldn't need to beg or demand for anything, because I'd know how to please her in every manner conceivable. And when I'm spent, my pack mates would take over, giving her everything she desires until she lacks the strength to do anything other than breathe.

Her cry of release pulls me from my fantasy, and I watch her face closely. Her eyes are closed, nose scrunched as she tries to extend the moment for as long as she can, but her expression tugs at my chest. She might have peaked, but that's the face of a woman who knows she'll be left wanting. The wolf howls, and his hips stutter as he spurts his unworthy load into her pussy.

My fist clenches on my knot almost to the point of pain, and my arousal is gone. Sex fills the air, but I can't see beyond the red haze filling my mind. He doesn't deserve the honor of filling her belly with his weak seed. He's an animal, prey, unworthy. Lyra is *mine.*

I have to stay still as the two put themselves back together. He keeps trying to apologize, saying that normally doesn't happen. That it'll be better next time. She just hums noncommittally, and I admit that a petty part of my heart sings as she turns her head when he tries to kiss her, his lips landing on her cheek instead before she saunters up the stairs and out of sight, leaving him behind to stare in disbelief.

"That little bitch..." Zane mutters to himself.

Or, at least he thinks he's talking just to himself. The insult to my little spark snaps the last shred of my control. Keeping my cloaking shield tight to my skin, I dart out from behind the shelf and wrap my hand around his meaty throat, shoving him back into the wall he just had Lyra up against. This close, I can smell her musk, like salted caramel and ice cream melting on my tongue and running like a hot river down my throat and straight to my groin.

"You aren't to touch her again, pup," I mutter, my voice deep and dark with my threat.

"What the–who are you? What's going on?" Zane chokes out as my fingers squeeze tight.

I laugh low in my throat, my other hand darting out and grabbing his cock and balls in a tight grip. He's not exactly lacking, but his equipment clearly wasn't sufficient enough to please my Lyra. I twist until he's screaming, or at least trying to. He can't breathe around my fingers, his face turning from red to blue and eyes glazing.

"If you don't want this to be the last time you ever disappoint a woman, then you won't touch her again. You won't speak to her, won't even think of her. Am I clear, pup?" I continue, twisting another quarter turn farther.

He nods frantically, clawing at my wrist, but his strength is fading. I could watch the light fade from his eyes and not lose a wink of sleep. Daring to touch what belongs to me and my pack is a crime worthy of such a punishment, but the tiny voice of reason in the back of my mind reminds me that his death would fall back onto Lyra. So instead, I release my grip, letting the mutt slump down the wall, gasping for breath.

I go back to the bar, content to finish my vigil from my hiding spot, but Dominic is prowling the floor now. In this lighting, it's hard to see details, but there's no doubt he's feeling the effects of our charms. It won't be long now, surely, until he doesn't have a choice but to give in to our demands. And if I play my cards right, I could win more than one prize in this exchange. It's that thought that comforts me as I slip out of Somnium and head back home.

CHAPTER 8

GAVRIL

I might not be able to read emotions like Viktor can, but when Felix storms out of the elevator and into the apartment, it's not difficult to sense the rage clinging to him. It drips from every pore, thick and heady.

I don't bother savoring the taste of the single malt in my hand, choosing instead to relish in the burn as I toss it to the back of my throat.

"Where the hell have you been?" Felix's eyes widen when he notices me. They're bright and steely gray, surrounded by thick lashes that brush his pale cheeks as he blinks in surprise.

Felix doesn't speak. Just watches as I round the kitchen island before he pounces.

His palm wraps around my throat, his thumb and fingers applying pressure while his mouth crashes onto mine. It's all teeth and tongue, filled with a feverish desperation that leaves me panting. Heat explodes low in my stomach, my cock hardening against the confines of my jeans. Felix might be smaller than me, but power runs through his veins like molten silver, unstoppable and all-consuming.

Wherever he's been and whatever he's been doing, he's worked up an appetite.

"I'm going to need you naked, spread, and ready," he orders, stepping back from me and stripping off his shirt. I do as he says, the authority in his tone leaving my knees weak.

"Yes, Sir," I reply, slipping out of one aspect of my personality and into another. Felix's instruction has always been enough to tame me, even if just for a while. Relief swells in my chest and my clothes are pooled at my feet before I even pull in a breath.

"Good boy, Gavril," he muses, walking in a slow path around me, surveying me like a predator would prey.

Viktor's office door opens quietly behind Felix, but Viktor says nothing. Instead, he chooses to watch from a distance as I position myself on the couch. I'm a big guy and it takes a second before I get myself comfortable. I hang over the back of the sofa, my knees spread and back arched to present my ass for his inspection.

The whole room buzzes with electricity, sparking across my skin with impatience. My heart pounds, but I don't dare look behind me. Not with Felix in a mood. Though I don't have any meetings this week. I don't need to sit comfortably. Maybe just a peek—

"*Calm,*" Viktor urges, emerging from the shadows, one large hand palming himself through his gray slacks.

The subaudible purr of his alpha bark makes my skin break out in goosebumps, and the involuntary shiver that runs down my spine like ice as I give in and obey. My cock is so hard that it's almost painful, but I don't dare take my hands off the back of the couch. I hiss through my teeth as Felix's long fingers wrap around the base and pull it backwards, jerking me with a harsh touch. His grip is slick with lube, and my eyes roll back with a groan as he pays extra attention to the ridges that run along the top.

"I've barely fucking touched you and you're already ready to blow. How fucking pathetic," Felix sneers, dropping my cock just as suddenly as he grabbed it.

I whine from the loss of contact, but it turns into a yelp as he brings his hands down on my ass, the blow stinging all the more from the lube coating his palms. I pant as the pain blossoms out across my body, and sparks arc off my shoulders and down my arms. Dropping my head to hang between my forearms, the frame of the couch creaks from how hard I'm gripping it. And then he's back, this time with something flexible in his fingers. I don't even get a second to process before Felix has the cock ring positioned perfectly around my balls and base. I tremble, wanting to buck and fight. Electricity jumps between my hands, across my shoulders, but a low warning growl pulls my attention.

"Control, Gav. Get it under control," Viktor warns.

He sounds closer, but I refrain from looking up or even breathing too hard. My power isn't the only thing I need to control. Felix knows, though, and acted without me needing to say a word. A few more hits like that and I would come all over his Italian leather furniture. But now, with the cock ring, I won't be able to come until he allows it. Behind me, Felix rustles around, and my heart stops as something smooth trail across my lower back, something a couple of inches wide and made of leather. It's the only warning I get before he brings the belt down hard across the swell of my ass, aimed perfectly to avoid contact with my balls. And then he grabs my cock again, mixing pleasure and pain with expert precision.

"Count them, and thank me for my time and attention," Felix snarls, words echoing strangely, sounding more like the beast lurking beneath his skin than man.

"Yes, Sir. One, Sir. Thank you, Sir," I reply, not hesitating for a moment.

Again and again, he brings the belt down across my ass and thighs, pausing long enough for me to feel the full impact and burn before torturing me with a few harsh strokes of my cock. My mind slips away by the time we get to five, and I sink into the hazy bliss that only comes from true submission by the time we hit eight. By ten, my soul detaches from my body, poised on the edge of oblivion but unable to fall.

"Good boy, Gavril. Such a good boy for me," Felix purrs, his fingers slick again and probing at my entrance.

I'm so relaxed that he doesn't even have to prep me for long, with one, then two of his fingers thrusting purposefully into my eager hole. I try to respond, but words fail me. Instead, I can only whimper like a lost pup, thrusting my aching hips back toward him.

"Don't worry, *my soul.* I've got you," Felix breathes, lips brushing the inflamed skin of my thighs before he backs away.

I mewl from the loss of contact, but the sound morphs into a keening moan as the blunt tip of his cock presses against my fluttering hole. I stay perfectly still as he thrusts forward, feeling every ridge along his length as it slips past my ring of muscle. He doesn't pause to let me adjust before he pulls back and starts again, going deeper and deeper until his knot is flush against my ass.

"Take it, just like that. What a good boy you are, taking what I give you," Felix babbles, lost in his own pleasure as he picks up speed.

"Thank you, Sir," I pant, hanging on for dear life.

Each time our skin meets, the welts from his strikes burn all over again. Felix leans down and I arch into him as his tongue runs in a long swipe through the sweat and sparks pooling in the hollow of my spine. My cock bobs between my legs, occasionally hitting my stomach and leaving a smear of sticky precum. I'm so close, teetering on the edge of a knife. But there's no relief in sight, not while that fucking silicone ring remains in place.

A hand on my chin makes me jump, but I let Viktor tilt my head to look at him as Felix continues to fuck me hard from behind. The gemstone purple of his eyes is lost to the black of his blown-out pupils, and I can only let the darkness swallow me. My mouth falls open on a gasp as Felix's cock spears my prostate over and over, battering me with the best brand of pleasure-pain. Viktor's arm flexes on the edge of my vision, and my gaze flicks down to find his cock out, the hand not holding my chin in a vice grip stroking it purposefully.

"Keep that pretty mouth open for me, pet. Just like that," Viktor pants, as close to losing control as he ever gets.

Obeying is second nature, and I let my jaw hang open, my tongue lolling out over my lower lip. Viktor's thumb finds my piercing and strokes it idly, eyes never leaving my face. Leaning down, Felix grabs my cock in a tight grip, squeezing my knot until it hurts. But my God, if it doesn't make me throb with longing. I want to beg, to plead for them to have mercy on me. But I can't, not with the way Viktor holds my mouth open. And even if I could, I doubt they would listen. So I settle on whimpering, eyes watering as I force myself not to blink.

"I'm going to count to five, and then you're going to come on Felix's cock. If you don't, then you don't get to come for a week. Understand, pet?" Viktor growls.

I nod, even as my mind races. I can't get there. Not like this.

"Five."

I try to close my eyes to hone in on the sensations running wild through my body, but Viktor shakes my chin in a wordless correction. I swallow hard, opening my eyes and focusing on his face above me. God, I'm on fire, but the flames refuse to consume me.

"Four."

Felix's hand works fast and furious, but I'm almost numb to his touch. The lack of circulation has kept me hard, but it's come at a price. He pulls away and spits into his palm before resuming his strokes.

"Three."

Felix's hips stutter, losing their steady rhythm in the race for the finish. His chest rattles against my back, a deep, animalistic growl shaking me to my bones.

"Two."

I can't get there. I'm too overwhelmed, unable to focus on anything. The soul-deep ache of failure makes my eyes water for a whole new reason.

"One."

I gasp as feel one of Felix's finger shift, turning to a claw for a moment before he slips a talon under the cock ring and pulls back, shredding it like tissue paper. I scream as feeling returns, and then white-hot pleasure streaks down my spine like lightning. The room brightens for a moment and then I'm coming harder than I have in months, painting the couch and Felix's hand with my seed. Felix follows right behind me, thrusting as deep as he can without knotting me as he spills ribbons of hot cum into my ass.

"Good boy," Viktor breathes.

And then his cock is pressed to my tongue and he's shooting his load into my waiting mouth. I moan, still riding the waves of my orgasm until he finishes. And like the obedient submissive they expect, I wait with Viktor's cum on my tongue until I'm given permission. Only then do I swallow, savoring every drop.

I lose track of time as Viktor and Felix work together to clean me up and apply healing balm to my welts, coming back down from subspace. They help me into our bed, and I'm nearly asleep in Viktor's arms when I hear him speak.

"What was that about, my heart?" The question is a whisper, directed at Felix. I keep my eyes closed, not wanting to interrupt.

There's a long pause, and I consider opening my eyes to look at our smallest pack mate, but then he sighs and runs his fingers through my hair.

"Just needed him. And you, for that matter. That is, if we haven't worn you out, old man," Felix teases.

Viktor growls, shifting until he's out from under me. I smile to myself as I hear the sounds of their heavy breathing and clothes hitting the floor. Rolling over, I relax into the pillow, the sound of Viktor fucking the attitude out of Felix the perfect lullaby.

CHAPTER 9

VIKTOR

The elevator drops swiftly and silently, down past the lobby, the basement level, and even the underground parking structure. Finally, at the very bottom of the shaft, the bell lets out a pleasant chime and the doors open to the best kept secret in Las Vegas.

Across the open space from the elevator, Gavril sweats over a kiln, red light glowing from within and throwing harsh shadows over the planes of his ruggedly beautiful face. Shirtless, his tattoos shine in the low light, and I lick my lips at the sight. I skirt the central pedestal, my steps echoing off the stone walls as I approach the forge. He doesn't look up as I approach his side, running my hand over the exposed plane of his damp back. God, what did I ever do to deserve this man?

"Almost ready to pour," Gavril grunts, doing his best not to react to my touch. But we've been together too long, and I know exactly how to get his attention if I wanted it. He's lucky this work is too important to risk.

"Is this the last one?" I ask, stepping away toward the

worktable.

A narrow mold box filled with tightly packed sand waits for my pack mate, the shape already pressed into the surface. One of the outer arcs, judging by the curve.

"One more. Still waiting for the last shipment to come in. Had to delay it."

Gavril's words are clipped, precise, and deathly serious. For all of his inner chaos, he always knows when the time and place is right to unleash it.

Sudden movement catches my eye and I spin, stepping out of the way as Gavril pulls a large crucible from the heat with a long set of tongs. In three strides, he's at the table, tipping the molten metal into the mold. It's red hot, but I can smell the rich, full-bodied bouquet rising in the steam. Like the best whiskey mixed with the best cigars and the sweetest honey. Every dragon's weakness: gold.

A thick river flows down the sand, filling the shape perfectly, with not a drop left to spare. Gavril lets out a satisfied exhale as he sets the crucible and tongs aside, then brushes off his hands. He looks up at me, the almost child-like glee in his smile making my heart skip a beat.

"So I was thinking..." Gavril starts, stepping back to lean against a wooden crate.

I nod, not looking up from the cooling metal. Gavril thinking is a dangerous game, but I'm willing to hear him out.

"If the plan doesn't work, I've thought up a new 'P.' Pacifica," he says, barely concealed laughter running below the statement.

I blink and do a double take, brow pulling down in confusion. "Like the car?" I question slowly.

"Yeah. I'm going to run Dom over with a minivan."

The earnest insanity in his face stops me from laughing outright. He...he really thinks that something like that would work?

"Listen, I know what you're thinking. But what if I was driving really, *really* fast?" Gavril replies hastily, shifting his restless legs.

Now I know he's joking. I roll my eyes and shake my head with a small, fond smile. "At best, you'd only destroy his vessel and send him back to his home plane. At worst, he'd have justification to finally retaliate."

He deflates a little, but doesn't argue. I look back at the gold, my smile widening. The liquid gold has solidified, the light of the forge gleaming off the top surface. I shrug out of my jacket and roll up the sleeves of my shirt, stomach practically vibrating with excitement. This is one of the largest pieces we've made, and it looks absolutely perfect. Without hesitation, I dig my fingers into the sand on each end of the curved bar, keeping my grip loose for the moment. It's still hot and malleable, but if we wait any longer, then it won't fuse with the others.

Gavril springs into action as I lift the piece from the table, facing me to support the middle. We walk sideways, completely in sync without needing to speak, as we move toward the pedestal at the center of the room, and the heart of this city.

We maneuver carefully, lining the piece up with its appropriate groove before ever-so-gently seating it in place. Stepping back, my heart flips at the sight before me. The mirror-polished surface of the moldavite base is carved with ancient Draconic text, passed down through the generations. The sweeping gold lines of the circle of power are dull, only faintly reflecting the light of the room. We're only missing a few pieces now. So close. So *fucking* close.

The doors to the council's audience chamber close with a resounding thud, and the gathered crowd goes quiet. Eyes of dozens of high-ranking dragons pierce through my skin to the bone, the malicious excitement in the air hitting my tongue like sour milk. I scan the room, logging faces in my mind. Every one of them

is reveling in watching me and my pack mates brought low.

Felix and Gavril are close enough to me that I can feel their body heat radiating onto the bare skin of my forearms. We're all dressed simply, in linen shirts and trousers, peasant garb. We'd been given no warning, no time to change or freshen up before meeting with the council. And now, it's clear that was intentional. The councilman's rebellious son and his deviant friends, in threadbare clothes and crusted with filth, is exactly the image they want people to have of us. Not three of the most powerful younglings to have been born in this millennium.

We move together, walking up the aisle toward the dais where the five members of the dragon council sit, like royalty of old. Five men, the oldest among our kind. They're supposed to be the wisest, too, but stagnation has rotted this body from the inside out. I lock eyes with the High Councilor, Yevgeniy Glazkov, as he reclines in his chair, looking for all the world like this is the last place he'd like to be.

You and me both, asshole.

My father, the finance minister, Zinon Kulikov, is at Yevgeniy's right hand, as he has been for the last two hundred years. The purple eyes I inherited narrow at me as I keep my chin high and shoulders back, refusing to show weakness. He didn't raise me to cower, and I'm not about to start now. Gavril's hand brushes against mine, a spark jumping between us. I don't bother to acknowledge it, because I can hardly blame him for being at the edge of his control. My father has never respected my pack mates, and I don't begrudge them their anger.

Once we reach the open space at the foot of the dais, there's a moment when the whole room seems to hold its breath, waiting. I incline my head in respect, but leave it at that. I won't get on my knees for old men past their time.

"Viktor Kulikov of Pack Kulikovich, Gavril Russo of Pack Russović, and Felix Devereaux of L'escadrille de Paris, you have been summoned before this council to receive your sentence for the crimes of which you have been previously convicted," Councilor Kazamir Tankov, the justice minister, begins.

My blood boils at the memory of that farce of a trial. They sat there and pretended like they didn't hunt humans for sport when they were our age, not caring if they ate serfs or kings. But Gavril shoots one Archduke in Sarajevo, and suddenly it's the end of the fucking world. Twenty years of exile in Siberia have done little to cool my resentment toward these arrogant windbags, it seems.

"We have reviewed the evidence, and heard from witnesses and others, and have reached a decision."

I don't move my gaze from Yevgeniy's face as he speaks, heart thudding like a war drum in my chest. I've considered every possible outcome, and we've planned for everything. But it always came back to one scenario, the most likely punishment: splitting us apart. Gavril, Felix, and I knew going in that this could be the last time we walk together among our kind, but I'd rather spend every moment from now until I lay myself to rest on the run than give them up. I won't let anyone hurt my pack, or rip us apart.

Gavril tenses beside me, his knuckles cracking as he clenches his fists. Felix is shifting from one foot to another, his fingers hovering over my skin. We won't be trapped here, not among our enemies. Felix will cloak us, and we'll escape through the hidden emergency corridor behind the dais before they can stop us. Our bags are already stashed at a safehouse. We're one step ahead of these ancient pricks. We always have been.

"You three will be sent to a newly merging leyline node. You are to secure the land, and assemble your altar. If you are able to do this, and the ritual to join your node to the network is successful, then you will be cleared of your crimes and be recognized as an official pack."

I blink rapidly, my mind grinding to a halt. We're being sent to...what? What the fuck? I stare into the High Councilor's black eyes, trying to find the twist, the catch. This is too good to be true. We aren't going to separated, but given a second chance at recognition. I want to shout for joy, to agree without asking any questions, but there's something too smug in Yevgeniy's deeply lined face.

There's a soft wave of silent disapproval that sweeps the room, the bloodlust cooling to malcontent. They wanted to watch us get drawn and quartered, but we're being given a boon. It should turn my stomach to feel how eager the crowd is for my pack's demise, but I only have eyes for the council.

As if answering my unspoken suspicions, my father shifts in his seat, leaning forward slightly. "This is not a task I would recommend you take lightly. You have already shown how...undisciplined you are. If you continue to act in a way unbecoming of a dragon of your standing, then we will be forced to do as many wished for us to do in the first place."

I nod, the message received loud and clear. But he need not worry. Now that we have a goal to chase, there won't be a being on any plane of existence that can stop us.

"Where is this node?" I ask hesitantly.

There's a chuckle that passes between the council members, and it makes my skin crawl. Kazamir smirks as he clears his throat. "It's a little train stop in the American west. The town hasn't been officially incorporated, but the locals have taken to calling it Las Vegas."

Had I known then what I do now, I wouldn't have agreed so eagerly to their backhanded offer for redemption. We'd been shipped off to the middle of the desert with not a penny to our names, and were soon cut off entirely from our kind. The closest flight, Los Angeles, has only started to acknowledge our presence in the last ten years, but even that is reluctant. We were sent here to rot, chasing after a goal we were never meant to achieve.

But despite their best efforts to break us, we have emerged all the stronger. And now, we're poised on the edge of achieving the impossible. "Have you decided where you're going to have them take yours from?" Gavril asks, voice suddenly soft and serious.

Looking up, I see him standing over one of the three empty obsidian plates along the outer ring of the circle. His thick fingers trace the indent, eyes distant.

I swallow, moving to his side. Threading my fingers through his, I pull our clasped hands to my lips. I kiss his knuckles fondly before letting them drop. He looks up at me expectantly, and I sigh.

"Not in detail. Have you?" I return, looking down at the obsidian plate.

"I was thinking it'd be pretty poetic if I make those bastards pull a scale out of my ass, but that's going to hurt like a bitch. So maybe not," Gavril says, shrugging with one shoulder.

I snort. Of course, even this would be an opportunity for my pack mate to cause chaos. Though I can't say I wouldn't want to stick it to the council if I'd been through half the shit Gavril has. Sighing, I look back to Gavril's face. I expect to see a smirk, but he's lost in thought. I squeeze our joined hands and pull gently toward the elevator. He doesn't fight me as we leave our sacred place.

"Felix says the charms are working a treat," Gavril starts once we're about halfway to the penthouse. "I know it's only been a few weeks, but Dom's looking rough. Not quite at death's door, but definitely approaching the front garden."

I smirk to myself. That's better than I would have hoped at this stage. We shouldn't need to wait much longer to make our next move. I'm about to respond, when my phone vibrates. I let go of Gavril's hand and extract it from my inner breast pocket, eyebrows shooting up as I see the name on the caller ID.

"This is Viktor Kulikov," I answer, holding the phone to my face.

"You dragon bastard," Dominic snarls by way of greeting.

"I'll have you know, my parents were happily bonded when my clutch was conceived," I snark back, smirk widening.

"I don't know if you think I'm stupid, or if you're just

desperate, but either way. I've got your number this time," Dominic goes on, not even bothering to acknowledge my retort.

The elevator arrives at the top floor, doors opening into the living area of my pack's home. Gavril shoots me a curious, questioning look as we exit, but I hold up a finger. I don't want to lose focus and give the game away too early.

"I hold any business owner in Las Vegas in the highest regard–"

"Oh, cut the shit," Dom snaps, speaking over my platitude. "You've wanted me gone from the moment we met. But really? Trying to run me out of business with free drink coupons?"

My heart settles a little. "Oh, those. Yes, I've seen flyers around. But I assure you–"

Dominic lets out a snarl that rumbles through the line. "Don't fucking lie to me! I know you–"

I openly grin as his words die in a ragged coughing fit. Oh, he certainly isn't doing well at all.

"I may have been born at night, but it wasn't last night. I know it was you. Who else would waste their time putting protection spells on literal garbage? Did you think it would stop people from cashing in the offer?" he goes on once he's recovered.

I let out a fake sigh, trying to sound defeated. But it's hard when I can't stop grinning like the cat that got the canary.

"I underestimated you, my friend. But it seems you've gotten the upper hand. I hope your business hasn't suffered too greatly as a result of our little joke," I say, picking my words with care.

"Joke? I don't know what counts as a joke to dragons, but this ain't it. And besides, the joke's on you. I haven't had this much business in years," Dominic replies, triumphant.

"Ah, then all's well that ends well," I say, shaking my head.

"For now. But try any shit like this again, and I assure

you, I won't be as forgiving."

I don't get a chance to reply as the line goes dead. I pull my phone away from my ear and slide it back in my pocket.

"What the fuck was that?" Gavril demands, taking a step toward me.

I turn my head slowly to look at him, my grin growing with each passing moment. Gavril goes a little pale, and I know I must look crazy, but I can't help it. This is the best news we could have received. Dominic may have found the enchanted flyers we swapped for his usual order, but he hasn't noticed the truly insidious charm we put on the other half of his shipment. And now that he thinks he's got the upper hand, he won't bother looking for it.

"I'm going to call the account managers and have them give Slyvester a credit. He has truly outdone himself," I say at last.

"I'm going to take a wild fucking guess and say that was friendly neighborhood demon dick?" Gavril quips, one eyebrow raised in cartoonish curiosity.

My cheeks ache with my smile as it widens even further, and I bite down on my bottom lip to stop myself from chuckling. Despite my glee, I have to keep a level head. There's still time for Dominic to figure out the rest of our plan. I only hope that if his brain does kick into gear and he realizes what we've done, that it's too late for him to do shit about it.

"It's wonderful, isn't it?" I sigh, straightening my posture and releasing a tense crack from my neck.

"What is? I gotta admit, Viktor, you're giving me the fucking creeps."

I ignore Gavril's concern and rub my hands together. "When things turn out just how I intended them to."

Gavril doesn't get a chance to respond as I cross to him and kiss him hard for a moment before breaking away and heading toward my office with a new spring in my step.

If demons thrive on pain and suffering, I sure hope Dominic is looking forward to his.

CHAPTER 10

Lyra

I wake up to the sound of rhythmic squeaking from the other bed in the glorified broom closet I'm forced to call my bedroom. I can smell the sex before I open my eyes, and I roll over to find Braxton rutting Ginny from behind. She looks over to me as she hears me move, giving me a sheepish grin, flashing her slightly pointed canines. Luckily, our relationship is beyond the point where this situation would embarrass either of us, so I roll my eyes and turn over to face the wall. If the Dressing Room Dick Rating Board is right, this should be over soon enough.

Living and working in a strip club means getting used to seeing people naked and engaged in all manner of carnal activities. This isn't the first time Ginny's woken me up like this, and I know I've returned the favor more than a few times. Not that it's been happening lately. After the quickie I'd had with Zane a few weeks ago, he's been avoiding me like the plague. I got checked out to make sure he didn't give me anything, and I'd come back clean. Maybe I should have at least kissed him after, but I'd been too busy being disappointed by his subpar performance to be nice. I don't engage with the customers of Somnium as a rule, and with Zane clearly not interested in another round, the pool of willing bedmates has dried up for the moment.

Minutes later, Braxton and Ginny finish up their business, and he scurries out without so much as a backward glance. I throw off my covers and start to get myself ready for the day. Ginny reclines on her lumpy mattress, face still flushed. Her golden eyes are on the door, full lips pulled up in a little grin.

"He's not so bad, if you don't mind the smell," she comments.

I snort humorlessly. "I'll take your word for it."

"Zane didn't do it for you?" she throws at me casually.

I sigh, jumping into my jeans and pulling a long-sleeved shirt down. All of my other work clothes are dirty, but I haven't been able to get a turn with the machine. There are about half a dozen of us who live here full time, so finding time to shower without someone banging on the door is hard enough, let alone to do other chores.

"He's got the equipment, but not enough blood for his dick and his brain to work at the same time. I could put a neon sign on my crotch with a flashing arrow pointing to my clit, and he still wouldn't be able to find it," I grumble, sitting on my bed to lace up my comfortable work shoes.

Ginny makes a pitying noise, and we share a laugh. The fact she can laugh at all is a minor miracle to me. She has to listen to people describing their darkest, most twisted fantasies every day as a Dream Lounge attendant, then watch them as they live them out in their heads. I don't know if I could do what she does for an hour, let alone five or six shifts a week. At least not without turning into a serial killer.

"You want me to try to hook you up with one of the guys in the lounge?" Ginny asks, bundling her blankets up to her neck as she sits up against her headboard.

I shake my head. "I'm fine, Ginny."

She squirms for a second, chewing on her lip as she considers my words. "Really? Because it looks to me like you're not letting the light steal away some of that darkness."

"You're my light, remember?" I grin, walking over to press a gentle kiss to her cheek. "And my darkness isn't the only thing you steal. I want my bottle of perfume back." I point a playful finger in her direction, catching the subtle notes of coffee beans and marzipan on her skin.

"What perfume?" Ginny's smile is blinding, stretching right across her angelic face as she tosses herself back against the mattress.

I raise an eyebrow. "The one you're wearing, genius. I should've known it was you that took it. Traitor."

I'm about to turn and make my exit when she reaches out and grabs my wrist. She tugs me back to her, gazing up at me with those familiar gold eyes. "Promise me that you're good?"

There's a shared moment of silence between us before I nod, just once.

"I'm good. I promise."

Ginny swallows, her throat bobbing. "I can't lose you, you know that?"

"Quit the sap, I'm not going anywhere." I frown, studying the concern written across her features. "What's brought this on?"

Perching on the edge of the bed, I wait for her reply. Her hand is tangled with mine, warm and comforting.

"We've lost three contracts this month," she admits somewhat reluctantly. "People I knew. People I *liked*."

It's the inevitable in this job, and I want to tell Ginny that, but I force the words back down. Sarcasm isn't going to do Ginny any good, not right now.

"The short-term contracts are the hardest, Gin. There's nothing we can do."

"Maybe you could talk to Dominic, or...or I could? Try to

convince him to give people longer? They were good people, Lyra."

My chest aches for Ginny. Back in the normal bar, we don't tend to get the short-term contracts. Instead, we're stuck with people mid or long term, ten years, one hundred. It's a blessing; one good thing about being out front and nowhere near the Dream Lounge.

"And what do we do when we lose one?" I begin, repeating the same thing I've told her time and time again.

"Remember them," she breathes, nodding slowly. "Remember them and move on."

I set my palm flat against the side of her face and smile. "Remember them and move on."

Leaving her with one last squeeze of our hands, I get my stuff ready for my shift, rolling out my stiff muscles. One day, I'll make a fuss about getting new mattresses, but with Dom in worse shape than I've ever seen him, that's a battle for another time.

I shoulder through the swinging door to the bar, taking a deep breath as I scan the room. It's midafternoon on a weekday, so there's only one lonely middle-aged man in a business suit watching Toyota perform. She's on the older side for a stripper, closer to forty than twenty, but she's got kids to put through college. And her pole tricks are the best out of anyone in the locker room, as far as I'm concerned.

I go around and start taking down the chairs from the tables, wiping them off, and getting ready for the evening crowd, waving to the dancers as they trickle in and head back to the dressing room to get ready. I'm bobbing my head to the classic rock track playing over the speakers, lost in thought. So lost, in fact, that I don't hear the person approaching behind me until he's grabbing me by my forearms and whipping me around to look at him.

"Where is he?" the man shouts in my face, spittle flying and making me cringe.

I try to struggle out of his hold, but his fingers are

clamped painfully into my skin, with no room for movement. When I don't answer, the man shakes me, my hair falling around my face from the force of it.

"Where the fuck is he?" The stranger's putrid breath in my face makes me gag, and after another heartbeat of struggling, I manage to slam my foot down on his instep, making him shout and release me.

I roll backward over the table, getting my first good look at my assailant now that I've put an obstacle between us. He's thin, almost skeletal, his clothes hanging off him like Spanish Moss. I couldn't put an age to him if I tried, his face gaunt, the skin pulled tight across his skull. His eyes are surrounded by bruise-like shadows, with no gleam or spark of life.

Another one of Dominic's less-than-satisfied customers. Just fucking great.

"Listen, pal, if you want to talk to the boss, you need an appoint–"

"No!" the man roars, charging around the table at me, bony fingers outstretched.

I circle around, keeping the furniture between me and the desperate intruder, heart pounding. I chance a look around, but Toyota has disappeared, along with her customer. Time to do what I'm good at: cause a scene.

"Get your fucking hands off me!" I screech at the top of my lungs, the pitch carrying through the empty room, even over the music still playing.

Tired of playing ring around the rosy, the man vaults over the table, and I take off backward, weaving around furniture to keep him from getting too close. All the while, I scream as loud as I can. I might be able to take care of myself, but I'm not stupid enough to try to fight someone who's on the edge of sanity. Thankfully, moments later, Phil and Wil, the co-managers of security and my favorite bouncers, come charging out from the back.

"Zombie creep!" I yell over my shoulder, heading in their direction.

Phil snorts, tossing his head and digging his hooves into the floor before charging at me. The dusty gray minotaur lowers his horns as we pass each other, and the intruder takes a headbutt straight to the sternum. Wil comes trotting up, his short Dwarven legs working to catch up to Phil.

I lean against the bar to catch my breath as I watch them eject the man from the club, tossing him outside with warnings not to come back. My heart has slowed back to normal by the time they join me.

"Sorry 'bout that, kid. You okay?" Phil asks, genuine concern filling his chocolate-brown eyes.

"Yeah, I'll be alright. Just wish Dom would deal with his fucking messes so we didn't have to," I reply with a resigned sigh.

Phil and Wil grunt in agreement, but we all fall silent. This isn't the first time one of Dom's customers has shown up demanding an audience with him, and this is the sixth time in the last week alone we've had to deal with these people. Dominic has been holed up in his office, not even coming out on our busiest nights to do his usual slimy salesman routine. I'd been okay with it, because the less I see of his demonic ass, the better, but this is crossing a line.

"I'm going to go talk to him," I declare, setting my shoulders and straightening my spine.

"You sure about that?" Wil asks skeptically, his gruff voice soft.

I nod, hoping my face doesn't show any of the nerves twisting up into knots in my belly. Dom can't hurt me, I remind myself. He can scream and rage, but he can't put his hands on me. I'm uniquely qualified to have this discussion. I've got nothing left to lose.

"Someone's got to pull his head out of his ass, and it might as well be me," I joke, but neither of the bouncers laugh.

"If things get out of hand, just shout," Phil says, clapping a hand on my shoulder.

My knees nearly buckle at the weight of it, but I still

smile up at him. "Thanks, Philbur," I reply fondly before setting out.

Their laughs follow me as I head toward the Dream Lounge curtain. I only pause for a moment before determination fills my chest again and I shove through the velvet. Even empty, this place gives me the creeps. Heavy drapes muffle all the sounds, and I keep my eyes forward to avoid looking at the alcoves lining the main path. The only way I can describe the atmosphere of this place is if an opium den had a baby with the stockroom of an abandoned dead-stock textile warehouse. Too many dissonant patterns and textures, and somehow everything still smells like mothballs and sex, despite how much cleaning the staff does.

I reach a door at the end of the hall, cleverly hidden behind a sheer curtain, and I don't even bother knocking before slamming it open. While I generally do everything I possibly can to avoid entering Dominic's office, it's easy to tell at the first glance that something is very wrong. His usually neat and orderly desk is piled with papers, bottles, food wrappers, and all other manner of detritus, so much so that it spills over the edges and onto the floor. It's sweltering, even for me, with the electric fireplace cranked up to the max, along with a couple of other portable space heaters. I don't get the chance to inspect the room further as Dominic lifts his head off the desk and glares at me.

"What?" he snarls, lip curling.

"Uh…well, you look like shit. Like, more than you usually do," I start, mind not able to move past his appearance.

Looking like shit is a bit of an understatement, if I'm being totally honest. A few weeks ago, he looked like he had a bad fever. But now he looks like death warmed over. Skin pale, and almost greenish, dark eyes sunken deep into his skull. His hair is thin, with bald patches I know weren't there before. He's dripping sweat, but his whole body shakes with uncontrollable tremors under the four blankets he has wrapped around his shoulders. Whatever bug he caught has taken a turn for the worse, and I almost feel sorry for him.

"Get the fuck out of my office," Dom snaps, words slurred.

"Actually, I don't think I will. Not until you stop hiding and deal with your fucking mess," I retort, crossing my arms over my chest stubbornly.

"What are–"

"Your clients. The ones you let go. They've been coming back and asking for you. One of them tried to kill me just now," I interject coldly.

"Maybe they'll succeed next time. Get you the fuck out of my hair," Dom grumbles, starting to lower his head back down to rest on his desk.

"You know what they want. Just give it to them and–"

"Does it look like I can do that right now, Lyra? Do I look like I can do anything right now?" he shouts, head snapping back up to glare at me.

I roll my eyes. "Just because you've got the Man Flu, it doesn't mean you get to fuck off and leave us to deal with the strung-out junkies you've created."

I catch the motion just in time to avoid the glass bottle Dominic hurls across the room at me, dodging to the side and letting it slam into the wall behind me, shattering. He's on his feet now, but just barely. He has to lean on his desk as he staggers around, advancing on me. Dominic was never a bulky guy to begin with, but he looks like he's dropped thirty pounds in a matter of weeks. Maybe he's actually caught something serious, though I don't know what sort of virus or infection could do this to a demon like him.

"If you don't get your fat ass out of my sight in the next thirty seconds, I'm–"

"You'll what? Sneeze on me? Give me a break. Listen, I'm not asking you to do cartwheels on the dancefloor, but you've got to deal with the assholes coming in here. Just let them sleep, and deal with the repayment when you're not knocking on Death's door," I interject.

Another bottle hurdles at me, and I'm not as fast this time. The projectile just barely misses me, but I hiss and flinch back as pain flares along my hands and face from the shrapnel that sprays out from the impact zone. In my moment of distraction, Dominic finds a burst of strength and advances on me, a hand going around my throat. I gasp as he slams me back into the wall, holding me up so my legs dangle uselessly. I try to scratch and claw at his forearm, but he doesn't let up.

And as I look up into his face, I freeze. His mask has slipped, just a little, and the red irises staring down at me blaze with hellfire. Sulfur fills my nose, and his touch burns, like he's putting out cigarettes on my jugular. Spots form on the edges of my vision, and it gets harder and harder to breathe. He squeezes tighter, and I choke, eyes rolling back in my head.

But then, he releases me with a shouted curse, dropping me like I've electrocuted him. I slump to the floor, sucking in deep breaths as my vision clears. Dominic stumbles back, shaking out his hand, and a flash of savage delight fills me as I see the slashes to his wrist and fingers. The No Harm Clause written into my contract strikes again, motherfucker. I gather myself, rubbing my throat. I hope he didn't leave marks this time. Phil and Wil do enough Mother Henning as it is.

"If you're so worried about my clients' well-being, then far be it from me to stop you. Congratulations. You've been promoted to Dream Lounge attendant, starting tonight," Dominic snaps, stumbling back to his desk.

The world shrinks to this room, background noise fading into television static behind the pounding of my heartbeat in my ears. No. Not this. He can't do this to me. My hands shake and I ball them into fists before Dominic can notice. Get ahold of yourself. Fight back. I wipe the shock from my expression before he turns back around, clenching my jaw and letting my anger override any stomach-churning horror.

"What? No, that's not–"

"That's an order, Lyra. Now get the fuck out of my office. You've got a shift to get ready for," he shouts, cutting off my protest.

The weight of his words settles over me, and I have to grit my teeth against the nasty things at the tip of my tongue. I can't ignore a direct order, not without violating the terms of our contract. But as I stomp out of the room, making sure I slam the door as hard as I possibly can, I seriously consider it. When the ache in my throat throbs again, I sigh. That's a fight for another day. I'm going to need all of my energy for what I'm going to have to endure tonight.

CHAPTER 11

VIKTOR

The area surrounding the strip is a strange liminal space between residential, industrial, and commercial. Once you're more than a block or two from the main drag, the gilded dream of wealth and excess flakes away to expose the rusted iron and sand-blasted stone that lies at the heart of this desert mirage. Plazas like the one Sly lives and works in are more common than dwellings, and most of those are eight-unit apartment buildings. Single-family houses do exist, but the ratio of occupied to condemned structures heavily favors the latter category.

My pack and I asked Antony to park a few blocks away so we could approach and get a look at the place before entering. I take point, with Felix and Gavril close behind me. Felix is nearly invisible in the shadows of the buildings, his dark hoodie and pants helping him to blend in and observe without being seen. Gavril buries his hands into the front pockets of his jeans, supremely at ease despite the shady surroundings. No one is out in the streets, but I can still feel eyes on me. Maybe

I shouldn't have worn my vintage charcoal suit. But I always believe in making an impression.

"I'm only going to ask this once," I begin, eyes fixed on the building across the street. Gavril pulls in a deep breath, puffing out his already large chest as he brings a hand up to stroke down over his beard.

"You're not getting cold feet, are you?" Gav asks with a smirk, eyes lingering on my face as he studies each micro-expression.

"We've waited a lifetime for this," I reply quietly. Felix moves in my peripheral vision, a twitch of nervousness hanging in the air.

"Two lifetimes," Gavril adds. "Maybe even three."

"I need to know we are all on board." My words are aimed at Felix, who shuffles from foot to foot, anxiety increasing. "Are we going to have a problem, darling?"

Felix doesn't immediately move to reply, instead choosing to stare intently at Somnium.

"Let's just get this over with," Felix mutters, stepping out onto the road. Instinctively, I reach out to grab his hoodie and pull him back. My eyes clash with his silver irises, and no matter how hard I try, I can't get a read on him.

"Are we good here?" I ask lowly. Felix has never been an open book, but his current reservedness has me on edge.

"We go in, we get Dominic to agree to our terms, we take over," Felix reiterates as though he's had the statement rehearsed and stored somewhere deep in his mind. I don't like it, but we don't have the time to change tactic. If we're going to strike, we have to do it now.

As we round the last corner and stop, waiting to cross the street, I get my first good look at the object of my obsession. The file of information I have on Somnium is nearly six inches thick, hidden inside of a cabinet, and locked away. I have photos of this ugly brick building from every angle, stretching back decades. Builders' diagrams, tax documents, shipping reports. Even a staggering list of former employees who've met untimely ends exactly one year after starting, going back even before my pack and I arrived in Las Vegas. Add in Felix's recent reports, and there's very little I don't know about Somnium and its owner. Gavril's the only one of us that has taken a more lenient approach, observing and gathering his information from the people who inhabit Las Vegas. He might not be as subtle as me or Felix, but he's learned a lot from his own list of connections.

Despite knowing all of that, nothing could have prepared me to approach the building itself. The bricks are dark, painted black, but sloppily. The workers didn't even bother to remove old layers, opting to just keep painting over the wear time and again. The name of the club is purple, and barely distinguishable from the background in the low light. There's a velvet rope and a queue of restless patrons, though the line stretches well beyond the barrier, curving around the building opposite the awning-covered entrance.

My pack doesn't break stride as we cross the road and shoulder past the people at the front of the line, even as they shout their protests. Gavril growls and I smirk as their shouting dies a swift death. I pull open the solid wood door, stepping into the belly of the beast.

Immediately upon crossing the threshold, I can feel the weak attempts at wards trying to shove me back out. But like cobwebs, they are easy to brush away and ignore. I swallow my grin. God, we really did a number on him. A shout draws my attention, and I blink. So Dom doesn't just rely on magical security.

"We don't serve *your kind* here," the larger of the two creatures snaps, stepping out of the shadows of the hallways and under the beam from a red canister fixture.

Gavril actually gasps out loud as the minotaur straightens to his full height, crossing his massive hairy arms over his broad chest, his plain black t-shirt stretching to its absolute limit. The red spotlight makes discerning color difficult, but the bull face glaring at us appears to be light in color, with a wide, flat nose and dark, wide-set eyes with no whites showing. His horns protrude from his temples for a few inches before turning sharply upward, adding several inches to his already impressive stature.

My eyes drop lower than I'd anticipated to find the second creature's face. Almost as broad in his barrel chest as he is tall, his dark skin gleams under the red light. Two bright green eyes glare up at me from above a thick mustache and waist-length beard. A dwarf. It's been a long time since I've seen one outside of their close-knit communities. Dwarves are almost as insular as dragons, and minotaurs, while not as closed off from the outside world, are herd creatures by nature. What the hell are they doing here?

But before I can think on it for very long, Gavril is leaning close, practically vibrating with chaotic excitement. "Oh my God. It's a fucking *minotaur*, Vik. Can I play, please?" he hisses into my ear. Though judging by the narrowing of the bull's eyes, I don't think he was being as quiet as he thought.

Ignoring my over-eager pack mate, I turn a genial smile toward the bouncers. "We have a meeting with your employer," I say smoothly, stepping forward.

The dwarf steps up to stop me, holding up a thick-fingered hand. "Dominic isn't taking any meetings today. And certainly not with you," he says, his words touched with an accent I've not heard in a number of years. Afrikaans, maybe?

This puzzle just keeps getting more complicated. And I do not have time for complications. I reach down and place a hand on his wrist, ensuring skin to skin contact. Instantly, exploratory tendrils of power ripple down the connection. His fear, mistrust, exhaustion, irritation, hit me in waves, along with the background noise of arousal that practically oozes from the walls. But I master the influx, pushing it aside to focus on the creature before me.

"We mean no harm to you or your friend. We need to speak with Dominic. And you're going to let us." My words are slow and deliberate, each one accompanied by a push of my will down my arm, through my fingers, and into my subject. Trust. Comfort. Ease. Relaxation.

There's almost no resistance, the lines on the dwarf's face smoothing out, his scowl lifting into a serene grin.

"Yes, yes. Very good. Dominic is in his office, in the Dream Lounge," the dwarf says, motioning behind him to the entrance to the club.

"Wil, what are you–"

The minotaur steps forward, but I catch him with a hand on his bare forearm. I repeat the calming process, and it only takes seconds before he, too, is stepping aside to allow my pack mates and me to pass.

"Aw, man. Did we have to do that? I haven't had a good tussle in ages. And I've never fought a minotaur before," Gavril whines, following as I turn the corner from the dark hallway and onto the main club floor.

I growl a warning, but it doesn't stop Gavril from letting out a sigh of longing. I look around, spotting the entrance to the Dream Lounge right away. The neon sign above a curtain-covered arch is tacky, but helpful. Most of the twenty-odd tables are full, some patrons just watching the stripper on the stage, while others are getting more private performances. The collective lust and anticipation cloud the room, but I lock my power down tight.

"Stay close," I mutter, looking over my shoulders.

Gavril is where I expect him to be, but as I look for Felix, I suck in a sharp breath. He's gone. And I can't spot his hoodied head anywhere in the crowd. Fuck. What is he thinking? My trick with the bouncers is going to wear off any second now, and we need to find Dominic before–

"HEY!"

–that happens. I turn on the balls of my feet, gritting my teeth as the minotaur and the dwarf charge across the club floor toward us. Gavril and I had nearly made it to the lounge entrance, where there's a little more open space, but the furniture would become an issue if a true brawl broke out. Gavril crouches, spine curling even as his face lights up like a kid who's just been told he's free to eat an entire candy store.

Gavril lunges, striking fast before the minotaur knows what's happened, knuckles cracking on the bull's prominent jaw. He lets out a bellow, sounding more bovine than human, staggering back a few steps on unsteady hooves. The dwarf barely manages to avoid becoming a tripping hazard, but then he's moving, sprinting toward me. In one smooth motion, I step into the oncoming force, dropping my shoulder to leverage his weight up and over my back before twisting to grab him by the beard. He's too stunned to fight me as I slam him down onto the hard floor with a crunch. A sharp crack pulls my attention, and I turn to see Gavril and the minotaur squared up against each other with their fists raised and, inexplicably, the shattered remains of a chair cascading over the bull's back.

There's a moment when nothing happens, only the music of the club filling the silence. Then, appearing like someone ripped an invisibility blanket off him, Felix is standing behind the bull, arms raised with the fragments of a chair leg clutched in each fist. The minotaur turns his head, chest expanding and contracting with each of the creature's puffing breaths. I'm about to yell out, to get the furious beast's attention away from my pack mate. But Gavril is faster. Like a cobra, his hand darts out, clamping onto the side of the minotaur's thick neck as bright white sparks crackle between his fingers and down into the bull's hide.

Another bellowing howl of pain, and then the minotaur drops like a sack of potatoes, sprawled out and twitching on the crusty strip club floor. The dwarf squirms, but a quick blow to his temple, and he's out cold, too. Readjusting my grip, I pull his limp form up with me as I get to my feet, tossing him onto the stage and nearly knocking over the willowy dryad in the middle of a spin. The music cuts out and panicked chatter fills the air. Adjusting my suit jacket, I nod to Felix and Gavril before turning to the curtain and pushing my way through.

CHAPTER 12

VIKTOR

T he magic of the portal zings against my skin, my scales rising toward the surface for a moment before I regain control. What sort of deal did Dominic have to make to get the juice for a spell like that, I wonder. Too many questions, and all of them irrelevant to the task at hand. We came here tonight to end this.

"Dominic?" I call out, almost in a little sing-song. "Don't make me send Gavril to come collect you."

Gavril grins in response, desperate for the chance, but he does well in holding himself back. I do revel in the image of him rubbing his large, eager hands together in preparation, though.

The staff flee at the sound of my voice, disappearing behind curtains and slamming doors. All but one. At the other end of the corridor, a woman stands perfectly still, back straight, chin lifted in defiance. Her copper hair is ruffled, like she's been pulling at it, and she's not wearing any makeup. She's dressed in the same sheer pink baby doll with faux feather trim as the rest of the staff back here, exposing the creamy skin of her arms and legs, and ample cleavage. Felix sucks in a sharp breath from my side. So he's noticed her, too.

We lock eyes, and despite myself, I let a single tendril of my power snake out toward her. The air around her is drenched in anger and frustration and fear, as I'd expected. But before I can get a better taste of her emotions, she's slamming down a mental wall and shoving me out. I blink, the only sign of my surprise.

"I should kill you where you fucking stand," a familiar voice snarls, pulling my attention away from the mystery woman.

I turn to find Dominic leaning heavily on the bar to my right, panting like he's just run a marathon. I glance back to the end of the hall, but the woman is gone. Another question to be answered later.

Dominic, in a word, looks like shit. His normally ruddy skin is a ghostly gray, with large dark circles under his watery eyes. Greasy hair hangs limply around his face, rather than being slicked back in his usual style. His chest is bulky, like he's wearing multiple layers of jackets and hoodies, but it's not doing anything to fight the chills that rack his body.

"You couldn't kill a snail, Dom," Gavril snarks, stepping up to my shoulder, hands back in his pockets. "Especially if you had to catch it first."

"Fucking try me, boy. You've got a lot of nerve showing up here after what you've done to me," Dominic snaps.

His threat is somewhat undercut when he tries to advance a step, but only ends up collapsing back against the bar, coughing like he's trying to eject one or both of his lungs.

"I have no idea what you're talking about, friend. We would never–"

Dominic growls, and I have to grin.

"Fine, I won't insult your intelligence. We've come to bargain," I finish, striding forward.

I tug my cotton handkerchief from my breast pocket and

use the fabric square to pull out one of the wrought-iron chairs set at a glass-topped table. Gavril and Felix maintain position at my flanks. Felix's attention isn't on the matter at hand, his gaze constantly moving around the room, on high alert. Gavril, however, is laser-focused on the demon before us. If he was less civilized, I suspect my pack mate would be openly drooling.

After a moment of hesitation, Dominic finally decides to play ball and flops down into the chair opposite me. I wonder vaguely how many people have been in this exact place, opposite the devil and trying to make a deal to save their own skin.

"Say your piece and get out. I don't have time for this," Dom grumbles, crossing his arms over his chest as he starts shaking again.

I notice the white bandages wrapped around his right hand, the white gauze stark against the sickly skin. Was he trying to cure himself with blood magic? Or did one of his slaves finally decide to rise against their master?

"Well, since you're in such a hurry, I'll get right to the point. We want Somnium, free and clear. And we want you out of our fucking city."

I press a finger to the tabletop for each of my points, my voice hardening from conversational to authoritative. For a moment, I swear Dominic considers laughing in my face, but then he stops, looking hard into my eyes. I don't dare try to read him with my power. He might be weakened, but opening a channel into my mind like that is still a risk with a creature like Dominic.

"What the fuck do you want with a strip club out in the 'burbs? You probably clear triple what I make in a week in an hour at one of your casinos," Dominic retorts sardonically.

"It's not about the money, my friend," I reply vaguely.

"Friends," Dominic scoffs, pushing his hair back. "Friends don't poison each other just to get what they want."

I smirk. "We haven't touched you, Dom. But we'll be

more than happy to offer you a cure if you agree to our terms."

That gets his attention. He sits for a moment in thoughtful silence. It's not a bad offer, all things considered.

"And what's stopping you from killing me the moment I sign on the dotted line?" Dominic asks harshly.

"You are smarter than you look," I tease, earning another growl. "Though that's not an unfair question. As long as you leave promptly and never return, then you will be free to live out the rest of your existence."

"And what's the word of a dragon worth," Dominic mutters.

Gavril lunges before I can respond, darting around the table and grabbing the demon by the back of his neck and lifting him off his feet to bring their eyes level. Dominic tries to shove at Gavril's chest, but his feeble attempts don't even faze Gavril. My pack mate lifts his other hand, electricity arcing menacingly between his spread fingers.

"The word of a dragon is worth a fuck ton more than the word of a demon," Gavril spits, disdain dripping from every syllable.

"Enough," I bark, eyes hardening.

Gavril takes another moment to stare Dominic down before dropping him back into the chair. Dominic rubs at the back of his neck, glancing nervously over his shoulder. I give Gavril another hard look, but he doesn't budge. Instead, he just settles his weight and clasps his hands in front of him, sparks occasionally skittering across his knuckles and up his arms. Any other day, the display of strength and power would make my mouth water. But right now, we can't push too hard, or all of this will be for nothing.

I reach into the inner pocket of my jacket and pull out a pristine piece of ivory parchment, folded into perfect thirds. I place it on the table and slide it forward, gesturing for Dominic to examine it. He picks it up like it's going to bite him, using only the tips of his fingers to unfold the paper and hold it up for examination. There's a long, pregnant pause as his eyes dart back and forth across the page. In the pause, I withdraw a fountain pen from the same pocket and place it deliberately on the table. The sharp edge of the nib catches the light, reflecting red back toward me like a drop of blood.

"So just so I understand: I sign over the club and get the fuck out of dodge, and you'll make this go away and never contact me again? I'm free to do whatever I want?" Dominic questions, eyes still on the paper.

I take a deep, calming breath before turning my attention back to him. "The club and the land beneath it, as well as your hasty exit, yes."

"We want your employees with long-term contracts, too."

Dominic and I both whip our gazes to Felix as he steps forward and nearly shouts the demand. What the fuck is he on about? We never discussed this. Gavril's eyes are wide, and for the first time since we entered Somnium, he's no longer focused on Dominic. I look back to Dominic and swallow my curse at the new light in the demon's eyes. Fuck.

"Those are some special deals, boy. What do you want with them?" he asks, suddenly more confident, with a touch of his usual smarmy attitude beneath his words.

Something about Dominic's word choice rankles, and I grit my teeth. But Felix lifts his chin proudly. Off to the side, Gavril raises a hand to cover his mouth, trying his hardest to keep whatever profanities he wants to spew at Felix locked away inside. We share a glance, an understanding passing between us. Our plan just changed and neither of us are happy about it.

"I'm not a boy, and what we want with them is none of your concern," he replies coldly.

Dominic chuckles, sounding more like himself by the minute. "Oh, it most certainly is. Those contracts weren't easy to come by, and I'm not just going to give them away on a lark."

"What do you want, then? Money?" Felix fires back.

I look at Dominic's face, and the blood drains from my

own as I watch the wheels turn behind his beady brown eyes. Oh, no. Fuck, fuck, fuck. The first rule of dealing with demons is to never give them a blank check. I turn my focus onto Felix, but his attention is still fixed on Dominic. His silver eyes flash with a strange heat, but otherwise, he's unreadable. At least he's smart enough for that.

"You didn't answer my question, boy," Dominic drawls, leaning forward.

"He told you not to call him that," Gavril snaps, and I sit forward, perching on the edge of my seat.

"You're leaving, and that means the staff is going with you. If we're getting the club, then we need people who are already familiar with the operation to stay on and train the new hires," Felix says smoothly.

That's a bold-faced lie if I've ever heard one. We've never discussed what would happen to the club once we obtained it. Even if we entertain the notion of leaving the doors open, using people who sold their eternal souls to a demon would not be the plan. And God forbid anyone connected to the dragon council finds out we, in essence, bartered for the ownership of another being.

Dominic seems to buy Felix's story, even if it makes my stomach churn. I want to shout this down, to move back to the original terms, but the damage is done. Trying to walk this back would damage the united front we've been presenting, and I won't give Dominic the satisfaction. So instead, I simply wait, all the while my temper rising. Once we're done here, Felix is going to have a lot to explain.

"There are six souls, and they aren't going to come cheap," Dominic says at last.

"Absolutely not," I interject before Felix can answer.

Felix shifts uncomfortably at my side, but I ignore him. One person, I could stomach. Two, pushing it, but doable. Six is out of the question.

Dominic shrugs. "Your loss. I've been wanting to downsize, anyway. This little move gives me the perfect opportunity to purge dead weight."

"What are you talking about?" Felix asks, strangely hoarse.

Dominic flashes a downright dastardly smile at my pack mate, and my blood runs colder.

"There's an...early termination clause in all my deals. If someone gets too rowdy, or if I need to make room for new blood, all it would take is a snap of my fingers, and they drop. No matter where they are in the world," Dominic says, speaking slowly through his grin.

"What do you want for them?" Felix asks, too fast. Too eager.

"A favor. One from each of you. For me to cash in at the time and place of my choosing."

The words are like a death knell. Gavril growls, his fists clenching at his sides. My eyes lock with his as I try to breathe. I'm ready to reject this whole thing, poised and preparing to call it all off. I would rather die than be in debt to a demon. We will figure out another way to get this plot of land.

"And you'll nullify the kill order part of their deals?" Felix demands, leaning forward.

"Oh, of course. But their souls are still mine once they reach the end of their natural lives," Dominic replies, waving a careless hand.

"Come on, you can't be fucking ser-" Gavril's words are cut off abruptly.

"Done," Felix says.

The exchange is over before I even have a chance to think, let alone react. Felix snatches the contract from Dominic's hand and picks up the pen. A quick slash along the heel of his right hand, and then he's scribbling his hasty amendment to the bottom of the page and signing his name. Gavril and I watch as he pushes the paper back toward us, wiping the pen on his jeans before putting it back on the table. I stare up at him in disbelief. Even Gavril's usual brutish confidence has vanished; he looks about as stunned as I feel.

What the fuck has Felix done?

We don't have a choice; Felix has forced both our hands. I sign the parchment reluctantly, handing it to Gavril, and he does the same. His large hand swallows up the pen and he scribbles his signature so roughly the paper tears a little.

"Excellent. A well-struck bargain, my good man," Dominic says, much too cheerfully.

He reaches out and grabs the pen, pricking his own finger and gathering up the black ichor that wells up. With a flourish, he signs his agreement and sighs. The terms of the deal take effect immediately, returning color and life to his face. I wasn't stupid enough to give him the full cure, but enough power returns for Dominic to create a duplicate of the contract with a lazy wave of his hand.

"Pleasure doing business with you," he drawls, gathering up his copy.

And before I can stop him, the demon snaps his fingers and vanishes into thin air.

CHAPTER 13

Lyra

I storm out of one of the velvet-lined "Dream Suites" I'd been assigned to for the night, seeing red. I want to throw the crystal vial in my hand to the ground and stomp on it until all that remains is glittering sand. But I'm already in enough shit with Dominic right now. If I want this punishment to end in the next decade, I need to play nice.

I stalk up to the tonic bar and set the vial down gently, grateful when the bartender comes up and takes it away. Franco gives me a pitying look, and I grind my teeth, crossing my arms over my chest.

"What's the dream?" the High Elf prompts, his voice showing no sign of judgment or condescension. Emotionless. Detached. Lucky bastard.

"He wants to…God, I can't even fucking speak it without throwing up in my mouth," I spit, swallowing hard as the client's request replays in my mind.

"Just breathe, sweetling. You just have to get through tonight," Franco says, a bit more feeling in his chocolate-rich baritone.

I look up at him and sigh. He's almost illegally beautiful, with high cheekbones sharp enough to cut a bitch to their bones, and eyes the color of spring grass. Like all fae, he's tall and lean, but the sheer mesh of his "uniform" shirt, such as it is, reveals defined chest and stomach muscles that are completely drool worthy. But his words make little sense. Is he under the impression that this is one-night only showing for me? I shake my head, not in the mood to sort through the layers of fae riddles right now.

"The sack of shit wants a girl. His...stepdaughter. His barely legal stepdaughter. And not with her consent. Don't make me repeat everything else. I'm sure you know what he wants," I grit out, dropping my eyes and speaking to the gleaming bar top between us.

Franco sighs, but doesn't say anything else before moving off to prepare the tonic, which I'm more than a little grateful for. Hearing all of the fucked-up things he wants to do to his wife's child was disgusting enough, and I'd barely contained the urge to smother him with one of the many throw pillows. I know Ginny must be pulling strings at the hostess station, because this is only the second client I've had to deal with. The other attendants have had four or five, and my first guy wasn't so bad. Just a little murder fantasy for a shitty boss. But if this rapist is tame enough for Ginny to send him my way, I shudder to consider what the others are having to deal with.

My thoughts are interrupted as Franco comes back with a stoppered flask, the liquid inside pitch black. He gives me one more sympathetic smile before moving off to help one of the others. Squaring my shoulders, I head back toward the alcove. I don't have to be in the room as the clients live out their fantasies, I remind myself. I just have to get this guy going and then I can leave him be.

I shoulder through the gap in the curtain, not looking up from the floor as I make my way to the ornate hookah-like device in the center of the circular room. I can see a man's bare and hairy leg out of the corner of my eye, and I force myself not to look. Especially when the wet sounds of skin on skin reach my ears. I pour the tonic into the reservoir and replace the top, the back of my throat burning with bile as I scramble out of the room.

There have been a few times in my hundred-odd years in this hellhole that I've considered taking the express route out of my contract. The year when Dominic only let me eat a slice of bread a day comes to mind. Or the time he dabbled with being a real brothel, until a John killed a few girls, girls I'd been close with. I had plans, too. Jumping off the top of Korona Drakona, running out in front of one of the billboard trucks that drive up and down the strip. But I'd always found something to keep me here. Usually, the knowledge that even if this was bad, it would be *nothing* compared to the torture I have waiting for me in Hell. Dominic has been waiting for a long time to give me a taste of my own medicine, and I don't want to give him the pleasure of having my eternal soul to play with any earlier than necessary.

But this...this might be my limit. I will be stuck back here, helping the rapists, murderers, pedophiles, and every other variety of deplorable being live out their sickest fantasies. Possibly for the rest of my very long life. Two clients, and I'm at my wit's end. I can't do this. And I would rather throw myself into the Grand Canyon than go to Dominic and ask him to reconsider. Like fuck would I let that scum-sucking demon get the better of me. But I don't know if I'll be able to finish this shift, let alone a lifetime of this. Sure, I might get used to it, but do I really want that? To become so numb to the depths of misery we sell here? What sort of person would that make me? And could I live with her, look at her in the mirror, or sleep at night knowing what I've allowed people to live out, even if it's just in their minds?

I stagger into a support pillar, leaning against it as my thoughts overwhelm me. My eyes burn, and I shake my head, grimacing. No. I won't let this break me. I won't let *them*, Dominic and his shit stain clients, break me.

I've just about talked myself into going back to the hostess station to get my next client, when a commotion near the entrance draws my attention. I would call the trio that stands before the curtained entrance "men," but such a simple word fails to encompass the immensity of their presence. The two in the lead are monstrous, pushing seven feet tall each, with a third, more average-sized but still statuesque man behind them. The smallest one's face is hidden in the shadows of his dark hoodie, and I can't tell much else about him from my quick glance.

The hairs on my arms and neck lift as invisible electricity crackles through the air, and I can't look away. I can hear my coworkers scrambling for cover, but I'm frozen in place. Every cell in my body seems to relax and vibrate with anticipation all at once. Something about them is calling to me, and it takes most of my strength to keep my feet planted. Because I wouldn't run away like the rest of the staff. No, it's worse. If my body had its way, I'd run to them and climb them like the California Redwoods they are.

The leader, because it's impossible to deny the waves of authority and dominance rolling off him like thunder, turns his head, and my heart stops as our eyes connect. His face is all hard angles, the line of his jaw sharp, even as I see a muscle twitch there as he clenches his teeth. But his eyes...the striking true purple of the irises takes my breath away. I've never seen a color like that before, not in any human I've ever met. And honestly, no being of any other race either. He's looking at me like he can't decide if he wants to eat me or fuck me, and my body is ready for whatever he chooses.

But just as I'm about to make a move, to challenge the predator across the room, he seems to remember himself. He blinks and looks away, and like some sort of magic spell, I'm slammed back into my body, and I suck in lungfuls of air.

"Dominic? Don't make me send Gavril to collect you,"

the purple-eyed sorcerer calls out.

His voice is deep, with the slightest hint of an accent, and it makes my knees weak for a moment. But then his words register and my heart twists. I can finally unglue my feet from the floor as I smell rotting garbage in the air, and I make a beeline toward the staff door.

The corridor beyond is blessedly empty, and I lean heavily against the wall, trying to catch my breath. Who the hell are those guys? I've never seen them in the club before, or anywhere, really. Though I don't tend to get out much, so that's not really saying anything. But I'm sure I would have noticed those three if we'd been in the same room before. Purple Eyes and his attack dog certainly would have stood out in a crowd. But if I've never seen them, why is there something so familiar about them?

I'm in the middle of trying to puzzle it out, when the door to my left crashes open again and Ginny comes barreling through, panic in her eyes. I straighten as she catches sight of me, and she lunges forward, grabbing my shoulders.

"Holy shit, Ly! Did you see them?" she whisper-shouts, shaking me.

"Kinda hard to miss," I grumble, shrugging to get her hands off me.

My skin is crawling uncomfortably, and while I'm not usually opposed to being touched, there's something about the feeling of her skin on mine that makes me truly sick. I shove down the half-formed thought my brain tries to conjure about who could put their hands on me, looking at her half-terrified, half-excited face. Her gold wolf-shifter eyes are bright in the semi-darkness, and she looks around to make sure we're alone.

"They're the dragons," she breathes, almost sounding reverent.

My heart drops like a lead weight. Dragons. *The* dragons.

"They're talking with Dom, and he's giving them the club. They're taking over," she goes on, but her voice sounds like it's coming from the other end of a tunnel.

Stories from my childhood flood my mind. The nuns at the orphanage would scare us into compliance with tales of dragons taking over cities in The Old Country, razing buildings, seizing all the gold and jewels for their hoards, and stealing away women and children for their sick pleasures. In hindsight, it was pretty fucked up that we were told explicit stories of the raping and violence these dragons would commit at such young ages. Yet the three of them seemed to move as one single unit. There is some invisible bond between them. One I can't see but can feel somehow, low in my belly and tangled with visions of them together. Like, *together*, together.

But the nuns couldn't possibly have made up the atrocities, not with every convincing detail. And now three of them are here, in the club. Oh, fuck.

"We have to get people out of here," I rasp, turning my horrified stare onto her.

"What are you–"

"There's no time. Get the staff out first. I'll get the clients," I order, moving away and leaving her stunned in my wake.

People are going to die if we stay here. Dragons only kill and destroy, and if they've set their sights on Somnium, then I have to do something. And as fucked up as their dreams are, the clients don't deserve to be left to the mercy of those monsters.

The first few alcoves I come across are already empty, thank God. But when I come to the next one, an older man in his Sunday best is just staring at the ceiling with a dopey smile on his face, completely oblivious.

"I think that would be lovely, Maureen. We'll get the kids together and have a picnic," he's mumbling, not even aware of my presence.

"Sir, it's time to go," I say firmly, crouching down and pulling the pipe from his hand.

He blinks a few times and looks at me, confused. His wrinkled face falls, reality crashing back down on him. I almost feel bad, but he needs to get out of here before it's too late.

"You don't want to stay tonight, right? Or what will you dream about when you come back?" I ask with a charming grin, tapping into a well of calm charisma and laying it on thick.

The older gentleman blinks again, a new clarity blooming behind his eyes that screams of loss and grief, but then he smiles, straightening. "You're right. There's always next time," he agrees.

I help him to his feet with a relieved sigh, guiding him toward the exit before moving on to the next alcove. The stepdad.

As I push through the curtain, my upper lip curls in disgust. He's spread eagle on his back, one hand holding the pipe end of the hookah to his lips as he strokes his cock with the other. He blows out a thick stream of black smoke as he groans, head falling back.

"Time's up," I deadpan, trying to look anywhere but at the revolting display in front of me.

I don't think he hears me, because he takes another drag, and I cough as I wave some of the noxious cloud away from my face. I move to the hookah and knock it over with my foot, spilling the rest of his tonic on the thick red carpet and pillows. When the sicko still doesn't react, I turn around, heading back toward the curtain. If I have time, I'll come back for him. Though it wouldn't be such a bad thing if–

A hand in my hair yanks me back, pulling a scream from my lungs. I lose my balance as I step on one of the pillows and I go down, hitting my elbow hard against the floor. I don't get a chance to recover, because a heavy body presses down on top of me. When I try to scream, his mouth is on me, tongue invading my throat and nearly choking me. His hands are everywhere, on my breasts, my stomach, my hips.

"My little girl is so ripe for me. Daddy just wants to play with you, just a little. Then we'll get ice cream," the client slurs in my ear.

I try to kick and claw at him, but even with all of my strength, he's too heavy. I can't get a full breath as his weight crushes down on my chest. My stomach rolls and I turn my head to the side, coughing and gagging as his hands push the feathered hem of my stupid top up, higher and higher, until he finds the top hem of the boy shorts I have under it.

My head spins, my vision blurring as I struggle to breathe. I can't get free. I can't escape. I'm trapped. I'm trapped. Trapped.

Then suddenly, a roar shakes me to my foundation, filling my senses. I suck in a deep breath as the weight lifts from my chest, and I lie there for a moment, tears leaking down my face. But I wipe them away, scrambling into a sitting position. A crunching pop pulls my attention, and I look up to find the smallest dragon kneeling on the chest of the client, fists flying. His face is twisted into a dark, savage snarl, rage filling every line of his beautiful features. He's halfway between man and beast, the hoodie that had been shielding his face from the mood lighting earlier having fallen back to reveal a mop of icy white hair. There's another punch, and another. His large, veined hands are splayed, sharp claws making his fingers look unnaturally long. The man, or monster, strikes the creep with a rage so palpable that I can feel it in my bones. I flinch as hot liquid splatters my legs. A few thick droplets pattern my chest and dampen my top, matching the lacerations now adorning the client's naked chest, or what's left of it. Finally, his struggles grow weaker, but the dragon keeps going, pounding his face with heavy fists until, at last, he stops moving.

When the dragon looks up at me, the silver inferno in his eyes nearly stops my heart.

CHAPTER 14

Felix

There's a moment after Dominic disappears where my pack mates and I sit still and quiet, but not for long.

"What in the actual fucking fuck was that?" Gavril snaps first, taking me by surprise. I'd been preparing myself for Viktor's onslaught, but not Gavril's. He's usually pretty laid back—at times arguably horizontal—but right now, his face has turned crimson. My eyes dart between Gavril and Viktor, who's sitting quietly with his large hands clasped on top of the table. Vik's true violet eyes are bright and unblinking, like he can't quite fathom what I've just done. How am I supposed to explain it to them without sounding like I've lost my mind? I love my pack. I love these men with my whole heart, soul, and every fiber of my being. The reality that I've been keeping this secret from them for a while feels dirty.

I swallow, my dry tongue almost catching at the back of my throat as I try to come up with the words. A way to fix this and make it better.

"I'll tell you everything," I state, glancing between the

two most important people in my life whilst a possible third lingers in the forefront of my mind. "But not now. We can't risk any sign of weakness."

Viktor's expression never changes. Never lightens. Every arch and twitch of his features are set in stone, the red glow from the bulbs above making him look like the real demon in the building.

"Felix is right," he says lowly, his voice an octave below its usual. Vik's lips part and the tip of his tongue taps against his front teeth while he studies me. "We'll discuss this later."

"I can't fucking believe this shit," Gavril mutters under his breath, but is quickly silenced by Viktor's palm as he lifts it up in front of his face.

"Not. Now." It's a sharp hiss, laced with threat, and it makes my insides drop.

"So what now? What are we going to do with these people? This fucking building?" Gavril goes on, despite my warning.

"Find the ones with these long-term contracts. We'll get them set up somewhere until we can figure out our next step. The others can follow that demon bastard to wherever he slithered off to." Viktor issues the commands with cold efficiency, the wheels of his mind turning behind his jewel-toned eyes.

"One of them needs to come with us," I interject.

Viktor gives me a harsh look, demanding I go on, but I shake my head. I won't speak of my little spark while we're inside these walls. Dominic might be gone, but we're still under his roof, surrounded by his employees. I won't risk anything happening before we can get to Lyra and get her out of here.

Gavril stalks off to follow Viktor's order, and I wait under his amethyst stare. The taste of whiskey on the back of my tongue tells me he's trying to read me, but I give him a stern growl. His gift is a blessing and a curse, but he knows he's not allowed to shortcut communication between the pack. He has the good sense to look a little ashamed before I feel him back off and give me a nod. I told him we'll talk later, and I meant it.

I turn on my heel, looking around the dim space. My heart is pounding with anticipation, yet there's a gentle twinge of realization that soothes the ache like a bucket of ice water over sizzling coals. We did it. Years of fighting and clawing have finally borne fruit. We own every inch of this city. The circle of power can be completed. I almost let myself dwell on the hundred-year victory before my thoughts return to the kink I've just put in our chain.

Lyra.

I whip my head around, nose twitching as I try to pick out her scent in the tangle hanging in the air around me. Viktor is speaking, but my mind doesn't register the words. I can finally act on the need that's been raging through my veins since we stepped foot inside this building.

I'd nearly blown Viktor's entire plan to pieces when I didn't see her in her usual place behind the bar. I'd slipped into my power, intent on hunting her down, but before I could so much as leave the club floor, Gavril started making a scene. Once the bouncers were dealt with, and we made our way into the Dream Lounge, my resolve to have her solidified.

Seeing her tonight pushed my control to the absolute limit. She'd been a sight to behold in her jeans and t-shirts, but the way she looked in the Dream Lounge uniform had been otherworldly. The baby pink chiffon was so thin I could see the outline of her nipples through the material, and the faux feathers lining the bottom hem barely covered the apex of her thighs. I suppose the get-up was supposed to be reminiscent of a nightgown, but it was more like lingerie. My heart went to war with my mind. I couldn't decide if I wanted to shred the scrap of fabric and ravage her in front of God and everyone else in the club, or if I wanted to rip out the eyes of everyone but my pack for daring to see what belonged to us.

Thankfully, she'd disappeared during the sit-down. I don't know if I could have focused if she'd been around. I knew it was going to be risky to jump in like that and add my condition to the contract, and I most assuredly will be hearing about it later. But after all of the research I'd done, all the nights I've spent inside this building, watching, observing, learning, it was the only way. If we didn't seize control of those employee contracts, Dominic would have picked up his entire operation and disappeared, and I couldn't let that happen. Not if it meant losing Lyra.

Now that it's over, and the demon-shaped thorn in our sides has vanished, I only have one goal.

Find her. Claim her. Protect her. Make her mine.

Finally, I catch a trace of salted caramel and vanilla ice cream, and I take off, not even bothering to excuse myself. My heart kicks, nerves rising like the tide in my belly. What will I say to her? How will she react to me? Will she sense this connection between us, too? A thousand questions race through my mind as I follow her scent like a bloodhound. It leads me to a curtained off room, one of the Dream Suites. At the last moment, I hesitate, swallowing hard around the sudden lump in my throat. I roll my shoulders, trying to psyche myself up. I can do this. This can't be a coincidence, to feel this way after all these years. She'll feel it too. She has to.

But my thoughts come to a screeching halt as a muffled scream comes from behind the curtain. There's another voice, a man's voice, but all reason abandons me at the sound of Lyra's distress. I rip back the curtain, pulling so hard that it actually detaches from the ceiling and pools on the floor at my feet. And as I look down to the floor, to the pasty, naked, middle-aged man, his hips thrusting down onto the figure beneath him, it only takes a glimpse of her copper hair to make my heart stop.

When it starts again, my vision goes red and my roar spills from my chest, louder than my human form could ever possibly make. But I'm not human. I'm a dragon, my blood thick with ancient magic, and this ant dares defile that which belongs to me and mine. My fingers become claws, stretching until the razor-sharp curves of my talons are free and I slice them into the mortal man's back, sending a spray of blood across the pillows and blankets covering the floor. The hot liquid splashes against my arms, scales appearing over the backs of my hands, up my wrists, and fading into normal flesh. I throw the man to the floor, my hood falling away as I leap onto him, straddling his barrel chest. My fists slam into his face over and over, claws shredding his flesh like hot butter. I've never felt such righteous fury in my life. I cannot control the animal instincts to destroy this scum, because he hurt my little spark. I can smell her tears in the air, and knowing he made her cry seals his fate. Punch after punch, I continue until my prey goes still beneath me. I still land another few blows. I'm nothing if not thorough.

I'm breathing heavily as I let my fists come to a stop, leaving them to dangle at my sides. I'm trying to focus on regaining control of my baser instincts, to come back into myself, when a faint whimper draws my attention. Looking up, I meet Lyra's eyes intentionally for the first time. I don't know what she sees that causes her to flinch back, but the movement is enough to quell the last bits of anger in my chest. I shake out my hands, willing them back into their humanoid shape and size. They're still covered in blood and gore, and I flush as it spatters the walls and cushions.

"Did he hurt you, *petite étincelle*?" I ask, glad my voice is steady and gentle.

She blinks, mouth working, but no sound coming out. I get a better look at her now that we're closer, and my hands ball into fists once more at the shadows of bruises on her throat she's tried to hide with makeup. My teeth crack as my jaw clenches and she flinches again. I swallow and take a deep breath. I need to focus and calm myself.

"Did he hurt you?" I ask again, nodding to the mangled corpse cooling beneath me.

She shakes her head, like she's trying to rouse herself from a dream, and clears her throat. "Yeah, uh...I mean, he was–I had it handled," she stutters, finding her strength again.

When I give her a skeptical tilt of my head, she glowers at me. I get to my feet in one fluid motion before taking a step in her direction. But I stop short as she scrambles backwards until she hits a wall. My brow furrows as she clambers to her feet, edging along the wall toward the exit. Now that she's vertical, I can see the blood that's splattered across her front, from her collarbone down to her knees.

Why does the sight of her covered in my enemy's blood make my cock twitch?

I try to push that feeling aside as she stares me down, not that it's very effective. I'm small for my kind, and I still tower over her. But she stands tall, not even remotely intimidated by me. Whatever earlier fear she'd had is now gone, replaced by the fight I've grown to admire.

"My name is Felix Devereaux," I say lamely, holding out a hand for her to shake.

I remember a moment too late that my hand is still sticky with blood, and a drop falls pointedly from my palm as it hangs in the air for a moment. She stares at it and then looks back to my face with a raised eyebrow. I flush hot as I pull it back and wipe it against my pant leg.

"Lyra Spanos. So, like, thanks for the assist, but I'm going to go now," she says, almost deadpan.

She takes a step toward the door and my heart lurches. No. She can't leave. Not now. Not ever. I growl and surge forward, grabbing her upper arm in what I hope is a gentle but firm grip. She looks up at me, eyes wide and mouth slightly open. This close, I can feel the heat rolling off her body, and her caramel and vanilla scent mixes with the metallic tang of violence and death still lingering around us.

"Stay," I murmur, stepping into her space.

"What the fuck, no! I'm not a dog–"

She starts to protest, but I silence her with another growl. Her eyes, hazel wells of defiance, narrow as they look up at me. But something else is stirring in my mind, pushing out all logic. It's hard to see in the red light, but my body reacts on instinct. Her hair has shifted, revealing softly pointed ears. Not the elongated points of the fae, but instead a more subtle, but far more familiar shape. My eyes trace over her face, breath hitching as more of her scent fills my lungs.

There's no way. How could she possibly–

But I don't get to finish my inspection or my train of thought as white-hot pain erupts from my cheek, the crack of her palm hitting my face ringing in the air. The blow is hard enough to stun me, and my hand spasms, releasing her arm. She doesn't hesitate, taking off before I can stop her.

CHAPTER 15

Lyra

I topple out of the room, almost falling ass over tits as I wobble on bare feet. The last fifteen minutes have been too wild, or maybe my brain is just overloaded with unwanted stimuli and muddied thoughts. Somnium is in chaos. There're a bunch of dancers huddled in a corner, talking in hushed voices while most of the Dream Lounge staff have already made a hasty exit.

Dragons scare the crap out of me, and it seems like the feeling is mutual, with ninety percent of the club having already made a run for it. I stumble through into a back room —the same one I was in earlier—and my body collapses back against the wall. I'm warm and sticky. Bile rises in the back of my throat as I remember that I'm covered in blood. The shitty baby doll did nothing to shield my skin from the spray caused by the dragon's well-timed Jack Torrance tribute act.

Hastily, I force myself to move over to the opposite end of the room, where there's a simple sink and a paper towel dispenser. My hands tremble furiously as I moisten a bundle of towels and begin scrubbing at my arms. The white tissue disintegrates within seconds, stained pink with streaks of gruesome crimson, and I let it fall into the sink with a stomp of my feet.

"Ew, ew, ew, ew," I mutter, dancing on the spot and simultaneously cursing myself for being such a wimp.

"Did you hear?" Hands on my shoulders whip me around, temporarily snapping me out of my thought spiral. Ginny's gold eyes widen as she takes me in, pulling her hands away to check for blood before looking back at me. "Shit, what the fuck happened to you?"

"Work in the Dream Lounge, they said; it'll only be mildly traumatic, they said." My voice is shaky, but I breathe through it, forcing air in and out of my lungs in time with the waves of nausea. "You know, I'm not even mad about the outfit. I hated this bullshit but, shit, is it in my hair?"

I'm hysterical.

I realize it just as tears start to well in my eyes and Ginny steps forward and embraces me in deceptively strong arms. She doesn't bat an eyelash as the blood soaks into her own baby pink teddy, just holding me tight as I struggle to keep it together.

"Did someone hurt you? Does this have to do with the dragons taking over our contracts?"

Ginny's words hurtle me right back down to earth with an almighty crash. I force myself away from her, gazing up into her face in the hope that this is some cruel joke.

"You're kidding, right? Our contracts?"

Ginny shakes her head, her expression unreadable. "Franco's been telling anyone he can. He overheard the whole thing. Dominic gave them Somnium, including us."

"Us?" I mutter, my brain struggling to clear the trauma-fog. "Like, us, us?"

A part of me is relieved. Relieved to be rid of Dominic. To be free from his insults and his abuse and everything that goes with working in this place. Until I realize, dragons aren't exactly warm and fuzzy. Hell, I had a front-row seat to that display just a few minutes ago. Two outta five stars, would not recommend. Even if he did technically swan in with his beautiful face and his lithe muscle, looking all terrifyingly adorable in a hoodie. And he was French. Or at least, I think he was French. Languages were never my strong point.

"Hello? Earth to Lyra," Ginny says, waving her hand in front of my eyes. "Look!"

Ginny's moved from in front of me and is now peeking through a crack in the door. I'm substantially shorter than she is, so like the comedy act we're apparently paying homage to, I duck down and look through the gap just below her.

"What are they doing?" she continues in a low whisper. The smell of her too-sweet perfume tickles at the back of my throat, and I let out a loud sneeze. To our horror, all three dragons turn to look toward where we're spying.

"Shit," Ginny gasps.

"Shit," I repeat, a little lower.

Yet for the life of me, I can't tear my eyes away.

The big boss man is the most commanding in his perfectly tailored suit. His dark hair is sprinkled with salt and pepper at the temples, pushed back to put his sharp features on display. Deep violet eyes are locked on me, fine wrinkles making them crinkle at the corners. He's not the only one staring. There's a huge beast of a guy at his side with a terrifyingly wide smile, his pearly white teeth flashing from beneath his auburn beard like neon lights. The look on his face tells me he's here for the chaos and the part of me that isn't frightened for my life finds that kind of endearing. When my line of sight finally settles on the smaller of the three, it takes all my strength not to let my fire simmer down.

Felix.

That's what he'd said his name was. It rolls around in my mind, and I mutter slowly to myself, allowing it to sit on the purse of my lips before letting it flick off the tip of my tongue with ease. He's more boyish looking than I'd realized earlier.

His mop of white-blond hair is tucked beneath the hood of his sweatshirt, just a few curls here and there managing to escape and fall in front of his silver eyes.

To my shock, his lips mimic mine. Only this time, the sound of my name coming from his mouth is loud enough to pique the curiosity of just about everyone in the room.

"Oh, girl, you're fucked," Ginny snaps, finally stepping back from the door and jogging off in search of a hiding place.

I frown, my eyes darting around the place as I try to make sense of what's going on. "What's that supposed to mean?" I ask, but Ginny is long gone, crouching behind one of the many boxes occupying the storage area.

"Don't tell me you're stupid enough to believe a cardboard box fort is going to hold up against a group of dragons." My voice trails off when they make their move, the big, burly one taking the first step. He marches with heavy booted feet across to the door and I'm so frozen in surprise that I don't even try to move away.

With a smirk plastered across his handsome features, he bends down to peek through the crack in the door. His eyes are dark, but it's impossible to discern their true color under the red glare of the light around us.

"You didn't think you could hide from us, did you?" he asks in a surprisingly sing-song voice. Jesus Christ, he's *enjoying* this.

I don't even make it a couple of steps back from the doorway before it swings open and he is setting a hand on either side of my waist. I kick and punch as best I can against the hold, but he lifts me from the sticky floor like I weigh nothing. And I can motherfucking guarantee I *do not* weigh nothing.

"Let me go!" I squeal, thrashing in his iron grip like my life depends on it. "Put me down, or I swear to God, I'll…"

He plonks me down, but keeps his bear-like hands on my waist, holding me in place.

"Go on, *vatreno*, what will you do? Whatever it is, I'd love to fucking see it."

I'm suddenly praying to whatever gods are listening that Ginny stays exactly where she is, hiding in the shadows behind the cardboard boxes. If she stays hidden, they won't take her, too.

"Gavril," Felix warns, taking a step forward, but he stops himself, glancing at the man in charge.

"Felix is right, Gavril," he says, eyes alight with something equal parts devilish and delicious. "Let's at least try to get her home before she starts biting at our ankles." His lips lift into a cruel smirk, and I immediately lunge at him, stunned when I'm hauled back by the dragon he'd referred to as Gavril.

"Who the fuck do you think you're talking to, Wall Street!" I yell, managing to strike him just once across the face with my open palm. He leans back to survey me with what looks like amazement. There are three long scratches on his cheekbone, and I instantly feel like I've made a very, very big mistake.

"Let's get her back to the penthouse," he announces calmly, and my stomach drops.

If it's between fight or flight, I choose fucking carnage.

CHAPTER 16

GAVRIL

A t Viktor's words, the little hellion screeches like someone is ripping out her toenails with rusty pliers. I flinch back at the sudden noise, but that's a big mistake. She takes advantage of my lapse, slipping from my loosened grip and taking off toward the curtain to the main club floor.

I chuckle darkly, eyes flashing to Felix and Viktor as my nerves spike with excitement. I spring after her, each eager stride of my long legs matching three of hers until I'm right behind her, wrapping my arms around her soft stomach from behind and lifting her off her feet just inches from the curtain. Her body is warm and supple against me, and I can't help but grin until my cheeks burn.

When Felix rattled off the names of the employees whose contracts we'd just acquired, I'd only had moments to ponder how he'd come to know those details. But then he'd pointed this little firecracker out, and something flipped inside of me. I'd taken notice of her earlier; it was impossible to ignore the absolutely stunning and fearless woman who'd stood her ground while others fled. Now that I've gotten a good look at her, and a little taste of her fire, I am ravenous for more. And now we get to take her home? I feel like my birthday's come early. We'll deal with those favors when they come. For now, we've got one sexy as sin redhead to wrangle.

"Ooh, you're a scrappy little one!" I exclaim with unbridled glee. There's something about her spark that has my blood boiling in anticipation and my cock twitching with sudden interest. It takes everything in me to keep a tight hold on the current of energy pulsing through me, but I don't get much time to focus on the feeling.

"Put me the fuck down!" she screams, kicking her feet and squirming like her life depends on it.

Viktor scoffs from his position a few paces away. His posture reads casual, the wrinkle between his brows the only sign of his growing irritation. "This can be as easy or as difficult as you wish to make it, but either way, you're leaving with us. And the longer you drag this out, the less patient you'll find me to be," Viktor drawls, almost bored as he hovers by the now-abandoned tonic bar.

"Go to hell, you scaly sociopath!" the tiny woman yells, scratching at my forearms furiously.

"Come on, you can do better than that, *vatreno*."

I'm doing my best not to hurt her, avoiding the furniture, but she's making it hard with all of her flailing. I admire her tenacity; it's the one thing that's still got me smiling like a fucking maniac throughout the whole ordeal. I've seen grown men wet themselves at the mere mention of Viktor losing patience with them, yet she's hissing and yowling like a feral cat. It's not that I can't take it, but when her sharp nails dig into my flesh and rip, it's not exactly comfortable. I can do scratching, hitting, and clawing. When she lunges forward and clamps her teeth down on my forearm, I instinctively shake her off as though I've just been stung.

She lets out a cry of triumph as she tries to make a break

for it again. I'm stunned into wide-eyed silence, staring at her with a mixture of annoyance and awe. I can't help but release a dreamy sigh as I study her tiny, curvy body jiggling with exertion. Each deep inhale she makes has those fucking tits bouncing in the ridiculous baby doll she's wearing. If I wasn't hard before, I definitely am now. Thankfully, Felix steps in and disrupts my lovesick daydreaming and blocks her path.

"Lyra, stop. If you'd just listen for a moment–"

She slaps his hands away as he tries to reach out for her, but doesn't move away. Lyra. The fire cat has a name. And what a fucking name it is. I roll it around my mouth for a moment, and I have to contain my groan as my cock twitches. As I adjust myself in my jeans, Viktor rolls his eyes.

"Stop playing with your food, Gav. We don't have time for this," Viktor sighs, approaching me.

I pout at him. I've been intentionally holding back the current running under my skin, not that I really know why. There's something in my gut telling me I don't want to use the normal *any means necessary* to restrain her. I'd happily stay here and watch her fight us tooth and nail for the next few hours, waiting patiently for her to tire herself out.

"If you think I'm going to just sit here and let you murder lizards lock me up and–"

"Murder lizards?" I interrupt with a surprised chuckle that rings out across the bar area. Don't tell me this little thing has a sense of humor, too? Jesus, I'll be lucky to make it through the night in her presence without losing my absolute shit.

"That's a new one. I sort of like it." I nudge Viktor with an elbow, the buzz of the hunt making me feel light and airy. Unfortunately, Viktor looks the exact opposite of amused when it comes to Lyra's antics, and I'm forced to clear my throat and bite down on my bottom lip to stop myself from smiling.

"If you don't subdue her, I will. And she won't like my methods," Viktor says, speaking to Felix now. Viktor knows how I get when I'm surrounded by chaos and it's nothing short of overzealous.

"SHE is standing right here, jackass. And she doesn't like your methods already. Did you fail fucking dinosaur kindergarten or something? Because your manners are piss poor, at best," Lyra says, whipping around and glaring up into his face, her arms crossed over her generous chest.

I wish she hadn't done that. Not because I'm afraid of what Viktor will do, but because I lose all focus at the sight of her tits in that sheer nightie, pushed up and nearly spilling out. I go a little lightheaded as blood rushes to my crotch, and I have to cross my arms to avoid outright rubbing myself through my pants like a horny teenager. I should have more control than this. It's one thing Viktor likes to remind me of. Somehow, little Lyra and her animated protests, although useless, have coaxed my own inner child to the surface. Where usually, said inner child would like to break shit and fuck people up, it now mostly just wants to tackle her to the ground and make her take my dick as punishment. It's a completely inappropriate thought that catches me off guard, but I don't have time to dwell on it.

"Lyra, please don't make us do this," Felix presses, taking a step forward to try to put a hand on her shoulder.

She dodges his touch and stubbornly lifts her chin. "Make you do what? Kidnap me? Pardon me for not making your abduction easy," she snarks, her upper lip curling in a sneer.

For the love of all that is holy, why does that look of open disgust make me somehow even harder? Is she a witch, enchanting me with her perfect breasts and condescension? If she insults me again, it's going to take all of my willpower not to thank her and ask for another.

But as Viktor steps forward, my stomach lurches with sudden protective panic. I don't want to see Lyra under his thumb, to see her fire reduced to a smolder. It seems like a crime against nature, like if someone tried to stop Niagara Falls or paint over the walls of the Grand Canyon. Unacceptable.

I shoulder him out of the way and tower over her. She's completely unruffled as she cranes her head back to glare up into my face. The top of her copper-haired head only comes up to my sternum, but she carries herself like she's ten feet tall. God, why is that so freaking adorable?

"You don't want Viktor to be the one to do this, *vatreno*. So let's save the fight for the bedroom games, shall we?" I say with a wink.

She rolls her eyes and pops her hip. "Keep dreaming, Jolly Green Giant," she spits.

I clasp my hand to my chest in faux offense. "Toss some more bullshit insults my way, Lyra. I'm really fucking enjoying it."

It's then that she flops down on the ground, legs crossed and spine curled as though she's protesting. I sigh and rub my eyes, though I do catch her glance up at me, and the way her eyes go wide at the sight of my sizable crotch bulge. I snort a singular chuckle to myself as she looks away, her entire face going a delicious shade of pink.

"I'm growing bored, Gavril," Viktor says, words very clipped.

Right. Playtime is over. Boo, Viktor. Boo to fucking you. Nevertheless, I crouch down as low as I can, balancing on the balls of my feet, even as Lyra stubbornly refuses to look in my eyes.

"We tried to do this the nice way. Keep that in mind," I murmur.

She whips her head around, but before she can protest further, I grab her by the upper arm. She gasps as I push a mild pulse of electricity through my fingers and into her system. There's no way for me to make it completely painless, especially as her body locks up and then goes limp in a fraction of a second. Toeing the line between paralysis and inducing cardiac arrest is tricky, but her chest is still rising and falling, even if she can't move. It's a relief that hits harder than I'd expected, but I'm thankfully distracted by Viktor's soft purr.

"Well done, Gav. Now get her into the car before she can cause a scene on the street." He strokes the back of my head affectionately, and I nuzzle into the touch, even as my mouth turns down in a frown.

Lyra can't move or speak, but her eyes are locked on me, and the very real terror swimming in their hazel depths shakes something in my core. Her scent is sour with fear, and even if my electricity has her incapable of voluntary muscle movements, she's still shaking like a leaf in a tornado.

I'm uncharacteristically tender, surprising even myself as I scoop an arm under her shoulders and knees, cradling her to my chest with ease as I rise from my position. I try to arrange her limbs so they won't dangle or flop around, but it's difficult to do without dropping her. But then there's Felix, carefully crossing her arms over her stomach and adjusting the drape of her legs on my forearm. All of his touches are gentle, almost reverent, and it makes me smile. He notices the expression, and blushes a little, but doesn't comment. Lyra begins to stir, and I give her a sharp look of warning, which she reads loud and clear. I don't want to have to do that again and, thankfully, she seems to agree with us on something. Finally.

I'm about to walk out of the Dream Lounge and back to our car, when Viktor stops me. He looks down at Lyra in my arms, inspecting her fully now that she can't fight or resist. Her face flushes a mortified red, and she averts her eyes, even if she can't look away. I turn to glare at Viktor, but stop short as I see him shrugging out of his jacket.

"Sit her up, Gav," he orders, barely loud enough to be heard over the ambient chaos still going on around us.

Lyra whimpers, the most protest she can muster in her current state, as I shift her in my arms until her head is resting on my shoulder. I miss her sweet violence already.

Viktor steps forward and, with quick but surprisingly considerate movements, maneuvers her arms through the sleeves. She's drowning in the soft silk, and once she's settled again, the coat nearly comes down to her knees. She almost looks like a child wearing her father's sports coat in a game of dress up.

Viktor doesn't speak as he motions for me to continue on my way, turning back to address the remaining Somnium employees. I don't waste time with sightseeing, heading straight out of the building and toward our waiting SUV. Judging by the experimental twitching, Lyra is gaining more control over her limbs, but she doesn't fight me as I climb into the backseat and position her across my lap, arms banded around her hips and waist to keep her from moving. And as Felix climbs in and closes the door, I realize suddenly that she's not shaking anymore.

CHAPTER 17

VIKTOR

I slam the front passenger door of our SUV and give a curt nod to the driver, head pounding. This night could not have gone less to plan. I touch the signed contract resting safely in the front pocket of my shirt, sighing. Well, that part went to plan. Somnium and the land under it now belong to me and my pack. Just over one hundred years of planning and work, and we're so close to our goal that I can taste it like sweet cream on my tongue.

We pull away from the curb and make our way through the streets of our city, the light of the billboards and signs creating artificial daylight. The car is silent, which is a welcome relief to the chaos we'd left behind at Somnium. We'll have to sort out which of the employees were included in the deal another day and get them added to the payroll. People may call me heartless, but I won't sink to slavery.

"Dick," a female voice grumbles from the backseat.

Great. The hellspawn is awake.

"Hey, we tried to do this the nice way," Gavril counters

with a chuckle.

I glare at her through the rearview mirror, not that she can see. Her copper-colored head is resting on Gavril's shoulder, and her eyes are decidedly fixed straight ahead. Felix keeps looking at her, pleading with his eyes for her attention. A tendril of my power snakes out to caress his neck, and I'm caught off guard by the intensity of his curiosity and desire for the scrap of a woman he's decided to bring home. But probing deeper, I can feel that this is more than lust or obsession. There's a current of white-hot need that almost hurts to approach. I back off, catching his eye as I settle back into my mind. There's no apology in his expression, and I blink in acknowledgment of his silent challenge. Yes, we will be discussing this before the night is over.

"You're still a dick," the woman snaps. Lyra. Felix called her Lyra. An odd name, but I can't deny that there's something pleasant about the way it rattles around my mind.

"Are you okay?" Felix asks, voice almost tender.

"Oh, I'm *swell*. I've been assaulted, kidnapped, and now I can't move my fucking legs. Totally having the best day ever," Lyra retorts.

Felix flinches back at the bite to her voice, but Gavril's growl draws my attention before I can reprimand her for her disrespect.

"Who fucking touched you?" he snarls, arms flexing to hold Lyra tighter.

"He's dead, Gav. I made sure of that," Felix responds, savage delight pulling at the corners of his mouth.

"Good," Gavril grunts, nodding with satisfaction.

Well, that explains the blood on his clothes. But it doesn't explain why my pack mates have lost their fucking minds.

"Not good! That's murder!" Lyra exclaims, hands lifting an inch as she tries to throw them up in exasperation.

"Is the body still at Somnium?" I ask, matter-of-fact.

Felix nods, not looking sorry in the least. I roll my eyes

and search my pockets for my phone. We need to get Martin on the job before the corpse-stench sets into the carpets. But I come up short, cursing under my breath. I twist in my seat, reaching for my coat.

"What the fuck? Get your scaly hands off me!" Lyra shouts, not that she can do anything about it.

I ignore her, finding my phone and pulling it from the inner pocket before settling back in my seat. My headache had been fading a few minutes ago, but thanks to this banshee's shrieking, it's back with full force. Firing off a quick message, I shove my phone into my pocket.

"Fucking dragons. Entitled, selfish, rude, barbaric–"

"Are you quite finished?" I snarl, whipping my head around to glare at her.

She has the nerve to lift her chin and glare at me. "Not even close," she deadpans.

Thank God we're pulling into the private underground parking garage beneath Korona Drakona. My seatbelt is off even before we've come to a full stop.

"Take her to the guest suite, Gav. Felix, a word," I snap, throwing open my door and launching myself toward the bank of elevators.

"Oooh, you're in trouble." Lyra's sing-song taunt fades as I put distance between us andgrind my teeth. The elevator door opens, and Gavril carries her away. Some peace, at last.
Finally alone, I try to calm my racing heart. I don't know what Felix is playing at, but I cannot allow that woman to get under my skin like this. We've worked far too hard to let one loud-mouthed, ill-tempered stray get in our way. Felix better have a good reason for bringing her back here.

He's silent for a long time, not even attempting to call the elevator back down to us. So he wants to do this here. Fine by me.

"Do you care to explain yourself?" I start, words clipped and tense. I have to keep a tight lock on my power. Despite my burning desire for answers, I won't force them out of my pack

128

mate. At least not without giving him the chance at honesty.

"You might have to be a little more specific," Felix says on a sigh, shoving his hands into the pouch of his hoodie.

I clench my jaw, taking a few calming breaths before replying. "Let's start with you deciding to go rogue and add slave contracts to this deal. Do you have any idea what will happen if the council finds out about this?"

Felix flinches at the soft but furious tone of my voice. A slightly guilty expression crosses his face before it goes back to impassive.

"They don't have to know. We just need to break the contracts as soon as–"

"Do you think the council will give a shit?" I turn on him, my shout echoing through the vast space of the garage. "We own people, Felix. Our laws are clear on what happens to slave owners. You've been there at the trials. There isn't a lot of room for negotiation. So I'll ask again: what the ever-loving fuck were you thinking?"

I expect him to challenge me, to fight back. He's never once backed down from my anger before. So when he stares straight ahead and chews his bottom lip, my surprise dampens my anger. His expression is indecipherable, and I can't stop the invisible tendril of my power from probing out for clarity. I'm met with a tangled mess of obsession, curiosity, longing, and something powerful running deep below the surface. But then he almost seems to shake himself from his thoughts, growling at me.

"Stay out of my head, Vik," he snaps, stepping away.

I catch him by the arm and pull him around until we're chest to chest. He still won't look at me, so I grab his chin between my thumb and forefinger, forcing his silver eyes up to meet mine. I keep my power on a tight leash, trying to respect his wish, but it's so hard when his eyes are cloudy and unreadable.

"What's going on, Felix? Talk to me," I urge, tone turning gentle.

Felix's gaze connects with mine, and the world falls away for a moment. The molten silver of his irises dances in the lights from below, and I find myself relaxing in spite of everything. After a long stretch of heavy silence, his shoulders slump and he frowns.

"Do you remember what happened to the Byzantine Flight?" he asks, voice distant.

I blink, pushing away the flashes of memories that come rushing to the surface. Blood-soaked streets. Bodies abandoned. So much fire and smoke. I clear my throat and swallow. I will never be able to forget that tragedy, and the insanity that followed.

"You know I do. What does that have to do with tonight?" I rasp, building up my wall so I don't get lost in my memories.

"I've been going to Somnium for a while, just to keep an eye on things. And ever since I laid eyes on her, I haven't been able to get her out of my head. I've tried to stay away, but I always end up back there. I've had dreams about her and..." he pauses, drawing in a shuddering breath. "She's the one I told you about. Or at least tried to tell you about."

Felix trails off, swallowing hard. My heart kicks against my ribs at the raw emotion in his voice, and the moisture pooling at the edges of his eyes. I move my grip from his chin to his neck, cupping his throat and nape and giving him a reassuring squeeze. He swallows again, blinking away the drops before continuing.

"What if you were right this whole time? What if... I know it's crazy, but she's got our ears, Vik. I can't think of another explanation. And with this feeling...what if...what if she's ours? Like, not just one of us, but *ours*?"

My heart stops as his words hang in the air. And as it kicks back into gear, my mind immediately and violently revolts against the idea. No. It's been centuries. We've gone down this path before, and only found heartbreak and misery. And besides, every single member of our species is accounted for, and this red-headed bartender certainly isn't on that list.

"It's not possible. They declared it a complete extermination," I regurgitate the line I'd been forced to obey, even if it still doesn't sit right after nearly two and a half centuries.

Felix doesn't respond, but then again, he doesn't have to. His eyes speak his disappointment and bitterness loud enough.

"Those favors you promised are going to come back to bite us in the ass. So keep this woman as long as she'll tolerate us, but just remember that they always leave. And when she does, don't let her take your heart. That belongs to me," I state, tone flat.

I kiss his forehead before releasing him and pushing the button to call the elevator.

As I leave Felix behind and step inside the car, my feet are heavy. His words bounce around my thoughts like angry bees, the buzzing growing louder and louder. It can't be possible, I remind myself. But even as I try to deny it, there's a tickle in the back of my mind. A little flutter of something I'd long since abandoned: hope.

CHAPTER 18

Lyra

The elevator doors close on us before I can get a good look at the drama in the garage. The older guy didn't look too happy, and despite my lack of a father figure, I recognize the disciplinary tone he had in his voice. If I wasn't currently paralyzed and in the middle of being kidnapped, I might have found the whole thing kind of erotic.

"So what now, Jolly Green? You beam me up to your cave and lock me in a cage?" My words are a little slurred and I presume it has something to do with the whole can't-feel-my-body thing. I'm fuzzy around the edges, like I'm passing between awake and dreaming.

They called him Gavril. An odd name, but it suits him. He's a big guy, really fucking big. With a gruff beard and auburn hair tied back in a short ponytail at the nape of his neck. His arms are thick and bulky with muscle and covered in ink. Clearly, they're not just for show, either, because he carries me out of the elevator and into a huge apartment with ease. Panic sets in the second the elevator doors close behind us.

I can't move, can't fight back. I'm left with nothing but a tingling sensation in my arms and legs and no matter how hard I try to squirm against this brute's hold, it's no use.

"I swear to God, if you don't put me down…" I grunt, but he pays no attention. He just keeps walking until, eventually, he shoves open a door into what seems to be a bedroom. I can't tell for sure because I still can't turn my head to the side to get a good look.

"You'll what?" Gavril chuckles. "Come on, firecracker, what are you going to do to me?"

He's teasing me. He's fucking teasing me.

Fear rips at my body like a thousand paper cuts. My heart is beating so fast, I know he must be able to feel it.

Still, he tosses me back onto the bed carelessly, letting my body bounce and flap against the comforter.

"You son of a bitch!" I squeal, halfway between fight or flight. Neither of which are possible in my current predicament.

He perches on the edge of the bed and grins wolfishly. "Watch your mouth, my mother was a good woman."

It's obvious he's only half serious, but I don't dwell on the shit he's spouting. I don't know these guys. I definitely don't trust them. Dragons are not good people. They take what they want, destroy it, and toss it aside without a second thought. I'm not about to be used and abused by yet more assholes. I've had enough of that crap in my entire godforsaken life.

My fingers grip at the duvet cover, sending sparks of life to the muscles in my forearm and bicep. It's coming back. Thank fuck, whatever this monster did to me isn't permanent.

Gavril moves from the bottom of the bed, walking slowly around to my side and dipping down to the ground. He opens his mouth to say something, but I don't give him a chance. I let saliva pool in my mouth before sending a glob of spit directly at his snarky face. A burst of pride fills my chest when it lands on his cheek and, for a split second, he looks surprised.

"There is quite a fire in you, isn't there?" he quips, smiling as he wipes the moisture from his face.

"I'm going to fucking kill you! Let me go!" I squeal, like it's doing me much good. Although the more I thrash and twitch, the more sensation I feel in my limbs. My mind won't stop reeling, spinning out of control as I consider all the things they might do to me. Some thoughts are darker than others. The unease tickles each corner of my mind incessantly, my imagination running wild. What's so special about me? Why would they take me and no one else? It's impossible to decipher whether they want to keep me or kill me, enslave me or free me. I'm spinning out of control; I can feel myself getting further and further away from my surroundings, slipping into a long tunnel of adrenaline-fueled survival instincts. If I'm going to make it out of this alive, I have to keep my wits about me, and as impossible as that sounds, I've got to give it my best try. My lungs expand to the point of pain when I pull in a deep, somewhat centering breath.

"Why the hell Felix wanted to keep you is beyond me," he sighs, like *I'm* the one ruining *his* day. "You're a pretty little thing, I'll give him that." His hand crawls close enough to twirl a strand of my hair between his fingers. He studies it like it's a foreign being. Despite his words, I can sense a pinch of uncertainty or mistruth, like he's trying to keep a dirty secret. I just wish my brain wasn't so fuzzy, then maybe I could figure the damn thing out and use it against him. I just need to find a way out of here.

"What? Never seen a ginger before?" I snap, recoiling as best I can, but he doesn't warrant the comment with a reaction. Instead, he stands up and trails across the room, stopping just short of a large window. I can only imagine the view outside. Even from my place on this bed, I know there'll be a sea of neon lights, flashing signs, and tourists below. An expanse of open space over the rooftops just begging to be breathed in and screamed out. God, what I wouldn't give to be out there now. Vegas's heady warm breeze spreading across my skin.

But no. I'm trapped in here with this jackass.

My body slumps to one side as I try to force myself off the bed. I fold like wet paper towels onto the carpeted floor. Each limb feels like it weighs a ton, and I'm exhausted just thinking about getting to my feet.

"Come on then, little one," Gavril muses, turning away from the window to watch me. He crosses his bulky arms in front of his chest and smiles.

The urge to reply with some smartass comment is overwhelming, but I hold it back, preserving my energy. I briefly wonder if the window would smash if I just outright launched myself at it. At least then I wouldn't have to deal with any of them. Dragons, demons, fucking Dominic. All my worries would vanish. In death, at least I'd be free.

With a growl, I fight to get to my feet. I wobble from side to side, using the bed for leverage.

"There she is," Gavril adds with a spark of mischief, like he's looking forward to seeing what I'm going to do next.

I might as well be crawling toward him at the speed I'm moving. One foot goes in front of the other, that's all I have to do. Just get close enough so I can rip his goddamn face off. Anger bubbles up from the pit of my stomach, taking over every single other sense until all I can see is red. Using all the strength I can muster, I lunge at him. My hands claw at his neck, face, and chest until I can see blood. He wrestles with me, grabbing my wrists in his mammoth hands while he does his best to get me under control.

"I hate you! Fucking dragon scum! I will kill you for this!" I scream and fight and yell, coming away with tiny fists full of his hair and palms smeared with blood.

"Calm down!" he orders. "Jesus fucking Christ, what are you?!" It's like he's shocked, completely taken aback by how much strength I have, or how much fear, I'm not sure. All I can see in the forefront of my mind is getting out that motherfucking window, letting my body float away on the humid breeze. Anything to just get out of here.

"It's like fighting with a fucking rabid trash panda!" The mumbled comment goes over my head as I continue to throw hands and feet in his general direction.

"Please, just let me go!" I shout, my face wet and lips salty with tears.

He's grappling to hold me still, anchoring my hands against his chest while he tries to keep me upright.

"Please, let me go," I repeat, out of breath and sniffling like the pathetic loser I am. Passed around from place to place, no home, no family, no one. Nothing. The thoughts come thick and fast as the adrenaline fades away.

"Please...let me go. Let me go. Just let me go." My voice is a mere whisper now, hoarse and breaking from the exertion.

"Sshh," Gavril tries to soothe, but it just sets me off again.

I squirm, reaching back over his shoulder to pick up an unused candle. With it in my hands, I crash the glass encased wax over the top of his head.

"Ow! Fuck!" Gavril drops me in his surprise, and I grab his shoulders, thrusting a knee between his legs.

It leaves him unsteady, but not immobile. I imagine to him this is much like being beaten up by an unruly toddler.

"Okay, that's enough," he breathes. Blood is dripping from his nose, and I've torn his neck up pretty good. Bonus points that he's still holding his junk in one hand as he grabs me around the waist and hoists me up off the ground once again.

A jolt of something runs from his hand where it's placed flat against my stomach. It stretches and ripples, and before I have a chance to say a thing, the world goes black once again.

I just have to hope that this time around, he's killed me.

CHAPTER 19

I had to take a lap around the underground parking garage to cool off from my conversation with Viktor. I don't want his cynicism to ruin this...whatever this is with Lyra. But I can't force them to like each other either. When I feel more centered, I finally head upstairs. The elevator door opens to the penthouse at the same time as Gavril is running out of the guest room. Viktor is in the kitchen, sipping on a neat glass of vodka. We watch together as Gavril slams his body back against the bedroom door. He's disheveled, like he's just gone six rounds with, well, something much bigger than him. His chest rises and falls in quick succession, and it's obvious he hasn't spotted us yet.

"Everything alright?" Viktor asks, taking quick strides toward Gavril, who practically buckles at the sound of his pack mate's voice. He takes Gavril's face in his large hands, bending down just enough to meet Gavril's feral gaze.

"I had to do it," Gavril stammers. "I didn't have another choice; it was like she was possessed or some shit."

"Do what, Gavril?" I spring to action, marching toward them and reaching behind Gavril to open the door to the guest room. Viktor shifts Gavril away from the door as I open it up, dreading the thought that I might find a bloodbath inside. Gavril isn't exactly the most controlled of the three of us, but I didn't expect violence. My heart is in my throat when I spot Lyra's tiny body curled up on top of the bed. I breathe a sigh of relief when I see her chest move as she pulls in a lungful of air and snores an exhale.

"What'd you do?" My temper has fizzled out, doused in relief, but my tone is still sharp.

Gavril winces dramatically, pulling a face as his cheeks flush pink. "I just had to knock her out, just a teeny bit."

"Explain to me how you knock someone out a *teeny* bit, Gavril." I tilt my head to the side as I wait for Gavril's answer, but he just shrugs. I'm about to tear him a new asshole when Viktor stifles a chuckle.

Both me and Gavril shoot him a look, wondering if perhaps he's finally lost the plot.

"What's so funny?" Gavril asks, sounding a little hurt.

Viktor covers his mouth with his fist, chewing down on his lips as he tries to control himself.

"It's just..." He cracks, giggling like he's just heard the best joke in centuries.

"Come on, Viktor, you're freaking me out," Gavril groans, studying him closely.

Vik calms just enough to steady his voice, a smile still tugging at his lips and making his adorable laughter lines more prominent. "We left you alone for ten minutes with the humanoid equivalent of a fucking Pomeranian."

There he goes again, with the uncontrollable laughter that this time has him doubled over.

"That's not fair! I couldn't do anything with her!" Gavril yells, storming past both me and Viktor and into the kitchen. He leans his elbows on the marble counter and covers his face.

"What? Was she nipping at your ankles?" Viktor jokes,

rounding the kitchen island and reaching for a bottle of vodka. I jump onto one of the barstools and swing from side to side, watching as he pours three decent measures into individual crystal tumblers. I'm not laughing. This situation doesn't seem as funny to me as it is to Viktor. I'm more concerned that Gavril's immediate instinct toward Lyra was to knock her unconscious. Sure, it's been a while since any of us have been around a woman like Lyra, but still. He could have talked her down or found some way to calm her without using his power.

"She was scared, and *crying*. There were literal tears, and she wouldn't stop yelling," Gavril explains quietly, like he knows he's about to set off Viktor's laughter yet again.

But Viktor settles, passing one of the glasses to me before pushing another across the counter to Gavril. Gav instantly knocks back the vodka with a subtle wince and taps the glass for a refill.

Viktor sips at his drink before breathing a long sigh. "Well, what did you try to do to de-escalate the situation?"

There's a moment of uncomfortable silence while Gavril digests the question. "What do you mean?"

I butt in, clearing my throat. "You know…food, water, an assurance that we weren't planning on killing her."

"I kinda just…" Gavril pauses, eyes shifting to stare at his hands. "I teased her a little. I thought it was all tongue in cheek, you know? She scratches me, I toss her over my shoulder. The usual. Like foreplay."

My eyes meet with Viktor's for a second, somewhere between disbelief and fucking hilarity.

"Okay, so from here on out, Gavril stays away from the Pomeranian. I'll take over and wait for her to wake up." Viktor sets his glass down and marches across to the guest room with his head held high. He means business. Those broad shoulders of his straighten, his posture strong and powerful, as always.

"Wait, wait, wait." I jump up from the stool, tangling myself in knots to get to Viktor before he can open the door to the guest room.

"Let me try," I urge, holding on to his arm to stop him from moving forward.

One gray tinged eyebrow raises in question as he studies me intently, waiting for me to explain.

"I don't think she needs to wake up to yet another seven-foot monster standing by her bed," I say, attempting to disguise the tremble to my words. "No offense, but you're not exactly the friendliest looking dragon in Las Vegas."

"Perhaps not, but I do know how to take care of someone in a vulnerable position," Viktor replies, true purple eyes blinking slowly.

"Yes, but *she* doesn't know that. To her, for now, at least, we're the bad guys. Which I understand is a pretty ridiculous statement, considering she's been under Dominic's thumb for a while, but…she's out of her comfort zone, stuck in fight-or-flight mode. The last thing we want is for her to make a run for it or hurt herself in the process of trying to fight."

Viktor ponders for a moment, biting down on his plump bottom lip with his sharp white teeth before he nods just once. "Fine. Any trouble, you find me, and I'll deal with it."

"Like you said, she's basically a Pomeranian, right?" I smile, trying to comfort Viktor.

"A fucking demon Pomeranian," Gavril chips in from behind us. "With really sharp fucking nails, might I add. Squirmy, too."

"Yeah, okay, sunshine," I quip with a chuckle. Gavril lifts his middle finger in my direction, but I ignore him, turning to twist open the handle on the door of the guest room. "Wish me luck."

It takes two hours for Lyra to wake. I've spent the entire time watching her from my place on the floor. The way her long lashes graze the tops of her cheeks and the sound of the tiny breaths passing her lips. She snores a little, just a muffled grunt every now and again. It's adorable. Her body is partially covered by blankets, but the indent of her narrow waist and the rise of her wide hips are still visible. She's so feminine; supple and soft. I imagine she's warm, too. All that pale skin flushed a delicious shade of pink in places. Like the tops of her pointed ears and the exposed skin of her chest. I shouldn't be looking at her like this, when she's asleep and vulnerable, but even as she stirs, I can't pull my eyes away.

I consider putting up my invisibility cloak, just so that I can continue watching her, but when her eyes flash open to meet mine, it's too late.

She jumps up, pushing herself back against the headboard, and tugging the blankets up to her neck.

"What are you doing?" The question comes out sharp and high-pitched, and the soothing sound of her relaxed breathing transforms into near hyperventilation.

"I...well, I'm just..." The words get jumbled while I try to formulate a response that won't frighten her or make this delicate situation even worse. "Just...watching."

Her face twists into something between disgust and fear, and I shrink back into the shadows, willing myself to vanish. The whole thing reminds me of times as a child, before my power had started to manifest. Times when I would hide any and everywhere, fighting not to be seen for fear of what would happen next. That same sick feeling settles in my stomach like I've swallowed a barrel of unset cement.

"Why?" The sound of Lyra's light, husky voice brings me back to the room and forces me to gather what's left of my confidence. I thought I could do this; make her feel better for at least a short while. Make her comfortable. But I remember the last time she was shut in a room with me and realize perhaps I've made a terrible mistake. The bloodstained clothes are gone, exchanged with spares I had in the trunk of our car, but I might as well have not bothered. One look at Lyra's face and the dark truth is staring back at me. I'm still that feral monster she was faced with just hours ago in Somnium.

I'm the reason she's so scared.

I'm the reason she's trembling.

I'm the reason all the blood has drained from her face.

The reason her eyes are wide and darting.

"I didn't want you to wake up alone," I reply finally, my own voice unsteady.

"You make it sound like I fell asleep," she scoffs, edging off the other side of the bed and putting distance between us.

I glance back and forth between her and the door. She's too close, and it isn't locked. Lyra must take note of my line of sight because she does just as I thought she would. She lunges for the door handle, but her legs get tangled in the bedsheets, and she falls with a huff onto the carpeted floor.

Leaping to attention, I try to gather her up and make sure she's not injured, but she throws her elbow back into my nose. I'm dazed for a second, but it's not enough to let her go. It takes all my strength not to hold her tightly, not to wallow in the feel of her body against mine.

"You can't leave, I'm sorry," I whisper softly, shifting us both backwards until she struggles out of my hold.

I don't know where the feeling is coming from, but panic fills my chest at the thought of her walking out now before we've even had a chance to prove ourselves to her. Why can't she see that she's safe here? Her wide hazel-gold eyes dart around me, looking for something I can't name. When I try to reach for her, she scrambles backwards like a crab, so I stop, my confusion more intense than ever.

Lyra's panting now, staring up at me from her place on the floor. "Why not? What are you going to do with me?"

Then the harsh scent of curdled vanilla hits my nose, my animal instincts recognizing it instantly. Fear. It's the questioning of a terrified person. Someone who's seen so much darkness that they can't find the light at the end of the shortest tunnel. My mind whirs, trying to puzzle out what to do next, something that won't make her shut down completely. I only have one shot here. One shot to convince her we're not as bad as she thinks we are.

"Are you hungry?" I ask. "Thirsty? I brought water."

Silence.

"I made sure it was bottled. You can check the caps...we haven't tampered with them or anything."

Again, silence. She's fuming, huffing and puffing like she can't catch her breath.

"I brought you clothes too. Just some spare sweatpants, a few hoodies. It's not cold by any means, but I figured you'd want something comfortable."

"I'm not staying here, so you can quit with the bullshit," she snaps, battling to get to her feet.

Gavril knows how to control his power, but no matter how gently he might have knocked her unconscious, she's still dizzy, wobbling like a newborn deer on bandy legs.

I open my mouth to speak, but I'm instantly silenced as a throw pillow collides with my head. It doesn't hurt, but it surprises me enough to knock me off balance.

"Wait, just..." My voice fades away as Lyra picks up a bedside lamp and smashes it against the window behind me. It's thick glass, so there's no risk of it breaking, but when it rains sharp pieces of porcelain across one of the rugs, I panic.

"Lyra, you're going to hurt yourself, please." Again, she ignores me.

"I." A hardback copy of Pride and Prejudice hits me in the shin.

"Want." Next, one of the many glass bottles of still and sparkling water I brought in smashes against another window.

"To." A throw cover I picked out a couple of years ago is torn to shreds and kicked aside.

"Leave!" On her last note, the antique bedside table from the art nouveau period makes a beeline for my chest.

I don't bother trying to catch it, just let it thump into my torso and fall to the floor in slightly worse condition than it was a few minutes ago.

Lyra is standing on the bed, breathing heavily and

looking exhausted.

"Please stay," I mutter, hating how lackluster I sound. "We aren't going to hurt you, we just... Look, I'm sorry for how Gavril acted. He's not great with people. He tends to go from zero to one hundred within seconds, but he'd never do anything to hurt you. And Viktor, well, he's a little formal and cold on the outside, but he's protective of the things and people he cares about." My eyes look down at the bedside table, and I tilt my head to the side. "That's one of the reasons we're not going to tell him about you trying to take me out with the bedroom furniture."

I take a second to prop the bedside table back onto his rounded legs, dusting off the top for good measure. Remaining on my knees, I stare up at Lyra as she bounces from foot to foot involuntarily on the mattress.

"Why don't we just get some food," I suggest. "I know a great pizza place. Or we could do Thai food, or Dim Sum. Just tell me what you want, and I'll get it for you. Please, just...stop trying to kill me, you're running out of things to throw."

"I could throw myself out that window. What do you think about that, huh?" Lyra argues, but I can see her resolve fading.

"I think the glass in these windows is an inch and a half thick," I reply, trying to shoot her a comforting smile. "So it's probably not the best laid escape plan, honestly."

Lyra's body collapses in a heap on the bed as tears well in her eyes. She tries to disguise them, covering her face with one of the few pillows she hasn't torn apart, but I can smell the sweet, salty liquid as it runs down her cheeks.

"Just leave me alone." The weakness in her tone devastates me. "Please," she adds on a sigh.

Knowing there's nothing else I can do, I get up and tuck my hands in my pockets. "Okay. But if you need anything, I'll be right outside."

I'm just about to slip out of the bedroom when I hear an almost silent weep from Lyra. "I don't need anything from you."

The pain of those words hit me right in the gut, branding me with a pain so much worse than anything I've ever felt before. I just have to hope I can change her mind. If I don't, I'm not sure I'll ever be able to move on.

CHAPTER 20

Lyra

I thought I wanted to be left alone, but after Felix closes the
door to my fancy prison cell, the reality of my situation
sets in. Everything I've ever known is gone, ripped away in
seconds by creatures I'm still not sure aren't going to literally
eat me.

That first night I fluctuate between nearly catatonic
shock and violent rage. I tear anything that isn't nailed down
from its place, launching them at that wide window that
refuses to give an inch. Even after hours of attempts, the glass
doesn't even have a scratch on it. But it doesn't stop me from
trying to break it. Over and over, until I'm spent and the entire
suite is upended. It's only then that I can sit, head blessedly
empty for a few moments. But then my panic creeps in, and the
cycle starts over.

By the time the sun rises, this room is absolutely
destroyed. Every plate, glass, bowl, and dish in the kitchenette
is broken to smithereens. The bedding is shredded, feathers
everywhere, and the couch is likewise destroyed. There's

nothing left to break in this room, except me.

And I refuse to let these scaly kidnappers break me.

About halfway through the night, during one of my rest periods, I resolved to escape. I need to get out of here before it's too late. I need to get back to Somnium, gather up what little belongings I have, and get the hell out of dodge. And in the light of day, my mind is made up. It's now or never. Every second I stay here is another chance for the dragons to finally snap and end this weird form of torture. But first, I need to change out of this blood-splattered outfit and make myself less conspicuous.

I will throw myself off a building before I ever admit it out loud, but the ensuite shower is the most outrageously luxurious thing I've ever had the pleasure of experiencing. Three showerheads, a digital thermostat that can control the temperature of each of them individually, and the perfect water pressure. If it weren't for the location, I could spend the rest of my life in that stall, and die a happy, shriveled raisin.

I've cleaned my body and hair multiple times, scrubbing until my pale skin is a bright pink and not a trace of blood remains. While the shampoo and body wash are nice, unscented stand-ins, they're just another reminder of how much I've lost in the last few hours. My green-apple scented products might have come from the bodega around the corner from Somnium, but at least they were mine.

After towel drying with infuriatingly fluffy towels, my mood only grows fouler as I shimmy into the clothes Felix brought for me. They're baggy and comfortable and soft, and goddamn him, just perfect. And he's even included some fuzzy socks with grippy bottoms. He's making it harder and harder to stay mad at him for ruining my life.

I stare at myself in the mirror, one of the few things I couldn't bring myself to destroy last night, and the harsh light is not doing me any favors. My round face is shadowed, and I suddenly feel my age. Two hundred is young for a fae, but the weight of the years drags my mouth into a frown. When I can't stand the sight of me anymore, I turn away and shuffle back into the living room part of the guest suite. Time to leave.

When I try the handle of the door to the suite, I'm ready for disappointment. But to my shock, it's unlocked. I only open it a crack, peeking out into the large living space beyond, ears straining for any sign of them. But the air is silent and still. My heart kicks a little faster in my chest as I push the door open more, slipping out of the suite and closing the door softly. I freeze, looking around, but nothing moves. There's no one in the ridiculously opulent sunken couch area, or the state-of-the-art kitchen. No one on the glass balcony overlooking the open space from the second floor.

My feet make no sound as I cross over to the elevator, but I pause before I press the call button. I turn to look behind me, chewing my bottom lip. This feels too easy. Someone has to be here, just hiding. But I don't have time to search the entire penthouse, and every minute I waste is a chance for them to come back. I jam my finger into the button, bouncing on the balls of my feet.

The bell as the doors open sounds like a gong crash in the silence, and I scurry inside the car, pressing the lower level button, and then hammer the door close button. If someone else is here, there's no way they didn't hear that.

Come on, come on, move.

I only relax as the doors finally slide closed and the car starts moving. I can't believe it. I'm leaving. My heart still pounds in my chest, but there's nothing to be done about that. The adrenaline filling my body makes me restless, and I shuffle my feet. Socks won't protect my soles for long, but stopping to acquire shoes isn't an option. I need to get out of this hotel and on the road as fast as possible.

The elevator opens, and a wall of casino noise hits me like a sack of bricks. I keep my head down as I exit the car, tucking my hands into the pouch of my hoodie. I keep my pace deliberately casual, doing everything in my power to avoid drawing attention. Navigating using the overhead signs, it only takes a few moments for the front doors to come into view. Dodging tourists, I push my way through the heavy glass door and out onto the sidewalk.

I keep moving, heading off in what I hope is the right direction. Las Vegas in the early hours of the morning is a lot less crowded than I'd hoped. Luckily, I blend better than in the casino, looking like one of the many homeless panhandlers wandering the streets. My mind races, trying to work despite the panic and adrenaline. Almost on instinct, I let my feet guide me to where I need to go.

I look around for the first time, trying to get my bearings. The view had been limited from Somnium's roof, but I'd still been able to see some of the strip. It takes me a minute, but I finally locate a landmark and adjust course. This is a stupid idea, far too obvious, but I don't have a choice. I can figure out what to do once I get back to the club and see what I have to work with. There's a small stash of cash I'd skimmed from the bar's tip jar. I just have to hope it'll be enough to get me a bus ticket out of here.

It takes far longer than I thought it would to find the squat brick prison I'd spent the last century inside of. The sun is almost directly overhead by the time I round the corner and come face to face with the black exterior. God, in the light of day, this place looks decrepit. Paint peeling, weeds growing out of the sidewalk, black awning now a sun-blasted gray, it looks...old. A relic of a time gone by. I can't believe anyone looked at this place and thought they were going to have a good time inside.

As I cross the street, my feet ache, the pavement rough even through my socks. I reach the front door and pull, but nothing happens. I try pushing, but the solid slab of wood doesn't give even a fraction of an inch. I push and pull with all my might, but it remains stubbornly locked. What the hell. We never locked the doors to this place. Refusing to be deterred, I take off around the building, through the narrow alley that lets out to the back where the dumpster is. The metal back door is firmly shut, and when I try the handle, it, too, is locked.

My stomach plummets as I look around, trying to find an answer. Somnium is a one-story building, so there's no fire exit to climb. Even if I managed to get on top of the dumpster, the gap between it and the building is too far for me to jump safely. There isn't a single universe in existence where I could shimmy my way up a drainpipe. But even if I ended up on the roof, what difference would it make?

I look back at the metal door as my world comes crashing down around my ears. Somnium is the only home I've ever known, even if it was hell on earth. It's only a matter of time before the dragons track me down, and I'm dragged back to that lush cage they insist on calling a penthouse. The world seems to tunnel around me, my heartbeat loud in my ears. I'm trapped. Again.

Something inside me snaps. Likely my last tether to sanity. The noise that comes out of my throat isn't human, a primal roar of pain and anger and fear and exhaustion that rips at my throat like claws. I wrap my hands around the smooth doorknob, shaking the door with all my strength. It rattles on its hinges, but nothing more. My vision blurs as I throw myself at the dull steel blocking my way, hammering it with my open palms. I scream and thrash and cry until there's nothing left inside of me. Defeat crashes down on my shoulders, and I collapse to my knees, the sting hardly even registering.

I've been alone for most of my life, but it hasn't felt lonely. I had the other kids at the orphanage, and then once I reached physical maturity and the nuns kicked me out, I had my desperation to keep me company. I met Dominic less than two years after my "graduation," and even if he was the world's biggest asshole, at least I could always count on him to be there. But he's gone, and I'm alone. Truly alone. Nowhere to go. Not a penny to my name. And not a speck of hope left.

There was a short while when I did have some company in the darkness. Ginny. I've forced myself not to think about her this entire time, somewhere between convincing myself she's alright and forgetting she ever existed. It's too raw, too painful to consider the alternative. That maybe the dragons abandoned her. Or killed her. No, I shake my head for my own benefit. If anything had happened to Ginny, I would have known. In some deep, mysterious place inside of me, I would have known. A little whisper perks up at the back of my mind that Ginny must be dead, because she hasn't tried to save me.

Suddenly, the sound of a rock skittering across concrete echoes off the walls of the alley behind me. I freeze, waiting. It could be an animal, a rat probably. But then there's a footstep, and then another, getting closer. My heart beats wildly in my throat. As my mind wheels and tries to form a plan, a cold, slightly accented voice cuts through the air.

"If you left something behind last night, you could have just said something."

CHAPTER 21

Lyra

T he lead dragon strolls out of the shadows, hands in the pockets of his crisp black slacks. Viktor. That's what the big guy called him. I stare up at him, partly in fear but mostly in shock.

"Left something behind? You motherfuckers didn't exactly give me time to pack a bag," I snap, curling into a defensive crouch, turning to put my back to the wall.

Viktor shrugs with a single shoulder, the pale blue dress shirt pulling tight over his muscles. He's a good half-dozen paces away from me, but it feels like the entire solar system has shrunk to the size of this alley. Every instinct in my body wants to run, but he's blocking the only exit. I know a predator when I see one, even if his cufflinks probably cost more than all the money I've earned in my lifetime.

"How did you find me?" I demand, unable to stop myself from asking.

The bastard has the audacity to roll his fucking eyes and sigh, like I'm some sort of child asking why the sky is blue.

When he looks back at me, the patronizing glint to his purple irises sets my teeth to grinding.

"After what it cost us to acquire you, did you really think we'd just leave you to your own devices?" he drawls, bored and annoyed in equal measure.

"I didn't fucking ask for you to *acquire me*," I shout, slamming a fist back against the door.

Viktor levels his stare at me, assessing. I slowly rise from my crouch, wanting to be closer to his level. Though, I'd be better off taking him out at the hips. Even then, I'm sure his legless torso would still be taller than me. Do dragons drink Miracle-Gro as formula or something?

"You're right, you didn't ask. But it doesn't change the fact that we're responsible for your care and comfort," Viktor says at last, settling his shoulders.

I blink at him, not sure how to react. He's responsible for my what now?

"I'm not sure why you felt the need to come back here, because I can assure you that anything you require can be delivered to the penthouse," he goes on, not even acknowledging my surprise.

His nonchalance finally shakes me from my stupor, and I let out an angry huff. "I don't want your charity. I want my life back," I spit.

Viktor cocks his head to the side, brow wrinkling in what appears to be confusion. "What life?"

The question hits me like a blow, and I curl backward away from him, leaning into the cold metal door. Two simple words, and he's cut me to my core. I fucking hate him for it.

"I want my stuff," I snap, avoiding eye contact.

There's a long moment of silence, and I brace for the rejection. I'm a prisoner in this scenario, so what right do I really have to make demands. But I can't let this go. I need something to anchor me, to keep me from going completely off the rails. And if I'm living on borrowed time, then goddamnit, I'm going to do this my way.

I look up at the sound of footsteps, jumping as I realize that Viktor has crossed the distance between us in a few silent strides, and is now basically on top of me. In the chaos of last night, I hadn't really been able to take him in. But now, the sheer intensity of his presence washes over me, and fucking hell, it's intense. He's just about as tall as Gavril, but there's something significantly more dangerous about Viktor. Like a cow and a grizzly bear might technically weigh the same, but one is more likely to tear me to shreds.

It could have been hours or mere seconds that I stand there, lost in the ocean of him. But then he reaches behind me and lays his palm flat on the door, breaking the spell. The lock clunks heavily, making us both jump. A blink of those hauntingly purple eyes, and then he steps back like he suddenly realized how close he had gotten.

I pull the door, almost stumbling with how easily it swings, and scramble inside the building before he can stop me. But only a few steps inside and I freeze. The building is completely silent, and as the door slams shut, I'm plunged into darkness. I scramble along the wall to find a switch, acutely aware of how hard my heart is beating. Once I find it, and white fluorescent light floods the space, I suck in a sharp breath.

I'm so used to seeing this place in a glow of red that I'd forgotten that the walls of the employee area were painted navy blue. The metal shelving units along the walls are rustier than I'd realized, the floor scuffed with dust bunnies huddling in the corners. But even as I take in the dingy space, it's the sheer chaos that strikes me hardest. Props are left scattered on the floor. Costumes abandoned, even someone's purse has been left behind. It's almost as if everyone just up and left without a trace.

But I don't linger in the feelings welling in my chest, heading toward the stairs in the corner opposite the rear entrance. I fly down them, not even hesitating in the dark. I've climbed up and down these steps every day for decades. I know every squeaky board and loose railing. But as I descend, the stillness and quiet only grow more unnerving. Where is everyone? There must be some people left, right? But once I reach the bottom floor, reality crashes down on top of me.

The bottom floor is where those of us with extended contracts lived. Since we don't have built-in expiration dates like most of the people who worked for Dominic, he'd been forced to give us basic facilities, even if he bitched every step of the way. A few bedrooms, a kitchenette, and one bathroom that six of us had to fight over. I'd been here the longest, with Ginny joining me in misery a few decades later. Phil and Will have always been a package deal, arriving within months of each other in the early seventies. Kelly, the dressing room manager, kept to herself, and Franco was always too wrapped up in his own shit. Even if we were rats trapped on a slave ship, at least we had each other.

But as I flip on the lights, my stomach drops. It's cold and empty, the doors to our rooms wide open. I'd say the place looks like it's been robbed, but we never had anything worth stealing. I wander for a moment, eyes wide and breathing shallow. The ship was sinking, and the rats have fled. All but me.

When I finally stagger through to the room I'd lived in for most of my life, I have to swallow back a sudden lump in my throat. My bed is untouched, just as messy as when I rolled out of it yesterday morning. My clothes are still in a pile under the bed, my shower caddy next to it. But as I glance over to the other side of the room, I can't see a single one of Ginny's personal items.

"Your coworkers are safe, if that's what you are wondering."

I whip around to find Viktor behind me, his massive form filling almost the entirety of the doorway. I take a step back out of instinct, hands balling into fists.

"What's that supposed to mean? How do you know that?" I snap, shoulders bunching defensively.

"When we acquired your contract, we also acquired

the others. We've been getting them settled into temporary lodgings until we can determine the next steps," he answers, unruffled.

Viktor slides his hands into his pockets and leans against the doorjamb. His calm in the face of my mounting anxiety grates on my already fraying nerves. Could he drop the Mr. Freeze act for one fucking second and act like a person?

"Why?" I grit.

Viktor blinks, but doesn't show any other reaction. "Because this place is hardly fit for habitation. How any of you lived here for as long as you did–"

"That's not what I fucking mean!"

I'm shouting now, but Viktor still stands, completely unfazed by any of it. My chest tightens with a feeling I don't dare to name, and I turn away before he can see the tears flooding my eyes. I hate how volatile these bastards make me. I can't push the feeling away anymore, and it burns me up from the inside. My friends left me. Just like everyone has. No one is coming to my rescue. No one is missing me. No one is out there wondering if I'm okay. There was a time when I would have gone to the ends of the earth for my friends at Somnium, but I'm beginning to understand that perhaps they never shared the same sentiment. All I have left are my kidnappers.

"Once you've gathered your things, I'd like to go to Dominic's office."

His cool and even tone cuts through the fog of emotion, and I swallow. I don't move, trying to gather myself. I have to get myself under control, or I'm going to end up doing something to piss them off. And unlike before, there isn't a No Harm Clause to protect me from their wrath if I push it too far. So instead of telling him to fuck off, I just drop down beside my bed and fish out a simple drawstring backpack and start shoving things inside it.

I don't take anything that has the club name on it, deciding on a whim to leave that part of my life behind. Dominic and my friends were happy enough to do that with me, so fuck them. But I realize quickly that leaves me with two pairs of jeans, some underwear, and one oversized hoodie I fished out of lost and found a few years back. Not even enough for a whole outfit. I do shed the destroyed socks I'd run here in, replacing them with my comfortable work shoes. Then it's just toiletries and a bottle of borrowed meds Ginny gave me.

Once I'm on my feet, I zip the bag closed and sling it over my back. It's lighter than I'd pictured, but I should have known better. The last thing I grab is an envelope from under my mattress. My small stash of cash. I tuck it into my pants pocket as I turn to face Viktor, feeling a little more like myself. He didn't say anything while I packed, and he continues to stare at me like he's lost in thought.

"Well?" I ask after several long moments of awkward silence.

That seems to shake him from whatever had been occupying his attention, his gaze coming back into focus as he looks me in the eye. The world-shrinking feeling returns with a vengeance and, suddenly, there's not enough air in the room for both of us. But the spell breaks as he steps out of the doorway and motions with one hand for me to lead the way. I consider telling him to find Dom's office himself, and walking back to Korona Drakona. But I'd rather save my energy. I'd learned the fine art of choosing my battles, and this just isn't worth it. So, with the literal dragon on my heels, I trudge out of my old room and back to the stairs.

CHAPTER 22

VIKTOR

When I'd noticed Lyra "sneak" out of her room and out of the penthouse from my office, I'll admit to being curious. I knew she didn't have anywhere to go, so I assumed she'd come to the same conclusion. Yet, as I followed her through the streets of Las Vegas, all the way back to Somnium, I had to admire her determination. And then she snapped.

It only took being in the splash zone of her breakdown for mere seconds for me to understand why Gavril panicked. Being near her as she screamed and cried and raged was like witnessing a hurricane making landfall. Wave after wave of emotion crashed over me, and it was all I could do to hang on and lock myself down so I didn't get swept out to sea.

And now, as I follow behind her up the stairs, I'm finding it hard to keep that wall up. She's in pain, and I don't even need my power to tell me that. Finding this place empty clearly struck a deep nerve, but I can't change the facts. Her coworkers made it clear that they just wanted out, to cut all ties with Las

Vegas and Somnium so they could move on, and I would not violate their trust to soothe one tiny hellspawn.

Once we reach the second floor, Lyra leads me down a hallway lined with identical doors. She's slumped over, clutching the strings of the woefully empty backpack she'd packed. All of her worldly possessions in one polyester sack. Felix seems keen on keeping her like a pet, so I'm sure he'll jump at the chance to provide her with creature comforts. I'd have to make sure he gets her more clothes, as a start. Then maybe a few pairs of shoes. A hairbrush. A proper coat.

My mental listing is interrupted as Lyra stops and opens a door, seemingly at random, not even looking back to see if I'm following. She disappears from sight for a moment as she shoves through a curtain, and my heart lurches. She seems to have calmed down, but it's clear that her mood shifts at the drop of a hat. And I don't feel like chasing her down again. But as I push through the curtain and find her standing there, waiting for me, my relief is short-lived as a new wall of emotion crumbles around me. This time, not from Lyra, but from the building itself.

I normally only pick up emotions from other beings, and I have to be in relatively close proximity to them. On occasion, if an object is of particular importance to someone, like a childhood toy or a book, I can pick up on traces of those feelings, but they usually fade within hours of being separated from their owners. I've only ever been able to pick up on emotions left behind in a physical location once, but that was the scene of a great tragedy. Being here last night, the air was thick with emotion, and it all washed over my senses like television static. But now, with no one around to interfere, the intensity of it nearly takes my breath away. It's desperation, and relief; the two mix together like bile and sugar in my mouth. I take a second to brace against the wall, my vision darkening at the edges and my legs feeling like jelly. Unfortunately, touching the walls only makes the tidal wave of emotions grow stronger, more deafening. By the time I come to my senses, Lyra's red brows are furrowed, a little knot forming in the center.

"You good, dragon boy?" she quips with a sharp edge of sarcasm. I nod, only once, as I straighten my posture and ease away from the wall.

"This place is a fucking abyss," I scoff, studying the poor interior decoration with a sense of disgust.

"Yeah, well, you get used to it." Her shoulders are slumped, but otherwise, she looks fine. There's the lingering sour taste of sadness, hurt, and anger rolling from her, but I'm coming to realize that's just her resting emotional state.

She picks up a discarded tonic glass and twirls it in her fingers. "After all, this wasn't just a whore house, it was a whore home."

If we were in any other situation, I might have laughed at her dark sense of humor.

I stall in the middle of the Dream Lounge, surveying the area with fresh eyes now that the place is empty. "Dominic's office?"

Lyra nods toward the far wall. "Behind the curtain, door to your left."

Scales ripple beneath my skin, itching to break free as more and more of the negative emotions from inside Somnium pile on top of each other. I need fresh air, open space, and a vast distance, some place that doesn't sting with each passing breath. I glance back at Lyra as she looks around the Dream Lounge with wide, unblinking eyes as I slip through the curtain and open the door to Dominic's office.

She's barely out of sight when I let my claws free. The ache of holding them back for even those few short moments makes me groan, and I have to roll my shoulders against the burn. Dominic's office is dark and simple, more akin to a cheap secondhand car dealer's office than one of a demon. But it's the volatility that strikes me the hardest. Pressure builds around me like cold cement walls, closing me in and making it hard for me to breathe at all. Yet beneath it are the subtle fragments of close-to-burning salted caramel and earthy vanilla. These are Dominic's feelings, coarse and unfiltered, and they're directed at Lyra.

Whatever Lyra did to Dominic has left an impression strong enough to make me physically ill. His disgust and anger at her lingers like sulfur, with undertones of bitter violence, and even sour notes of sexual violence strike like white-hot pokers. If this is what is left over, I fear for the day he comes to collect on their deal. As the thought of Dominic taking Lyra away from me crosses my mind, another flash of rage streaks across my vision. No. He won't ever put a finger on her, not as long as I draw breath.

The fierceness of that protective instinct finally knocks me back into the present. What the hell is she doing to me? She hates me, hates my pack, yet I'm ready to fight to the bitter end to protect her from the consequences of her own actions? No. Out of the question.

I roll my shoulders and gather my wits. I'm here for a reason. The faster I complete this task, the sooner I can be back where I belong.

I brush aside the debris littering the desk, scanning the paperwork beneath it. Expense reports, inventory sheets, payroll ledgers.

Straightening, I look around, eyes finding the singular painting in the room. Pulling it away, I contain my eye roll as I find a wall safe.

It doesn't take much for me to crack the code. There aren't any wards or protection charms around the lock, and I can hear the tumblers fall into place as I turn the dial. Opening the door, I grin as I find what I came for. The contracts. Demons are an old-fashioned sort, keeping paper copies of their deals. I slide the sheaf of parchment out, thumbing through them to confirm the identities of the people now under my rule. Six contracts, including Lyra's. I stare at the page with her name on it, seeing but not reading. I have every right to know the terms of her deal, but learning this way makes something in my gut churn. So I tuck it away. I don't have time to really look at it now anyway.

I look back into the safe, curious about what else he might have been hiding. No cash, though I'm not surprised. It probably vanished into his pockets the moment he left. There are a few odds and ends, though. A keyring with a dozen assorted keys, probably to the different rooms in the building. The deed to the land, which I take. And then a box, about the size of a shoebox, tucked into the back.

I carry it over to the desk, admiring the craftsmanship of the walnut box. It's unadorned, with simple hinges and a clasp holding it closed. I don't detect anything outwardly magical about it, except a strong cloaking ward. He was trying to hide something. I set the box down, using one finger to lift the lid, bracing for any sort of trap. But once the lid is open, I frown in disappointment. It's a jewelry box. There's a set of rings on a blue ribbon tucked into one velvet-lined partition, a simple gold chain in another. But my eye skims over the other objects until it lands on a pendant that has my mind racing.

About the size of a casino chip, a bright red jewel is set into platinum filigree, the swirls and loops of the metalwork encasing the gem to form a teardrop shaped pendant. The simple leather strap that runs through the top is a striking contrast to the absolute beauty of the piece, but it's not the beauty that makes my heart stop. To most eyes, the red gem would appear to be some sort of semi-precious stone, perhaps carnelian or garnet, but this is no stone. No, this is a dragon scale, and the way it's been honed and polished and set...

How the fuck did some low life demon end up with a dragon's betrothal gift.

"Where did you get that?" she rasps, less of a question and more of a demand.

I blink a few times, caught completely off guard by her sudden appearance. Shock and disbelief roll off her in waves, tasting like buttercream frosting on my tongue. I look at the necklace and then back to her, my confusion growing with every moment.

"It was in the safe. Why?" I ask cautiously.

"He said...he needed an anchor, something to make the locator spell work. I can't believe...I would have thought he would have tossed it years ago," Lyra says faintly, and I'm not sure she's even aware of me anymore.

"This is yours?" My voice is nearly a shout, but I don't care. Dominic coming into possession of a dragon heirloom, while highly unlikely, could be explained. Demons aren't exactly known for their honest dealings. But *Lyra*...

She seems to come back into herself then, shaking her head as if to clear away cobwebs. She inhales sharply through her nose, lifting her chin defiantly. "Yeah, it is. Now give it back."

She holds out her hand, fingers splayed wide, mouth set in a firm line. I growl and close my fist around the pendent and tuck it to my chest. She doesn't move, not even a flinch as I level a warning glare in her direction. If my head wasn't already full, I'd admire her tenacity. I've seen men twice her size and three times as powerful wither like grass under the desert sun at the sound of my growl.

"No. This is a relic of my people. I don't know how the hell you managed to get your hands on it–"

Lyra tosses her head and shows me her teeth. "You can cut the judgment, lizard dick. I didn't fucking steal it. It was my mother's. The nuns gave it to me when I aged out of the orphanage. So fuck your people. That's mine, and I want it back. Now."

Her words land like blows, one after another, stunning me into silence. My mind is moving too fast, and connections are slipping through my fingers. But a question rises above all the noise: who the fuck is Lyra Spanos?

We're silent for another long moment, but not for lack of things to say. I want to ask more, to demand answers, but she snarls and drops her hand before I can get my mouth to function. She crosses her arms over her glorious chest and turns away, teeth grinding hard enough for me to hear from across the room.

"Fuck it, whatever. I don't need that shitty necklace anyway," she grumbles, storming out of the office and out of my sight.

I find Lyra in the backseat of the car I'd parked out front, hugging her meager possessions to her chest as she obstinately stares out the window, not even acknowledging me as I slide in beside her and close the door. A nod to the driver and we're off, heading back home. The air is heavy with words unsaid, but I hesitate. Why am I hesitating? She has information I want. If she were literally any other being on the planet, I'd have her singing her darkest secrets in minutes. But I can't bring myself to exert that sort of pressure on her.

I mull over my thoughts and feelings, unable to ignore the pulsing ball of anguish and disappointment beside me. Glancing out of the corner of my eye, I'm forced to do a double take as a single tear rolls down her cheek. She reaches up to wipe it away, but I'm faster, hand moving before my brain can think better of it. She gasps at the touch, and finally turns to look at me. I snatch my hand away from the feel of her velvet skin like I've been burned. Her hazel eyes sear into mine with hurt and anger, and I take a deep breath as something cracks in my chest.

Reaching into my pocket, I pull the pendant out and look down at it, conflicted. Dragons don't shed their scales like snakes or lizards. Removing even a single one is arduous and painful, symbolic of the depths of one's commitment to the recipient.

"How did your mother come to possess this?" I ask into the silence, my fingers drifting to her chin to cup her face and force her eyes to stay with mine.

She blinks, swallowing hard. She's trembling under my touch, and I probe just a little. Confusion, anger, and distrust swirl at the forefront of her mind, but there's a slow, deep undercurrent of heat and desire that sparks something inside of me. I want to pull that feeling forward, to replace the negative energy with positive, to reassure her she's safe. But she pulls away, looking out the passenger window.

"I don't know. She died shortly after giving birth to me. The nuns said she was holding this when she passed, calling out for a Quintus. My father," Lyra replies, words a breathless whisper.

I don't sense any attempts at deception. I realize with a jolt that this might be the first truly honest thing she's ever said to me. The implications of her answer crash over me in waves. But I don't have the room in my head to unravel this mystery, at least not right now. But with that admission, she shuts down again. The rest of the ride back to the casino is as silent as a grave, and she takes off once we're parked before I can even open my mouth. So I'm left alone with more questions than answers, and no clue of how to uncover them.

CHAPTER 23

GAVRIL

A lot of people say that silence is more disconcerting than screaming, depending on the context. Like with children. If they're quiet when they should be playing, something serious is going down. So when the elevator opens up to the penthouse and absolute silence greets me, my adrenaline spikes. I thought it was risky to leave Viktor alone with Lyra, but Felix and I had to deal with the rogue dryad clan today. He's still downstairs, picking up the day's requests and messages from the concierge.

"Hello? Anyone home?" I yell, my words literally echoing in the vastness of the penthouse.

Going from room to room, finding no evidence of a struggle, only leaves me more anxious. What the fuck did those two do to each other? Did Lyra leave?

A strange twist in my stomach catches me off guard as I think of losing that little fireball. I've known her less than two full days. Why should I care if she stays or goes? But I can't deny that my world has been brightening with her in it. More exciting, less routine. I don't want to lose that so soon.

I call out again from the back hallway, knocking on Viktor's bedroom door, only to receive no answer. But then the distant chime of the elevator pulls my attention.

The doors hum as they open, revealing Viktor and Lyra. She has her arms folded across her front, a bag clutched to her chest as she stares daggers at Viktor's back. He steps out first, signaling for her to follow. His face is twisted in its usual scowl, whilst hers is pink and flustered.

"Felix with you?" I ask, knowing the answer, since the elevator doors are already slipping shut.

Viktor shakes his head, moving into the kitchen and opening the fridge. He surveys the contents before plucking a few things from inside and setting them down on the counter.

"Sit," he orders calmly, and I find myself immediately settling onto one of the stools at the island. "You too, Lyra,"

She isn't quite as keen to do as he asks, and I watch her closely while she toys with her options. Eventually, she puts the bag she's been carrying down on the floor and takes a seat one away from me.

"Felix will be here in a second," Viktor adds. His hands are busy chopping green onions, tomatoes and avocado.

"So..." I muse, pursing my lips as my eyes shift from Viktor to Lyra. "What have you guys been up to?"

Silence cloaks the three of us once more, and I suddenly feel like the naughty child in a classroom. The one that clearly can't follow social cues.

"Do I have to be here, or can I go back to my tastefully decorated prison cell?" Lyra offers a forced, tight-lipped smile, glancing between Viktor and me.

"No," Vik snaps, unwrapping a parchment covered pack of raw chicken. "You will sit, you will listen, and you will eat."

Lyra's nostrils flare, her chest rising and falling with shallow breaths as she tries to tackle her rage. As much as I would love to enjoy the fireworks, I don't like the look in Viktor's eyes. He's at the end of his patience, and if Lyra keeps pushing, she won't like the results.

"Help me polish off these berries, *vatreno*," I offer, hopping off my stool and crossing to the fridge before pulling out a plastic container of strawberries.

"I'm allergic," Lyra spits, still glaring at Viktor.

Viktor lets out a warning growl, and I swallow hard. All right. Time to call a bluff.

I plop down on my stool again, grabbing a small red berry and slicing off the top with a sharp talon. I brace myself for impact, before poking Lyra in the ribs with my other hand. She shrieks like I've electrocuted her again, but I seize the opportunity and shove the strawberry in her open mouth before she can stop me.

I can feel Viktor's stare on the side of my face, but I don't look away from Lyra as she turns her heated glare on me. I try to keep my expression innocent, even a little playful. Seconds tick by until, at last, she starts chewing.

"If I'd actually been allergic, you could have killed me," she grumbles after she swallows.

To my relief, she picks up another strawberry, removing the leaves with her thumbnail.
I glance at Viktor, my heart flip-flopping at the pride shining in his amethyst eyes. The side of my mouth lifts in a smirk before I eat another strawberry.

"Good thing you're not," I reply simply.

And to my eternal relief, she doesn't curse or shout or storm away. She just rolls her eyes, trying to sulk while demolishing the fresh container of berries I'd bought this morning.

Viktor is still visible out of the corner of my eye as I watch Lyra. Her mouth settles around each strawberry, and she sucks as she bites down, gulping every morsel of juice released by the fruit. My cock hardens, but I ignore it, reminding myself that this isn't the time for hard-ons, especially when Viktor is so tense. Luckily, I'm distracted by the sound of the elevator bell announcing Felix's return.

He appears moments later, disheveled, and generally looking worse for wear. His black sweatpants hang low on his sharp, narrow hips. The matching t-shirt clings to every lithe muscle, his sculpted abs and shoulders creating harsh lines. Usually, he's covered up in a hoodie, face barely visible in the shadows.

His pale grey eyes flash at Lyra, twinkling in the warm hue of the chandelier above the kitchen island.

"Felix," Viktor addresses casually. "Nice of you to join us."

Lyra's scowl deepens, and she pushes the tray of berries away from her with the tips of her delicate fingers. Something happened between those two. I might not be the most perceptive member of this pack, but even an idiot could sense the tension lingering in the air like clouds of smoke.

We all sit in silence, each waiting for someone else to talk. Naturally, Lyra is the first to speak up.

"So is this a new form of torture you're trying out? Awkward silences?" she asks nonchalantly.

Viktor growls lowly while he scrapes the chunks of raw chicken into a hot pan alongside onions and peppers. His large hand darts out on instinct, picking up three jars of various spices in one palm.

"We have some ground rules to cover," Vik replies, sprinkling and stirring like it's the most natural thing in the world. Not once does he turn to look at any of us.

"Ground rules?" Lyra chuckles, venom lacing each word from her pretty pink lips. "Are you for real?"

Felix and I go still. Viktor draws in a breath and turns around, abandoning the pan as he grips on to the kitchen counters hard enough that the veins in his forearms ripple.

His eyes are the most vibrant purple when he finally lets his lids flutter open. "No more trying to sneak out."

"Yeah," Lyra laughs, moving to stand. "Sure thing, boss. I'll just head back to my cell like a good little girl. That's what you want, right? Some silent lap dog that just sits in the corner wagging its tale and waiting for you to return. No fucking deal, lizard dick."

The second her perky ass is off the stool, Viktor's voice booms like thunder. "Sit. Down."

I look at Felix and pull a face. Daddy's mad as shit.

"In case you hadn't noticed, the doors are not locked. The windows do open. And the elevator only requires a keycard downstairs. This isn't a prison, Lyra. Perhaps if you'd spend a little more time thinking and a little less time wreaking havoc, you'd have realized such a thing."

Her butt meets the stool once again. *Lucky stool.* And she stares, slack-jawed, at Viktor.

"You're telling me, I could have just waltzed out the front door?"

Viktor turns to stir the contents of the pan before he grabs a pack of organic soft-shell tortillas from the cupboard above his head. He tears the pack open with his teeth and sets the pile down on a baking tray. We all watch as he puts them in the oven to warm; his backside does look extraordinary in those suit pants.

"Vik..." Felix begins in warning. It seems he's just as lost as I am.

"You could have." Viktor shrugs. "But where would you go?"

Lyra is visibly taken aback, and I have to suffocate the urge to put my hands on her and soothe her ruffled feathers.

"The truth is, Lyra, you have no money, barely any belongings, and no family. If you stay with us, you will be taken care of, protected. Even if you don't want to admit it, you are safe here."

"For how long?" she huffs. "So I'll just be your burden, until what?"

Viktor doesn't look up, but what little color is left in Felix's face drains. My heart gives an unnatural lurch at the thought of Lyra leaving, let alone anyone else having her. She's ours, my instincts scream. She can't leave.

"You know that's not—" Felix begins, but is instantly cut off by Lyra.

"No, let me just say this out loud. I need to make sure I'm hearing this right." Lyra wiggles in her seat and raises her hands whilst Viktor continues cooking. "I stay here, and you keep me like a pet. One that no doubt you'll tire of eventually. Maybe not this week, maybe not even this month. But eventually, you'll get sick of me. And just like Dominic, you'll ship me off to the first person that offers to take me off your hands. Sound about right?"

"That's not exactly what I was getting at, no," Viktor replies, pulling four plates from the cupboard and setting them down alongside four wineglasses on the countertop.

"Then what are you getting at, boss man? Hm?"

Lyra disguises her hurt well. Cloaked in confidence and anger. My chest aches; she sounds just like me, back in the day, before Viktor and Felix. When I was stuck competing with my brothers for my parents' affection. She's never been the favorite, never even been in the top three. Felix seems to share my hurt, looking at Lyra like all he wants to do is bundle her up in blankets and protect her from the rest of the world. Maybe even protect her from herself.

"You stay with us, you don't just get a room and an allowance like some child, you are our guest. We won't make you leave, and you stop trying to run away to nowhere. You do as you please, go where you want in this penthouse, or casino, or even this city. All we ask is that you let one of us know. It's the same courtesy we offer each other."

Vik is busy plating up, filling the tortillas with spiced chicken, peppers, and onions, and topping each one with a generous helping of the fresh guacamole he's put together. This whole time, he hasn't even blinked. Unlike Felix and I, this is Viktor's strong suit. Talking. Bargaining.

He passes a plate to us all and fills the glasses with a floral smelling white wine. Lyra does nothing but stare down at the plate as if it's about to bite her.

"You'll also eat," Viktor announces, leaning his arms on the counter so his face is just a foot away from Lyra's. "You'll have three meals a day and you'll hydrate. And I'm not talking about coffee and energy drinks. Water and food will be provided, and you are expected to consume without argument."

"Why? Want me fattened up for the bi-annual dragon feast?" I chuckle at the joke, stifling it with my fist.

Viktor casts his eyes to the ceiling and shakes his head. *"Jesus Christ. Why is nothing simple with you?"* He mutters the words in Russian, but his tone is clear. "We don't plan on eating you, darling." Viktor sighs as though he's exhausted himself.

"Speak for yourself." I grin widely and shoot Lyra a wink.

Lyra narrows her eyes at me, then at Viktor, and last at Felix. I don't react, digging into the delicious meal Viktor's made for us. He might not be the most affable dragon to have ever lived, but goddamn is he a good cook. Felix does the same, though his gaze is locked onto Lyra like she's the most fascinating performance on the planet.

"I don't want you in my room," Lyra says at last.

Viktor doesn't even blink. "Easy enough. Once the repairs are complete, your door will have a lock on it, with one key in the safe and the other in your possession."

"Why-"

"If the fucking building's on fire, I'm not going to knock politely," Viktor counters before she can even speak than the first syllable of her protest.

I snort into my food as her jaw snaps shut with an audible click of her teeth. She clears her throat, and finally picks up her fork.

And it feels like the Christmas Day Truce on the Western Front when she takes that first bite and doesn't have a single smartass comment.

CHAPTER 24

Lyra

Harsh sunlight streams in through the expanse of windows covering the far wall of the dragon boys' sunken sitting room. I pull the soft blanket over my head, burying my face in the pillow in an attempt to will myself back to sleep. It's useless. Day has broken, and it seems I'm destined to break alongside it. After last night's dinner, in which I'd sunk a solid four glasses of wine and eaten six of Viktor's homemade and annoyingly delicious tacos, I'd collapsed into a heap with the television on in the background. Gavril had made the bold choice to sit beside me, flicking through channels until he settled on some crime show I'd never had the pleasure of watching. The drone of background noise and Gavril's occasional 'I knew its!' were a welcome distraction that lulled me to sleep within what must've been just a few minutes.

I still haven't digested Viktor's so-called ground rules. I want to be mad at the requests, but fuck. Dominic never gave a shit if I was fed or if my room was secure at night. My brain has been mush, too full and tired to comprehend that maybe these dragons don't want to sacrifice me to their dragon overlords. Or if they are, why they would want to keep me comfortable in the meantime. And I mean, if this is how I'll live before I meet my maker, then fine. But not knowing the whys of it all is going to drive me insane before I ever get to the not-so-pearly gates.

Despite the emotional overload, the sofa I've slept on is comfortable, but the cushions are soft, and my body has made some kind of Lyra-shaped indent. My back aches and I'm pretty sure I've pulled a muscle in my shoulder. Years of sleeping on a cheap, hard mattress have left me incompatible with the softness of expensive couches. In fairness, the bed in the guest room was firmer and more palatable but, of course, I chose to rip that room to shreds during my last temper tantrum.

"Coffee?" Felix's voice rings out from behind me, quickly followed by the bitter scent of freshly made coffee. I arch my neck around to catch a glimpse of him, and he shoots me that one-sided, boyish smile of his. My insides melt, the scent of the coffee giving way to jasmine and winter spice. My lips part and it coats my tongue, leaving me breathless and flushed. Those feelings, as quickly as they appear, are all pushed down into that box I keep locked away deep inside.

"Cream and sugar, please," I reply finally, doing my best to shrug off whatever it is I'm choosing to avoid.

Felix sets a silver tray on the coffee table and kneels down, pouring coffee into a fancy ass cup. He's dressed in all black today, tight jeans and an oversized hoodie. But he's left the hood down for once, leaving his tousled white hair in a tangle on top of his head. He's so pale in the sunlight that every glint or shadow seems to dance across his features. His plump, pink lips are parted in concentration when he takes a spoon and stirs the two cups before passing one to me.

"It'll be hot," he mumbles, shuffling backward on his butt until he's resting against the sofa opposite me. Seeing him like this, in the sunlight, I realize he looks inherently elven, but not in a realistic way. Elves of reality are small, more closely related to dwarves than any fae creature. He's more akin to what humans think elves look like. Like those lace-front wearing guys in Lord of the Rings.

I nurse the cup of coffee in my palms, blowing on it every few seconds to cool it quicker. After the shitty sleep I've had, I'm going to need all the caffeine I can get my hands on. I take a quick sip, then another. It's the best damn coffee I've ever had. At Somnium, there were always a couple of pots on the go for staff. We kept it behind the bar and, most days, I'd devour at least three cups. But in comparison with the rich, chocolatey tasting coffee, with the fluffy foamy top that Felix has made me, it was straight up liquid shit.

As if reading my mind, Felix chimes in. "How did you sleep?"

I chuckle, shrugging nonchalantly as I take a sip. "Not great."

"I'm sorry to hear that." I hate how formal he sounds, and my first instinct is to get pissy with him, but he doesn't give me much of a chance.

"What's your favorite color?" He stares at me with those gray eyes of his, thick lashes framing them as he blinks slowly.

"Excuse me?" I scowl, genuinely wondering if he's lost his mind.

"I thought we could redecorate your room," he replies casually.

I pause for a second, my brain running through all the reasons why they'd want to do anything to make me feel at home. This is my cage. Why bother making it look pretty?

"Why?"

Felix seems caught off guard and I'm waiting for him to stumble over his response as his cheeks flush pink, but he merely clears his throat and straightens his shoulders. "Because you destroyed the other one, but also because it might be nice for you to have an area you can call your own."

I remain silent, digesting his words as best I can.

"We all have our own spaces," he adds. "Our own place

in this penthouse that we can do with what we feel like." His light French accent leaves his words bleeding together, making them sound like the softest poetry.

"I'm guessing you weren't a fan of Viktor's art nouveau pieces, since they were some of the first things to end up smashed."

I'm about to go on the defensive when I notice Felix's smirk, a dimple appearing in his cheek.

"I'm not much of an interior decorator," I quip light-heartedly, my defenses slipping away minute by minute. Something I've picked up on, in the short time I've been here, is that it's hard to stay mad at Felix. He's too calm, collected, and quiet, like the soft hum of white noise, lulling me into a false sense of safety and security.

"One second," he says, holding up a finger as he climbs gracefully to his feet. Within seconds, he's back, settling on the carpeted floor in front of me, a laptop in hand. He opens it up and types in a quick password before opening the web browser. It doesn't take him long to start pulling up pictures of artistically decorated bedrooms.

"So you designed this place yourself?" I question, watching as he favorites different bits and pieces on a website where the prices are longer than most phone numbers.

He shakes his head, tendrils of white-blond hair covering his forehead. "Viktor did most of it. Gavril and I don't take much interest in that sort of thing."

"What's your room like?" The question comes out of nowhere, and when his eyes flash to meet mine, I realize I've made a mistake.

"I can show you sometime," he says, voice trembling with hope and excitement. "It's basic, but it suits my needs."

"I'm good, Invisiboy."

Guilt wracks me when disappointment clouds his boyish features. I'm forced to remind myself that I'm not here as a "guest," as Viktor so kindly called me. I'm here as a prisoner. A glorified one, perhaps, but a prisoner, nonetheless.

"How do you feel about blue?" he asks, ignoring my previous insult and moving swiftly on.

I scrunch up my face. "I don't know, it's a color, I guess."

Felix exhales loudly through his nostrils and turns his attention back to the laptop. "Pink?"

"Of course, because every girl dreams of a perfect, pink, princess bedroom with all the fixings. Oh, kind sir, won't you hire someone to fluff my pillows at night too?"

I get the sense that I'm annoying him, but he's calm enough that he doesn't let on. I watch as he aimlessly scrolls through Pinterest board after Pinterest board, pausing every now and again to shoot me a side on glance to gauge my reaction.

With a groan, I fall back against the soft sofa cushions. "Fine, if you're so intent on redecorating the guest room, I like white."

"White?" he asks in surprise, a little frown tugging at his fair brows.

I run my finger around the rim of the coffee mug, avoiding his eyes. "I spent years in a dingy shared bedroom, with no windows, no natural light. It was dark, okay? White reflects the light, makes things look bigger. Or at least that's what I think, anyway."

Felix keeps quiet, neither agreeing nor disagreeing with my possibly nonsensical explanation for the color choice.

"White," he muses. "I'll get some sheer curtains, too."

In that second, I'm unsure if he's making fun of me. I'd get it if he were. There aren't many people that can say they went from one unlit cage to another. I've never had much of a choice about anything in my life, which makes my stomach hurt just to think about. Dominic even went as far as buying my clothes. So it comes as no surprise I have no sense of taste. I've never been given the opportunity to even think about such mundane, everyday things.

"Why sheer curtains?" I question, finally breaking the silence.

Felix lifts his shoulders in a casual shrug. "They'll let the natural light in more than the blinds that are up there now. That way you can see the sun rise and set without even moving from your bed."

I drain what's left of my coffee, already mourning the taste, and set the cup down. Shimmying to the edge of the sofa cushions, I study him with odd curiosity. Where did he come from? Him and the others. They're the weirdest people I've ever met. Either that or they're just good at playing pretend when it comes to niceties. I can't decide if I'm just getting used to being a captive, or if these three dragons are growing on me.

I've spent most of life terrified of dragons, hating the fact that they existed in the same universe as me. Purely because I never wanted to cross paths with the monsters I'd been told about all my life from various sources. Hell, I didn't trust Dominic as far as I could throw him, but the fact he seemed so concerned about dragons only fed into my fear. Big so-called scary demon like him being scared of a few reptiles? It was enough to make me want to steer clear of the species. Yet Felix, Gavril, and Viktor don't seem so bad. Not once have they honestly tried to hurt me. Yeah, Gavril went a little electro-guy on me when I arrived here, but I was unharmed, aside from my bruised ego.

Felix shuffles on the floor and I'm reminded that he's waiting on an answer about sheer curtains, of all things.

"Okay," I agree, finally. "That sounds nice."

Joy lights up Felix's soft features, though he fights to disguise it. There's something about the way his face changes, losing all signs of stress or tension, that gives me a warm feeling in my stomach. Close to butterflies, but not so nerve-wracking. It's as if seeing him relaxed and happy in turn makes me feel the same way. I can't explain it. So I resign myself to watching him as he taps away on the computer, ordering a bunch of bedding, throw pillows, and curtains that go with a natural color scheme. He adds in the odd pop of color, a large faux cactus in a pastel green pot, and a few cushions with

178

colored tassels of the ends. There's a mix of white, pale greens, and sandy yellows that, despite trying my hardest, make my insides warm and my skin prickle. By the time it comes to paying, I can picture what the room will look like in my mind's eye. And it's *beautiful*.

Not too showy, not fancy. Just a normal room, with normal things. No garish colors or blacked-out windows. No red lights or squeaky leather. I've not even seen it in person yet and it already feels strangely like my own. Not so much a cage, but a space I truly wouldn't want to leave because it'd bring me peace.

I'm beginning to feel like perhaps I'm not as temporary as I thought I was. Maybe they do want me here...or maybe I'm just really susceptible to Stockholm Syndrome. My messed-up brain can't make sense of it, but I'm not even sure I want to. Do I belong here? Do they want me here?

A swell of panic claws at my throat, turning my stomach over in uneasy waves. Out of nowhere, my breathing has quickened, and I clutch at my chest and neck.

"Lyra?" Felix asks as I scramble to my feet.

I pace up and down the sunken living room, waving my hands in front of my body in an attempt to distract myself from the rush of anxiety. It's just a room.

It's just a room.

I repeat the words to myself inside my head, trying to let them sink in as best I can, but it's no use.

"Deep breaths," Felix whispers, in front of me now. He places his hands on either of my arms and draws in a dramatic gasp. "In through your nose, out through your mouth. Try to hold it." The touch of his skin on mine does nothing to calm me down; instead, my heart races to catch up. His hands are soft and warm, delicate just like the rest of him, and I'm sent spiraling into a frenzy at the forbidden thought that those hands would feel nicer elsewhere.

Shaking my head, I fumble over my words. "I'm fine. It's fine. Everything's fine."

"No, you're having a panic attack," Felix stresses, maintaining his example of breathing as though I've forgotten how to do the damn thing.

Oh shit, maybe I have forgotten how to breathe.

"Was it the stuff? We don't have to buy anything, we can wait, I just thought..." His voice trails off helplessly, cool gray eyes darting back to look at the laptop like he's considering typing into Google *'how to not let your house pet die.'*

House pet. That's what I am. A stray cat they brought in off the streets, who they're dressing up and giving a pretty cage, to be kept until they're bored and can dump me back where they found me. Nothing permanent, no hope of actually belonging, no hope of anything, really.

"Okay, uh..." Felix gives up the breathing demonstration, finally. "What side of a dragon has the most scales?"

My eyes steady, fixating on Felix with the feeling that perhaps he's having a fucking stroke. "What? I don't know. Why would I know that?"

Felix pauses for a second, going still. "The outside."

There's silence. Never-ending, suffocating silence. Then I laugh. And laugh. And laugh.

Everything about this situation is absolutely coconuts. But I keep laughing until tears leak from my eyes and my sides ache. My body flips the bird at "fight or flight" and finally releases some of the built-up fear and tension in the form of hysterical cackles. Felix smiles at me, his eyes soft as I calm down. He's not judging me or yelling at me or questioning me. He just looks...happy. Happy because I'm happy.

That's when I decide to hell with it. I deserve sheer curtains and a cactus, even if this weird roommate situation I'm in doesn't last. At least I'll get to see the sun rise and set every day without having to climb onto a roof.

CHAPTER 25

VIKTOR

I set my desk phone back in its cradle, sighing to myself. Well, I'm never going to get that hour and a half back, but I'll take the small victory that came from the call.

My contacts finally managed to track down Dominic and confirm he's out of my city. When he'd vanished after our "meeting," it had been chaos. Questions from the dozens of people who'd been working that night, and then more still from the people who showed up at Somnium to find it closed and condemned. But at last, it's been confirmed that Dominic has been spotted in Reno and most of his employees are back to their usual grind at his new club. I was hoping he'd move a little bit farther away than this, but fuck it. As long as he's not here making a mess of my plan, then that's good enough for me.

But now comes the part I've been least looking forward to: those fucking contracts Felix saddled us with. Since bringing them back with me, I haven't had the chance to really look at them and see what we're dealing with in regard to terminating them. But it's imperative that we do so as fast as possible, before any of the nearby packs get word and rat us out to the council. Because it won't matter to those dinosaurs if we're actively working to free these people. Owning people is owning people, no matter the intention.

When I open the folder and start reading the tiny text on the sheets of parchment, the sad stories of these people's lives unfold, one after another. A high elf who wanted revenge against an unfaithful lover, who had to watch others live out their wildest dreams. Two unlikely friends who wanted different lives than what their monstrous appearances dictated, only to lose everything in a few bad games of roulette and have to use their forms to earn their keep. A nymph who just wanted a family, being forced to take care of an ever-rotating cast of young, desperate women she couldn't save. And a wolf shifter who willingly sacrificed herself to keep her sisters from starving, serving addicts their fix every night for the rest of her very long life.

Each of these contracts is nearly identical, with the same boiler plate legalese that outlines the terms and conditions of the deal. My blood boils when I find myself reading a paragraph labeled "No Harm Clause," feeling the fool all over again. Dominic bluffed hard, and Felix fell for it, hook, line, and sinker. According to these documents, the demon would have been better off throwing himself into the Grand Canyon than laying a finger on any of these people. Any damage done to their person would reflect back onto him, even if Dominic wasn't the one inflicting it. Even ordering someone to do his dirty work would have triggered the magic of this clause. And even now, he still can't hurt them as the document makes no mention of the clause transferring away if someone else were to come into possession of the contract. I scribble a note to make sure that information is relayed when I have my sit-downs with the creatures I now possess. It's a cold comfort, to be sure, but they deserve to know that right now, they are probably the safest they've ever been in their entire lives.

Unable to avoid it any longer, I take a deep breath and pick up Lyra's contract. The first thing I notice is the difference in size. The other five contracts are about as large as a piece of legal-size paper. Lyra's contract is twice as long, and the words are so densely packed that it takes serious concentration to discern the text. Her sad story isn't entirely surprising; a little orphan girl who was desperate enough to sell her soul for answers is almost cliched. And as I scan over the document, my brow furrows in confusion. Some parts are the same as the others, but some make next to no sense. Why would Dominic need to include terms that expressly forbid her from leaving Somnium without permission and an escort? Why would he need to cap the amount of alcohol she consumed on any given day? And why the fuck was she required to disclose any romantic relationships beyond casual hookups?

The level of control Dominic exerted over Lyra's life makes my stomach turn, especially the parts that limit her privacy and bodily autonomy. I can't imagine anyone willingly subjecting themselves to this sort of treatment, let alone enduring it for over a century. It strikes a deep chord in my soul, the one I've felt since my early years. The expectations placed on my shoulders by my father and the entire Siberian flight, the comparisons between me and my clutch mates. These terms and those judgments are chains forged from the same cruel, unyielding steel. It wasn't until I met Gavril, and subsequently Felix, that I was finally able to break free and live my life the way I wanted.

And after everything Lyra's been through, she deserves to feel the same weightless joy when her shackles are finally broken.

I run through one of the other easier-to-read contracts, searching for the nullification and termination clauses. My temples throb with the beginning of a headache as I sort through the dense text. Even though I'd love to string the demon bastard up on an iron hook and exorcise him so thoroughly that his own mother wouldn't recognize him, killing Dominic doesn't void the soul contract. In fact, it seems that in the event of his untimely demise, the souls he possesses would be given to his superiors, along with any souls possessed by the lesser demons in Dominic's employ. *Just when you think demons can't get any fucking worse, they start engaging in pyramid schemes.* Somehow, even killing the idiots who sold their souls won't work, because despite Dominic selling us the contracts, he's worded this deal so that he retains possession of the soul after death.

It takes most of the afternoon for me to find something I can work with. But I still want to check with my legal department to make sure I'm interpreting this clause correctly. Like any good charlatan, Dominic did include a way for his victim to earn their soul back through an "act of great sacrifice," but there aren't any details on what that means. For Dominic, it would be a way to dangle the carrot without having to pay up, because he could claim that any sacrifices the person makes aren't great enough. For our purposes, there's a chance that I could ask for something as simple as a monetary payment and declare it a "great sacrifice." I place a yellow sticky note under the first line of the clause, marking it for review before turning to the others. The other four simple contracts have the same clause, but sure as the fucking sunrise, I can't find it in Lyra's contract.

But as I'm scanning the document for what feels like the fiftieth time, something catches my attention that I hadn't noticed before. Tucked between a clause that prevents Lyra from ever eating more than her "authorized number of calories" and an amendment giving her the privilege of a pillow is a block of words written in spikey symbols I can't understand. And the longer I stare at it, trying to grasp some sort of meaning, the more my head pounds until the pain forces me to look away. My chest tightens as I sit back in my chair, mouth suddenly bone dry. I've studied dozens of languages during the course of my lifetime, and I've never seen anything like that. I run my fingers over the text, pulling my hand away as I feel a sudden, sharp pinch on my fingertips, like the prick of a rose thorn.

I'm out of my chair and scanning the shelves of books lining the walls of my office until I come to the one I need. Pulling the ancient tome from its place, I bring it back to my desk, flipping through the pages of spells rapidly. At last, I find the page and begin to recite the incantation. My heart thunders against my ribs, fighting to escape whatever truth I'm about to reveal. If my instincts are correct, what I'm looking at is abyssal, the language demons use to perform their blood magic and the translation spell I'm casting will reveal exactly what Dominic wrote all those years ago.

As I finish speaking, a warm tingle runs down my spine, pulling at the scales hidden just beneath my skin. I watch as the spikey letters shift before my eyes, reforming into Russian Cyrillic, my native tongue. And to my surprise, hidden glyphs appear between and behind other parts of the contract, written in an ink so light that I missed it until it was forced to be revealed by my spell. My eyes go wide as I read, mouth falling open in a mixture of shock, horror, and fury.

This is more than a bargain for possession of Lyra's soul. Dominic has been actively leeching her power without her knowledge for over a century and using it to power his own operation. Lyra was the one-creature battery for all of the wards and enchantments that fucking demon cast over Somnium.

But why? And how has he not drained her dry? A ritual this powerful would kill a lesser creature in twenty years flat. A powerful High Fae might be able to withstand it, but she'd have to be the shortest High Fae to have ever been brought into this world. She could be a jinn, but Dominic wouldn't stop at siphoning her power when she would have reality-altering magic at her disposal. And if she's neither of those things, the only other possible explanation would be...

I sink back into my chair, trying to sort through my racing thoughts. This contract makes no sense, yet my mind keeps trying to push an answer forward. But there's no way. She can't be. We would have felt her from the first moment we stepped off the train in 1930. I look back at the necklace sitting next to the contract on the smooth mahogany surface of my desk.

Fuck this speculation. I need answers. And there's only one person I can think of to call.

I put my desk phone on speaker as I dial the number, waiting for the line to connect. I won't miss this part of communication once we're connected to the network. But after several long minutes of silence, the line finally starts to ring. It takes eight rings for my call to be answered.

"Hello? Who call? How you get this number?" the wizened voice snaps through the receiver, his accent thick over his broken English.

"Good afternoon, Igor. This is Viktor Kulikov," I answer genially, speaking in my native Russian.

Igor lets out a pleasant but surprised noise, which makes me smile slightly. I've always liked the older dragon. He's an academic, working as one of the draconic historians in the de facto capital, the Siberian Flight. I grew up there, spending much of my time in the hall of records, trying to satiate my ravenous curiosity. Igor was always there to feed my mind. I probably would have ended up as his apprentice if I hadn't found Gavril and Felix.

"I was starting to think you'd forgotten about me, my boy," Igor chides, though it lacks any true heat.

I sit and listen as he launches into a monologue, recounting the latest news and gossip from home. I make noises of interest and engagement at appropriate intervals, but I'm only half listening. A few of the youths have come of age and a new pseudo-pack has formed. A dragon pack isn't official until it settles within a flight or, as me and my pack mates chose to do, establishes a new point on the leyline network. Another reason for us to deal with Lyra as fast as possible.

"It's good to catch up, but I haven't called to gossip, old

friend," I manage to interject into one of the lulls in Igor's speech.

"Then why have you called?" Igor asks, suspicion already creeping into his words.

"Have you ever heard of a dragon having their soul bound and siphoned for magic?" I start cautiously.

"Of course not!" Igor replies indignantly. "A dragon would never allow themself to be caught in such a position."

I clear my throat softly. "Right. But I thought I'd heard of a story, more of a legend, from the beginning of the blood war, where something akin to that happened."

Igor hums, but doesn't answer right away. If anyone would know if this type of magic is possible, it will be him. Despite his advanced age, his memory is still as sharp as ever. He's read nearly every book, scroll, and document in the great library. If he can't recall the information directly, then he'll at least know where to find it.

"I don't recall that story, but I suppose it's possible. Demons stooped so low as to descale alphas alive in those days, so it wouldn't be that much of a stretch to think they would attempt to extract magic from betas or omegas," Igor says at last.

I slump a little in my chair. I was hoping I'd misread that part of Lyra's contract. But if it's possible for that type of magic to exist, it's going to make breaking this contract that much more complicated.

"Though, I suppose many atrocities were committed during that time. It's impossible to sort fact from exaggeration in those accounts. I would have to look into this matter further if you need a concrete answer," he goes on, his attempt to bait me as transparent as glass.

"Perhaps. I'm still in the first stages of my research," I say dismissively. "Last we spoke, you mentioned that you'd found new documents from the Byz–"

"No," Igor interrupts firmly. "You've been told to let that go."

I frown petulantly. "My interest is purely academic, I assure you," I insist, hoping I'm not laying on the innocent act too thickly.

Igor barks a harsh laugh. "You have always been a bad liar, Vitya. But let's say I was to entertain your "academic interest." What do you want to know?"

I smirk at the nickname. He's the only one outside my pack I've ever tolerated using a diminutive of my name. It never feels condescending coming from him.

"Was there ever a Quintus Spanos among the Byzantine Flight? Did he have a family?" I ask softly, picking up the necklace again.

Igor hums, but this is a lighter, more curious sound. My heart gives a little triumphant kick. I've hooked him. Now all I have to do is reel him in.

"I'd have to pull out the genealogies again, but the name does ring a bell. What's your interest in him?" Igor says, much less suspicious now.

"A contact of mine thinks he's come across an artifact that may have belonged to him," I say, picking my words with care.

"What sort of artifact?"

His betrothal gift, and possibly his daughter. "My contact didn't say," I drone.

Igor lets out a huff, but I don't take the bait. Better to keep him chasing the carrot.

"I'll look into it, and I'll give you a call if I find anything," he says at last. "But if we do find something, the council won't be pleased to see you still digging into that tragedy."

I sigh. He's right, of course, but that doesn't mean I like hearing it. I'd always disagreed with the council's decision to close the book on the Byzantine Slaughter, even though many dragons were left unaccounted for. Being ordered to stop looking had rankled at the time, and finding Lyra has reopened that old wound.

"Let's cross that bridge when we get to it," I reply. "It

could be nothing, after all."

"Yes, very well. I'll be in touch once I find the information you're looking for," Igor says, effectively ending the conversation.

We say our goodbyes, and I slump back against the leather of my office chair once I've ended the call. I don't like the knot of unease that's formed in my chest, but I trust Igor. He's the one who taught me to seek out knowledge and truth, especially when the powers that be tell you not to. But that is something I can tuck away for now. No use worrying about it until I have more information.

For now, I'll focus on something I can actually accomplish. I slide the first contract out again, deciding what "great sacrifice" I could ask for from the high elf known to his friends as Franco.

CHAPTER 26

GAVRIL

My hand wraps around the door handle, and the second I shove it open, I'm hit in the face with the scent of freshly baked bread and cinnamon. The place is simple, and small enough that when I step inside, there's barely enough room for anyone else on this side of the counter. It's familiar and heavenly, every surface feeling like it has been lightly dusted with confectioners' sugar.

"I always know it's you. The door sounds like you've taken it off hinge." Aga's voice is light and sing-song today, which is good. It means the short and stout lady is entirely human, but terrifying all the same.

"How are you, Aga? You look gorgeous, as always," I reply with a grin, leaning my elbows on the glass counter as she rounds the corner and stops right in front of me.

She throws a hand toward me in distaste. "Stop it, I tell you every time, flattery get you zero, nothing."

"You still think I'm trying to rob you, Aga? Come on, how long have we known each other?" The answer is years.

Decades. I've known Aga since her little Polish bakery was nothing but a person-pulled wagon. She was just a child back then, mischievous and round-faced. It's one of the bittersweet sides of being immortal. I knew Aga's mother and father well, as they arrived in Vegas not long after us, nothing with them but the clothes on their back. I watched them go from a young married couple, to a couple with three mouths to feed and a tiny kitchen where they made fresh bread to sell on the street corners at dawn.

"Too fucking long and always trouble. Always trouble," she tuts, shaking her head. Strands of grey and black hair poke out from underneath her hairnet, and she pushes them back in with arthritic fingers. "Kremówka?"

"Three please, as always," I wink, watching her pluck three custard filled pastries from the display and put them messily into a paper bag.

"Coffee or tea?" she asks, still shaking her head in dismay, as though she doesn't want my business. I've been coming to this bakery every Thursday for eighty years. Even helped Aga's parents find a proper shop with a larger kitchen. It wasn't until the fifties that they got this place, right around the corner from Korona Drakona, rent controlled for as long as I'm alive.

"Tea, please." Aga hovers at a cauldron pot bubbling on a hot plate behind her, taking a takeaway cup from the stack at its side and ladling potent herbal tea until it's up to the rim.

"Cold? Flu?" she asks in her harshly accented voice. You'd think growing up in the U.S., she'd have lost the rough edges, but no. She sounds just like her mother did.

"Oh, Aga, you care?" I tease, planting a hand to my chest. "Such a sweet old lady."
Aga scowls, setting the takeaway cup down on the counter by the paper bag. "Big dumb oaf. Next Thursday."

Passing her a twenty, I pick up my order with a wide grin and a mock salute. "Thursday at eleven, Aga."

I bump out of the door and sit down at one of the

few outdoor sets in front of the bakery, diving into the paper bag of custard-filled pastries and devouring one whole. I'm busy trying to swallow, when my phone buzzes in my pocket. Everyone knows I take this hour out every single week; the pack wouldn't disturb me, so immediately I'm concerned. Unlocking the screen, I chug hot, bitter tea, and read the message from none other than the Head of Security back at Korona Drakona.

Lyra left the penthouse 11:04AM, moved Southwest, on foot.

I wolf down the last two pastries as I'm standing up and dust the crumbs from my t-shirt. Once I've tossed the bag and cup into a nearby trashcan, I set off on foot to track down our wandering pain in the ass.

I'm back outside the casino in a matter of seconds, eyeing the streets of people in the hope I'll catch a glimpse of red hair. The heat is close to unbearable, especially after downing half a pint of hot tea, but as always, the view across the strip takes my breath away. The penthouse is high enough that it allows us to see the city from above, the neon lights and bustling crowds. Down here, it's different. The energy is palpable, the thrill of tourists and locals alike as they move as one unit. Excitement leaves me feeling buzzed.

I'm not worried about Lyra being out on her own, not exactly. She's tough; she can take care of herself for the most part, even if my pack mates don't necessarily agree. I don't spot her at first, but my nostrils flare and my chest fills with sweet caramel and vanilla. I'd know her scent anywhere. It's engrained in my mind, just the same as Felix's and Viktor's are. I follow those familiar notes for about a block, maybe two, before I spot her.

The last twenty-four hours at the penthouse have been rife with tension, and for the first time in hours, I let myself relax into the thrill of the hunt. Lyra hadn't said much about Viktor setting some ground rules at the time. She had snapped back with some pissed off comment, her face twisting into that adorable little rabid puppy expression she likes so much. But now, watching as she weaves in between people, her gaze focused up at the tall buildings and flashing signs, she looks childlike. Giving her permission to roam free was a great idea. Especially now, as the sun beats down on her ivory skin, heat making the tops of her bare shoulders turn pink. I get the overwhelming urge to go tell her to put more sunscreen on, but that would ruin my plan for the day.

Instead, I watch the way her body moves. There's an elegance about it. Her wide hips have a natural sway, her spine is straight and shoulders back. It's a confident kind of walk. The kind you'd expect from someone like her, who's had to put up with bullshit her entire adult life.   Despite her small stature, she exudes power. Watching her closely, I'm still unsure if she's playing a part, portraying herself as cool and self-assured when inside she's a nervous wreck. It's times like these that I wish I had a power like Viktor's, able to slip unnoticed into someone's mind and feel every little thing they're feeling. The only thing I have to rely on is her scent. It's faint in the air, but it has me collared and leashed. I follow cautiously, making sure to keep myself just out of sight.

Lyra's gaze turns to the side, and she stalls, shielding her eyes from the sun as she peers into a store window. I dart behind a crowd of women on a bachelorette party, hoping their sparkly sashes and over-the-top squeals will help keep me hidden. Lyra turns away from the window a few seconds later, folding a strand of red hair behind her ear.

Stealth is Felix's jam. I tend to stick to the brute force side of things. But following Lyra as she walks, I get a new thrill that warms in my veins. She has no idea I'm walking a few paces behind her, my steps matching hers despite my legs being twice the length. I shoulder through the crowds, dipping behind shrubs and people holding advertising boards. At my height, staying hidden isn't easy. I let myself fall back from Lyra a little more, depending on her vanilla and salted caramel scent to lead the way.

She walks into a large mall, one with multiple floors and a massive marble front. I study her as she moves from store to store, pausing every now and again to peer into a window. She wrings her hands at her front, looking around like she's worried she's about to get in trouble. Sadness tickles the back of my throat as it sinks in that she's never been allowed this level of freedom before. Something that me and my pack take for granted. We can come and go as we please, never having to ask permission for anything, unless it's in the bedroom. It makes me want to shout or scream or punch something, knowing that she hasn't been able to truly *live*.

I push those bigger feelings aside, choosing to enjoy watching Lyra out in the wild. Eventually, she builds up the courage to go into a store. It's your standard tourist trap, Las Vegas snow globes and tacky beach towels, magnets, t-shirts, little miniature figurines of Vegas landmarks, the whole nine yards. I can't risk going inside the store, but I do find myself a good watching spot behind an information panel, the large map of the mall making for a perfect hiding place.

Lyra roves in and out of the aisles, picking up a large snow globe and shaking it. Her eyes light up as the fake snow flutters over the tiny buildings. Her plump pink lips lift at the corners and my whole body warms as she clutches the tacky treasure to her chest. Seriousness quickly returns to her beautiful face, though, as she fumbles around in her pocket, pulling out the odd dollar note here or there. It doesn't take a genius to realize she doesn't have the money to buy the damn thing.

Everything inside me is telling me to march over there

194

and buy her every fucking trashy souvenir in the shop. But I don't want to ruin this for her. This adventure she's taken herself on. It's too much fun watching from the side-lines.

Hours pass like minutes, Lyra roaming through the mall at a snail's pace and me following unseen behind her. She smells candles, touches blankets and pillows. Holds outfits up to her chest to see if they'll fit before placing them gently back on the rack. When she gets to a jewelry store, though, she doesn't even bother going in. Her eyes merely roam over the sparkly diamonds in the window. So far, I've gathered that she's a little like a magpie. Anything that shimmers or moves, she's eager to touch it. I love that. Mostly, I love the image of her wrapped up in gold and jewels, dazzling and expensive. My breath catches as I picture her all dressed up, sparkling like a star against a dark velvet sky. Pearls would complement her skin, and diamonds would accentuate her eyes. God, what I wouldn't give to see her like that, above me with a delicate palm around my throat.

I swallow, hard. This is not the time to pop a rich guy boner. I've never felt the need to flash the cash as much as I do in this moment, but fuck, what a pretty picture she'd be.

It's only when she reaches the food court that her excitement becomes truly palpable. She surveys each vendor with a smile; Chinese, Indian, burgers, fried chicken, sushi, and ice cream.   Her delicate hands fumble with the few dollars in her pocket again. Is she hungry? Can she afford to get herself some food? Viktor would never let me live it down if I left her to starve.

Thankfully, I'm allowed to watch her for just a bit longer. She takes out her money and spends it on two slices of pizza and a small soda. Finding a free table, she settles down into her seat and demolishes the food in just a few minutes, her gaze flitting over the other shoppers with curiosity.

Nightfall is approaching, the sky turning to vivid shades of purple and dark blue through the arched windows. I remain standing around a corner, staring at Lyra as she packs up her trash and tosses it away. She looks sad, like she knows her day has come to an end. The mall will stay open for hours yet, but it seems Lyra is ready to leave. Her last dollar spent and her posture beginning to slump with tiredness. It's been a long day, so she must be exhausted. I tackle the urge to go to her and bundle her in my arms, carry her back to the penthouse. Instead, I keep following.

She casts a few looks toward stores she missed but doesn't stop walking. Every now and again, she turns her head to frown one way, then the other. Her steps quicken as the crowds start to dissipate. There's no natural flow of foot traffic; everyone is going in different directions.   When I breathe in and hold it in my lungs, her sweet caramel and vanilla scent has begun to turn sour. Like milk left on the counter for too long. I urge her to turn around or glance at one of the maps, but she doesn't. Her legs take her left and right, turning her on her heel over and over. I'm so busy watching her that I don't notice the couple that has come to a standstill in front of me.

"Just ask," one of them mutters.

"You ask him," the other says.

I'm about to step out of their reach, when I feel a tap on my arm. I look down with a scowl, finding two young guys with a paper map in their hands.

"Excuse me, sir, do you know how to get here?" The smaller of the two points to a spot on a map of the strip. His nose twitches, pushing his glasses high up on his face.

"Head out that way and find a cab. I'm not a tourist information center." My eyes were off her for a second. A fucking second. And now she's vanished.

There's no flash of red hair or pale skin. The mall is quieter, but Lyra is nowhere to be found.

I shove away from the two guys, my steps quickening as I scan the area. Fuck. Drawing a lungful of air in through my nostrils, I close my eyes and try to focus. Her scent isn't just sour now. It's putrid. Burning caramel and curdled cream choke me, and I break into a faster pace. She can't have gotten far.

When her scent wavers, I change direction, darting past shoppers as it grows stronger and stronger. I halt when I come to a service exit, barely pausing to shove my way through the black outdoors. Her scent slaps me across the face, making my eyes water. Lyra is anxiously chewing on her thumb, peering down the alleyway she's ended up in. Dumpsters and discarded cardboard packaging litter the small area, a cool wind whipping around the corner of the building and sending her hair fluttering over her shoulders.

"Lyra, you good?" I ask without thinking, marching toward her until I can set my hands on her arms and turn her around.

There's a split second of relief, where her scent turns thick and sweet again, before she sends her fist flying toward my nose. I step back, mostly from the surprise of her hit landing.

"I fucking knew it!" she yells, attempting to throw a second punch. I put my hand flat against her forehead, arm outstretched to keep her a safe distance from me. A growl roils from between her lips. She's frustrated, angry, but not scared. And for that, I'm relieved.

"Why the hell are you following me?" Lyra asks with a huff, pushing herself away from me and folding her arms across her middle. "Viktor said—"

I cut her off, "Viktor-schmikter. I got a heads up you'd left the building. I wanted to know you were safe. How was I supposed to know you were just taking a trip to the mall?"

"I left a note, duh," Lyra snaps, a frown deepening on her forehead. "Which you'd know if you'd thought to go back to the penthouse before you started following me like some deranged stalker."

"You were scared. What did you want me to do? Just hang back and pretend you didn't need help?"

"Exactly! I was fine. I wasn't even scared."

I raise an eyebrow at her, taking a cautious step forward.

"I could smell your fear."

"Fuck you and your superhuman sense of smell. I was *fine.*"

"So you meant to end up in the service alley?" I ask confidently.

She shuffles from foot to foot, kicking at the concrete beneath her shoes. "Maybe I did."

"Listen, this can do one of two ways," I begin with a sigh. "I can leave you here to figure out how to get home on your own, or we can go get you a silly fucking snow globe and head back to the penthouse. Your choice."

Lyra's eyes go wide, her posture straightening as she holds her head up high and tilts her chin to the sky. "Did the others come too?"

"No, they're tied up with work," I reply simply. "Make a choice, trouble. I don't have all day."

She stays silent, clearing her throat and looking between me and the mall. "They're called snow globes?"

My heart sinks, stomach twisting. "Yes. And I'll buy you ten of the damn things if you'll just stop being a stubborn little asshole."

"Oh, I'm the asshole?" Lyra scoffs, but she's relaxed. Her scent has returned to normal, and she's quit chewing at her nails. "Fine, bigger asshole. You can buy me a snow-globe, but I want ice cream too."

A smile breaks out on my face, the grin making my cheeks hurt. "Hey, hey, if you're making demands, I want something in return."

She pouts, watches me, waits. "What?"

I lean forward, tapping my cheek with my pointer finger. "A thank you. Or a please. I don't care what you want to call it, but put it right here."

"You're fucking infuriating," she groans, still scowling at me.

"You too, babe. Put it here."

Her lips meet my cheek for a fraction of a second, but my

God, is it incredible.

"Happy, shithead?" Lyra asks with enough venom to bring a grown man to his knees. Luckily, I like being on my knees.

"The happiest," I say with another smile, holding my hand out for her to take. "Come on."

I walk us both toward the service exit, but she chuckles. "It's locked, dipshit. I was stuck out here, remember?"

With a grunt, I slam my shoulder against the door, her hand still nestled in mine, and it swings open. The alarm howls in retaliation, but I ignore it.

"If we get arrested, I'm telling the others it was your fault."

I drag her along, her short legs struggling to keep up. "Smile for the camera." I shoot a wave at the security cam, and Lyra chuckles.

"You're insane," she laughs, the sound ringing in my ears and warming me to my very core.

"Snow globes or ice cream first?"

Lyra shakes her head, pondering the question for a few seconds. "Snow globes."

CHAPTER 27

Lyra

After my misadventure the other day, I'd decided that I'm better off sticking to the casino for the moment. At least until I'm more familiar with the layout and exits. But I can't help the feeling of eyes on my back any time I leave the "safety" of the penthouse. The fact that Gavril "Walking Garden Shed" Russo got away with following me for an entire afternoon without my noticing unsettles me more than I'm willing to admit. I'm sure it's all part of their plan to make me uncomfortable outside the walls of my new digs.

I haven't had much interaction with the oldest of my three roommates, or whatever he's trying to pretend we are. Most days, I wake up long after he's gone, the only evidence of his presence, the smell of espresso in the air and a breakfast plate left on the counter for me under one of those fancy silver domes. Felix flits in and out of the penthouse, usually bringing up a new delivery of stuff for my room when he returns. I think he's giving me space, because he doesn't initiate interactions often. Honestly, it's sort of nice to just be near each other but doing our own things, and not have to be forced into awkward conversation all the time. When Gavril decides to be around, though, he's impossible to ignore. Everything about him demands my attention.

I don't know how long it's been since they dragged me out of Somnium, and that unsettles me. Days are passing without my notice, and without me trying to figure out what my fallback plan is going to be when these scaly bastards finally get tired of me. Felix is having fun playing interior designer, and Gavril is amusing himself by getting on my every nerve, and Viktor is content enough to ignore me. But this won't last. Nothing good ever does. And the waiting and not knowing will kill me long before the dragons ever get the chance.

That's how I've ended up in their fancy-pants kitchen, rummaging around in the cabinets like I'm trying to rob the place. I know for a fact that Viktor is upstairs in his office, but I'm not bothering to keep my exploits a secret. Jars and boxes are everywhere, and I've made no attempt to put things back the way I found them. I'm slamming cabinets closed whenever I get the chance, though it's much harder to do when most things have soft-close hinges. But I'm nothing if not persistent.

Maybe it's boredom. Maybe I actually do have a death wish, like Ginny always said. Or maybe I'm sick of being a passenger in my own life. But I'm determined to get some answers today to the questions that have been burning holes inside of me. Why did they come into Somnium and take over? What do they want with that shithole? And what do they want from me? I know I could ask Gavril or Felix any of those questions, but there are bigger unknowns that I need answered, and Viktor is the only one who can do that.

What happened to the No Harm Clause in my contract? And if it's no longer in effect, will these dragons kill me if I become more hassle than I'm worth?

In the beginning, before I got sick of his shit and started fighting back, Dominic would "playfully" slap my ass or pinch my cheek or otherwise touch me in ways that were always condescending and vaguely creepy. But he didn't start getting backlash from the No Harm Clause until he started trying to hit me with the intent to cause me physical pain. It didn't take me long to figure out that I could do just about anything to him and he couldn't follow through with physical threats. Could he make my life miserable? Oh, for sure, and he rarely hesitated to do so.

I don't know what sort of deal the dragons struck with my former employer. They say I'm safe with them, but I know better than to trust anyone at their word. My instincts tell me that Felix would never hurt me, and I'm ignoring all of the weird feelings that knowledge stirs up. Based on Gavril's behavior that night at Somnium, he might be the size of a midsize sedan, but he wouldn't be able to conjure the malice it would take to trigger the effects of the clause. But Viktor is an entirely different beast.

I look up at the stairs as I hold the cutlery organizer out in front of me, taking a deep breath. But even after I turn it over and listen to dozens of forks, knives, and spoons clatter across the marble floor, there's no movement or response. At this point, I've run out of things to destroy. I look around and huff out a breath of frustration. Okay, so he's not going to take the bait. I wander over to the fridge and look inside, a grin pulling at my cheeks as I spot the clear plastic bag of sour dark cherries, an idea forming. Time to take a more direct approach.

My bare feet slap against the cool stone of the stairs, and I don't bother trying to be quiet as I march my way up to Viktor's office, cherries cradled against my chest. There's still a nervous twist in my stomach as I close in on the door, but I push it aside. He can't ignore me forever.

The door swings open on silent hinges, hitting the bookshelf behind it with a satisfying crash. Viktor doesn't flinch behind his massive mahogany desk, just gives me the side-eye as I cross the room with my head held high.

"'Sup, lizard dick," I chirp, throwing myself into one of

the leather chairs opposite him.

"Dragons aren't lizards, you know," he replies, sighing and rolling his eyes.

I snort derisively, looking around quickly. His office is nice, though the decor doesn't quite line up with the ostentatious modern vibe of the main living space. Downstairs, it's all clean lines and glass and marble and gold. In here, it's dark wood bookcases built in to nearly every wall, leather furniture, and an honest to God fireplace. But I don't let my gaze linger to take in any other details. Instead, I lean back and bring my feet up to rest on top of the gleaming surface of Viktor's desk and pop a cherry into my mouth.

"Can I help you with something, Lyra?" Viktor asks, staring at his computer screen like it insulted his mother.

I hum thoughtfully, using my teeth to strip the flesh from the cherry pit. I look around for a moment and smirk as I spot the small wastepaper basket across the room. Cocking my head back to get a better angle, I spit the pit out with a satisfying '*pthwop*,' watching it arc through the air but land a few inches short. I have to contain my impish grin as I see a vein in Viktor's forehead throb.

"Not really. Just wanted to grace you with my sparkling presence," I say, my heart racing at the thrill of the game. Or maybe the threat of death is making my heart pound. Potato, tomato.

I spit another cherry pit, and Viktor looks up for this one, his purple eyes tracking the red dot through the air and watching it bounce off the wall and miss the basket. A muscle in his jaw jumps as he turns his attention back to his computer. As if I'd let him off that easily.

"So, like, what do you even *do*?" I ask, trying to channel as much disrespect as I can possibly manage into the words.

Viktor's shoulders lift and fall as he tries to calm down, but I send another cherry pit flying. I don't know why, but the slight flinch I catch as the pit misses makes my stomach dance with a strange sort of delight. Mr. Calm, Cool, and Collected isn't as unflappable as he'd like everyone to think.

"I am the owner and operator of Korona Drakona and its subsidiaries," Viktor answers at last, every word stiff with forced steadiness.

"Okay, but what does that even mean?" I push, speaking through a mouthful of cherry.

"It means I run this casino and this city," Viktor snaps, glaring at me for a moment before he catches himself, and speaks more calmly. "It means that nothing happens in this city without my knowledge and blessing."

I snort before spitting another cherry pit. This time, I manage to make the shot, and I can't help the celebratory air punch. I can feel Viktor's gaze on me like a touch, and goosebumps run up my bare legs at the spark in their amethyst depths.

"No wonder you've gone gray. It must be hell on your blood pressure to micromanage everything in this godforsaken town," I reply, trying to keep up the casual tone.

"I'm not a micromanager," Viktor counters, a little too quickly.

"Yeah, okay, lizard dick," I return, laughing sarcastically.

"And I'm a California 10."

"Well, in that case, I'm glad you and I finally agree on something."

The implications of Viktor's words take a moment to hit me, and then my face flushes red hot. Viktor's turned back to his computer, smirking like the cat that got the canary. My lower belly clenches for an entirely different reason, but I seize on my irritation instead of acknowledging the fact he might have just given me a compliment. I spit two cherry pits in quick succession, not even caring that one of the pits doesn't have the power of the other, and it lands on top of a pristine piece of white paper on Viktor's desk, staining it instantly.

"I don't even know why you overgrown iguanas came here in the first place. I've been here for nearly one hundred years, and I can't say it's gotten—"

"Wait, you've been here for how long?" Viktor interrupts urgently, turning his body to face me fully.

"I came here with Dominic right after the rail company connected this town to the line. You showed up not long after that, if I remember correctly," I return, fiddling with a cherry stem in the bag.

I don't think I could forget that day if I tried. Dominic bitched up a storm at first, but then decided it was better to keep off their radar. I can't say I disagreed with his strategy at the time, especially with a lot of the stories from the orphanage still fresh in my mind. I thought we'd be long gone before Viktor and his buddies cared enough to make any moves. Egg on my face.

Viktor looks at me for a long moment, but I don't back down. His eyes go distant, like he's trying to remember something. But then he nods to himself, just a quick dip of his chin, before he settles back in his chair, crossing one elegant leg over the other.

"We were sent here by the governing council of our kind about one hundred years ago," Viktor starts, his attention fully on me.

All thoughts of trying to get under his skin fly out of my head. Is he saying there are…more of his kind? And they have a governing body? But I don't get to question him further, as he continues speaking.

"This place is magically significant to my people. So we were tasked with gaining control of it."

My brow furrows at that frustratingly vague answer. As I consider my next response, I bite into another cherry. A little bit of juice runs down my chin, and I catch it with my thumb before it can drip onto my favorite oversized hoodie. Viktor's eyes lock onto my fingers, an almost hungry glint to his gaze. Moving slowly, I lick the juice from my thumb, then pop the rest of the cherry into my mouth. I swear I hear a low rumble, like distant thunder, but it must just be a passing plane, or traffic from the street below. I don't know if he sees the question on my face, or something else, but Viktor doesn't wait for a response before he goes on.

"Eons ago, dragons discovered wells of magic at various points around the world. These nexuses of power, as we came to call them, leaked energy randomly, throwing out bursts of catastrophic magic like solar flares. But dragons learned how to tame the nexuses, and found a way to direct the magic, creating a web of leylines that spans the globe.

"There are only about a dozen nexuses, but the points where their leylines meet are also highly volatile, magically speaking. Dragons have established seats of power anywhere these nodes occur, to keep the magic from falling into the wrong hands. Control of a node also comes with official recognition of a pack by the council. Which is what brought Felix, Gavril, and me here."

Viktor's deep voice takes on a calm confidence, like he's told this story a thousand times before, and it's a little hypnotizing. It takes me a few moments after he finishes to truly absorb his words, and then my brow furrows with concern and confusion.

"You've been here forever, so what's the hold up?" I ask, the first question that crosses my mind tumbling out before I can stop it.

Viktor sighs, that stupid patronizing sigh that makes my teeth grind, and rubs his temple. "The laws that govern magic are...unique. In order to control the node, one must control the land. And until recently, there was a certain landowner who wouldn't cooperate like the rest of the people here."

He's talking about Dominic, of course, but that answer only creates more questions. "What does that mean?"

"We may own the land, but realistically, land is only worth so much in this day and age. Back when my kind was first seizing control of the nexuses and the nodes, we could rely on fear to ensure the people living on the land continued to work it and pay their tribute. Now, things are different," Viktor says, chuckling at his own joke, though I don't find anything he says particularly amusing.

"So the stories of destruction and enslavement by entitled dragon tyrants aren't so far-fetched," I spit, rolling my eyes.

Viktor's eyes narrow at me, but I don't care. I'm angry, mostly at myself. I was starting to let my guard down, but I should know better. Dragons are merciless and cruel, and completely unrepentant. Add on top of that this superiority complex, and it just makes them entirely insufferable.

"Those stories are just that: stories. The truth is that the days of serfdom and dragon kingdoms are long gone. Tribute of gold and silver has been replaced with rent and union dues and business loan payments. Farm labor has been replaced with store clerks, poker dealers, sex workers, restauranteurs. The land may be ours, but many of the buildings on top of it belong to banks or developers. That's not to say that we don't control who gets the building permits, and that we don't manage disputes between the many clans and factions of non-humans that live here. We aren't tyrants, Lyra. And I'd thank you to stop judging my people on the basis of bedtime stories meant to scare children into compliance."

My jaw physically drops at his words, shock flooding my system right before my defenses slam into place. He can act like this sophisticated, modern businessman all he likes. But he's just as lethal as all the stories say. I saw what he did to Dominic, what he was willing to do to gain control of Somnium. How many other people did he poison or intimidate or torture just to get his hands on their land?

"That's quite the fucking saintly tone, lizard dick. Setting aside the question of how you went about acquiring the land, who fucking died and made dragons rulers of all the magic? What gives them the right to decide who gets magic and who doesn't?" I throw back, hackles rising.

Viktor has the nerve to roll his eyes at me again, which only infuriates me further. "It's not about who gets magic and who doesn't. It's about keeping the planet in one piece.

Because, trust me, you wouldn't want to see a world where dragons aren't in control," he answers.

"Don't take that fucking patronizing tone with me. It's a fair question," I snap, sitting up at last, my feet hitting the floor with a slap.

"My people have been fighting off demon attacks on nexuses and nodes since before humans crawled out of their caves, and you want to argue about whether that's fair? There isn't another race of beings in existence strong enough to keep these near infinite pools of pure magic out of the hands of truly malevolent creatures literally from the depths of hell," Viktor fires back, sitting up straight as well.

My jaw clenches, rage building like an inferno in my gut. The arrogance of this asshole! I throw the bag of cherries off to the side, neither of us acknowledging them as they scatter across the hardwood.

"Dragons kill people," I state simply, lifting my chin.

"And demons fucking don't?" Viktor nearly shouts back, and it's only thanks to years of Dominic's abuse that I manage to contain my flinch. "Tell me, Lyra. How many people walked out of Dominic's club, whole and healthy? How many more did he trick and con into giving up their souls for a few nights of cheap thrills?"

I close my eyes for just a moment, but dozens of faces flash through my memory. Years of people who lost themselves to Dominic's sick drug. People I liked, before I stopped letting myself get close to the short-term crowd. "You shut your fucking mouth," I snarl.

Viktor gets to his feet and slams his hands on the desk, and this time, I can't stop myself from visibly jumping. "You can sit there, acting all high and mighty, but you're hardly any better than your employer. You were there, every day, as he lured in helpless victims—"

"Fuck you, and the fucking high horse you rode in on!" I shriek, standing at last. "You don't know a goddamn thing about me, or my life!"

"And you don't know a thing about my kind!" Viktor shouts back. "We've lost good people, better people than you, fighting to save the nexuses."

I rock back onto my heels, a watery laugh of disbelief escaping before I can stop it. So there's the truth, how he really feels about me. He can play nice all he likes, but I'm just like the rest of the peons he controls in this city. And I'll never be as good as the worst of his kind.

"I'm sure you fucking did. There's not a whole lot worse you can do than me," I say, shaking my head and walking away.

CHAPTER 28

VIKTOR

Watching Lyra walk away stings more than her verbal slap, and for a moment, I'm frozen. I can't believe I let her get to me like that, but I'm even more embarrassed by the outright lie I told her, knowing it would cut deep. Almost as soon as the words passed my lips, I wanted to take them back. And now she's walking away, not giving me the chance to apologize.

I rush around my desk, striding after her out into the hallway. "Lyra! No, wait—"

"Save it, Viktor. I don't want your empty apologies."

Lyra's already at the end of the hall and starting down the stairs by the time I catch up with her. Without thinking, I grab her elbow and pull her around, backing her against the glass railing of the balcony overlooking the main living floor. It strikes me again how small she is as I step closer, boxing her in with my arms and preventing her from leaving.

"I shouldn't have said that, Lyra. It was cruel, and I didn't —"

"Didn't what? You didn't mean it?" Lyra interrupts me again, and it sets my jaw. But she just barks out a hollow laugh. "If you want to lie to yourself, that's on you. But don't lie to me. I've been around the block enough to know people are the most honest when they're drunk, high, or angry."

I blink as the implications of her words hit me, and then a wave of hot fury barrels through my system. I'm not exactly the sunniest optimist, but I've been alive for nearly eight hundred years. Lyra is so young, too young to be this cynical and bitter. Someone made her like this, and even imagining it makes me want to break bones.

"You doubt my sincerity, *moye plamya,* but I am truly sorry for saying all of that. It's not how I feel about you, and I don't know why I even thought it, let alone said it out loud," I reply, speaking softly and looking directly into her eyes.

I have to hold my power back, willing myself not to intrude on her emotional privacy or influence her. She looks up at me, her guard coming down millimeter by millimeter as she inspects my face for signs of dishonesty. After several long, tense heartbeats, her shoulders slump.

"It's not like you're not right. I'm not that great. Certainly not by dragon standards," she grumbles, looking down at her bare feet.

I can't help myself, my eyes flickering down to her shapely legs, letting myself drink her in. The very bottom hem of her sleep shorts peeks out from under her oversized hoodie, giving the illusion that she's not actually wearing anything on her bottom half. This close, her body heat radiates into my skin, making my heart race. I take a deep breath and nearly regret it. Her scent is mouthwatering, the green apple of her shampoo mixing with her natural caramel and vanilla musk to create fresh apple pie in my nose. I inch forward, leaning in even closer so our chests almost touch when we breathe.

I'm about to answer when something shiny catches my attention. And as I look up over her head and down into the kitchen, my eyes go wide. It's an absolute nightmare, with cabinets wide open and their contents spread across every available surface. The silverware is scattered on the floor, along with all the cooking utensils. Nothing appears to be broken, but the disorganization of my personal workspace still makes me see red.

"Is that so? You seem to be quite skilled at causing trouble," I growl, hands gripping the glass on either side of her until my knuckles go white.

Lyra's head snaps up, and she gasps softly before immediately trying to slip under my arm. Without thinking, my hand darts out and grabs her throat in a loose but firm grip, and I force her face up to look into my eyes. Her pulse hammers under my fingers, and I can feel her trembling slightly. True fear takes over her face, banking some of the heat of my anger.

"Do you have anything to say for yourself?" I prompt, frowning down at her.

She swallows hard, the muscles of her throat working under my grip. My hand nearly circles her entire neck, only an inch separating my thumb and middle finger near her spine. It would be so easy to squeeze, to watch her struggle—

"You shouldn't leave your pets unattended, you know. Never know what sort of destruction they can cause when your back is turned," she rasps out, eyes sparking and one side of her mouth lifting in a smirk.

I growl, her bratty tone flipping a switch in my hindbrain. I give her another long look, really considering my next move. If I cross this line with Lyra, there's no going back. But her caramel scent is getting stronger, and her cheeks are flushed the most beautiful shade of pink.

"You know what happens to naughty pets who misbehave, don't you?" I murmur, squeezing just a little.

"Are you going to spank me with a newspaper, Daddy? Or rub my nose in my mess?" she sneers. And that taunt, hearing her call me that name while looking like sex on a stick, snaps the last shred of my control. I press forward, trapping her body against the glass with my hips, making sure she can feel how hard she's made me in such a short time.

"You'd like that, wouldn't you? You'd enjoy being bent over my knee and having your ass turned red," I return, matching her mocking tone. "I bet you're getting wet just thinking about my hands on you, you naughty little slut."

Her jaw drops open, but she doesn't make any attempt to deny it. In fact, I feel her shifting against me, trying to get friction against my leg. I chuckle and squeeze a little harder, bending her backwards over the railing until her toes barely touch the floor. She squeals, hands coming up to cling to my shirt. I grab her waist, holding her steady with ease, even if she feels like she could fall at any moment. Exactly how I want her. Her fear and arousal is a heady mix of caramel and salt coating my tongue, and I can't contain my power anymore, not when I'm this close.

"But I don't need to lay a finger on your perky little ass to punish you, *my flame*. I just have to do this," I hiss, grinning like a fiend.

Invisible tendrils of power wrap around Lyra like vines, and she gasps, eyes rolling back in her head as I take over and dial up the arousal coursing through her veins. She's shaking now, this time from raw pleasure. I keep pushing her higher and higher, manipulating her emotions to make her feel more pleasure than she's probably ever felt in her life.

"Holy shit! That's—oh, fuck! Please, I can't—"

I chuckle again. "You act out like a child, desperate for my attention. Well, you have it, Lyra. Is this not what you wanted?"

She screams as her body convulses, her orgasm ripping through her like claws. There's no gentle build, no time for her to adjust to the ecstasy coursing in her veins. And I don't relent, pushing her body even harder. She scratches at my arm, trying to wriggle free from me and what I'm doing to her body.

"It's too much! Please, it hurts! No more!" she moans, cresting the peak again and then again in quick succession.

I tut, pulling her back toward me and holding her close.

Her legs shake, unable to support her weight as I keep going, not letting up even as she babbles for mercy. Something primal in me hums with satisfaction as tears stream down her face, sweat beading on her forehead. I slip a leg between her thighs to support her better, and she starts grinding her hips against me, soaking my slacks with another release.

"Look at you, all your defenses stripped away to reveal the good little slut you try to hide. But Daddy knows better. And he makes you feel so good, doesn't he?"

She nods mindlessly, and I squeeze her throat slightly before relaxing my grip, resting my fingers against her throat as my other arms bands around her waist to hold her against me. She whines, still trying to grind into me. One of her hands is on my wrist, the other trying to undo my belt buckle. I growl a warning, but she's beyond reason. So in a few quick movements, I manage to get her wrists behind her back, held tight in the hand that's not around her throat.

"Does my pretty little slut need something?" I coo, and she nods frantically, wriggling in my grip. But she stills as I squeeze her throat and push a more intense wave of pleasure through her body. I've lost count of the number of times she's climaxed, but I feel her thighs squeeze mine as a particularly strong one pulses through her. "Use your words for Daddy, and maybe he'll give you what you want."

Lyra whimpers, shivering despite radiating heat into my chest. She looks up at me, her pupils blown wide and tears in her eyes. "It's so…please, I'm so—it's too much. Please," she pants, licking her dry lips.

I lean down and take her bottom lip between my teeth and tug, making her moan. When I release her, I only pull back far enough to look into her hazy, come drunk eyes.

"Say you're sorry," I prompt.

She whimpers, closing her eyes and letting her head fall back as she comes again. I back off a little, still keeping the waves of pleasure crashing through her but lowering the intensity. And then she chokes out a sob, shoulders shaking as she struggles to obey. Taking pity, I release her throat and slide my hand down her body until I reach the apex of her thighs. Her shorts are absolutely ruined, and I push them aside until my fingers brush along the outside of her swollen sex.

"You're going to come again for me, and if you say you're sorry when you do, then I promise it'll be the last one. Can you do that for me, *my flame*? Can you do that for Daddy?"

I keep my tone gentle, along with my touch, and she shivers under my hand again. But at last, she nods. I purr my approval and push two of my fingers deep into her core with ease. She gasps at the sudden fullness, her whole body slumping forward until her head rests against my shoulder. As I pump in and out of her tight channel, I ease off my influence until all that's left is the genuine pleasure of my fingers stroking the spongy spot on her upper wall with firm precision.

"Oh, my God. Yes, that's—holy shit!" Lyra pants and moans, her hips matching my rhythm perfectly.

"I can feel you clenching on my hand. So ready to come for me, my desperate little cum slut. You want one more, don't you? Come on, and give it to me," I growl, voice sinking into my chest and vibrating with my purr.

"Oh, yes! Fuck! I'm sorry, Daddy!"

She screams as she explodes one last time, soaking my sleeve with her release. I work her down from the high, releasing her wrists to tuck them against her chest as I cradle her close. When I finally slip my fingers from her pulsing pussy, I can't stop myself from licking them clean, even though I almost immediately regret it. She's sweet caramel with just the right hit of salt and musk to balance out the sweetness. And now that I've had a taste, I desperately want to drink her dry. But she's had enough, and I made a promise.

I gather her in my arms, wrapping her legs around my waist as I carry her down to the couch where she's been sleeping. She doesn't fight me, thank the heavens, and even lets me wrap her in a soft blanket before settling her into my lap.

And even though I know it won't last, I let myself enjoy this moment of peace.

"I'm sorry about the kitchen," she mumbles after nearly fifteen whole minutes of silence.

I kiss her forehead, brushing her hair back from her face. "I know, my flame. You're forgiven."

"Not going to make me clean up my own mess?" she grumbles.

I chuckle a little, squeezing her tighter. "No. I'll call housekeeping later to take care of it."

"Well, aren't you full of surprises."

She says it so low that I'm not sure she intended for me to hear it, so I don't comment. We're quiet for another long few minutes, but neither of us makes a move to end this fragile truce. But then something she said earlier hits me.

"You're not a bad person, Lyra," I mutter, kissing her hair again.

"Oh, really?" she breathes out on a laugh. "And what kind of person do you think I am?"

A brat who needs to be taught a lesson every now and then.

A lonely girl who just wants to be safe.

A lost soul who's had to endure far too much heartache for someone so young.

Those thoughts and more cross my mind, but the one that settles on my tongue might be the most honest.

"I don't know. But I don't think you know either."

CHAPTER 29

Lyra

Long after Viktor leaves me on the couch to sleep, his parting shot haunts me, and keeps sneaking up on me for the next week like a creep in an alley when I least expect it.

I don't know. But I don't think you know either.

Where the fuck does he get off with that shit? I know who I am. I'm Lyra Spanos. I might not know what species I am. Or who my parents are. Or where I'm from. But I know who I am. And it's not someone who will let that scaley motherfucker get under my skin. He can judge me however he likes. I've never needed a man's approval before, and I'm not about to start now. Even if this particular man can make me come harder and more times than I ever have in my life, without even sticking his dick inside me. Which I'm not disappointed about. Not in the slightest. And I'm not disappointed when Viktor goes back into Phantom Mode, making himself scarce once more.

I shouldn't be pissed about him not interacting with me.

I've had plenty of one-night stands and have never felt this level of...abandonment after the fact. I want to be mad about him doing that—whatever the fuck it was—to me without asking. But having him take control like that, pushing my body to what felt like its absolute limit, was thrilling in a way I've never experienced before. And then after, when he just held me and stroked my hair until I fell asleep, was intimate on an entirely different level. I've never done after-sex cuddles; it was sort of hard to fit more than one person on the prison cots Dominic oh-so-generously provided us. And being in Viktor's arms after such an intense moment was nice, enjoyable even. But admitting that to myself strikes fear deep in my soul, so I shove all of that in the mental box labeled "shit to deal with later" and try to forget about it.

When we set my "ground rules," the dragons tried to say that I could go anywhere I wanted. I've been out on walks in the casino, but I haven't gone any farther afield than that. Gavril tracking me down was embarrassing enough. God forbid Viktor's the one to find me stuck in an alley. Again. So despite my roomies' best intentions, I'm still trapped inside this building, no chains or prison bars needed. And, for some reason, every time I remember that fact, my skin crawls. I never felt like this with Dominic, even if the circumstances are remarkably similar. Maybe it's because it felt like Dominic was trapped in Somnium with me, and I'm painfully aware that I'm trapped in this penthouse with these infuriatingly accommodating dragons.

Felix ordered so many new things for my room that I'm able to make a cozy fort out of the empty boxes. Well, I've stacked them around the part of the sofa I've been sleeping on while the renovation process continues. It's better than sitting out in the open, that's for fucking sure. Not that I'm avoiding anyone. I just want my own space. And if certain residents can't judge me with their weird purple eyes, then all the better. I brace myself for the comments about how childish having a cardboard fort is, but other than a weird side-eye from Gavril when I erected the edifice, none of them have complained about it. In fact, a string of fairy lights appeared inside of my Cave of Cardboard Solitude the next day. And it's so hard to sulk under the warm, twinkling glow of fairy lights.

Gavril has made it his personal mission to keep me "entertained, so I don't start chewing on the couch cushions." He'd earned a swing at his kidney—the highest point I could reach when we're standing side by side—for that comment, and he couldn't even do me the favor of pretending like he didn't enjoy it. Instead, he's made me watch marathons of his favorite television shows and movies, given me a stack of books as tall as I am to read, and even lent me a tablet to play games on.

And the whole time, I'm just bracing myself for the other shoe to hit the floor. I learned early that nothing good comes without a price tag attached to it. First at the orphanage, and then with Dominic, I know better than to expect people to do things out of the kindness of their hearts. And the longer this bizarre roommate arrangement goes on, the jumpier and more irritable I get. I refuse to give Viktor any form of satisfaction after...the incident and ask him for anything else, and I can't bring myself to ask Gavril or Felix what they want from me in return for all the stuff they've done. Because I'm not sure I could handle the answer.

I find myself once again inside my cardboard fort, huddled under one of the fluffy blankets with one leg tucked under my hips, my chin resting on the other as I stare out of the opening toward the open door to the guest room. I can't see Felix, but I can hear him singing to himself in French as he paints the walls. Despite not understanding a word, his tenor isn't unpleasant to listen to. As I clutch the blanket tighter around me, I try to ignore the feeling of my skin crawling again. Willing my body into stillness, I concentrate on my breathing. I will not let them break me. I won't admit defeat. This is a test, and I will pass.

A soft knock on one of the boxes makes me jump

slightly. "Housekeeping," Gavril sing-songs in a comically high-pitched falsetto.

"I've got enough Girl Scout cookies," I call back, my words short.

"That's okay. I've got something better," Gavril says, crouching down to look through the doorway.

It's almost funny to see this brute of a man bent nearly in half and grinning at me through the opening of a box fort. One wrong move, and he could make the whole structure collapse. But instead, he moves with an acute awareness of his size, carefully maneuvering around my little sanctuary. He doesn't try to force himself inside, but waits for me outside. Is this what people mean when they talk about "personal space" and "boundaries?"

"Viktor just texted me, and he's got a new toy for us to play with," Gavril says, grinning so mischievously I expect him to start twirling his auburn mustache at any moment.

And that alone has my attention. I've seen Gavril get excited over cheap souvenirs and pastries and a good plot twist, but this is an entirely different sort of anticipation. One I've felt on nights when I've had to defend myself against handsy patrons and strung-out creeps. Despite almost everything about us being polar opposites physically, the dinner bell to the feast of violence and chaos rings inside both of us. Viktor might be the one ringing it, but I'd be a fool to ignore an invitation to such a prime meal.

"Give me ten minutes."

It only takes me five minutes to throw on a pair of jeans and a hoodie, bundle up my hair into a messy bun, and slip into my old worn sneakers. When I come out of my bathroom, Gavril is standing in the middle of the empty space that used to be my bedroom, shoulder to mid-bicep with Felix. The room is only half painted, but it already feels twice as big as it did before. Which is to say, it feels like an airplane hangar.

I open my mouth to let Gavril know I'm ready, but stop short as Gavril leans into Felix, and then bends down so Felix can bestow a chaste kiss to his cheek. A deep rumbling purr emanates from somewhere in his chest that doesn't seem physically possible, like there's a cavern below his sternum, and the sound of primal satisfaction is echoing to the surface. My cheeks heat, and I force myself to look away. It's not like I haven't picked up on the more-than-friends thing these three have going on, but in my world, affection wasn't something we could afford. Our lives inside Somnium were too short for that old song and dance. This moment between them shouldn't surprise me, but it feels too intimate for my eyes...even if a deeply selfish and delusional part of me wants to be a part of it.

"Ready, *vatreno*?"

Gavril's voice pulls my gaze back, and I try to will the blood from my face. But I can still feel Felix's keenly observant stare on me, and I only give a curt nod before striding past them and out into the main living space. I hear Gavril's steps behind me, but I hold my head high. Silence falls between us, and it hits me again how quiet the penthouse is. There's no noise from the street, or even the casino below us. But once we're in the elevator, and we've descended a few floors, slot machine pings and faint music fills the small space. Oh, and the most awkward silence to have ever existed.

"So," I start, drawing out the word for effect, "where are we going?"

Gavril chuckles, grinning like a fiend again. "You'll see."

The elevator dings as we reach the lobby, and I let Gavril lead the way out onto the busy casino floor. We cut a swath through the crowds, everyone practically jumping out of Gavril's way. It strikes me again just how big he is, especially compared to normal sized people. But then I'm swept up in the buzz of life around me. Even for the early afternoon, the casino is bouncing with the highs and lows of Las Vegas. People with their heads in their hands, others with arms in the air and smiles on their faces. I'd basically become nocturnal while working at Somnium, and I'd never considered that this city could be just as busy in the daylight hours.

"Are those little legs of yours keeping up?" Gavril calls over his shoulder.

I grit my teeth and try to swing for his kidney again, but he dodges with entirely too much agility for a man his size. I try for another right hook, but my attention catches on the door Gavril has been leading us toward. A plain wood door marked with a simple "Employees Only," that just so happens to require a handprint scan and a six-digit code to open. When Gavril finally pulls it open and motions me inside, my curiosity is officially piqued.

A short dark hallway opens into a room full of screens, dozens of camera feeds from all around the casino. The images flicker every few seconds, revealing more of the building. I'm almost overwhelmed by the vast amount of information before me, but then my eyes catch on an all-too-familiar form straightening and turning around.

Viktor's stern profile is lit by the black-and-white screens, but somehow his amethyst eyes still manage to spark with disapproval as he looks me up and down once before turning to Gavril.

"What is she doing here?" Viktor asks, running a hand through his salt-and-pepper hair in irritation.

"She's out on day release, lizard dick," I reply with a tight-lipped smile before Gavril has a chance to answer.

Viktor growls low in his throat, but Gavril just chuckles. "You told me to come down," he says simply.

"Yes, *you*. Not her," he snaps back.

"Aw, come on, Vik. Let her have some fun," Gavril whines.

Viktor sighs and pinches the bridge of his nose, closing his eyes. I look him up and down, noticing his choice of attire for the first time. All black, with a vest unlike anything I've ever seen. It cinches his entire waist, emphasizing his sinful shoulder-to-hip ratio. At last, he opens his eyes and stares me down.

"If you want to stay, you will behave, understand? This is not the time or place to backtalk or argue. If I tell you to do something, you will do it without question. Am I clear?"

My instinct is to do exactly the opposite, but the expression on his face gives me pause. There's a simmering violet fire in his eyes, a tension in his jaw that I haven't seen before. Not even when we had our blow up. Whatever is happening is serious, that much is obvious, but he's not pushing me away or telling me to mind my own business. He probably told Gavril a lot more than just "come down here," but he brought me anyway. They're letting me into their world. And it would be a waste to squander this opportunity.

"Yes, Daddy," I quip back.

The fire in Viktor's eyes flashes hot for a second, and one of those impossibly deep purrs rumbles out of his chest. "*Khoroshaya devochka*," he murmurs before turning back to the screens.

One of these days, I'm going to run out of room in my "Shit to Deal with Later" box. Especially if these dragons keep making me feel all these weird, stomach fluttering feelings whenever they look at me a certain way. But that's a problem for future me. For now, the warm little flip of my stomach and the blush in my cheeks his words cause will be forced inside of that box to be examined another day.

CHAPTER 30

Lyra

Viktor leads us out of the security room without speaking, typing on his phone as he walks. The sea of people parts around him, every creature seeming to recognize a predator and fleeing on instinct. When we reach the gleaming gold bar, I can't help the flash of envy as I look over the setup. Everything is so clean and organized, with plenty of cut crystal glasses ready to be filled with expensive liquor. There isn't a single scratch or dent in the bar top, and they even have a computer for their point-of-sale system. I bet they don't have to put the cards they keep for open tabs into an old cigar box. Lucky bastards.

The bartender, a kelpie, judging by the seaweed green hair piled on top of their head, hands Viktor a double vodka soda, which the dragon immediately downs in two gulps. My neck is going to get sore if I can't stop myself from staring at him. But the fluidity and grace to not only his movements, but Gavril's, is hypnotizing. They're both well over 6'5", and muscular as hell, but they move like ballet dancers. Completely in control of every twist and turn of their massive bodies.

Viktor nods to Gavril, who turns to look out over the casino. I try to follow their eyeline, but I can't see beyond the first line of slot machines.

"The one at the blackjack table?" Gavril murmurs, a gravelly rasp of a question that makes me shiver.

"The drowned sewer rat," Viktor replies with a nod, disdain dripping from every word.

Gavril stalks off, leaving Viktor and I alone for the first time since our fight. He seems perfectly content to ignore me, but I've never been good at being seen and not heard.

"So, what'd the sewer rat do to earn your...attention?" I ask, unable to keep the curiosity out of my voice.

One corner of Viktor's mouth lifts in a smirk. "He thought he could get away with counting cards," he says simply.

It takes me a second, but then I let out a little ironic chuckle. I almost pity the guy. But, as the saying goes, play stupid games and you win stupid prizes.

A sudden commotion pulls my attention, lots of gasping and yelling just out of sight. But a moment later, Gavril reappears, carrying a squat, middle-aged man over one shoulder like a sack of potatoes.

"Hey, man! Wait, I was in the middle of a fucking game!" the weasel argues, thrashing against Gavril's iron grip as he approaches.

"You ready to have some fun, baby girl?"

Gavril grins wildly, leading the way through the casino floor. No one even bats an eyelash at the sight of the hulking beast of a man with some business casual schmuck slung over his shoulder like a sack of potatoes. Viktor's hand is on my lower back, forcing me to keep pace with him as we follow behind Gavril. It hits me right then that *this* is what Gavril meant when he said we've got a new toy to "play" with. And something tells me we're not about to sit down to a rousing game of Candy Land.

And what's even worse is that it doesn't occur to me to run or try to talk my way out of this. My mind still reels as we head beyond another Employee Only door and stalk down a hallway for another few paces. But then, seemingly at random, Viktor shoves open a door and Gavril goes inside. I look around and see that we've ended up in some back room that looks like it's meant to be used for storage. But in this case, it seems the only thing they're storing in this is a single dining chair and a few dim spotlights. It's seedy in the most familiar way, reminding me of Somnium's backrooms and dim hallways. I'm met with a rush of cool air from the air conditioner in the corner and I revel in the blast as it re-centers me. This situation is looking more and more fragile, like I'm about to see something that would make me an ideal candidate for the witness protection program. In fairness, that could be a step up from my current position as dragon captive. I wonder if they'll send me somewhere tropical. I hear Fiji's nice.

Gavril shoves the man into the chair and swiftly clamps a bear-like palm against his chest to stop him from moving. I'm immediately on high alert. I hadn't really considered what the dragons were going to do with the cheater once they got him away from the crowds. Now I just feel like an idiot. Have I just signed up to watch yet another display of dragon bloodlust? Fear and intrigue writhe together to mix a somewhat intoxicating cocktail and I'm left feeling unsure whether I want to shut my eyes or keep them wide open.

With a click, Viktor locks the door behind us and watches alongside me, although he seems far calmer. I'm guessing he's used to this kind of thing. There's not a casino owner in all of Vegas that hasn't gotten their hands dirty at some point.

There is one similarity between Viktor and I in this moment, though. It seems we're both in awe as Gavril rolls up the sleeves of his navy-blue Henley.

The first punch lands with a resounding crack against the smaller man's jaw, sending a glob of blood and spittle toward the ground. Fear and shock take a swing at my stomach and I almost double over. What was I expecting them to do? Dance the cha cha? Still, I'm caught off guard.

Viktor steps forward, out of the shadows and beneath the yellow spotlights. "Let me ask you a simple question, Mr..." He waves an elegant hand in front of himself, urging the man to finish his sentence.

"Semple," he replies shakily. "Johnathon Semple."

"John, can I call you John?"

He nods, confusion crinkling the corners of his too-small eyes.

"John," Viktor begins. "Do you think I'm stupid?"

A dark cloud settles over us all, the weight of Viktor's authority and threat covering me like a weighted blanket. I can't move. Can't leave. Shit, I can't even breathe. Even now, my lungs are holding on to a breath of air, unwilling to let it go. Do I want to be here? I've asked the same question a thousand times upon following the man into this room, yet here I am. Glued to the spot. Can't move. Can't breathe. Can't look away. I'm no stranger to violence. I spent most of my life as its next-door neighbor. Yet this is different. I realize with a shudder that it's because I'm not in any danger. I know, on some level, that Gavril and Viktor won't hurt me. That right now, amongst them, I'm... safe?

John Semple, however, is not safe. Panic rises in his face as he struggles against the chair. "Wh— Man, I don't know you, but I swear I never said nothing 'bout you to no one."

Viktor looks back at me, eyebrows raised in amusement as I keep my own eyes on Gavril, his smile widening with the promise of violence. God, Gavril's teeth have never looked quite so sharp. So menacing. My throat constricts and I swallow, hard. Heat spreads up my chest to my cheeks, leaving me feeling unsteady and confused. Am I enjoying this? The thrill of the whole scenario is certainly doing wonders for my heart rate, since it's kicked up a couple of notches just in these past few seconds.

"You see, I think you must think I'm stupid," Viktor continues, tugging up his suit pants to allow himself enough give to sink down onto the heels of his leather shoes.

"You thinking I'm a fucking moron is the only explanation I can come up with. Because why, oh why, John, would you attempt to steal money from me unless you were under the impression I was as dim as the day is long?"

I've never seen this side to Viktor either. The pure control he has over the situation, and Jesus, Mary, and Joseph, the way his ass looks in those tight suit pants. What is wrong with me? I'm about to witness a fucking murder, and I can't stop drooling over the assassin in charge. I'm starting to think that if I found out I was next, I'd merely bow down and say, *"thank you, Daddy."*

"Steal? No, man, I didn't steal anything. I promise!" Realization is setting in, even I can see it from my place against the back wall. It's in the nervous tremor of Johnathan Semple's clammy little hands.

"Hey, do you like tricks, John?" Viktor asks with a tight-lipped smile. When he doesn't reply, Viktor merely nods at Gavril and stands to full height.

The moment Viktor is out of harm's way, Gavril's hand sparks with electric blue static.

The chair doesn't survive the impact, but by the sound of Johnathon's whaling, he's still very much alive. I'm unable to look away as his body convulses ghoulishly, limbs jutting and pulling of their own accord long after Gavril's hand has left his chest.

My eyes leave Jonathon Semple's wriggling body and move on to watch Gavril. He's breathing heavily, but he hasn't broken a sweat. His bear-like knuckles are smeared with blood, but it isn't his own. That heat I felt earlier dips lower and lower, until I'm pressing my legs together to soothe the growing pressure in my core.

Please tell me I'm not fucked up enough to be finding this attractive.

But I'm not the only one. Gavril's jeans are tighter around the crotch than they were just minutes ago, the outline of his cock visible even in the dim lights. Flickers of electricity still travel between the tips of his fingers and a brief, intrusive thought wonders if there are more intimate ways he can use such a skill. Moisture builds between my legs, leaving my panties damp and sticky with arousal.

"Beautiful, pet." Viktor's praise brings me crashing back down to earth, and I watch when he pats Gavril on the shoulder before turning his focus back to Mr. Semple. "Let me make one thing very, very clear, John."

Johnathon's body relaxes, eyes finally rolling to their rightful position.

"Step foot inside one of our casinos again, and I'll take your dirty fucking hands and make you eat them. Do we have an understanding, John?"

He nods furiously, scuttling backwards in a futile attempt to put space between himself and Gavril.

"Lovely," Viktor says, clapping his large palms together. "Gavril, would you mind giving this newly changed man a little taste of the services we offer to cheaters."

"Up you get, little guy. We've got at least forty-five minutes together before I get bored." Gavril chuckles.

My mouth is too dry to swallow, and I realize my body is slumped against the wall, exhausted from a mixture of adrenaline and lust. Viktor takes position beside me, nostrils flaring as he turns his head to study my face. Oh God, can he smell me? Can he smell how turned on I am? I'm about to begin babbling about how this is all some big misunderstanding and I'm just as confused as he is, when Gavril's movement in front of me stills.

"Can I interest you in a little stress relief?" Gavril asks, holding out his hand for me to take. Out of fear or stupidity or intrigue, I let him pull me up to standing and walk me over to a table opposite Johnathon's weary body. Viktor's eyes are on me, following my every move, while Gavril shows me a selection of *tools.*

"This one could be good to start with. How's your aim?" Gavril asks, lifting a fucking crossbow like it's the most natural thing in the world.

"Who do you think I am, Robin Hood?" I snap in disbelief. Gavril shrugs and sets the thing back down with a heavier hand than makes me comfortable.

"Suit yourself," he sighs, picking up a baseball bat and making some stupid face that makes him look like he's offering me a choice of takeout as opposed to weapons.

I hum to myself, trying to ignore the sickly feeling in my stomach. "This guy stole a lot, huh?"

Gavril nods simply. "People like him are scum, Lyra. Like black mold that just keeps coming back no matter how much you paint over it."

"Are you going to...you know." I run one finger across my neck and stick out my tongue, hoping Gavril knows the universal sign for killing someone.

He chuckles, and I swear I even hear Viktor letting a small laugh escape from behind me.

"No, just make it so he knows he's not welcome here." Gavril pauses, pondering his next words carefully. "Think of it like a rage room. I can cover his face with a towel if it makes you feel better."

I inhale deeply through my nose, puffing out my lips as I exhale and nod. "Okay." I take the bat in my shaky hands and move it around a bit, trying to get used to the weight so that I know how hard to hit.

I've never held a bat before. It's not like Somnium was known for hosting employee baseball games. And any time I've ever had the pleasure of hitting someone, I've always just used my hands, like a normal person.

I walk toward the cheater, preferring to think of him that way than use his real name. Guys like this used to come into Somnium all the time. Little rat-faced men with grabby hands and crooked teeth. God, the number of times men like him have reached over the bar or under a table to grab me, like they were entitled to my body just because we happened to be in a strip club. Suddenly, I feel dirty. Images of that stupid Dream Lounge outfit Dominic made me wear flashes through my mind, so vivid I can almost smell the bitter magic in the air.

The bat swings seemingly of its own accord. Nervousness gives way to rage in a matter of seconds. The wood collides with the cheater's face, and he lets out a breathless *"hmph,"* which is overshadowed by the sound of teeth rattling onto the concrete floor.

"That's it," Gavril enthuses, circling me like a predator. "Again."

Thump.

One in the guy's ribs.

Thump.

A hit to his legs.

Thump.

Down on the top of his head.

Thump.

Fuck it, one more to the face.

And another.

And another.

And another.

My arms ache with the weight of the bat and the force of my hits and it isn't until Viktor's arms encircle me, pulling me away, that I realize I've left the guy half dead.

"Shit," I breathe, panting with exertion. "Shit!"

Viktor forces my back to his chest as his hands cover mine. It doesn't take much for him to make me drop the bat. Specks of blood cover my hoodie and Gavril is eyeing me like he wants to devour me whole.

"Is he dead?" But the question is lost as Johnathon's head lolls to the side and he spits out a mouthful of blood.

"That's my fucking girl," Gavril purrs, and it's then, with Viktor's arms around me, that I realize, Gavril isn't the only one popping a violence boner. Viktor's dick is rock hard against my back, twitching with each erratic heartbeat. My mind overflows with the image of being filled by Viktor. Fuck it, *and* Gavril. One beneath me and one behind me, pulling and pushing and making sure I'm so full I can't think anymore. Their huge bodies and thick cocks taking everything I have to give and demanding more and more until there's nothing left. No fear. No rage. No sadness.

Gavril takes a step or two forward, closing the distance so that I've got one dragon pressed into my back and the other crushed against my chest. He looks over my head, green eyes so bright that I'm sure I can see the reflection of Viktor's own violet irises in their pools. A small, breathless groan leaves my parted lips. I'm soaked, my thighs sticking together despite the oversized sweats I'm wearing. Without thinking, I push my ass back against Viktor and tangle my hands in Gavril's bloodied t-shirt.

A low growl rumbles against my spine, as another starts beneath the tips of my fingers. For a second, I just stay there, using Viktor and Gavril's overbearingly huge bodies to keep me upright, sandwiched between them. I pant as though I've run a marathon, fighting to catch my breath and free myself of the spinning in my head.

The adrenaline fog clears, and clarity starts to build up my walls, reality settling in like a lead weight tied to my heart. I break free of Viktor and Gavril's bodies, hot and delirious with such powerful desire I'm worried they can smell it all over me.

"I have to go," I grumble, turning and reaching for the door handle. I sense someone about to follow me, but I turn just in time to hold up my hand. "I'll take the elevator back up to the penthouse."

For some reason, they seem to trust me. Although, when I reach the elevator and mash my finger against the button, I sense someone loitering in the vicinity. Not Viktor or Gavril, but maybe a security guard. That feeling remains as I step into the car and wait. It only vanishes when the doors open into the penthouse and I hear Felix.

"Lyra?" he yells before poking his head around the doorframe. There's a smear of white paint on his cheek and he's holding a paintbrush. He looks fucking adorable. The exact opposite of the two dragons I left downstairs.

"Yeah, it's um, it's me, yup," I babble, stepping farther into the apartment until I can grab on to one of the kitchen counters to steady myself. My eyes meet with the door of the freezer, and I immediately open it up. Just as I had expected, there's a perfectly chilled bottle of vodka in the top drawer. Snapping open the bottle, I pour a hefty measure into a glass from the draining board. I down the three fingers' worth of vodka with a grimace, sticking my tongue out in an effort to soothe the subtle burn.

"You hungry?" Felix asks, eyebrows knitted together as he watches me. "I could order pizza."

I'm so foggy with mixed emotions and vodka that I don't even bother to argue. "Sure. Pizza. Yeah."

Felix's face lights up with a grin. "Okay, I'll order now. Any preference?"

"Could we, like...go out? I want to get outta here for a bit," I reply, hoping he doesn't notice how unsteady my voice sounds.

Surprise widens his silver eyes at the suggestion. "Out?"

"Yeah," I reply, acting as calm as possible. I realize with a pinch of bitterness that if I'm going to be convincing, I need to tell him a speck of truth. "I just need some open space. No walls. Ya know?"

Felix nods. "I'll just grab my wallet."

He bounces off toward his room, seemingly too happy to pay much attention to the tremble in my hands or the spots of blood on my clothes.

CHAPTER 31

GAVRIL

Watching Lyra leave, I wonder if we did the right thing. Then I'm reminded of the way her face lit up when I passed her the bat. How she held it tightly in her small hands, checking the weight and considering her next move. God, how her eyes sparkled with the thrill of that first hit. The sound was deafening, and she didn't let up, not once. If Viktor hadn't pulled her off the weasel, I'm certain she'd have beaten the poor guy to death.

Viktor calls in the cleanup guy to get rid of Johnathon Semple. It's a quick call, his tone never changing. I'm just heading out of the "storage" room, leaving Semple groaning on the floor behind me, when Viktor's voice rings out from behind me, curt and elegant as ever.

"Gavril, a word."

He makes an excellent boss man, looking sleek in his obnoxiously expensive suits and fine leather shoes. I turn to meet his waiting gaze. He's leaning against the wall with his large, sinewy hands clasped in front of himself. One foot is tucked behind the other, and his usually dark purple eyes are alight with something carnal that I recognize all too well. It's like the rest of the world disappears the moment I lock my eyes with his.

The image of his arms wrapped around Lyra's waist makes my heart race. All it would've taken was for him to bend her over and rip through her clothing and he could've fucked her right there in the pool of blood she'd created, like a pair of feral fucking animals. The way Lyra had clung to both of us, her hands buried in my t-shirt and her backside up against Viktor...there was a second there when everything felt right. Natural. As though she were a missing piece we didn't even know we needed. I want to ask Vik if he feels the same way, if that spark of belonging struck him in his cold heart, too.

"Something wrong, Viktor?" I ask delicately, my feet moving of their own accord until I'm just a few feet away from him. He's just two inches shorter than I am, but I'm twice his width, yet you'd think he was a ten-foot-tall marble statue the way I worship at his feet at a moment's notice. Viktor's broad shoulders taper off into a narrow waist, cinched in by the corset suit vest he's wearing. Powerful men and their slutty little waists always did make me crazy.

"You did wonderfully in there," he purrs, pink tongue coming out to dart across his bottom lip as his focus trails from my face down to my heaving chest.

I melt with the slightest offer of a compliment. "Thank you, Sir."

Viktor doesn't miss the desire in my tone, matching it with just a twitch of a smile.

"You know what happens to good boys that do as they're told, don't you, Gavril?"

My knees buckle, my entire body begging to drop to the floor in pleading. Already, I can feel my cock hardening in the confines of my pants, straining against the material as if desperate to get close to Viktor.

"They get rewarded, Sir." The words travel on a breath,

my heart pounding in my throat.

"They do indeed, pet." Viktor pauses, the perfect picture of control as he holds out a hand for me to grasp. "Come with me."

We exit the service hallway where the storage room is located and pass through the casino. Eyes follow our every move until we enter a simple broom closet by the bar.

"Classy," I tease. "You run numerous five-star casinos, but you plan on fucking me in a closet?"

Viktor locks the door behind him and lunges at me, his hand tight around my throat and his face so close to mine, I can feel the warmth of his breath on my lips.

"I'll fuck you wherever I want, darling," Viktor croons, running his tongue over the seam of my lips, grinning wolfishly in the dim light. "And you'll fucking love it."

He captures my mouth with his, his tongue laving mine with attention as the hand holding my throat runs down over my chest. Neatly trimmed nails rake at my skin as that hand slips under my Henley.

"On your knees," Viktor orders between kisses, teeth catching on my bottom lip and nipping just hard enough to make me wince.

"Always." The one word has Viktor moaning, and I drop to my knees with pleasure, trembling hands fumbling in the dark to undo his belt and the button and zipper beneath it.

"Now, Gavril," he groans, his back flush to the worktop behind him. There's a rumble of falling cleaning supplies and the smash of a mop as it falls to the ground when our movements grow urgent with need.

"Yes, Sir," I obey gladly, tugging down his suit pants and fitted boxers, letting his length spring free. A bead of moisture pools at the tip, and I greedily lean forward to steal a taste of him. The purple head is salty against my flattened tongue as Viktor's hand shifts to take a fistful of my hair. He pulls harshly, forcing my mouth away from his thick cock and ordering my eyes up to his.

"I love watching you work," he says with a lazy smile. "I love seeing you bring grown men to their knees. But most of all, I love seeing you on yours."

"I imagine there was someone else you enjoyed watching this time, *Sir*," I grunt, my hands still running up and down Viktor's steel length. Viktor's face twitches in anger, his hold on my hair tightening to the point of pain.

"Do as you're fucking told, Gavril. Or I'll whip your ass so you can't sit for a month."

The temptation is too much, and my mouth opens, letting the words out before I can stop them. "Did she feel good pressed up against your hard cock, *Daddy*? Was she just as soft and warm as you had imagined?"

Viktor releases a sound just close enough to an alpha bark that I shudder. That's a strong response from someone who claims not to give a shit about her. But I don't get the chance to ponder that further, or press for more details, as another sharp tug on my hair makes me gasp, leaving my mouth wide open for him to thrust his cock inside. He's got the perfect way to shut me the hell up, and I moan as he pushes my face flush to his pelvis, my mouth opening greedily to take him all in. His cock hits the back of my throat, those narrow hips sharp beneath my open palms as he thrusts eagerly into my mouth. I draw back just enough to tease him a little, swirling the length of my tongue around the tip and pulsing the flattened muscle against the underside. The sound of his rushed breaths and the whisper of filthy words leave me throbbing against the inside of my jeans. I wrap one hand at the base, where Viktor's knot is already pounding, and squeeze. Hard.

Viktor's next move is so quick it leaves my head in a spin. He tugs me off his dick, leaving it to bob against the solid planes of his stomach before he whips me round and bends me over the dirty worktop. My face is flush with the wood, held there by Viktor's hand against the back of my neck.

"What have I told you about teasing, pet?" Viktor growls

while he rips my jeans down, his palm landing against my bare ass with a resounding *smack*.

My sharp intake of breath curtails into a gruff chuckle. "I wasn't teasing, was I?"

He steps closer, his cock pressing between my ass cheeks while he roves his hand up and down my spine. I can feel him shifting at my back, rummaging in his fallen suit pants before a glob of something cold hits my hole. Viktor's long, elegant fingers run in soothing circles, making me clench on emptiness.

"Prepared, as always, Sir." I smile, pushing back against his fingers.

Viktor is always the strong, silent type, not much for taking dirty unless things aren't going his way. He likes control, yearns for it, and I am more than happy to oblige. Most of the time. Although I have to admit that the temptation to bring Lyra up again is overwhelming. I want to see his reaction. The moment I saw between them back there, surrounded by chaos and carnage, was something spectacular. And I certainly didn't miss the moment after she left when Viktor readjusted himself in his suit pants. And him shutting me down a few moments ago is enough to make me wonder if something has happened between them and they just aren't talking about it. But I have meetings this week, and I can't imagine standing through a three-hour security briefing first thing in the morning. I'll just tuck that away for now and focus on the matter at hand.

With my ass slippery with lube and my cock painfully hard, I reach down just enough to palm myself once or twice, chasing whatever sweet release I can find.

"You know the rules, Gavril," Viktor reminds calmly, the tremor in his voice barely noticeable.

My grin widens against the wooden bench, faltering only as Viktor slips two fingers inside me and scissors them tortuously.

"Fuck, Vik..." I sigh, rocking back onto him again and

again.

"Be a good boy and ask nicely." His lips press onto my back, tongue slipping out just enough to taste the thin layer of sweat covering my flushed skin.

"Please, *Daddy* fuck me," I beg, hoping it'll be enough to convince him. He does have a habit of keeping me waiting. It's a game Viktor enjoys playing a little too much.

"Such sweet words from that filthy mouth of yours, pet."

I am rewarded with his blunt head pushing against my greedy ass, and the feeling is overwhelming. Viktor moves slowly, making sure I feel every ridge along his substantial length. Full. Almost full.

"You best keep quiet for now. We wouldn't like to cause a scene, would we? You know how this town likes to *talk*," Viktor coos, snapping his hips and forcing his entire length inside me. A guttural moan spills from between my parted lips, the hand I held on my cock long forgotten as I'm consumed by Viktor.

"Sshhh, pet," he continues, offering me sharp but slow thrusts. One hand remains against my hip as the other snakes to the front, pushing my hand away and gripping my throbbing cock in his capable grip and working me in tandem with each snap of his hips.

Harder. Faster. I need all of him, all of Viktor's cruel, dark energy, all at once.

Voices fall to hushed pants, echoing in the small, dark closet. I'm swallowing him up, pulling him deeper and deeper until I can feel him in my bones, in my soul. Viktor's pace never falters, each slide of his thick cock inside me causing sparks behind my closed lids. My skin tingles, pressure building deep in my stomach.

"Viktor, I'm..." I cry breathlessly, limp in his grasp as his cock grazes beautifully against my prostate.

"Such a good boy for me, Gavril. Such a good fucking boy." He's struggling now, his gravelly voice straining with each word as he ups his speed.

The free hand that had been dragging me back against

his cock walks up over my shoulder, settling around my throat. Warm fingers press on either side of my windpipe, and my eyes all but roll to the back of my head.

"More," I beg. "More, Viktor, please."

For once, he obeys without question and increases that delicious pressure that has me delirious.

Viktor hums approvingly as I spill ropes of hot cum against his hand, my ass squeezing his cock.

"That's my good boy," Viktor mewls, holding himself deep inside me as he explodes, muffling his roar against my back. The blissful weight of his body on top of mine, pressing me into the counter, is the one feeling I'll never grow tired of.

But even as my body sings with receding waves of pleasure, something feels missing. *Someone* is missing. I look down at the desk, and the overwhelming need to have a certain red-headed hellion below me, with her face covered in bloody freckles, catches me off guard. I push the dream to the back of my mind, coming back to the present as Viktor fusses, cleaning us both up.

Once we're presentable again, he leans in and gives me a soft kiss, a question in his eyes as he pulls away. I shake my head. Of course, he could sense my mood shift, but I'm not sure I'm ready to look it in the face, let alone talk about it.

For now, I'll just have to find another cheater to work out my feelings with.

CHAPTER 32

We both take fifteen minutes to tidy ourselves up. I decided to keep things simple, worried that if I dressed up, it would scare her off. Lyra changes into a pair of yoga pants and a clean black hoodie that hits mid-thigh, her red hair still a little damp and tied back into a ponytail, with a few escaped tendrils curling around her face. When she stepped out of her half-decorated bedroom, which still smelled like wet paint and MDF, she looked utterly mesmerizing to me. The knowledge that she was comfy, warm, and about to be well-fed sparked a deep-rooted sense of pleasure inside me.

She offers me a polite smile as we step into the elevator. We stay quiet even as the elevator dings, opening onto the ground floor of Korona Drakona. I slide my hands into my pockets to stop myself from reaching out and touching her. There are so many questions I want to ask. So much that I want to know. I just have to hope that food is enough of a bribe to get her talking.

Just as we're stepping out of the elevator, I spot Viktor and Gavril leaving the security office.

"I'll just let them know we're heading out," I say calmly to Lyra, leaving her to hover as I make my way over to my pack mates. A smirk lifts the corners of my mouth when I smell sex in the air.

"Having a fun, productive day at the office?" I quip, making both of them jump.

They whip around to face me, both of them sporting the characteristic just-fucked flush to their faces. Viktor gives me a chastising look, but Gavril just laughs.

"You could say that. Where are you two going?" Gavril asks, eyes peering over my shoulder to look at Lyra.

I snap my teeth at him with a soft growl, a small warning not to mess up the first chance I've had to take Lyra out on some semblance of a date. "She wants out of the penthouse, probably to get away from you two after whatever the hell you did with her earlier," I grumble. I'd noticed the tangled scent of fear and excitement ripe in the air around her almost immediately.

Viktor rolls his eyes, but doesn't say anything, which makes me even more suspicious. I'd noticed the blood on her face and clothes, but decided against asking her about it. These two are fair game for interrogation, though.

"We just—" Viktor cuts off Gavril's protest with a low growl of his own.

Gavril rolls his eyes and starts again. "I brought her in to help with a cheater."

I blink at him, waiting for him to go on, but I'm acutely aware of Lyra standing just a few feet behind me. I don't know how good her hearing is, but I don't want to risk her overhearing anything she shouldn't.

"Can I come for dinner too? I'm starved," Gavril asks with a grin, winking at Lyra over my shoulder.

If Gavril wants dinner, he can order his own. I'm sure he's starving after a day of traumatizing our already traumatized house guest.

"Abso-fucking-lutely not. She came upstairs looking like she saw a fucking ghost. I'm going to get her to eat something and hope like hell she doesn't have another panic attack." I glare at Gavril and Viktor, straightening my spine.

Viktor perks up, brows pulled low with sudden concern. "Another panic attack? What do you mean?"

I sigh, shaking my head. "I'll tell you later. Have fun with your...work. Use plenty of lube."

I walk away as they protest but, thankfully, they don't follow me.

When I reach Lyra's side, I smile as comfortingly as I can. "Shall we?"

She nods, frowning. "What's up with the murder-twins?"

I chuckle at the nickname, but shrug. "Nothing, just wanted to know where we were going."

We exit the casino, leaving the air-conditioned environment behind as we head down the strip. The sidewalks are packed with people, as always. Folks elbowing through the crowds as they weave in different directions. Tourists stop to look through the windows of stores or pause in front of casinos as they discuss where they want to go first.

Lyra remains close to my side, so close that her arm is almost touching mine. I want to capture her hand, or at the very least link her arm through mine, but I resist the urge. It's enough of a miracle that I've got her to go out with me. She admires the tall buildings and greenery, even shooting me a smile when we walk past a pink Cadillac parked on the side of the road. The overweight Elvis impersonator driving it winks at her, shooting finger-guns in our direction.

"God, this place is like a fucking fever dream," Lyra mutters as we pass, and I can't help but chuckle. It's been years since me, Viktor, and Gavril arrived here. Stepping off the train into a dusty desert wasteland. We spent the first ten years chasing our tails, trying to figure out what the fuck we were supposed to do and how to do it. Las Vegas built itself up from the ground, people and creatures from all over the place finding themselves on the doorstep of this new micro-world. It wasn't easy, taking over the land, taking people beneath our wings, so to speak. It's not unusual for dragons to bide their time, though. Something which is easily misunderstood by humans. Our species have all the time in the world to get our shit in order.

"So you haven't explored Vegas much?" I ask. It's a simple question that hopefully won't have Lyra putting her guard up from the get-go.

She shakes her head, curls of red hair shimmering in the sunlight like fire. "Nope. I spent what felt like an eternity going from bar to bed, rinse and repeat. Not much allowance for tourism."

There's an uncomfortable pause, but I do my best to pretend I don't notice.

"You still fancying pizza?" I ask, clearing my head of bustling thoughts and returning to the present. It's too easy to get lost in my memories.

Lyra nods, just once. "Yup. Maybe pasta, too. I'm not sure." She's definitely not her usual feisty self. Whatever Gavril and Viktor had her doing back at the casino has either calmed her or frightened her into silence. I make a deal with myself right then and there to get her out of whatever daydream-like funk she's in.

"I know a great little Italian place. Super casual, outdoor seating." I glance at her out of the corner of my eye as we walk, watching for any reaction. She merely nods, her pointed chin tipping down.

"Sounds great," she replies, her tone flat and indifferent.

I wish I could pull her out of her shell. See that flash of chaos that's always shining in her bright eyes. But I'll take the simple approach. Open her up with good food and general chit-chat. Make sure she feels at ease before I try to get to know her better.

We round a corner, and the alfresco dining area comes into view. I watch Lyra as her steps slow, and she studies her surroundings with avid curiosity. The outdoor seating is covered by a clear gazebo, intended to protect the area from the sun and rain. Green vines twirl and coil around the metal frame, entwined with delicate fairy lights that, even in the fading afternoon sun, twinkle ethereally. It's one of the nicer places to eat along the strip. Calm and oddly quiet, given its surroundings.

"I don't get to come here as often as I'd like," I say, ushering her toward the restaurant.

"Yeah, I get the sense Viktor isn't much of a carbs guy." The reply comes naturally, and I smile, relieved that after her apparently traumatic afternoon, she still has the ability to joke.

"He likes to cook," I say, drawing in a nervous breath. "He doesn't see the point in eating elsewhere when he can make a better meal than most of the chefs in the city."

"Fair." Lyra shrugs, following me into the small Italian restaurant. It's chilled, with a display up front and a counter where you can order.

"Any preferences?" I ask, hovering in front of the counter with my hands tucked in my pockets. I'm not used to feeling so on edge. Usually, I watch situations from a distance before I put myself in them. I practice, rehearse, repeat. This dinner date has caught me off guard, and I feel uncharacteristically unprepared.

"Food," Lyra snaps back, eyes twinkling beneath the lights.

"Why don't you go choose a table and I'll order for us?" I suggest, hoping that she'll see me trusting her not to make a break for it and relax a little. It seems to work because she smiles, turning on her heel and marching off toward the alfresco dining area. She picks a table right at the open window and her cheeks flush a delicious shade of pink from the heat.

I take the liberty of ordering enough food to feed eight

people. Pizza, breadsticks, a spicy sausage pasta, and a basket of warm chocolate chip cookies. When the woman asks if we'll be wanting the food brought to us all at once, I say yes, smiling like a maniac. Something tells me that a banquet of food being laid out in front of Lyra might make her happy.

My hand ruffles through my mop of blonde hair as I walk over to Lyra's chosen table and take a seat opposite her. She's so busy people watching that she doesn't even notice me approaching, and I love that. It's a prime opportunity for me to just watch her. She's got her chin leaning on her palm, face scrunched up against the sunlight. Her long lashes graze the tops of her cheeks, where a faint blush has lit up her ivory skin. I'd give anything to watch her like this for hours. To absorb and connect with every millimeter of her face to the point where every time I close my eyes, I have a perfect rendition of her features in my mind. There's not enough time in the world that would allow me such a privilege, but it won't stop me from praying to every god for just a second longer to gaze upon her.

The hustle and bustle of food arriving has both of us jumping with surprise. My face heats when Lyra realizes I've been here, watching her, this whole time. The waitress sets up a second table beside ours, placing our plates in front of us and leaving the numerous dishes of food on the temporary table at our side. Lyra's eyes widen at the cheese and pepperoni pizza, and as her hand moves to grab a slice, I interrupt.

"Careful, it's—"

Lyra completely disregards my warning, pulling a slice out and shoving it into her mouth. She groans her approval and devours the slice in a minute flat. It takes me a moment to shake free of her spell. She's already halfway through her second slice before I gather my wits and serve myself a slice.

We eat in silence, demolishing one pizza together and starting on the pasta before Lyra finally slows down. I'm focused on my own plate, working quickly through the food even as I clutch the plate to my chest. I can feel her eyes on me, but it's background noise, a distraction from the task before me.

"Who used to steal your food?" Lyra asks into the silence.

I jump, cheeks flushing hot. When I look up at her, her gold-green eyes stare into my soul, seeing everything. I straighten a little from the defensive slouch I'd fallen into, chewing the bite of food I'd just taken slowly, as I think. It only takes a moment of hard eye contact, her eyes full of a deep understanding, before I have to look away, choosing to focus on her chin instead.

"Um...some of my cousins. I don't think they ever meant me any real harm, but I've always been something of an easy target," I admit, picking my words carefully.

Lyra snorts her derisive agreement. "Kids can be real assholes," she grumbles, finishing off her breadstick in two bites.

"Do you have siblings? Or cousins?" I ask cautiously, sitting up ever so slightly.

I know it's pushing my luck, but I have so many questions about Lyra and her life. My chest has been filled with an overwhelming need to know her since the first time I laid eyes on her. But the longer we sit in silence, the more nervous I get. I don't want her to shut down again.

"I don't have any blood siblings. My mother and father struggled to have me, and were warned against having any more children. But that's seventeenth century medicine for you," I go on, chuckling a little at the end.

"You're that old? You don't look a day over twelve," she tosses back.

The dig stings, but I shrug it off. "Dragons aren't meant to have single birth clutches. The offspring tend to be smaller, weaker. You'd think we'd end up bigger, with no one else to compete with for resources, but *la vie est un mystère*."

I laugh at my own joke, and my heart twists as I hear her let out a singular chuckle. We fall back into silence, and I hardly dare to breathe. Her eyes have softened around the edges, less defensive and more curious. A bubble of hope appears in my stomach. I feel like I'm trying to talk down a feral cat; one false move, and she'll bolt.

"You're French?" Lyra asks, trying to be casual and mostly succeeding.

I nod with a warm smile, and it doesn't escape my notice that she's relaxing more with each minute we talk. Baby steps, I remind myself. She needs to learn to trust us, and interest in our backgrounds is a good start.

"I was born into the Parisian Flight, the collection of many packs in one place," I explain, responding to the confused twitch of her brows. "Where are you from?"

She hesitates again, biting the inside of her lower lip. I swallow the urge to apologize for prying, but that insane curiosity won't let me walk the question back.

"New York City. Lower East Side, when it was still a slum. Grew up in an orphanage," she admits, words coming out stilted.

My face falls before I can stop it, eyes softening. Lyra snaps her head around, looking away from me with a scowl. Shit. No, no, no. We can't stop now, not when we're making such good progress. I follow her eyeline to the basket of cookies, and an idea strikes me like lightning.   Grabbing the basket, I pull it toward me before she can stop me. I pick up a clean napkin and start breaking up the cookies into even-ish chunks.

"Why would you ruin perfectly good cookies?" she exclaims, more outraged than I've ever seen someone be over baked goods.

"Making things interesting," I reply with a smirk. "You've been drooling over these since the waitress set them down, and I want to get to know you. So let's play a game. One bite for one answer. The bigger, more detailed the answer, the bigger piece you can take. If you don't want to answer, the other person gets to take your bite."

CHAPTER 33

Lyra

Felix takes it upon himself to clear the table as he talks, piling the empty plates and dishes onto the small table that the waitress had brought out with our food. The only thing left on the surface of our table is the napkin covered in cookie pieces. I stare at them, swallowing as my mouth waters at the smell alone. These are homemade, for sure. Probably based on a recipe someone's nonna brought over from The Old Country. And Felix is holding them ransom in exchange for my life story.

"Ask me whatever you want," Felix challenges, pulling my attention back to him.

There's a playfulness to his expression that makes my heart skip a beat. He doesn't look like a kid anymore. No, he's all man, fire in his eyes as he waits for me to do my worst. The part of me that's been pulling a full Benedict Arnold all night wants to melt and show him my belly, but the larger, more truculent part of my brain puffs up like a turkey.

"The man you killed at Somnium, was he your first?" I

ask, spitting out the first thing that comes to mind.

I expect him to balk, but he just lifts his chin. "No, and he won't be the last. Anyone who so much as thinks of harming a hair on your gorgeous head will meet a similar fate."

He takes a small piece, popping it into his mouth and licking melted chocolate from his fingers. I should be panicking, my voice of reason asserts, because he's just admitted he's murdered before, and will do it again without batting an eyelash. But instead, my brain is too busy losing its shit over the fact he called me gorgeous. Thankfully, he doesn't dwell.

"How old are you?" he asks, tone light.

I hesitate, more out of instinct than anything else. But this is a safe answer. "I stopped counting around one hundred fifty. But I think I was born in…1825?" I say, words lifting in a question as I struggle to remember.

I take a medium-sized cookie chunk and pop it into my mouth. The moan that escapes my throat is primal, and my eyes roll into the back of my head as pure, uncomplicated pleasure spreads to every corner of my body. I rarely think of anything as perfect, but these cookies just might be. I take my time chewing, letting the flavors melt into my tongue and slide down my throat. When I open my eyes, I flush as I find Felix staring at me, undisguised lust in his molten gaze. A shiver runs across my skin, and the silence between us crackles.

"When's the last time you got laid? And was it good?" I blurt, tongue a little too big for my mouth.

"That's two questions," he returns, tilting his head and smirking.

"So you can count," I snark, mirroring his smirk.

"I'll answer, but then you've got to answer two from me," he says in warning.

I lift my chin, mouth set in a stern line. "Bring it, lizard boy."

Felix laughs and shakes his head, settling back against the worn wooden chair, stretching one arm out to the side as he lounges. There's something so fluid about the way he moves, like he has complete mastery over every muscle fiber in his body. It almost begs the question of what he might look like under his jogging pants and hoodie.

"The last time I got fucked was maybe a week or so ago. Viktor needed a playmate, and we'd already worn Gavril out," Felix starts, completely unashamed.

My brain short circuits at the mental image of this small, angelic creature lying under the hulking mass of stern muscle, his head thrown back with ecstasy, Viktor's salt-and-pepper hair ruffled and hanging over his brow. But I stop myself before I finish that fantasy. That's going to have to be something I think about later, when I'm alone.

"But I think you mean the last time I was with a woman. Rest assured, *petite étincelle*, I haven't been with a woman since the late 1700s," he finishes.

"Why?" I ask, leaning forward, enthralled by the sound of his smooth, slightly accented voice.

"Because my pack and I have been searching for our mate. I've taken oaths to be with no one but them until we find her," Felix says, tone softening and going a little distant.

I sit back, honestly shocked by the level of honesty he's displaying. I look down into my lap, toying with the hem of my sweater as he eats his reward cookies, mouth going dry. I don't know if I could do what they've done. If I'd spent over three hundred years searching for someone, I'd have given up, for sure.

"How long have you been at Somnium, and how did you end up working for the demon?"

My heart stops for a moment before kicking back on, slamming into my ribs. I look up, ready to tell him to mind his damn business and take the rest of the fucking cookies, but his face stops my protests in their tracks. There's no judgment, no condescension, just cool, guileless curiosity. The air is warm, the background chatter an indistinct hum.

"One hundred fourteen years. I made a deal with a two-timing slime ball, and he dragged me to this godforsaken city back before the Depression," I say, picking my words with care.

I can hear the blood rushing in my ears, but I grit my teeth. My eyes are burning as memories tumble out from the box I normally keep them in, but I refuse to cry in front of this man. I turn away as I eat my cookie bits with more force than is strictly necessary.

"What was the deal?" Felix asks, just above a whisper.

"No," I snap, closing my eyes as I fight to keep my breathing even.

"You can tell me, Lyra. I promise I won't tell anyone, not even Viktor or Gavril," he presses.

And fuck me with a cactus, but I believe him. This is a man who hasn't had a girlfriend since before indoor plumbing became a thing, all because he pinky promised he wouldn't.

"It's so stupid, but I wanted what all orphans want: to know why my parents didn't keep me. The nuns told all the kids their mothers were dead, so I didn't believe them when they fed me the same line. I was only a few years out of the orphanage and following a lead down to New Orleans. I was poking around, asking questions in this hole-in-the-wall place, and Dominic overheard. When he told me he could help, I took the bait," I drone, speaking to my open palms.

Felix doesn't speak, though I wish he would. Because it's too quiet in this safe space we've made on the patio of this restaurant, and my head echoes with the conversation, the last one I had as a free person. Dominic sold his grift hard, and I bought every fucking word. He promised he'd not only help me figure out what happened to them, but he'd help me find them, too. God, I was so naive.

"What did he find?" Felix's voice is full of forced calm, but it sounds like it's coming from the other end of a tunnel.

I let out a single bark of watery laughter, squeezing my eyes shut. "He brought me to a field in Turkey. Turns out my dad was tried and executed for treason, and they buried him and other criminals in one communal grave and wiped all mention of them from the records. And my mother did actually die giving birth to me. I'd sold my immortal soul to find out I'm the offspring of a traitor and a whore. So fucking stupid."

My voice cracks and I rub my eyes, wiping away the moisture before it can fall. I growl softly in frustration, trying to get myself together, but I can't. I hate Felix for making me think about this shit, and I'm about to fire off a string of insults when suddenly, arms wrap around my shoulders. I'm lifted out of my chair before settling again, this time draped across Felix's lap.   I'm so shocked that I forget that I'm angry and hurt, so overwhelmed by the comfort of his warm chest that my tears dry. He holds me close and tight, his cheek resting on the top of my head.

"You're not stupid, Lyra. Wanting to know about your past is natural, and I can't imagine how hard it must have been to be alone for so many years," he whispers into my hair.

I choke on my inhale, his voice cracking open my heart like a chisel. No one has ever said those words to me. No one has ever attempted to understand. And here he is, basically a complete stranger, offering me genuine empathy and comfort. I look up at him, and our faces are only inches apart. His breath is sweet with chocolate, but there's something under it that makes my heart pick up speed. A scent that's deeply, intrinsically Felix. His gaze flicks between my eyes and my lips, and I go still. But like magnets, the pull between us is impossible to fight.

At the first brush of his lips against mine, a shock goes through me, like I've stuck a fork in a socket, but in the best possible way. But he pulls back, hesitating. Waiting. Never one to back down, I lean in, claiming his mouth. My eyes slide closed as he moans, hands tightening around me. He tries to guide our movements, and I find it all too easy to relent and let him take the lead. For someone who hasn't kissed a woman in four hundred years, he's remarkably good at making something so simple feel like a deep, thorough, full-body experience.

We pull away for air, and I want to dive back in, but Felix retreats, looking at me with a serious frown. I flush hot, my better judgment coming back.

"I'm sorry–"

"You don't have to–"

We speak at the same time, both going quiet as we wait for the other to finish what they were going to say. Felix recovers faster, clearing his throat.

"You don't have to do anything you don't want to, Lyra. I'm not–this wasn't about–there's no pressure for–"

I cut off his adorably awkward rambling with another quick kiss. When I pull away, his cheeks are pink, and I can't help but smile. He relaxes as I do, and I sigh. Maybe he's right. If he were any other guy, we'd already be halfway through foreplay by now. But there's something really...nice about eating dinner out in the open, listening to the busy Vegas strip as people rush around, getting on with their day. It's like the world is as oblivious to us as we are to them. Just two people on a date, cuddling and kissing, all clumsy limbs and stolen smiles. It's natural. Normal. I can't remember the last time I've done anything even remotely like this. Then I realize with a jolt, I've never done this. Never had this simple normality. No one has ever taken me out to dinner, no one has ever warned me the pizza's too hot, or tried to get to know me. So I do all I can do and settle back into his arms, resting my head on his chest.

"I deserve the rest of these fucking cookies for that," I grumble, only half-serious.

Before I can reach for them, Felix has the plate in hand and brings it close enough for me to take some.

"You do, *petite étincelle.* You deserve this and so much more," he whispers.

I flush hot, choosing to pretend like I didn't hear him instead of admitting that the reverence in his voice makes my heart flip and stomach clench. I'll just add that to the ever-growing pile of feelings that can be dealt with another time.

"Okay, my turn to pick the game," I announce, lifting my head from Felix's shoulder and shooting him a smile.

He matches my expression, silver eyes twinkling. "Oh yeah? What are you thinking?"

"It's something Ginny and I used to do," I explain, recalling all the nights spent up on top of Somnium. The two of us make-shifting a bed out of cushions and blankets on the dirty rooftop. "You have to choose a person and make up their life story."

Felix's brow furrows, but he's on the edge of a laugh. "Right..."

"The goal is simple." I put on my sternest expression. "You have to make the other person laugh."

"That doesn't sound so hard," Felix replies, though he doesn't sound too certain. I'm going to take a wild guess and say he and the others don't spend their free time playing games.

"I'll go first." I sit up a little, trying to ignore the fact that my ass is nestled against Felix's crotch. Surely, he can't be comfortable, since I definitely weigh more than he does. As if reading my mind, Felix settles an arm around my middle, holding me to him.

"See that guy over there?" I point as subtly as I can at a guy walking along with a much younger woman. His hairy-knuckled hand is wrapped around hers, and while she's slender and stylish in a white and gold dress with sandals, he's in flip-flops, orange board shorts, and a white vest. "Definitely mafia. Not big leagues, but he's got those Tony Soprano vibes, if you know what I'm saying."

Felix sets a hand over his mouth, stifling a giggle. "What about his wife?"

"Oh, totally not his wife." I chuckle. "I'm thinking...the nanny? No! His daughter's college roommate. See the way she grimaces every time he pulls her a little closer? In it for the money, one hundred percent."

255

Felix breaks and offers up a laugh, but it's not the kind of belly-wobbling laugh I was looking for. I fold my arms over my stomach and huff.

"Okay, Monsieur Party Pooper," I announce in my best fake-French accent. "Your turn."

Felix shifts in his seat, eyes narrowing as he studies the crowds. "Hmmm…"

"Come on, hurry up!" I prod at him, silently hoping to throw him off his game.

"Got one," he starts, lifting his hand and pointing toward a much older woman. It takes me a second to spot the clear plastic backpack she's wearing on her chest.

"Is that a fucking *cat*?" I giggle, staring at the woman in awe.

Felix nods furiously, tossing his head back. "I bet that cat isn't just a cat."

"You're going to have to give me more than that," I reply, tilting my head to the side.

"She's a powerful witch," he begins with animation, already taking the game much more seriously than I did. "Found out her husband was betting all their money away, poker, maybe. Blackjack on the weekends. She could've just divorced him, but that wouldn't have been punishment enough."

My legs are kicking up and down like a child as Felix crafts his elaborate story.

"No, she decided to turn him into a lowly household tabby and now she walks the streets of Las Vegas with him in his little plastic box. She weaves in and out of casinos, forcing him to watch as others come alive with the thrill of winning big. Jackpots are her favorite method of torture. She hunts them out, listening for the ring of the slot machines, knowing her husband will never indulge in his treasured pastime ever again."

We both fall silent. Our eyes meet and he's the first to crack. A loud chuckle spills from his lips, rumbling in his chest beneath the tips of my fingers. It's not long before I join him, laughing and laughing, until sweet, happy tears stream down my cheeks.

"You took that way too fucking seriously," I say between hiccups, wiping at my eyes.

"Dragons are terribly competitive, *petite étincelle,*" he muses, studying my face with a grin. "You'd be wise to keep that in mind the next time you challenge me."

It sounds close to a threat, one that builds a delicious fire low in my belly.

CHAPTER 34

VIKTOR

When I flick the switches on the bare cement wall, it takes a few seconds for the basement to illuminate. The fluorescent tube lighting blinks once or twice, casting every dark corner in a too-bright yellow glow. I stand for a second, rolling my sleeves up as I survey the sigil with mixed emotions.

Gavril and Felix have been working hard on this, enough late nights and long hours to last a lifetime. I almost feel like I got the easy job; securing land, maintaining the casino, and making sure our relationship with the council was on decent terms. Politics. Dragon politics, to be exact, are exhausting. I do wish I'd been more involved in crafting the sigil, though. I walk slowly around the outskirts of the hardened gold circle, admiring every glimmer of the precious metal as the reflections ripple across the surface.

I'm so caught up in admiring the view that I barely notice when Gavril and Felix enter the room behind me. A large hand comes down on my shoulder and I glance back, catching Gavril's eyes. He smiles, not the predator-like grin I'm used to seeing, but the subtle, sincere smirk of someone who's genuinely proud.

"You did so well," I say, setting my hand on top of his. "It looks perfect."

"You think?" Felix asks with a chuckle. "I thought the right edge looked a little wonky."

"Fuck you," Gavril snaps, but there's a warmth in his expression. Felix is only teasing, and as much as Gavril pretends to hate it, he eats it up with a lick of his lips.

I pull in a long breath of air, the scent of my pack mates mixing with the musky smell down here in the basement. It brings a short-lived comfort, and I force myself to unclench my jaw and relax my shoulders. Enjoy this. Just for a second.

"What's left to do?" I ask, knowing full well that we're in the end stages. An uncomfortable silence hovers in the air, the weight of the question sinking like a lead weight.

Felix raises an eyebrow, and Gavril peers between me and the sigil.

"Just the ceremony," Felix mutters. "Are we in a good position to organize it?"

I toy with the sharp edges of my teeth with the tip of my tongue. I knew I would have to tell them sooner or later, but that doesn't soothe the ache.

Felix steps forward, folding his arms across his middle as he frowns at me. "Viktor?"

They both knew the ceremony would be risky, given our recent acquirement of Somnium and the contracts. It's a crime for our species to master slaves. If we get caught with our panties around our ankles, we could be up for execution before we even mention the ceremony.

"We have an issue," I admit finally, succumbing to the infinite swell of dread that comes along with it.

"Does it have red hair and a great ass?" Gavril chips in, his usual dirty humor missing its lighthearted charm.

I nod, loosening my tie and undoing the top button of

my shirt. "When Felix took the contracts, we found ourselves in deep shit. We know that. We've accepted it and, for the most part, we've tried to move past it."

"But we're at a point now where moving past it isn't an option anymore. Right?" Felix replies, leaning his back against the dusty basement wall.

"We either fix the issue of the contracts or we can't move forward with the ceremony." I'm tiptoeing around the real issue here. It's not all the contracts that I'm worried about, it's just one in particular. I recall the feeling I had when looking over the demonic text in Lyra's contract. Remember the overwhelming sense of apprehension when the words were revealed to me. All of the controls and constraints written into her personal contract that weren't found in any of the others. The acceptance that perhaps there is a chance Lyra is one of us.

As much as I recoil at the possibility, it still sits there in the forefront of my mind, willing me to find answers.

"So we fix the contracts, and fast. Easy peasy," Gavril says with a shrug. "Lemon squeezy."

Felix and I both eye him with impatience. It's not the time for lightheartedness.

Gavril must sense the tension because he raises his eyebrows. "Or are we looking more like difficult pifficult lemon squifficult?"

I pinch the bridge of my nose, attempting to find some semblance of calm. "If you take anything seriously, Gavril, can you make it this? I beg you to just plan your words in your head, repeatedly and silently, before you decide to grace us with their presence."

"Copy that," Gavril mumbles, pursing his lips as he attempts to hold back a smile.

"Lyra's contract is different from the others," I begin. Felix perks up, stepping closer.

"Different how?" he asks with a scowl, studying my expression for any hint of a clue.

"I managed to decipher some demonic text that wasn't present in the other contracts. There were details there that have me concerned."

Nobody speaks, even Gavril remains quiet.

"Dominic has been siphoning power from her to maintain the spells over Somnium, making it bigger on the inside, the portal between the strip club and the Dream Lounge. All of that was powered by the magic he was stealing from her. Or at least, he was, until we acquired her contract." I pause, planning my next words very carefully. "The amount of time she's been under his thumb and the amount of power she must have to maintain Somnium's protections means there are only a few options as to what species she is."

"Dragon," Felix breathes, gray eyes wide and sparkling. "She could be a dragon."

I swallow, having predicted that Felix would come to this conclusion. He's made it clear how he feels about her. The pull he senses between them. It's no secret that this would be Felix's dream come true. The only problem is, if this is the case, it's closer to a nightmare.

"When I visited Somnium to retrieve the contracts, I found something else that may be further proof she's one of our kind." Felix is about to speak, but I hold up my hand. "Before we jump to conclusions, I've been in touch with Igor. He's looking into the Byzantine Flight."

"The Byzantine Flight?" Gavril asks. "How did you connect the Lyra dot to the Byzantine Flight dot? Pretty farfetched, don't you think?"

"Let him tell us what he found at Somnium," Felix whispers, expression stark and unblinking.

"A betrothal gift," I reply, squaring my shoulders as I try to regain control over my posture. "Lyra mentioned it was her mother's."

"It wasn't just any old betrothal gift, was it?" Felix pushes. "It was a dragon's."

Gavril looks as if he's watching a game of tennis, his focus switching back and forth between Felix and me.

"If she has a dragon's betrothal gift, there's no doubt about it, Viktor," Gavril states matter-of-factly, maintaining his usual demeanor.

"Or her mother was a thief," I retaliate, the words coming out sharper than I had intended. A large part of me wants to trust my upbringing. The understanding that no dragon flies beneath the radar. The council knows every dragon ever born. There's no way Lyra could have gone undocumented for her entire life without setting off alarm bells.

Except that the clauses in her contract with Dominic would do just that. She fell into her snare shortly after she left the orphanage that raised her. Dragons reach physical maturity before they come into their magic, so it's possible she was years, possibly even decades, away from her powers appearing. As a survival tactic, one meant to keep dragon younglings safe until they can defend themselves. But if Dominic got to her in that window of vulnerability, forced her to live in secrecy...hidden away behind the walls of Somnium...

"We need to tell the council," Felix adds, excitement turning his cheeks pink. My sweet boy, always erring on the side of hope. I hate to crush him like this. To stomp on his dream of finding his fated mate. But I must.

"If Lyra is a dragon, and the council finds out she willingly sold her soul to Dominic, she's dead. We'll be lucky if they don't slaughter her on the spot, but it's the same outcome if they drag her back to Siberia and put her through a farce of a trial. And it's not just her that'll suffer the same injustice. We took on the contracts from Somnium, Felix. We agreed to become masters of slaves, and that too is punishable by death." I pause, letting the words sink in as the tension in the room becomes almost stifling. "Nothing good can come of this."

"But good did come of it."

I expect the words from Felix, but not from Gavril. His stance has changed, and now he's slunk down. Any hint of confidence and tomfoolery has dissipated.

"We found Lyra," he adds. "I know you have your issues with her, Vik, but she's good for us. Her broken pieces and ours, they fit."

"Fuck the ceremony." Felix laughs, shaking his head. "We go rogue. We don't waste any more time on this leyline bullshit and we disappear."

"Felix," I warn, stunned that he'd be willing to throw years' worth of hard work down the drain if it meant we could keep Lyra as ours.

"You feel it too and you're a fucking bullshit liar if you say otherwise!" Felix screams, voice cracking. He mutters something indiscernible in French, pacing the room back and forth as he fists at his blond hair.

"We wait for Igor to come back with more information," I say, approaching Felix with caution and setting my hands on both of his arms. He stills, just long enough to lock his wide eyes with mine.

"We don't rush to make decisions. We've worked hard for this life we have built, and if there is a way for us to achieve our goals and keep Lyra safe, then I promise you, we will do it. But until then, we have to keep ourselves in check."

Gavril sighs, fingers toying with his beard. I watch as he plucks at the wiry hairs, a nervous habit he's had for years.

"So we wait," Gavril adds, stepping toward us and wrapping an arm around our shoulders.

"I won't let anything happen to her." Felix's words settle between the three of us. "Or us."

It's a promise. Or a thinly veiled threat. Whichever one it is, I know that all three of us feel it as deeply in our bones as we do our love for each other.

CHAPTER 35

Lyra

It's been a few days since I poured my heart out to Felix at the restaurant, and I've felt a little unbalanced ever since. I'd never been inclined to let my guard down like that before. The kiss we shared hasn't left my mind either. The way his lips felt on mine. The rush of warmth and comfort he provided was like nothing I've experienced. I've thought about it over and over again, so much so that it's kept me up at night, longing for more.

But since then, it's felt as though he's pulled back. Instead, throwing himself into finishing decorating my room. We haven't spoken. Haven't even looked at each other since the kiss. And I think that hurts more than anything else.

I gulp down the tumbler of ice-cold water Viktor laid out for me on the counter, along with a handful of homemade pecan granola and a banana. The note he left for me specifically asked that I use a bowl this time around, but I take great joy in leaving crumbs of granola and a banana peel on top of his elegant cursive writing.

I've barely set the glass down on the counter when my vision goes black. Warm, soft hands cover my eyes and as I go to swing an elbow back, I take one panicked breath, my lungs filling with familiar jasmine that melts all my fear and worries.

"Felix, what are you—" My words die in my throat as he presses his lips against my ear.

"I have a surprise for you," he whispers gently, the comforting heat of his breath on my skin causing the hairs to rise at the back of my neck.

Excitement wells up in my chest, a burst of unexpected child-like glee. "Is my room ready?"

His chest is pressed flush against my back, and I feel the push and pull of his muscles as he nods. "Wanna see?"

A grin spreads across my face as I hop down from the stool and follow his lead. Felix keeps his body close to mine, hand still over my eyes as he walks us to my room. I hate to admit that I've missed him, but to my relief, it seems that any awkwardness over our kiss has dissipated.

Our footsteps walk in time with each other, bare feet padding against the floor until Felix brings us to a halt. "Keep your eyes closed, okay?"

I nod as his hands leave my eyes, clenching my eyelids shut despite being desperate to be back in control of my senses. That's the thing with Felix. Even though I've spent years promising myself that I wouldn't trust another person, he makes me yield with just the sound of his soothing voice.

"Just a few more steps," he urges as the door clicks open. He sets his large palms on the curve of my hips as he moves us off the hardwood floors and onto a fluffy carpet.

"Can I open them yet?" I ask, breathless with anticipation.

He offers me a squeeze of my hips before the contact is gone.

His body shifts past mine before he announces, "Go ahead. Open your eyes."

Bright light floods in through the huge windows, sheer

coral curtains letting the sunshine through the thick panes of glass while the material pools on the neutral-colored carpet. I swallow as my eyes move over the room. There's a row of rattan drawers that line one wall, topped with succulents and candles. The walls are half painted white, the other half in a shade of forest green that's so similar to the plants that I gasp. It feels like the desert. All sandy hues, with splashes of subtle color. I step forward, eyes trained on the bed draped with numerous thick blankets and plump throw pillows. There's a set of two keys sitting on the bedside table, and I look to Felix in question.

"The silver one is for your door, and the little one is for the fireproof lockbox in the closet. Viktor suggested that, so you can have a place to put anything you want to keep safe. And you have the only key," Felix rambles, shuffling his feet.

The implications of that don't hit me right away, but the wave crashes, and I have to look away so Felix doesn't see the tears in my eyes. On the wall behind the headboard, that's laden with books and lit up with a salt lamp, is a selection of three simple paintings. All done on white paper with blank ink or paint. They're all simple curves and gentle swoops and it takes me a few seconds to realize they look like a woman, voluptuous and feminine.

"I did those," Felix says quietly, clearing his throat. I'd almost forgotten he was in here with me. "It's you."

My neck snaps around to look at him. There's the hint of a blush at the tops of his cheekbones and his eyes are trained on the floor.

"You...drew me?" I ask in disbelief.

Felix nods, just once. "I couldn't find any art I liked. Even tried going through Vik's dealer, but there was nothing that felt like..." His voice trails off as I take a few steps toward him. "Nothing that felt like you."

"I've never had anything like this before." My mind can't focus on any one thing. Every time I look at something, I see something else. It's a blur of greens and corals, desert and lush forest.

"It wasn't a problem," Felix says, dismissing my words. "I actually enjoyed doing it. I might give Viktor a run for his money in the interior decorating department."

I shake my head. "I don't think you understand. I've never had my own space before. My own room."

Felix ruffles his white hair and smiles coyly. "So, you like it?"

I'm too deep in my head to even register his question, a surprised laugh escaping my parted lips. I went from the orphanage to working for Dominic, but even before Somnium was built, I'd had to share sleeping quarters with at least one other person. Having this, a space of my own, a space that feels so inherently *me* almost overwhelms me. No prison cell could ever feel this welcoming, down to the smallest details. My eyes meet Felix's. We're a few feet apart and he's chewing on his bottom lip with his sharp white teeth.

"If there's anything you want to cha—" His words give way to an audible gasp when I throw myself at him. My arms wrap around his neck, my face buried against his shoulder. I balance as best I can on the tips of my toes, breathing in waves of his earthy jasmine scent as tears well in my eyes.

"Thank you," I sigh, as my lips settle against his soft skin, his pulse battering against them.

Without thinking, I open my mouth and kiss that sweet spot where I feel his heartbeat. He audibly groans, arms coming to circle my middle as he hoists me up off the floor and lifts my legs to settle on his sharp hips. I'm about to move, torn away from my innocent thank you by the warmth pooling in the pit of my stomach. Nerves swell inside me, making my own heart race to keep up with what's happening. Felix's jasmine gives way to sweet, toasted oats and cinnamon. He smells like the home I never had.

I reluctantly lift my face away from his shoulder to stare at him. Our eyes are level, both wide and disbelieving. That first kiss is nothing compared to this. Everything inside me is melting and mixing with everything that makes Felix, *Felix*. His large hand trails up my side, across my chest, over my throat, until he buries his fingers in my hair. My mouth clamps down on his, a clash of tongue and teeth, until he's walking us backwards.

The backs of his knees hit the bed, and he crumbles down against the mattress, holding me on top of him without breaking our kiss. Heat blooms between my legs, and I feel the slickness coat my panties. Beneath me, he's hard. Rock solid as he presses up into my core. There's too much between us, too many layers keeping us apart. I want to rip at his clothes, want to christen my brand-new bed with the taste and feel of every inch of him. The wafts of lavender from the scented candles are nice, but it's not what I want my new room to smell of. I want his scent everywhere, on the bed, the sheets, my skin, inside me.

Felix's tongue tangles with mine, sucking me further and further in as I roll my hips against him. I've never felt so blindly out of control. So desperate, so wanting. My hands travel up his chest, clawing at the flimsy cotton t-shirt he's wearing until I can grasp at his neck. Beneath my wandering fingers, his heart flutters, and he swallows deeply, Adam's apple bobbing as though he's fighting for air.

He tears his mouth from mine, gently tugging my head back by my hair so that our lips are just a breath apart. "We can't do this."

"Why?" I whine, running my tongue across the seam of his kiss-swollen lips.

"There's a reason," he argues, capturing my tongue in his mouth and sucking. "I just can't think when all I can smell is you." On the last word, he flips us, leaving my legs spread wide beneath him. My pelvis tilts and curls, begging him for the lightest amount of pressure.

"What do you smell?" I ask breathlessly. His head falls between my breasts, his back arched beneath my touch.

A growl simmers low in his throat and he shakes his

white-blond hair. "Sea salt and brown sugar caramel, poured over sour green apples." His mouth opens, teeth clamping down on the thin material of my cami and releasing it with a snap. "French vanilla, soaked in warm milk. So fucking warm. Soft. Everything."

I mewl beneath him, hands settling on his narrow waist as we writhe like horny teenagers atop the sheets. His palms grip at my ribcage, riding farther up until his thumbs are on either side of my breasts. Hot breath fans across my covered skin, his face roving farther down as he scatters open-mouthed kisses across my stomach. Even through the thin material, I can feel the moisture of his mouth as he sucks and licks every millimeter he covers. My hands tremble as they bury themselves in the sheets beneath me. When Felix reaches the bare skin where my cami meets my sweats, he pauses.

"If I don't stop now, I'll never stop. I'll drink you dry," he pants, his voice taking on a new air of desire as his words mix with the growls rumbling in his throat.

"Then don't stop," I plead, pushing off the bed in the hope that he'll put that mouth exactly where I want it. He dips lower, until his face is between my thighs, and he pulls in a never-ending breath.

"I have to, *petite étincelle*."

The warmth disappears, and I look down to find Felix staring up at me from between my thighs. "I need to know that when I take you, I get to keep you." His silver eyes plead with mine.

Panic rises in my chest. He wants to keep me, like a bird in a cage. No. Not when I've just begun to taste what freedom could really be like.

"I can't give that to anybody," I reply sharply, pushing myself up the bed and holding my legs to my chest. The distance has my head clearing, has the feelings of lust and want floating away like dandelions in the wind.

Felix stands up, stepping away from the mattress. His cock is tenting his sweats, but you wouldn't know it from looking at his face. Pain taints his delicate features, and he swallows heavily. "A man can dream that perhaps that will change."

I shake my head, pressing my face into my knees to avoid looking at him. "No." I pause, ignoring the bitter sting of tears in my eyes. "I could never promise all of my heart to anyone. After everything that's happened...there's just not enough of it left."

But if that were really true, then I wouldn't feel the shattering of that stupid, blackened, shriveled, worthless organ in my chest as he walks away, closing my door softly behind him.

CHAPTER 36

GAVRIL

As is my norm for a weekend, I roll out of my pit at eleven and slump onto a stool at the breakfast bar, hoping that the coffee machine would spit out an espresso all on its own. Coffee is Viktor's secret passion project, and he normally makes enough for everyone. But with the carafe empty, and a pounding caffeine headache building, I have no other choice than to figure it out. I just manage to slip a pod in the obnoxious contraption, when I hear the gentle pad of bare feet on the floor.

"Oh." An apathetic voice, groggy with sleep, sounds from behind me, and I turn away from the coffee machine just long enough to catch a glimpse of Lyra. She's standing with her arms crossed beneath her ample bust, the large t-shirt she's swimming in doing nothing to disguise the round curves of her hips and nip of her waist. Pale, bare legs peek out from beneath the simple cotton, showing off a few delicate freckles spattered across the ivory like constellations.

"Coffee?" I ask, clearing my throat as I slip a cup beneath

the spout and push what I hope is the right button. The machine whirs and hisses before the divine scent of rich coffee fills my nose. Despite trying to stay calm, the minute Lyra steps closer, and I catch a whiff of her shampoo, my stomach clenches. We've never lived in such close proximity to a woman. Shit, we've never even had a woman in this penthouse apart from the odd maid or occasional escort. But this isn't just any woman.

This little ball of chaos and violence has turned my pack's entire world upside down in a matter of a few short weeks. And if Felix is right about her, then she's not going anywhere any time soon. I could almost picture what that version of the future could be. Lyra on patrol in the casino, helping to find the cheats and scammers who think they could outsmart us. Eating dinner together, and then taking her to bed to fuck her to sleep.

Ah, shit. I just popped a fucking boner over morning coffee.

"Please," Lyra sighs, bringing me back to reality with a thump.

She brushes past me and walks over to the fridge. It takes a second for her to figure out how to open it, but when she does, her frown deepens.

"What the fuck is this?" She stomps her feet, puffing a stray strand of red hair from in front of her mouth and turning her scowl in my direction.

"Sorry, were you expecting Felix's balls on a platter?" I chuckle, and she shoots me a look that could drop a man dead.

"Fuck you. What is all this crap?" Her hand disappears into the refrigerator and reappears a second later with a bag of spinach.

"That is a vegetable," I quip as she tosses the bag over her shoulder in the hunt for something more appealing. "A leafy green, to be exact. Excellent source of iron."

"I get my iron from stout like a normal person," she scoffs, picking up a carton of blueberries and staring at it like they're an alien lifeform.

"Explains why you're so pale," I mutter, passing her a cup of steaming coffee.

"Aren't you supposed to be meat eaters? Where's the bacon? Everything in here is pre-food!" Lyra takes a single sip of the espresso before gagging like she's swallowed raw sewage. She slams the coffee down on the breakfast bar and kicks the fridge door shut in her fury. Releasing a high-pitched squeal that's loud enough to rival a banshee, she starts jumping up and down on one foot, her hands reaching down to nurse what I presume is a stubbed toe.

"You are a fucking liability." I laugh, reaching forward and picking her up with ease. She squirms, slapping at my shoulders until I plonk her ass down on the counter.

She draws in a breath and stares down at me from her perch. Well, sort of. The cabinets were built extra tall for mine and Viktor's comfort, but she's so small that it hardly makes much of a difference. We're just about eye to eye, but she's looking down her nose at me with such disdain that I feel six inches tall. And my God, does that make my cock throb. I slump my shoulders, trying my best to shrink, but I'm not exactly pocket-sized.

Lyra grumbles and shifts petulantly. "What is it with you dicks just picking me up and throwing me around? Contrary to popular belief, I'm a person, not a plaything."

"Oh, but you make such a pretty plaything," I tease, smiling up at her, a hand resting on either side of her.

Without a second thought, she sends an open palm flying against my face. It cracks on my cheekbone, echoing through the open kitchen. Her face falls, lips opening and closing like a fish out of water, as if she's trying to come up with something to fill the silence.

A purr settles deep in my chest, rumbling beneath her hand as it slips down from my face, over my throat, until it eventually settles against my racing heart.

"Would you like me to make you breakfast?" I ask, toying

with the hem of her t-shirt as excitement buzzes at the tips of my fingers.

"The big bad dragon wants to play chef now?" she says through gritted teeth, but her expression has softened, leaving her looking younger and oddly more fragile. I'm not sure I like it.

"If you want food, too, I can do that. But I know something I'd like better," I toss back, trying to get her hackles back up. Anything except this exhausted, defeated frown.

She doesn't reengage, though. She just stares at her hand over my heart, like it's suddenly started speaking in riddles.

"Slap me again," I suggest, squaring up to her a little.

Lyra raises one ginger eyebrow. "Excuse me?"

"It made you feel better, didn't it?" I add calmly. "You're mad we have no food and only fancy ass coffee. Hell, we grabbed you and transported you here without your permission. We've apparently done nothing but make you furious for weeks on end. Slap me. Take it out on me. Trust me, I'll enjoy it as much as you will."

She shoves her hands against my chest, but I remain stoic. "Go on, you know you want to. Hit me. Treat me like a little fucking bitch and show me just how big and strong you are."

Her confusion is palpable, but there's a dark twinkle in her eye, as if the temptation is too much.

"I'm not going to hit you. Do you think I'm that stupid to fall for that crap? You'll be on the phone crying to Daddy the second my fist touches your nose."

I try to disguise my smile, flicking my tongue out to run over my bottom lip as I fantasize about all the ways this woman could ruin me. "Ah, so you figured out all on your own that Viktor loves that Daddy shit, huh?"

A blush spreads up Lyra's neck, lighting up her features and settling into a deep crimson across her cheeks.

"Don't go shy on me now, princess." I lean forward, my lips so close to her ear, I can almost taste the velvety skin.

"Those dirty boys have been pushing and pulling, vying for your attention every minute of the day. Begging for just a taste of you. But I'm the only one who's willing to get down on his knees."

"Then do it," she whispers, pushing her chest against mine.

"What? What do you want me to do?" My cock is straining against the confines of my sweatpants, moisture beading at the tip as my breaths come in short rasps.

Lyra, with mischief in her gaze, pushes against my chest and points one elegant finger to the floor. "Get on your fucking knees."

CHAPTER 37

Lyra

The heady rush of power that sings through my veins as I watch Gavril, the hulking brute, who has proven over and over again that he can manhandle me without breaking a sweat, sink to his knees before me, makes my head spin. My blood comes alive like I've never experienced before, not with any of the men I've talked into my bed. His ocean eyes stare up at me, waiting.

I spread my thighs just slightly on the counter, leaning back as best as I can. Gavril purrs, honest to God, *purrs*, as he realizes I'm only wearing thin cotton panties below my sleep shirt. But he doesn't move, doesn't even blink, as he watches my hand pull the hem of my shirt up and out of the way before trailing back to my core and stroking the growing damp patch.

"Is this what you want, big guy? To have a taste of this for breakfast?" I coo, not sure where the words are coming from, but going with it because they just feel *right.*

Gavril swallows and pants, licking his lips as his eyes follow my fingers. "Yes. I want to taste you."

I hum as another little spark of power flows through me. Gavril wasn't entirely wrong; my head has been six kinds of fucked since the dragons barged into my life and upended everything. But I don't need to beat the shit out of him to feel like myself. I need to be back in the driver's seat of my own fucking life, even for just a few minutes. And if I get a few orgasms out of the deal, all the better.

Whimpering, I slip a finger under the now soaked fabric of my panties, teasing my entrance without revealing it to my captive audience. I'm wet and aching already, and we've hardly begun to play. God, it's been too long. But I want to live in this moment for as long as I can. So as I withdraw a single finger, shiny with my essence, and hold it out for Gavril. I conjure up my best holier-than-thou glare and lift my chin.

"Have a taste then, you pathetic, thirsty snake," I sneer, only feeling the tiniest bit of guilt for laying it on so thick.

But Gavril doesn't care. If anything, he seems to enjoy my insults far more than any sane person ought to. He clambers forward, taking my finger in his mouth and palming himself through his sweats, eyes rolling back in his head as he closes his lips around the digit. His tongue runs up and down the length, and I can't help the gasp as I feel the smooth, round ball of a piercing against my skin.

"You taste so good, so fucking good. Please, I need more. Let me taste your perfect pussy, please," Gavril begs between obscene sucking, his determination to get every microscopic drop of my cream from my skin admirable, and unbelievably hot.

"Get your hand off your dick, and maybe I'll believe you," I snap, pulling my hand away and grabbing a fistful of his hair.

He puts his hands behind his back, the movement so fast I almost don't pick up on it. I pull hard, cranking Gavril's head back until he gasps and moans. Glancing down, I swallow roughly as I see the outline of his fully erect cock against the thin material of his pants. And fuck me...if I didn't know any better, I would have thought he had a whole ass can of spray paint in his pocket. But no, he's just *very* happy to see me.

"Please, Mistress. Let me taste you, let me make you feel good. I need to feel you come on my tongue, even just once. Please."

Gavril's fervent plea catches me off guard. I've never been addressed as mistress before and I can't decide if it's fucking weird as hell or if maybe, just maybe, I kinda like it. Nevertheless, despite the surprise, it draws my eyes back up to his face, and I'm stunned into silence by the absolute vulnerability sparkling in his midnight eyes. There's no ulterior motive pulling at his features, nothing in his expression except sincere, uncomplicated desperation. My heart kicks in my chest, flipping and flopping with desire and excitement. I've never had a man look at me like that, and I can hardly stand it.

So instead, I lean back and use my grip on his hair to pull his mouth to my core.

I close my eyes and tilt my head back as Gavril goes to work, not wasting a single moment. He uses his teeth, suddenly much longer than they had been a moment ago, and shreds the crotch of my panties, leaving me exposed to his mouth. My usual hookups don't typically involve a lot of foreplay, and if anything, I'm the one on my knees giving head. But this...this is something a girl could get used to.

He licks and sucks and moans like he's a man on death row and my cunt is his last meal before execution. Simultaneously ravenous and reverent, he explores thoroughly to find the places that make my toes curl before focusing his undivided attention on them. I feel the ball of his tongue piercing as it flicks over my clit, the difference between metal and flesh somehow enhancing my pleasure rather than distracting me from it. Before I know what's happened, I'm on the edge of release, hanging on by a thread.

"I'm going to soak your fucking face with my come, and you're going to drink every drop, you hear me?" I pant, legs shaking as I clamp them around his ears, hanging on for dear life.

His response is a muffled groan, and a renewed focus on my pleasure spots, alternating between flicking my clit and fucking me deep with his thick, muscular tongue. My chest heaves, and I feel the sweat pooling on my back as my voice climbs higher and louder. And then, all at once, he bites down on my pleasure bud, and I crack, shattering into a million dazzling pieces. He purrs again, the vibrations adding to the symphony of pleasure ringing through my body. And he doesn't stop then, doesn't let up as I crest one wave, quickly building me back up to a second.

"Gav...oh, fuck, I can't," I moan, releasing his head and falling back onto my elbows as my whole body shakes.

"More, *prelepa vatra*. Give me more," Gavril growls, the words low and deep, like they're echoing up from the depths of an ancient cavern.

One of his arms bands around my thigh, stopping me from escaping even as he slides two fingers into my spasming entrance, twisting and curling them at just the right spot to make me gasp and arch off the marble. I reach out, trying to find anything to hang on to, but there's nothing within arm's reach, leaving me exposed as pleasure spills over me again, another orgasm spreading like molten gold through my veins.

"Please let me fuck you, *prelepa vatra*. I'm so fucking hard for you. Please," Gavril pants, finally slowing his onslaught to work me down from my high.

Twisting around, I find him looming over me, eyes wide with anticipation. I look away, not exactly pleased that I let him take my control away again, but too blissed out for the moment to care. Especially as he slows his fingers to a rolling, leisurely pace, like he's using my pussy as some sort of fidget toy while his mind is elsewhere. I glance around, a grin spreading across my cheeks as I spot the perfect location.

"Clear the table, and then lie down. On your back," I command, lifting my chin.

Gavril leans in for a kiss, but I turn my cheek. He hasn't

earned that yet, especially after taking liberties. He kisses my neck and nips at it slightly, sending a shiver down my spine before he pulls away and rushes around the breakfast bar. I catch my breath for a moment, shoving aside the suddenly empty feeling in my core, and the longing for the bulk of another body on top of me before I have to look too closely. Swinging my legs around, I crawl over the breakfast bar as I watch Gavril carefully remove the place settings and table cloth, revealing a massive slab of thick glass. Strong enough to support both of us. Perfect.

Gavril carefully picks up the centerpiece, something glass and definitely antique, and goes to move it away before I clear my throat, halting him in his tracks. A deviant little grin pulls at the corners of my mouth, and he swallows.

"Smash it," I order, settling on my heels with my knees spread, giving him just a peek at the patch of curls at the apex of my thighs.

Gavril hesitates, looking between me and the centerpiece. I scoff and roll my eyes. "You want to smash it for me, don't you, big guy? If you do, I'll let you come inside me," I coo, tapping into my well of charm and laying it on thick for a moment, batting my eyelashes and everything.

Without another second of thought, Gavril lifts the piece over his head and spikes it into the marble floor, sending glass in every direction. God, I hope that was expensive and irreplaceable. Viktor will probably have my ass on a platter later, but right now, I couldn't give less of a fuck. Especially as Gavril sheds his clothes like they're on fire and climbs up onto the table, cock nearly purple and throbbing as it sticks straight up.

I shed my shirt and what's left of my panties, glad I decided to go braless, and pad across the space, careful of the broken glass. The table doesn't even shudder as I climb on a chair and then onto the slick surface, moving to stand with one foot on either side of his hips. He looks up at me, hands twitching at his sides, and I swear I see little white sparks dancing between his fingers. But I get distracted by the absolute magnificence of his cock. Thick and long, with ridges running up the underside and a barbell pierced through just below the head. At the base, I blink as I see the beginnings of what I think is a knot starting to form. Huh. Didn't know dragons have knots. But good to know, especially if I want to torture him a little next time. I can see now that Gavril's nipples are pierced too, little silver rings catching the light as he pants.

"Please…" Gavril rasps, trailing off as he struggles to stay still.

"Please, what?" I tease, drawing out the game for just a moment longer.

"Please fuck me, Mistress. Use my cock to make yourself come. Please–"

His begging ends with an abrupt shout as I drop to my knees, grab his cock by the base and hover above him, rubbing the head along my slick folds. The muscles in his neck bulge as he strains not to touch me, and I laugh, lifting my hips and sliding the tip of his cock inside of me. The stretch is incredible. I've had some big guys, wolf shifters mostly, but none of them has ever felt like this before. Each ridge that slips inside of me feels like magic against my nerves, as if my body was made to receive pleasure from this specific form of dick. I only take about half of him before I withdraw, and I moan long and low in my throat. If the ridges felt good going in, then they feel like heaven coming out.

"You can take it, *prelepa vatra*. You're so perfect, so tight, so wet. Thank you for fucking me, thank you," Gavril babbles, and I'm not even sure he knows what's coming out of his mouth, especially as he slips into another language I don't recognize.

The only sound for a few moments is our breathing as I work more and more of his impeccable dragon cock into me, until at last, I reach the base. His knot presses against my outer lips, fully swollen now, but I don't think I could take that on my best day, and if it's anything like a wolf shifter knot, then I don't want to be stuck on Gavril for God knows how long.

I lean forward and balance myself with my hands on his stomach so I can shift my hips, slowly at first, just to get a feel for what I'm working with. But all rational thought flies out the window as those damn ridges drag along sweet spots I didn't even know existed before. Stars burst behind my eyes, and I shout a string of curses at the ceiling, my body moving of its own accord.

"Can I touch you? Please?" Gavril moans, pulling me back down to earth for a moment.

I nod, hips stuttering as he reaches up and takes my breasts in his huge hands, massaging them just right, flicking and tweaking my nipples to add just that little bite of pain. We find a rhythm, the sound of our hips slapping together over and over, faster and faster, filling the air. I can lose myself in this, the simple act of two bodies coming together to seek mutual pleasure. And the pleasure that's building promises to be something mind blowing.

But a sudden sharp zap brings me back, and I snap my head down to stare at Gavril. His hands have moved to my hips, and are big enough that his thumbs can nearly brush my clit. He's grinning up at me, his hips slowing. I open my mouth to question him, but then I see another little arc of electricity jump from his finger and across my skin. I squeak and squirm, my nerves feeling more sensitive, like he's plucking strings on a violin and leaving them vibrating with aftershocks.

"What the..." I start, trailing off in confusion.

"Want me to show you what my sparks are really good for?" Gavril asks, his cocky grin playful and less irritating now that he's inside me.

I nod, curiosity getting the better of me. I'm not disappointed as he traces his fingers along my skin, little jolts making the hairs on my arms stand on end. But it doesn't hurt, at least not in a bad way. He stays away from my heart and lungs, trailing over my stomach and lower until he deliberately bucks his hips, putting me off balance and needing to lean backward. One of his hands holds me back, and the other slides between my folds, finding my clit and circling. He doesn't make me do any of the work, fucking up into me as he works my clit and thrusts deep and slow, making my toes curl and eyes slide closed. A zap across my clit makes me jump, but I let out a long, loud moan as his thumb rubs away the hurt. I'm way more sensitive now, but he doesn't stop, shocking me over and over, even sending a jolt through his cock and into the walls of my pussy as he picks up speed again.

"Come for me, please. I want to feel you," Gavril moans, words distant as pleasure screams through me.

His hands grip my hips, helping me move faster, fuck harder than I ever have before in my life. I swear I can feel his cock bruising the undersides of my lungs, but it all feels so good, too good. I scream, coming hard and soaking us both in my release. He growls in response, a feral sound that only makes me smile as he holds me still, pounding into me from below. Wave after wave of pleasure crash over me, and I let my head hang back between my shoulders, my whole body singing with euphoria. I'm falling and soaring all at once, my mind free and light.

Another bolt of electricity makes me gasp and then he's coming, filling my channel with rope after rope of hot, thick cum. He slowly fucks himself through it, eyes shut tight against the pleasure, until all at once, he loses strength. I realize that he's been holding me up for the last several minutes, because as soon as he lets go, I flop down onto his chest, completely boneless and sated.

The top of my head only reaches his diaphragm, but I don't have the strength to move into a more comfortable position. As the thought occurs to me, though, Gavril is there, lifting me from his softened cock and pulling me up higher on his chest. I don't let myself think about the manhandling, but instead choose to focus on the thoroughly fucked ache appearing between my legs, and the warmth of his arms holding me close.

"I normally don't do after-sex cuddles," I murmur into the silence.

"Me neither. But we can try it once, see how it feels? If we hate it, we never have to do it again. Deal?" Gavril says, still a little breathless.

"Deal," I mumble.

I close my eyes just to rest for a minute, a grin spreading across my face. This has to be the first non-shouted, insult-less conversation we've had. And I have to admit, I don't hate it.

CHAPTER 38

I slam the back passenger door to the black SUV, slumping into the backseat beside Viktor. Antony, our driver, pulls away from the building and heads down the lonely desert highway, silence filling the vehicle like chlorine gas. I'm not exactly displeased with today's chore, but every moment away from Lyra makes me twitchy.

"I'm glad Philip and Wilbur were agreeable to our terms. Having men like them in our organization will be quite beneficial, I think," Viktor says conversationally, sighing contentedly.

I grunt a response. We'd broken the minotaur's and the dwarf's contracts today, asking them to give us their miniscule savings in return for their freedom. Once Viktor deemed the act a "great sacrifice," the contract dissolved into a pile of dust on the table and we'd given the money back, along with offers for employment. As far as I'm aware, they are the only ones so far who've accepted the offer.

"One more to go," Viktor goes on.

"Two more," I correct lowly.

Viktor sighs and looks at me. I don't feel him trying to read my emotions, which surprises me. Not that he'd find much beyond my anxiety to get back to Vegas in a hurry.

"We aren't going to be able to break Lyra's contract this easily, Felix. We've discussed this be—"

I snap my head to him, cutting across his patronizing placation. "Yeah, I know we have. I just…"

I trail off, not sure how to finish that thought. I just want her free? True, but that's not all I'm feeling. But I don't dare think beyond that. I'm hopeful that my theory is correct, but I'd be a fool to lean too heavily on that hope. Even if Lyra is what I think she is, there's still a chance she could reject us. But I refuse to dwell on that possibility. We've still got a long way to go, but Lyra's seemed to settle in more lately. And that's something, right?

Viktor's about to respond, when his phone goes off. He answers, immediately switching to Russian, which simultaneously makes me melt and puts me on guard. There's something musical about the way he speaks his mother tongue, but he only does when he's talking to someone from home. And the short list of people who could be calling isn't full of friendly names.

The call is brief, and Viktor looks significantly more troubled as he lowers his phone to his lap, staring at the black screen.

"Who was that?" I ask, unable to contain my curiosity any longer.

Viktor jumps slightly, like I've startled him out of a memory, and then turns to look at me. There's moisture lining his jewel-tone eyes, and my jaw falls slack at the sight. But he blinks it away quickly, clearing his throat.

"Igor. I asked him to look into something for me, and he's just informed me of what he found," Viktor explains hoarsely.

I wait, raising my eyebrows slightly in silent prompting for him to go on. I don't know the historian as well as Viktor does, but I know he's trustworthy. Viktor hesitates, which only makes my heart twist.

"This is about Lyra?" I ask, though my tone suggests that the words are more of a statement than a question.

Viktor nods simply, and my stomach swoops. Just as he's about to respond, his phone goes off again. This time, Viktor's brow creases with annoyance as he pulls up the notification.

"Can't leave them alone for five minutes," he mutters under his breath, chuckling almost fondly.

"What's wrong? Is Lyra okay?" I ask, sitting up, attention recaptured.

"She's just fine. But I think you'll feel better once you see this," he says, turning the phone into landscape and passing it to me.

I'm about to object, but then my eyes go wide. It's the security feed from inside the penthouse, specifically overlooking the dining room table. In the middle of the table are Gavril and Lyra, both naked. He's on his back, with Lyra kneeling over him, one of her hands between them. My jaw drops as I watch her sinking slowly onto my pack mate's cock, eyes closed and lips slightly parted.

I'm instantly hard, my cock tenting the soft material of my jogging pants, and I can't help but moan as I watch the screen, completely entranced. Every inch of Lyra's skin is smooth, and I take great delight in studying the delicate freckles that cover her arms and stomach, the little scars that tell a story of a hard life. I'm looking at her from the side, but her profile is just as beautiful as the rest of her.

"How is it, *my heart*? Is our little house guest treating Gavril well?" Viktor asks, almost too casually.

Transfixed, I nod, as Lyra works herself up and down on Gavril's length. He's the thickest of us, but she's taking him like a champion. The volume is faint, but they aren't saying much, too focused on the race toward pleasure.

I jump as Viktor's hand strokes me, his touch proprietary in the best way. He owns me, mind, body, and soul, and he belongs to me and Gavril just as completely. I reach out to touch him, but he shushes me and nods to the screen.

"No, Felix. Let Daddy take care of you," he purrs, sliding off the seat and into the space between the seats at my knees.

I swallow and let out a shaky breath. This feels like a distraction, a way to avoid answering my questions about his call with Igor, but fuck me. It's not often that Viktor gets on his knees, so I'm not going to waste this. And being able to watch the woman who's got me wrapped around her little finger? Even better. His eyes sparkle like amethyst stars as he frees my cock, spreading my precum over the head with a thumb.

"You can take it, *beautiful flame*. You're so perfect, so tight, so wet. Thank you for fucking me, thank you. *I'm yours. Use me, just like that. Yes, beautiful flame. Yours, take me. I'm yours,*" Gavril babbles, a mix of English and his native Serbian.

I wonder what Lyra would say if she knew that the beast between her thighs is pledging himself to her cunt. Not that I blame him. I've dreamt of how she's going to feel when I finally get the chance to please her. I don't begrudge Gavril this, especially when it's clear by the way Lyra's face twists and bunches as he fucks her hard and deep that she's enjoying it.

"Fuck," I hiss, pulled from my thoughts as Viktor's mouth closes around my tip.

He chuckles, but doesn't pull away as he sucks, his tongue running along my ridges with each pass. He doesn't try to match Gavril and Lyra's pace–they're going too hard for that–but it's a perfect counterpoint. I can imagine us sitting in the living room, just off screen, watching as Lyra rides our pack mate, using him to chase her own pleasure. She'd smell like caramel cupcakes and sex, her perfect body shimmering with sweat.

Gavril begs to touch her, and I growl, even as she nods her permission. I wouldn't let him have that privilege without earning it. He'd bring her to climax at least twice before he would be able to touch her bouncing tits. Even better, Viktor and I would tie his hands to the table legs, leaving him stretched out for our pleasure. Lyra would fuck him until she was satisfied, and then Viktor and I would have our way with our pack mate. I'd make sure Lyra was seen to while Viktor plays his games. Maybe I'd fill her with my cum and make Gavril lick her clean before filling her again and again, each time letting our plaything clean up the mess Viktor and I make.

Viktor sucks me deeper than ever, and I have to stop myself from thrusting up into his mouth, bruising the back of his throat even as he swallows around me. His teeth drag along my length, adding just a hint of pain to enhance the pleasure. My crotch is soaked with his spit as he uses one hand to work what he doesn't have in his mouth. I fight to keep my eyes open, not wanting to miss a moment of what's happening on the screen and what's happening in front of me.

"Come for me, please. I want to feel you," Gavril moans, the desperation in his voice making me twitch between Viktor's lips.

I watch Lyra's face, determined not to even blink until she peaks. And I'm glad for it. The pup I watched her fuck not that long ago truly didn't know how to please a woman as special as Lyra, but Gavril is world's better than some dog. Her scream of pleasure is the music of the angels, making the hair on the back of my neck stand on end and my balls tighten. I can feel my own release just out of reach, each moment watching my little spark riding the wave, bringing me closer and closer.

But then I have to do a double take. My eyes go wide as I stare at Lyra, not watching her face, but the sudden shifting on the skin of her back. Gavril is holding her still as he pounds into her from below, lost in her body and the race toward orgasm. Neither of them aware of the scales appearing along the column of her spine. Elegant, blood-red scales, overlapping and shifting with her movement. And her eyes...the pupils...

"Viktor, stop. Look at this," I nearly shout, grabbing at his collar to get his attention.

He releases my cock with a *pop* that's frankly

pornographic, looking up at me with an annoyed glare.

"Watching is your thing, Felix. I was perfectly content to–"

"No, shut up and look!" Turning the phone around, I nearly shove it in his face.

He blinks and reels back, brow furrowed for a moment, before his lips part on a silent gasp. But then he blinks, shakes his head, and looks at me.

"I don't know what–"

"Lyra! Didn't you see her eyes? Her scales?" I demand, turning the phone around to look again.

Lyra is lying on Gavril's chest now, both catching their breath. One of his hands is running up and down her back, her completely smooth, scaleless back. I hit the pause button, bringing up the timeline of the recording and rewinding a few moments. Viktor tucks my softened cock away, and I catch the sullen frown pulling at his mouth. But my own pleasure hardly matters. Not when things are finally starting to make sense.

It takes me a couple of tries, but I let out a shout of triumph as I freeze the video at just the right moment. And I was right. Her eyes have shifted to a true gold, vertical pupils running through them as she stares at the ceiling, lost in ecstasy. And along her back, in a crisscross pattern, are definitely protective scales.

I turn the phone around and push it into Viktor's hands, watching his face closely. He stares and stares, not speaking and hardly blinking. The silence stretches on, and my heart hammers in my chest. I've had my suspicions for a while, but this all but confirms them. I knew she was special, knew she was more than just an orphan bartender. This connection I've been feeling means something, means everything.

"No. Trick of the light. There has to be some sort of reflection, something that's–"

"What the–are you serious? That's no trick!" I shout over Viktor's vehement denials.

"There's no way. She can't be–we'd know. Everyone is

accounted for, Felix. The council would know about her, would have brought her into a pack decades ago," Viktor goes on, shaking his head, even as he shoves his phone back into his pocket.

Everything Lyra told me over our pizza and pasta slides to the tip of my tongue, but I bite the words back. She told me those stories in confidence, and I won't ruin the progress I've made with her by spilling her darkest secrets just to win an argument.

"Denial isn't just a river in Egypt, you know," I mutter, turning to look out the window.

Viktor sighs heavily, and I don't even have to look to know he's pinching the bridge of his nose.

We don't speak for the rest of the ride back into the city. Viktor keeps pulling out his phone to look at the still from the security footage, staring at the scales over and over, like he thinks they're going to change one of these times. But I hardly care. My heart soars with triumph. I was right. Lyra is a dragon, just like us.

CHAPTER 39

GAVRIL

Fucking hell, that was insane. My naked body is still lying against the cool glass table, muscles twitching and spasming like I've just run a marathon. Lyra is settled atop me, her face against my chest as my hand runs lazy circles against her hip. She was relaxed for a while, a few moments that felt like the sweetest eternity. But now, I can feel her beginning to tense up as the realization sets in.

I don't want her to leap up and run from me, but I get the feeling that's exactly what she's about to do. I've never known anyone quite so skittish. She was just as into this as I was, but in the gray afternoon light, I can see the red tint of her flushed skin fading into pale regret.

My body sits up in time with hers. She's so small against me, her thick thighs tucked around my waist as she arches to get away from my touch.

"I can't do this," she mutters, blinking rapidly, like she's just woken up from a dream. My brain runs through all of the things I could possibly say to make her feel better, but in reality, I know the only thing that'll cure her nervousness is some distance. My large hands almost meet as I set them at her waist and gently lift her down off the table, making sure her bare feet don't come into contact with the broken glass littering the floor. Lyra stands there awkwardly, shuffling and attempting to cover herself up despite not having enough hands to keep her breasts and glistening pussy from my eager eyes.

"Why don't you take a shower," I suggest, spinning around so that my legs are flung over the edge of the table. "I'll take care of all this."

She is silent and unsure as she nods. On clumsy legs, she stumbles away from me, giving me a great view of her plump ass before she disappears into her bedroom. I'm pussy whipped. There's no point in denying it. My traitorous stomach is doing little flips as my mind casts back to how Lyra looked above me. The way her pretty pussy swallowed up my cock with ease and the expression on her face. Lips parted while she panted and moaned. It didn't feel like she was putting on a show. It felt raw and natural, like I was simply her throne to sit atop.

I stop myself just short of a girlish sigh and hop down off the table. Picking up bundles of discarded clothing, I pause when I find Lyra's torn underwear next to one of the stools at the breakfast bar. I bring the simple cotton to my face and inhale, her lingering scent of smoky salted caramel and heady vanilla already starting to wane. Still, I make a mental note to keep these panties as a reminder.

Just as I'm tugging on my sweatpants, a shrill ringing sounds from my pocket and I fumble with tingling hands as I hit the answer button.

"We need to talk," Viktor announces simply on the other end, his voice gravelly and urgent.

I lean my elbows against the marble counter. "Miss me already?" My lips twitch with a smile.

"Is Lyra there?" Felix's question comes from somewhere

just distant enough that I instantly know he's listening in from Viktor's side.

"What's the prob, boys?" I might not be the smartest of the three of us, but I can sense there's something wrong. There are only two reasons why they call me during daylight hours; either there's someone I need to take care of, or I'm in trouble. I'm too sated to imagine all the ways I might be about to get punished, so I don't bother to tease them like I usually do.

"We need to talk. Get to my study and wait there. We'll be back in ten." Viktor is all business, which isn't unusual for him. What is strange is that he doesn't wait for my answer before hanging up. I stand in the kitchen frowning at myself, my brain cloudy from sex and working at a relative snail's pace, unlike its normal steam train chug.

Nevertheless, I walk over to Viktor's study and open the door. Closing it behind me, I perch on the edge of a too-small leather chair on the opposite side of his antique swiveling counterpart.

Ten minutes pass slowly and when I hear the front door click open and footsteps approaching, I start flicking tendrils of electricity from finger to finger. It's a nervous habit, but I revel in the gentle tickle of distraction it offers me. Viktor walks in first, unbuttoning his suit jacket and ruffling a hand back through his perfectly styled hair. He's silent as he takes a seat behind his desk and opens his laptop.

Felix follows second, slipping the door shut behind him. His dark hoodie is pulled up over his head, leaving just a few disobedient tendrils of white-blond hair peeking out over his forehead. Oddly, he avoids my eyes and hovers in the corner of the room, trying to disappear against the walnut bookshelves.

"Anyone mind telling me what's going on, or can I expect a riveting game of charades in just a few moments?" I ask finally, unable to take the heavy silence any longer.

Viktor lifts his chin and ponders for a second, violet eyes twinkling. "Felix, how do you say in charades 'don't fuck the houseguest?'"

"Depends, is it a book? Movie?" Felix mocks as my stomach drops.

Viktor shakes his head, his fingers drumming against his chin. "No, just a dragon who can't keep his dick in his pants for longer than five fucking minutes."

I suck my lips into my mouth as I try to hide a wide grin, but it falters a few seconds later. "Wait, how'd you know?"

"You broke my vase," Viktor sighs, typing furiously against the keyboard before he spins the screen toward me. My focus settles on the image of Lyra riding me, clear as day. There's no denying it.

"To be fair, Vik, you should thank them for that. It was a hideous vase." Felix chuckles, white teeth toying with the sleeve of his hoodie.

Viktor tilts his head to the side and sighs. "Not the fucking point."

"Listen, it just kind of happened. What do you want me to say? I'll buy you a new ugly vase."

"Not the point, Gav," Viktor replies. "Look at this."

We all huddle around the laptop as he presses play. The sound is down, but the image as it plays out is enough to get me hard all over again. Fuck, she's majestic.

"There," Felix snaps, lunging forward to slap the space bar and pause the video.

"That ass, right?" I smirk. "Fucking glorious."

"You can see it, can't you?" Felix's attention is on Viktor, who is poised just inches from the screen as his eyes roam over Lyra's pale skin and the pattern of freckles glittering at the base of her spine.

Red freckles.

My head cranes to the side. "They're not freckles."

"You're a genius, Gav. Really." Viktor zooms in on the image, making it blurry but not unreadable.

"Scales. I told you," Felix adds. "I fucking *told* you."

"Why would Lyra have scales?" I whisper, not expecting a direct answer.

"The feelings I've had, the feelings I know you guys have felt. That need to protect her? To covet her?" Felix has marched away from the computer screen, pacing up and down the room. "She's ours. She's a dragon and she's ours."

I look to Viktor and wait for his response to this whole situation. Of all of us, he's been the most skeptical of this "Lyra is a dragon" idea. But here we are with undeniable proof. And he's silent, staring at the image as if he can light it on fire.

"Is this what Igor told you on that call?" Felix prompts, whipping around to stare at Viktor from across the room.

My brow pulls down in confusion. "Igor? Like Igor the Bookwyrm?"

Viktor rolls his eyes at the nickname I'd given his mentor, but doesn't answer. He just sits at his desk and opens a drawer. Felix takes a few steps closer, and we both gasp as Viktor extracts a beautiful pendant. A red jewel wrapped in intricate platinum.

"This," Viktor starts, "is the heart scale of Quintus Spanos, an alpha belonging to the Byzantine Flight. It was given to his mate, a beta named Phoebe in 1824, only two months before the Slaughter."

His voice is grim, his eyes focused entirely on the betrothal gift in his palm. I've never seen him like this, so completely unreadable. He's only occasionally guarded his emotions around me and Felix, but never to this extent. It's like he's completely shut down, or holding something back, something terrible and dangerous.

"Lyra was born in 1825. So that means..."

Felix trails off as Viktor nods. "Quintus was captured by the enemy before we could reach him and several others. From what I understand, they were interrogated for information relating to the missing lodescales."

So this is where Lyra gets her strength and stubbornness, then.

"Well, considering they're still missing, I'll say those hellspawn didn't get anything out of them," I mutter, my heart aching.

Viktor shakes his head. "No, but they were executed before our people could rescue them. Our records, according to Igor, say that Phoebe was lost in the carnage when the demons overran Constantinople."

"Well, that's obviously not true," Felix scoffs, shifting restlessly.

"No, it fucking is not. And because of the fucking council, and their fucking order, one of our people was left alone and unprotected!"

Viktor suddenly stands and swipes a full stack of papers off his desk, sending them flying in every direction. I jump to my feet, unsure if I should back away or approach. But Viktor's shoulders heave with ragged breaths, his eyes wide and distant. He picks up a paperweight and launches it at one of the bookshelves, shattering the glass trinket and splintering the shelf that it hits.

"I fucking *told them* there was something we were missing. That we couldn't let something like this rest until every single motherfucking soul was accounted for. I *knew* it. I fucking knew it. But they didn't listen, did they."

Viktor speaks almost to himself, and I take a half step forward, reaching out to my pack mate, but Felix gets there first. He slides between us, putting his hands on Viktor's slumped shoulders and looking up into his face, twisted almost beyond recognition with fury.

"You were right, Vitya. You knew she was out there, waiting for us to find her," Felix says, words soft and soothing.

"What she's been through...no one should have to suffer that way. And because they gave up on her, she's..."

Viktor cuts himself off with a snarl, fists shaking at his sides. I close the distance and wrap my arms around Felix and Viktor, holding them close as we all press our heads together.

"Those fuckers in their frozen shithole gave up on her, but we won't, Vik. We won't give up on her," I whisper, voice trembling with my passion.

"We can't change the past, but we can do everything in our power to protect her, and care for her, and…"

Love her.

Felix doesn't have to say the words out loud, but I can hear them clear as day in my head. She's one of us, and we're the only ones who can protect her now, even if she's going to hate it. But there's no world in which I breathe and Lyra doesn't. Those dinosaurs can kiss my scaley ass if they think they're going to take my little hellion away from me.

"She deserves to know the truth," Viktor says at last.

"Then let's go find her," Felix says eagerly.

As we break apart from our huddle, a flash of lightning brightens the entire room, followed closely by a roll of thunder. I grin wildly, but Viktor gives me a warning look.

"Lyra probably won't take this news well, Gav. You need to keep it together," he says sternly.

My smile fades, but I nod. I can't play in the storm today, not when we have something much more world altering to do. Viktor looks me up and down once before nodding and leading the way out of his office to find our girl.

CHAPTER 40

Lyra

I 've set all three heads in this fantasy shower as hot as they can go, but it's no use. Nothing is burning away the deep ache of satisfaction Gavril has left in my bones.

The girls at the club used to bitch about my lava-hot showers, and how there was never enough hot water left over for the rest of them. So I'd gotten used to taking what I considered lukewarm showers at best. But now, as I stand in the billowing steam, trying to get my racing thoughts into some sort of order, I realize that I'm actually comfortable for the first time in a long time. I'm not racing to get in and out before someone pounds on the door demanding their turn. The water is warm and my skin prickles with awareness rather than pain. It's almost enough to make me relax and forget about the last hour.

Almost.

Every time I close my eyes, I can feel Gavril's hands on me. Not claiming, not trying to demand or rush, but grounding, anchoring. He wanted me to make me feel good, and mission *fucking* accomplished. I've racked up a respectable body count during my time at Somnium, but not a single one of those cocks ever made me feel what I felt on that dining room table. What's worse, none of the men attached to those cocks ever made me feel the way Gavril did.

And that alone has me wanting to run screaming for the hills.

Feelings only complicate things, and my "relationships" —if you want to call being kidnapped and then escaping and then coming back and then agreeing to be roommates with three creatures from my childhood nightmares in a penthouse a "relationship"—with these dragons are complicated enough. I want to smother Viktor in his sleep, but getting a rise out of him is a strangely fun game, seemingly for the both of us. Being around Felix is like holding a stick of lit dynamite with an uncertain fuse, only I'm not sure if I'm going to lose my hand at the end, or my heart. And Gavril...he's just as likely to shank me as he is to fuck me, and that's a level of crazy I'm usually bringing to the table, but it's nice to have a kindred spirit.

They've proven themselves to be morally bankrupt, yet somehow, fair and just in their own twisted ways. Any sane person would be trying to escape at every possible opportunity. But me? I must have a cell in the looney bin on standby because I can't make myself leave.

More bored than anything, I turn off the shower and towel dry before slipping into another pair of leggings and a perfectly oversized t-shirt, one of many that keep magically appearing in my closet. All of which smell faintly of jasmine and manly musk. Felix is the hardest to hate. I wish he would, I don't know, call me a bitch or stare at my ass for too long. And even though Gavril does all of those fuck boy things and more, it's so fucking charming that I can't even be mad at him for it. The audacity of them.

I'm just exiting the bathroom and running a brush

through my hair as the first rumble breaks through the silent air. My heart flips over, and I perk up, head whipping around as I try to find the nearest window.

I drop my hairbrush and haul ass out of the guest room and out into the main penthouse. The glass is gone from the floor, but Gavril is nowhere to be found. But as I hear the first pattering of drops, I forget all about him. There's a storm to be witnessed.

Rain in the desert is unlike anything I've ever experienced. Because of the Rocky Mountains and the Mojave Desert, the only storm clouds that can survive are the biggest and meanest of the bunch. There are no gentle showers or misty drizzles so fine it hardly even counts as precipitation. No. In the desert, when it rains, it truly pours. And judging by the roiling mass of black stretching from horizon to horizon, this one won't be any different.

I pad on bare feet to the balcony doors, staring up into the sky as the first heavy drops start to fall. I can almost feel the electricity in the air moments before the sky flashes blinding white. There are several seconds of silence before the slow roll of thunder, and I can't help but smile. It's coming, but still a bit out. Perfect.

Looking down at the gold handles of the doors, I chew the inside of my cheek. They couldn't possibly have been stupid enough to leave these unlocked, right? We're up high, but one really determined burglar could scale the building and get in this way. But then, when I give them the slightest tug, the huge panes of glass glide open on silent hinges. The wind up here is insane, but it's angled away from the balcony, letting me stay dry as the rain starts to come down harder.

I test how far my safety bubble extends, and I'm surprised to find I can get almost halfway to the railing before the rain hits my face. But a pull in my chest keeps my feet moving, until I'm there, standing on my tiptoes to see over the edge of the metal barrier and look down on the strip. I don't know if anything could have prepared me for the sight of Las

Vegas from this high up. It's not fear that pulls the air from my lungs, but awe. I can see everything from here, the perfect perch. Korona Drakona is in the dead center of the action, and I can see it all. One end to the other, completely uninterrupted. And even farther, I can see where the lights fade and the desert begins, the mountains blending with the storm clouds to create a perfect dome over the city that has become my world.

"Lyra? What are you doing?"

I whip around at the sound of Gavril's voice, spine stiffening as he strides across the living room toward me. Felix and Viktor are hot on his heels, faces drawn into stern frowns. Thankfully, Gavril stops at the edge of the dry zone, while the other two hover just inside the balcony doors. I want to back up, but there's nowhere to go. So I do the only thing I can think of: climb onto a metal chair and sit my ass on the edge of the railing. They all flinch forward, but a simple tilt backward has them all freezing in place. It's a stupid power move, but right now, having this one ounce of control settles my racing heart.

"Enjoying the weather. What can I do you for, Jolly Green?" I chirp, folding my arms across my stomach.

It didn't matter ten minutes ago that my t-shirt was white. Now, as the rain gets more intense, it definitely feels like a tactical error. But changing means getting past the wall of dragons blocking the door. My self-control is shaky on a good day, but that dicking down crossed wires in my brain and I'm not going to take any chances.

"Just realized I never asked, but what the hell are you?" Gavril shoves his hands in his jean pockets and rocks his weight backward and forward from the balls of his feet to his heels. Like a child, impatient for his reward after being a good boy.

I blink at him, trying to see past the charm and forearm muscles to his motive. "A Virgo, I think," I respond flatly.

Gavril chuckles and smiles, a bit too fond for my liking. "No, I meant your species. Because the boys and I...well, we think we know," he quips, still doing that rocking thing.

I blink again, tensing against a gust that threatens to knock me off balance. Viktor steps up to be level with Gavril, hands twitching at his sides. His jaw works like he's chewing on his own tongue. What's got him so tense?

"My mom died before anyone could ask. My attempt at fact finding...well, let's just call it the biggest bust in history. If it weren't for the fact that I've kept this fat ass and youthful skin for over a hundred years, I'd say I'm just a human with weird-shaped ears," I retort, falling back on self-deprecation like an old friend to hide the pang in my chest.

The sky flashes and thunder cracks, closer now, but the heart of the storm still hasn't hit. Taking a deep breath, the air smells like ozone and clean water, such a welcome change from the piss and exhaust at street level. I look over my shoulder as the lights start to flick on, their solar-powered timers activated as the sky gets darker and darker. God, why does such a filthy and corrupt place have to be so beautiful?

"See, we have a different theory. We think you might be one of us," Viktor says, pulling me back to reality.

I stare, brain flat out refusing to comprehend anything he just said. One of them? What the fuck does that mean? I'm not some soulless, selfish, entitled prick. Well, technically, I don't have an eternal soul. I bartered that away to a double-crossing bastard, who then used it as a bartering chip in whatever fucked-up deal he made.

"You have scales, Lyra. We saw them. And your–"

"When? Where?" I demand, speaking over Felix as my spine straightens and eyes harden.

He has the decency to flush and look ashamed, but Gavril must have damaged that part of his brain, because he just grins.

"We have cameras, you know. Smashing that vase set off the sonar alert, and I received the notification on my phone," Viktor explains, oddly calm.

I let out a shriek of wordless outrage, even as my skin heats. Viktor watched me fuck Gavril. My first thought should be 'how dare he,' but instead, all I can think is 'was he jealous?' I don't know what sort of upside-down land I've fallen into, but I've just about reached the end of my rope.

"On your back, there were scales. We can show you, if you just come inside," Felix says, taking the tiniest step forward. His arm twitches at his side, like he wants to reach for me, but thinks better of it.

"I don't have scales," I counter, even going as far as to reach behind me to check. But there's nothing unusual hiding beneath the soaked fabric of my shirt.

Felix sighs and nods, toying with his sleeves. "I don't know what triggered them to appear–"

"Probably that orgasm I gave her," Gavril mumbles, laughing under his breath.

Viktor growls and grips his arm tight enough for his knuckles to turn white. But Gavril never loses that shit-eating grin. Objectively, I can't deny that he rocked my world, but making me grow *scales*? No fucking way.

"We have some things we'd like to talk to you about," Felix implores, motioning for me to get down.

My spine straightens as I look at the three of them. Gavril is bouncing around like a puppy at the end of a leash. Felix's face is pale, but at least the concern there seems genuine. Viktor isn't even looking at me, like he's already decided that I'm not worth his time. Well, fuck him. I don't owe him shit.

"Then talk," I grit out, settling more securely on the railing.

The wind is really picking up, and I feel goosebumps on my skin, but now it's a matter of pride. I won't be moved, even if lightning were to come down and strike me where I sit. Which, considering how the rate and intensity of the thunder keeps rising, might actually be possible. Gavril looks up at the sky, edging toward the line on the balcony floor, rain splashing on the wet pavement. But Felix and Viktor are there, grabbing his arms and giving him warning looks.

"It's just rain. It's not like he's going to melt," I scoff, holding up a hand to catch a palmful of water. I try to fling it at Viktor, but the wind carries it away before it even gets close. Still, Viktor flinches back, and I roll my eyes. Probably doesn't want to get his expensive suit wet. Prissy dragon.

"It's the lightning. With Gavril's power..." Felix starts, trailing off as another flash of light paints the sky, followed closely by a near-deafening crack of thunder.

"It can't hurt me," Gavril whines, trying to make a break for it, but Viktor grabs him this time before he can step out into the downpour.

"But you're not alone. *Settle*."

Viktor's command takes on a strange, otherworldly echo, like his chest is suddenly the size of an oil tanker. My bones turn to jelly, eyes drooping with sudden exhaustion. I yawn, swaying in the wind. Settling sounds nice, like *really* nice. The best idea in the world. I could just lie back in a cloud of pillows and sleep for days.

"Lyra, NO!"

Felix's shout cuts through the haze, but the spell breaks completely as I recline, only to find open air. My arms shoot out, trying to find anything to grab on to, but it's too late. I'm past the point of recovery. Everything is slick, and the wind is too strong.

The last thing I see before I fall backward off the balcony is Viktor sprinting toward me, two feet shy of being able to save me.

CHAPTER 41

VIKTOR

F ear tears apart my heart the second I see her succumb
to my Alpha bark, there's no time for questions, for
logical thinking.

"Lyra, NO!"

My feet are moving before my mind catches up. She's
tipping backward, arching farther and farther into the rainy
void until she's past the point of no return. Her arms go wide
like an eagle taking flight, whirling in a vain attempt to right
her balance, but it's not going to work.

As her eyes meet mine for a fractured moment before
she disappears, the desperation and fear rips through me like
claws. I feel her fall. Sense the drop in her stomach and the
static-like fizzing in her limbs. Felix is screaming somewhere
in the distance, but I barely hear him. I don't even break
stride as I step up onto a chair, the table, and then swan dive
over the railing and plummet after her. Everything falls away
around me. The wind whips its punishment around my face,
whispering and taunting.

You'll never catch her in time. You're too late. You did this. This is your fault. She's dead because of you.

Lyra's hair is like an ember in the premature darkness, and I streamline my body to catch up, tucking my chin to my chest and straightening my arms by my sides. I realize too late that there won't be enough time for me to grab her and shift. I don't even think I could get my wings out fast enough. So I settle on the next best thing: scales.

Eighty floors.
I can't catch her.
Seventy floors.
I can't get to her in time.
Sixty floors.
Lyra is going to die.
I blink against the rush of wind
and rain that hits my face and clouds my eyes.
Fifty floors.
I'm on top of her.

Her high-pitched scream is in my ears, piercing and filled with distress. Yet despite her fear, she still fights me as I try to put my arms around her. A growl builds low in my chest, reverberating against my taut rib cage as my scales slip into place.

"*Stop*," I bark, and sigh in relief as she goes limp instantly.

The relief is lost in a swell of urgency. If I don't position myself correctly, she could still be the one to hit the ground. If I fuck this up, my pack will never forgive me. I'll never forgive myself. The grief will rip our pack apart. Felix will succumb to a broken heart, Gavril's anger will swallow him whole, and my regret will run like poison through my veins.

My grip on her tightens, arms encasing her as I fight against the wind to turn us. My scales. I need to get my scales out. There's no time for wings, no time for a full shift. The scales feel as though they're shredding my skin and flesh. Sharp edges poking through and shifting into place. The armor will only be enough to protect my back and organs from the impact. If I don't shift enough, there's a good chance I won't survive this. I'm at peace with that realization. If I can ensure that Lyra is safe, then sacrificing myself is the smallest of prices to pay.

God, I never realized how small Lyra is until I tuck her into a ball and hold her flush to my chest.

Desperation forces the scales to slip into place more rapidly as we're thrown past the thirtieth floor of Korona Drakona. I wrap as much of my body around her as I can. My arms lock in place, hands holding on to my biceps as I squeeze. There needs to be as little wiggle room as possible so that my body absorbs the majority of the force from the fall.

My focus zeroes in, this is my last chance. I'm out of time. Even with seventy percent of my body now covered in scales, it's still going to hurt like a bitch. I try to reassure myself that dragon scales are better than any body armor. Nearly impenetrable, flexible to move with us but strong enough to repel all but the most advanced weapons. I will shield Lyra with my body, even if it means breaking a few bones in the process.

Fuck, I will shield Lyra with all I have for the rest of my days on this earth if it means we don't lose her. I will take every ounce of pain and suffering, every tear, every sob, I will steal it all away. I'm bartering with someone, something. I don't know who, but I sure as hell hope they're listening.

The people on the strip look less like ants; they're bigger, getting closer and closer and closer. My breath holds still in my lungs, cars and buildings rushing past us, with Lyra still buried against my chest and in my arms. The last time we were alone, and I held her this close, I had her screaming my name and begging for mercy. If we live through this, I need to apologize for that, and maybe show her that being with me isn't all sharp edges and pain. She deserves that much, as a start. I hope whatever being is considering my bargain will let me have another chance to treat her right.

The concrete crumbles under the impact, but I keep my hold on Lyra even as she compresses my torso. Stupid fucking laws of physics. There are screams from around us, but my head spins as whiplash settles over me. Rain cloaks my vision, and I groan, trying to take stock of my body. I'm alive, but my back is going to be sore for a good while. I can still feel my arms and legs, which is a good sign. And as I move to sit up, my scales shift along my back, all intact.

"Lyra?" I groan, looking down at the shaking ball in my arms.

My heart stops dead as I stare, only to kick-start again like a cannon. Through the water-soaked white shirt, plain as day, are scales. Blood red ones, arranged almost exactly like the ones I can feel along my own back. Carefully overlapping plates, the largest of which is only about as big as my palm, wrap around her back and shoulders before disappearing from view, but I don't need to see them. I know her belly is going to be covered in narrow scute-like bands, protecting her vital organs. But it's the differences that make my blood run cold. I run my fingers in a line, following the curve of her spine, and I have to swallow hard. No hard edges, no spines. Just a smooth protective shell, designed to protect the most vulnerable subset of my kind.

"Omega," I breathe, hardly able to believe the word coming out of my mouth.

No matter how hard I try to explain the things I can see and feel, my heart and soul cannot deny the realization. Everything slots into place without any more questions; the pull she has on my pack, her ears. That goddamn heirloom. The fact that she's still breathing after falling nearly eighty stories. And the final nail in the coffin: when she snaps her head up to me, her eyes are fully gold with vertical pupils. Dragon eyes. They lock with mine like they're seeing me for the very first time, alight with terror and belonging.

I can't get my limbs to work as she snarls at me, scrambling away like some sort of feral animal. I don't know if she's noticed the change, but she's staring at me with open contempt and fear in her eyes and what little of her scent I can pick up in the rain. I try to get up, to go to her and do my duty as an alpha, her alpha, but she snaps her teeth at me, making me freeze.

"You want to stay right there, don't you," she croons, voice silky smooth despite the rage pulling at each inch of her face.

My heart slows, and I settle back on my haunches. She's right. I shouldn't move just yet. I'll just catch my breath for a minute and assess before doing anything rash. I close my eyes and take a deep breath, running another quick check over my body. Nothing broken, just sore. Felix and Gavril are probably going to have my ass for this, but it doesn't matter. Nothing before this moment matters. Lyra is one of us, and what's more, she's an *omega.*

I smile lazily at the thought and open my eyes, ready to get back to our pack. But she's gone. I sit up, spinning on my knees in the crater our impact created. There's no sign of her anywhere in the gawking crowd, not a flash of fiery hair, or gold eyes. I inhale deep, my ribs screaming in pain, but my heartbreak is somehow even louder. Her scent is lost in a twilight sea of rain, wind, and neon lights.

She's gone, and it's all my fault.

The story continues in...

Neon Nightmares

Coming fall 2023

Also by Thora

Pack Saint Clair Series

Lilacs and Leather

Lavender and Lightning

Laurels and Liquor

The Complete Edition

Also by Shannon

Beneath the City Sleeps Series

Silver Vein (Book One)

Dark & Damned Fairytales Collection

California Snow (Part One)

Contemporary Romances

Behind His Eyes (Standalone)

Filthy Delicious (Book One)

The Shadow Wolves Saga

Tempt

Covet

Ignite

About Thora

Thora Woods is a lifelong writer, reader, and creator. Born in New Orleans, LA, she began her writing journey in her pre-teens, growing her skills at SUNY Fredonia in their Creative Writing program. Lilacs and Leather is Thora's Prst published work. Thora lives in Western New York with her two dogs, Fritter and Pepper, two cats, Impala and Hoagie, and her husband.

About Shannon

Shannon French dwells in a small seaside town in Scotland with her husband, two kids, two cats and therapy dog Zepp. She began writing from bed a few years back after a run in with Bacterial Meningitis left her with a couple of neurological parting gifts, a.k.a. Intracranial Hypertension and Functional Neurological Disorder. Shannon writes to escape the darker days and has a certain penchant for werewolves, witches and vampires.

Made in United States
Troutdale, OR
08/27/2023